TINSEL TOWN

CATHERINE MANN

SIMON AND SCHUSTER | NEW YORK

This novel is a work of fiction. Names, characters, places and incidents
are either the product of the author's imagination or are used fictitiously.
Any resemblance to actual events or locales or persons, living or dead, is
entirely coincidental.

Copyright © 1985 by Catherine Mann Productions, Inc.
All rights reserved
including the right of reproduction
in whole or in part in any form
Published by Simon and Schuster
A Division of Simon & Schuster, Inc.
Simon & Schuster Building
Rockefeller Center
1230 Avenue of the Americas
New York, New York 10020
SIMON AND SCHUSTER and colophon are registered trademarks
of Simon & Schuster, Inc.
Manufactured in the United States of America
3   5   7   9   10   8   6   4   2
Library of Congress Cataloging in Publication Data
Mann, Catherine.
Tinsel Town.

I. Title.
PS3563.A5353T5   1985   813'.54   85-10740
ISBN 0-671-55262-7

ACKNOWLEDGMENTS

I would like to express my immeasurable gratitude to Pam Bernstein, my agent, for believing; Patricia Soliman for her impeccable editorial vision; Linda Dozoretz for her unwavering encouragement and support; my friends at *Entertainment Tonight,* especially Rex Hosea, for his kindness, even though he'll deny it, Gary Herman, for always understanding, and Clay Smith for sharing his vast knowledge of the record industry. I would also like to thank my very good friends Susan Haymer, Sally Jewett, and Bill Olson for being there when I needed them. And I owe a special debt of gratitude to Gary Diedrichs for showing me the way. Without his assistance this book would not have been written.

This is for my parents, who first kindled my creative spirit.

For Jerry, who recognized it.

For Gary, who helped channel it.

And for Gregory, whose love has given me strength.

— CHAPTER —
One

In the chill of a March dawn, the champagne-beige 380SL took a careening right off Sunset Boulevard, barely missing the International Network gate.

Old Charlie, the parking-lot attendant, jumped as if someone had sent a thousand volts surging through his seat. His third cup of early-morning coffee slopped over the *Daily Racing Form*.

"Gawd Almighty! Miss DuRand again. In an all-fired hurry."

Christine DuRand was always in a hurry. Always late. But this morning more than any other demanded every split second she could steal.

Today she would do the celebrity interview of her television career. Roland Williams. The Roland Williams. The aloof, mysterious, scintillatingly sexual Latin recording superstar who for years had refused all interviews. That Roland Williams—hers for the questioning today at noon. Sharp.

Finally it's all paying off, she thought for the dozenth time that morning. She'd been trying to get an interview with Williams for two years. This is it. My God. This is it.

She could hardly believe it.

Christine snatched up the buff leather briefcase, the lavender St. Laurent suit, the clear plastic makeup bag, and walked briskly toward the main entrance.

Good idea, not drying my hair, she thought, running a hand through the long, thick blue-black curls, still damp from the shower.

The massive glass doors parted.

"Mornin' Miss DuRand. In very early this mornin'."

It was Jake, the beefy black night-security guard. Doomed to the graveyard shift.

"Yes," she said, returning his smile, not breaking stride as she passed by on the way to the elevators.

Jake watched her backside approvingly. He let out a low whistle.

Wonder what lucky dude gets his hands on that? Got her own show, what? Six months now? Talkin' to the stars. Nice gig. Least she ain't stuck-up like a lotta them folks. Nooossir . . . friendly . . . but a hard worker. Seems all business, that one.

Christine got off on the fourth floor.

Read Williams file. Find out what Maggie knows. Do makeup. Fix hair. Have wardrobe press suit. She made a mental checklist as she unlocked the door to her office and dressing room.

She flicked on the light switch, revealing a hodgepodge of country French furniture. Sturdy, rough-hewn cherrywood tables and chairs. An armoire. Couches with comfy floral-print cushions. And a huge walk-in closet, which Chistine adored most of all.

She ducked inside the closet to hang up the suit.

Thank God I didn't spend the night at Blair's. All the way out in Malibu.

Usually Christine was willing to juggle her schedule for Blair Montgomery. Their time together was reward enough for whatever accommodations she had to make. They'd been "an item" for a year and a half. The same amount of time Christine had been working for the International Network.

Blair was in his late forties. More than a decade her senior. A strikingly handsome, highly sought after movie producer. And the first man in Christine's life who made her feel the way millions of television viewers perceived her. Beautiful. Vibrant. Relaxed. Alive.

They'd met at the celebrity-studded party following the premiere of Blair's movie *Speedway 500*. Christine barely remembered shaking his hand. She had just joined the network, and as she rushed back to the studio that evening, her mind was on meeting her 10 P.M. deadline, not Blair Montgomery.

The next day, when he phoned to thank her for the excellent coverage, he suggested lunch. She almost declined, considering her hectic schedule. But something about his voice, the authority and hint of intimacy, made her accept.

They met at Ma Maison. Blair was sitting at one of the first tables off the patio entrance when she arrived. And by the familiar way the owner, Patrick Terrail, treated him, Christine knew she should be impressed.

Despite herself, she was. Blair had a keen sense of humor, knew everyone in Hollywood, and had the most sensual mouth she had ever seen.

A month later they were seeing each other exclusively. All her free nights were spent with Blair in Malibu. It had been years since Christine had been so completely swept up in a man. They talked about love. But never commitment.

Tugging off her pink cashmere sweater—a Christmas gift from Blair—she thought about an evening they'd shared earlier that week. Blair was lathering her with aloe vera soap in his enormous Spanish-tiled shower. They'd just taken a fast plunge in the ocean. Then his strong hands moved demandingly over Christine's body, which glistened like alabaster sculpture beaded with a sultry mixture of salt water, sweat, and the cleansing gush of water overhead. His tongue traced a straight line downward from her throat.

"Blair, you idiot, you're going to drown!"

Christine quivered.

Stepping out of her Sasson jeans, she reminded herself there was no time for distractions. None.

Is that what he is—a distraction?

No. She knew he was more than that. Much more. Blair was her mentor. Her helpmate. The strongest man in her life. He was the one person she could always count on to make things happen.

Where would I be without him? she thought, tossing the jeans over a hanger. The question had been on her mind for the past few months—ever since she'd started to hit her stride with her own show.

The DuRand Report aired twice weekly for Hollywood-hungry audiences in every English-speaking nation in the world, plus most of Europe, several South American nations, and Japan. Christine knew it could catapult her to international fame. The numbers in the WorldWide Ratings were climbing. There was an increasing flow of favorable publicity. She was set for the cover of *TV Guide* next month.

Christine DuRand was coming into her own. And she knew it. She could feel the energy almost overwhelming her. At last. This was her reward—for all the rejection she'd endured, the obstacles she'd overcome. The news directors who'd turned her down. The bewildering, seemingly impossible task of switching from print to television journalism. The endless list of public-relations representatives she'd phoned daily to plead for celebrity interviews. The constant edit sessions. The all-nighters, boning up for interviews. The continuous cups of coffee and resultant bout with a stomach ulcer. Finally it all seemed worth it.

Could she have done it without Blair? Yes. Maybe. No. Christine had to admit it. Without him she probably wouldn't have her own show. Not that he'd pulled strings at the network. What he did was better than that. Blair had introduced Christine to the people who count in Hollywood.

It was through him that she'd managed to land a number of exclusive interviews with stars usually off-limits to reporters. Barbra Streisand, Woody Allen, Diane Keaton, Paul Newman. Even Warren Beatty had agreed to sit down and chat with Christine.

And it was Blair who'd inadvertently helped her win an Emmy for excellence in reporting. He'd arranged for her to do a story on special effects during filming of a science-fiction movie called *Extended*. The movie cameras rolled at sunset. Seconds after the director yelled "Action!" the scene rocked with an unexpected explosion. A tragic accident.

The leading actress and three extras were set afire and literally burned alive. Christine had it all on tape. A lead story for the news.

It was one of those emotionally jarring situations many reporters must face. Christine felt paralyzed with horror. She'd just watched four people die. But her journalistic instincts told her to move fast. Interview whomever she could. And race back to the studio with the tapes.

She covered all the follow-up stories as well. The grieving families. The ongoing investigations and litigation. The studio's ultimate two-hundred-million-dollar loss.

The night she received the Emmy, Blair was there wrapping his arms around her when she came off stage.

Several weeks later he was toasting her with champagne over dinner at The Ivy because she'd just landed her own show.

Blair even hired famed lighting director Gavin Aimes to make sure Christine's raven-black hair was illuminated properly in the studio.

She had never looked better on television than she did on *The DuRand Report.*

"*UHHHHahhhhh,*" came the moan from the huge woman with the mass of damp chestnut hair.

"Can't . . . do it. . . . Can't . . . get 'em together. F'crissakes, Brad, crank it back a notch or two."

Maggie Rafferty was lying on the Nautilus Hip Adduction/Abduction machine. Spread-eagled. Her least favorite position, under the circumstances.

Again she tried to force her massive, tremulous thighs together. Sweat poured off her quivering flesh onto the padded red vinyl leg braces.

"C'mon, Maggie. Where's that old fighting Irish spirit this morning?" urged her trainer, Brad Larson. "Just pretend there's a great big shlang right here—" He pointed to her crotch. "And you want to squeeze the life out of it."

"Can't . . . too much weight," Maggie rasped, inching her aching legs slowly inward, too strained to enjoy the tingling sensation in her groin.

"*Uggggahhhhh—*" Legs almost closed now.

"Getting closer. Just a tad more and you get a big smooch," taunted Brad, a stocky sandy-haired onetime Mr. Universe who Maggie suspected relied on daily doses of steroids to keep the biceps bulging.

One thing about Brad, though. He knew how to make Maggie move. "Almost there, Maggie me girl! Harder! Tighten up those saggy baggy muscles and—"

"*Ooooooosh . . .*" Maggie's head flopped to one side as she finally felt her knees touch.

She'd started these torture sessions on a dare.

Almost from her first day at the International Network as Christine DuRand's assistant, there'd been the little hints, nudges that Maggie do something about her humongous bod. All of Christine's "suggestions" had been deftly eluded. Until the dare.

"If you can drop fifty pounds with Brad Larson, I'll send you to Hawaii. The Kahala Hilton for a week."

Maggie couldn't resist, although on mornings like this she wished she had.

"Okay. Let's move over here and work off some arm flab."

"Oh, no—that's it," Maggie announced.

She unhooked the seat belt and lifted her largeness off the machine.

"Cutting it short today? A little tuckered out from all that depravity last night?" Brad snapped a damp towel at her backside as she headed for the showers.

"Make it up tomorrow," mumbled Maggie, waving him off.

Yeah. Last night. What a scene. Outrageous party.

Her thoughts now flashed back to the elaborate manse in Trousdale with the obligatory gorgeous view of the twinkling lights of Hollywood below. Standard issue to your upper-middle producer, in this case one Mort Finestein.

Maggie's mission impossible, as usual—conversational interrogation. Snoop snoop snoop. Find out *anything* about Roland Williams, since almost nothing on him existed in print.

She stalked the place in search of childhood chums who had taken the plunge into the biz as actors or actresses, writers, musicians, studio or record-company execs, hairdressers, makeup artists, techies. . . .

And as usual, the search led her into some bizarre and unexpected corners.

How about those two in the sauna? Hah! Sweet Jesus, shooting heroin! Two royally messed up starlets. Couldn't be over nineteen, either one of 'em. Tuck that away in the futures file!

Maggie stepped into the shower and turned on the rewarding torrent of cool water. She smiled to herself, calculating just how she would break the spectacular news of last night's endeavors to Christine.

"Hans Siegfried, you sure are kinky!" she laughed, soaping up her pendulous breasts.

But what a gold mine. Maggie had spotted Hans at the party just before midnight, dangling his feet in the large mosaic-tiled pool, watching half a dozen nearly naked women float around on mini-banana boats overladen with fresh fruit. Maggie couldn't figure out whether he wanted to bite into one of those ripe, sweet cuties or into a papaya. But he did look a little lonely. And slightly depressed.

Here comes Big Mag to the rescue, hon. . . .

Actually, Maggie was desperate. Two solid hours of working the six jam-packed party rooms, plus the patio, and her intelligence haul on Roland Williams added up to exactly . . . nothing. Zip. *Nada.* He had umpteen gold and platinum records and kept to himself. So big deal.

She was about ready to give up. That's when she saw Hans. If anyone here knew about Roland Williams, Hans Siegfried did.

He knew everything, or so it sometimes seemed. He was a fixture at every party in town, but his real base of operations was the Beverly Hills Hotel. It was the perfect listening post, a kind of show-biz Demilitarized Zone, neutral turf for both East (New York deal makers, money men, and executives of the multinational corporations that own the movie studios, TV networks, and record companies) and West (Hollywood).

Hans was at least forty-five, but he possessed one of those ageless faces made possible by the fortuitous combination of good genes and loads of money. His mother was Scandinavian, his father a fair-skinned German Jew who had salted away his fortune in the meat-packing business in Schleswig-Holstein. Hans himself had fled the family years ago to encamp in Hollywood, calling himself a producer and quickly ingratiating his way into the movie colony social scene. It wasn't difficult. He had too much money to turn away.

Hans talked a great game about movie deals "in the pipeline," but no one could remember a film of his actually getting made. Not that it mattered. Hans played the role of successful producer, so in the eyes of most, that's what he was.

The Beverly Hills Hotel was his "office." By day he usually lounged at poolside, his "uniform" a skimpy European bikini which showed off to best advantage his lithe and boyish body. Hans also held sway on business matters in the hotel bungalow reserved expressly for that purpose.

Bungalow Eight. No one knows precisely why, but Eight—along with Six and Nine—has special status even within the already highly privileged confines of the Beverly Hills. A characteristic salmon-pink, with ocher tile roof, bordered by privet hedges and shrubbery in perpetual bloom, shaded by spruce and maple and palms, it offers a tranquil, almost hushed, serenity—the perfect illusion of a secluded country hideaway. It is the only one of twenty-one bungalows on the hotel grounds with a private walled patio. The living room inside is spacious and cheery, with a walnut mantel framing the fireplace and a gorgeous Oriental tapestry hung above a lemon-yellow sofa. A formal dining room offers window views of the lush greenery on three sides, and of course the hotel supplies fresh floral arrangements daily. A more pleasant setting in which to pretend that work was being done would be hard to imagine.

Maggie had long been curious about Hans. She knew he tried to hide his Jewish heritage, yet apparently felt no qualms about living off his trust fund. She wondered how any one person could possibly be the receptacle of so much . . . information.

15

Maybe he eavesdropped on the constant flow of phone calls into the cabanas surrounding the pool, or it was his incessant chatting up of the hotel's VIP clientele and their bikinied bimbos while they preened on fluffy towels and soft pillows, sipping tall drinks. Or perhaps the goods were spilled during the lavish late-afternoon soirees he hosted in Bungalow Eight. Maggie didn't know.

But one thing about Hans: he was on the money. He didn't spread false gossip; he always had the facts.

It took the rest of the night to procure all the titillating details available on Roland Williams. One of the weirdest nights she'd ever had. But worth it. Definitely worth it.

When Hans suggested a "private party"—not at his hotel bungalow but at his much larger residence high in the hills off Mulholland Drive—Maggie figured he just wanted someone to talk to. She was positive he was gay.

She got a surprise. She got an education. From the moment they entered the mansion. Now she knew the secret life of Hans Siegfried.

It was like walking into a medieval nightmare. Suits of armor, pikes, lances, maces, and broadswords mounted on the bare stone walls, heavy oaken furniture, long wax tapers throwing off a flickering eerie light. When Hans urged her to strip down and suit up, Maggie wasn't at all certain what he had in mind.

He handed her a short black leather caftan.

What happened next wasn't really that bad. It didn't hurt. Didn't hurt Maggie, anyway. Hans was the one into pain. Maggie played the dominatrix, the punisher, the mistress of the shackles and chains and wielder of whips. She was S&M Queen for a Night.

Hans unloaded the latest developments in Roland Williams's life while hanging head first from the high cathedral ceiling.

"Hot damn!" yelped Maggie as she shimmied dry with a large plush bath sheet. "Wait'll Christine hears this. It'll scald her Midwestern ears."

"Shit!"

Blair Montgomery slammed down the phone.

He was angry. Angrier than he'd been in months. He felt like putting his fist through the sparkling glass table perched on his deck overlooking Malibu beach. Even his early morning run hadn't helped. Now, his bathing suit still dripping from a bracing charge into the chill surf, Blair paced the redwood deck like a cornered stallion.

"Mista Mongumly wan mee-mow-zah now?" It was Shanu, the prize Chinese houseboy Blair had managed to lure away from close friends of the Gregory Pecks. In a community overrun with Mexican maids and gardeners, having an Oriental cook/valet was pure prestige. Usually Blair wallowed in it. Today he was too steamed up to care.

Shanu balanced a stemmed glass of orange juice, champagne, and chopped ice on a silver tray. A mimosa. Blair's favorite waker-upper.

He yanked the glass from the tray and gulped greedily. "No breakfast today," he snapped, dismissing Shanu.

What the hell is it with her? Where was she last night?

For the third time within fifteen minutes, Blair dialed the International Network. This time, at least, a receptionist answered.

"Where's Miss DuRand?" he nearly yelled.

"Not answering, sir. Is there a message?"

You bet. Ask her where she was strutting that cute little ass of hers last night. I sure didn't get any of it.

"Tell her to call Blair. She knows the number." He hung up.

That prima donna. Couldn't drive out here last night. Even though I've been away three days on location. Had to wait for a phone call from a flack, she said. So why isn't she home at seven A.M.? *Who's she screwing if it isn't me?*

At forty-seven, Blair Montgomery was a bona fide Hollywood success story. He had been raised in the shadow of the studios. Daddy held a string of fancy titles at several. These days Blair produced an average of a picture a year—usually a blockbuster, with the odd colossal bomb to keep things interesting. No half measures for Blair, never Mr. In-Between. There was always a way to keep the old bank balance bulging. Structure that deal with some imagination. Skim the cream. Use your leverage. So what if the small-minded might call them kickbacks? Anything's legit if you don't get caught. Even if you do. Look at Begelman. Got his hands slapped. A little bad press. Didn't stop David. Won't stop Blair.

He'd never been married, and wasn't planning on it. Why bother? Women were always irresistibly drawn to the blinding light of success, but Blair was the ultimate. Not another paunchy, cigar-smoking sugar daddy. A muscular six-footer with dark-brown wavy hair and a perfect smile. A "catch."

In his youth he scored with anything in a skirt. Now he was more selective. It wasn't that he was slowing down. Just smartening up. He needed someone to show off. A top-of-the-heap gal. Flashy. Stylish. A pacesetter. A cinch for frequent mentions by Army Archerd in *Variety*.

By his standards, then, Blair had been "monogamous" for the past three years. First with Marva Collins—until her TV sitcom was axed. Next with Andrea Rhodes, until her film production company went bust. Then came Lana Miquelle—until she dumped her fashion-modeling career to discover she couldn't act.

Now Christine DuRand. Perfect for him. Fresh-faced and freckled, a nice body. A tigress in bed, once he'd unleashed her libido. Showed no signs of maternal instincts. Didn't want marriage.

Best of all, she was a comer. Hadn't she just locked up an exclusive interview with Princess Diana? That was Blair's kind of maneuver. She'd be ahead of the pack for a while. And during that time, nobody was going to poach on Blair Montgomery's territory.

He dialed Christine's home number. Maybe she went out early to swim. But each time the unanswered phone rang, Blair felt his blood pressure soar a little higher.

Christine checked her watch as she reached for the short blue terry-cloth wrapper. Seven-thirty. Maggie should be in soon. With a side-long glance at the full-length mirror, she half smiled. Pleased with her thirty-one-year-old body. She could still pass for twenty-five. Easily, even naked. Five-foot five-inch frame. Nicely curved to the waist. Tummy flat to the tip of the soft triangle where her lacy panties met her thighs; a pleasing flare of hips; legs well toned from a daily forty-lap swim.

She cast an appraising eye at her long, trim legs. Not bad for a former fatty from Minneapolis. Christine secured the wrapper snugly around her small waist and moved to her cluttered desk. Thinking about how far she'd come since high school.

Her name then was Cathleen Rand. A sweet whirlwind at St. Anthony's High. Bright. National Honor Society. Talented. President of the Dramatics Club, a fixture in student theatrical presentations. And one of the loneliest girls in school. Everybody's pal. Nobody's date.

Pride can be a powerful force in a young woman. Only turkeys ask fat girls out, she lamented, so Cathleen stayed home. The night of her senior prom, slumped on the couch in her family's modest living room, watching a jumpy rerun of a Katharine Hepburn movie, she made a vow. In her own life she would always show that same Hepburn spunk. Everyone else be damned! And in her own good time, when she was ready, the svelte star inside her would emerge and shine.

The metamorphosis came in her sophomore year at Northwestern University. Determined to become an actress—no, a leading lady on Broadway—she put herself on a strict diet. Eggs and grapefruit, fish and chicken. And an exhausting exercise program. Aerobics for a full hour, followed by a half-mile swim—every day. Within four months she'd trimmed down. Suddenly she was thought of as pretty. Even beautiful. It amused her to see what new powers she held over men, but inside she felt the same as always. Overweight. Insecure. Driven to do something with her life.

After graduation, she couldn't wait to be off to New York, pounding the pavement as a hopeful model and actress. Her weight was down to a hundred and three, borderline anorexia. But perfect for television-commercial calls for a fresh young housewife pitching decaf or a cute girl-next-door peddling soap.

Now, a decade later, Cathleen Rand, a.k.a. Christine DuRand, was aloft in her starry galaxy just as she had planned. The "popular" girls back in Minneapolis fantasized about big-city glamour, money, romance. Especially romance. And Christine had it. Had it all. Lived it all.

Funny, though. Before Blair she never thought of herself as a sexual being—certainly not a provocative one. There was something about his animal maleness, his domineering ego, that brought it out in her. Christine wasn't quite sure what it was. Or whether *it* was really the best thing for her. . . .

Bless me, Father, for I have sinned. It's been three weeks since my last confession—

—Go on, my child.

—I kissed my boyfriend with my mouth open, and he put his hands up my . . .

Men. Sex. Intimacy. That thrilling flush which always seemed to accompany the feeling that you were falling in love. She'd learned to repress it in high school. The nuns said sex without marriage was bad. Nice girls didn't.

The older Christine became, the more she realized you couldn't be "just friends" with boys. They always wanted more. She struggled not to give it to them. And with Kent Michaels she succeeded.

Kent was her first love. The college football hero from her hometown. Good-looking, tall, blond, with pale-blue eyes that made her churn inside. Every girl in Minneapolis was after Kent Michaels. But the summer before her senior year at Northwestern—he fell in love with Cathleen Rand.

On steamy nights they gasped and petted on her parents' sprawling front porch, straining against each other in the swaying hammock, his hands moving up her skirt and down her blouse. "I want you, I want you—" So close to doing it. But they waited. Too long. She broke their engagement.

Next came Steven Jacobs. She, a struggling actress; he, a Manhattan investment manager, married. It was he who urged her to change her image, to take the more alluring-sounding name of Christine DuRand. They fell in love "forever." It lasted four years. "I'd make you a damn good wife. Why can't you get a divorce?" Twenty-five years old and heartbroken. She needed a new life, in a faraway place.

She found it in Los Angeles. Working as a secretary for *Celebrity* magazine. Her self-confidence daunted, she no longer had the drive to go after modeling or acting jobs. She just needed to pay the bills. Living with a girlfriend. Answering phones and typing at work. Trying to shake off the memory of Steven. The good times. The private jets and limousines. The tenderness they'd shared.

She was also determined never to let that happen again. Never would she let another man get control of her. Use her. And leave her, betrayed and alone, to fend for herself.

Aloneness. It was her greatest burden.

She desperately needed a new direction. And once she set her mind to it, she found one. Late one Friday afternoon, Polly Millan, the magazine's highly talented but dreadfully disorganized editor in chief, began shouting from her office. Polly was in an unusually frenzied state. She'd forgotten about an interview she'd scheduled with Stefanie Powers early that evening. All the staff reporters were busy or out of town. Polly herself was catching a plane for New York in an hour.

Christine volunteered to do the interview. Obviously taken aback at first, Polly quickly gave the girl a once-over. Found the Gucci shoes and Ann Taylor dress acceptable. Then asked about Christine's studies at Northwestern.

"All right, then. Might as well give it a go, Chris," she finally shrugged. "Here's the research. Meet her at the Polo Lounge at six-thirty. The more personal the questions, the better. And don't forget to take a tape recorder."

Christine spent the weekend transcribing the Stefanie Powers interview and shaping the piece. On Monday Polly read it through, removed her glasses and gave Christine a long, scrutinizing look. "How'd you like to do some more reporting, Chris?" she asked, smiling.

That was the beginning. Through her work, Christine started to find herself again. Now she could shrug off the painful memories. She was too busy to care. She was learning. She was improving. And she loved every minute of it.

Within six months Christine became one of the magazine's most valuable reporters. And for the next two years she traveled all over the country, her eye fixed on the glittery firmament of the entertainment industry. She tracked the show-biz comets as they crossed the heavens. She recorded the fiery crashes of the unlucky and the burned out.

The work was consuming. Her social life was limited to occasional dinners with men she met on the job. Publicists, journalists, technicians.

One of them, a news cameraman, suggested that Christine make the switch to television. "You're certainly talented enough," he said encouragingly. "You should see some of the space cases I work with. Their interviews sound like laundry lists. Why don't you tag along on a couple of stories and see what goes on?"

She did. Television reporting didn't look easy. The standups. The quick interviews. Jamming a microphone under somebody's chin when they really didn't want to talk. Writing a story in the back of a van to meet a deadline.

Somehow, though, Christine knew she could do it. If she got the chance—that was the hard part. For a whole year she tried to get a TV job. The news directors in Los Angeles were polite but uninterested. She needed time to make mistakes in a small market, they all said. Find a job in Palm Springs or Sheboygan.

She was willing to move by then. Writing for *Celebrity* had lost its luster. She needed a new challenge. Christine contacted thirty-five news directors and got thirty-five rejections. Without on-air experience, it seemed, she didn't have a chance.

But the next week Christine literally ran into her opportunity. Rushing out of the ladies room of the Century Plaza Hotel, she took a swift left turn and bumped into a tall, graying man in a dark brown suit, wearing a nametag.

"Donald Winston, KQV-TV," it read. Despite the confused circumstances, the name registered: News Director for Channel 8, a small independent station here in town. You spoke to him last January, she

21

remembered. Quickly she apologized for the collision, introduced herself, and began telling Winston about her recent interview with Katharine Hepburn. Then she thrust an advance copy of the magazine into his hand.

It all happened so fast and Christine had been so, well, ballsy, that she wondered afterwards what he really thought. But Winston must have been impressed, because when she phoned the next day, he agreed to see her.

The truth was, Don Winston had been searching for a specialist in celebrity news—someone with journalistic credentials. He had a solid news operation, and now he wanted to round it out. Take on the big boys at the owned-and-operated stations. Channels 2, 4 and 7 each had an entertainment reporter. He needed someone who could do interviews, reviews, and cover the party circuit without coming off like a puffball.

Christine sat there listening, hardly believing what she heard. She knew she was perfect for the job. And it was in L.A.

Winston asked her to audition, and she threw herself into the tryout with typical energy and determination. Through her magazine contacts she arranged an interview with Dolly Parton. Winston was impressed. He gave the piece three minutes of airtime. And with Christine's gentle prodding, Dolly talked frankly about her phantom marriage to media-shy Carl Dean, whom she had met in a Nashville laundromat at the tender age of eighteen.

Two weeks later Christine became KQV's entertainment reporter. She had never been so nervous. Her hands shook when she gave the suggested lead-in to her first story to anchorman Curt Allison.

"Too long," Allison huffed after barely glancing at the copy.

"But we have to say something about . . ."

"I only have ten seconds to say it, Ms. DuRand," he replied brusquely. "Cut it down. Fast."

The newsroom was not the friendliest of environments. At least not at first. Even at this non-network station, most of the staffers had paid their dues. They'd worked in Grand Rapids or Sioux City. They were legit. Christine wasn't. She was a greenhorn. And despite Don Winston's confidence in her, few of Christine's co-workers offered any help or advice.

She sweated through terrible twelve-hour days. Turning out a story took her twice the time it did other reporters. The videotape editors lost patience with her almost immediately, throwing up their hands at her indecision about which soundbites to use.

"Listen, sweetheart," one of them said stormily, "by the time you decide what to go with, tonight's news will be over. If you can't feel it in your gut, you shouldn't be here."

It was 9 P.M., her second week at the station. She was exhausted. She was hungry. She wasn't thinking straight. And she felt like giving up. There was never enough time to concentrate on what you wanted to say. At the magazine she'd had hours to ponder over her angle on a story. Working TV news was machine-gun journalism. You just had to blast your way through and trust that your instincts were on target.

After a few moments, Christine regained her composure. "Okay, Eli," she said authoritatively. "Take the second bite and cut out at thirty-five seconds, when Jane says, 'It's what I do best.' " Then Christine walked resolutely out of the editing room.

Eli's thick mustache spread out evenly over a satisfied smile. Kid's going to be okay, he thought. Tough underneath. Just needed a little kick in the ass.

Christine never hesitated in the editing room again. She began to trust herself, realizing no one else could make her decisions for her. Her pieces became sharper, more substantial, and at the same time more fun.

Don Winston was pleased with his choice. His entertainment reporter was winning a reputation in Hollywood as a talented, incisive, but sensitive interviewer.

Three years later Christine heard about a position at the International Network, went after it, and got it. Twice the money—three times the work. She signed on eagerly and didn't look back. The job—Hollywood reporter for the network's twenty-four-hour news—was exhilarating. And exhausting. Day after day of running from one assignment to the next, turning out four or five stories by early evening. Often covering parties or openings at night.

Now, with her own show, the pace was even quicker, the pressure even greater. She found herself working constantly. Keeping up the contacts. Fighting for exclusive interviews. Poring over stacks of research material late into the night.

And, of course, there was Blair. It seemed to Christine that she was forever juggling her schedule for him. Doing as few evening interviews as she could get away with. Slipping out of town with him on weekends when she knew she should be working. Attending every Hollywood party and dinner with him she possibly could, even though she was often dead tired.

Is Blair really making more demands on me now? The thought occupied her as she walked over to the makeup table and flicked on the blaze of small round lights. *Or am I just feeling the pressure of carrying my own show?*

As she reached for her hairbrush, the phone jangled for the third time that morning. Her private line.

"Damn," she muttered.

She knew who that was. She let it ring.

Roland Williams hadn't felt in such a dark mood in a long time.

I don't need this, I really don't, he was thinking, as he navigated the shiny metallic black Jeep up the bumpy side road toward his Soledad Canyon ranch. The gloomy refrain had echoed through his mind the whole hour's drive, since he had left the house in Bel-Air shortly before seven A.M.

But he was almost there. At least now he could steal a few hours' time with his "family." His precious animals. Sixty-five of them at last count. Exotic wonders from around the world. Hand-picked . . . for their weaknesses, their frailties.

A five-foot-high Australian emu with a broken wing. A cud-chewing hartebeest from the savannas of Kenya with a deformed foot. Rhesus and capuchin monkeys. A lemur from Madagascar. Even a platypus. All ailing or defective; all pampered by the finest veterinarians Roland could find.

With each and every one of these abandoned and vulnerable creatures he felt a special kinship, a private, personal bond.

Roland came to a quick stop in front of the elongated white adobe ranch house, yanked on the hand brake, and sprang to the ground with the ease and grace of an acrobat. If he hadn't had such a gift of music, he might easily have been a successful professional athlete. He was lanky. Six feet three inches, with the loping, powerful strides of a gazelle. His skin, smooth and burnished, like a lovingly tanned leather, seemed created for the public eye, as did the strong, blunted nose, the huge, inquiringly sensual green-gold eyes, deeply set above prominent cheekbones, powerful jawline. He was born to be noticed, loved, emulated. If not on the stages of the world's concert halls, then on its playing fields, where he might have summoned unheard-of resources to propel his team to victory in World Cup soccer play . . . or made the impossible end-zone catch to capture the Super Bowl . . .

or, twisting and turning and spinning, magically arced the winning basket through the hoop in the final seconds of the NBA Championship playoffs. Roland Williams was born to be a star. Every move he made was star quality and picture perfect.

Yet he'd spent most of his life avoiding photographers. Hiding from the media leeches. Protecting his tender core.

Roland slid off the green crash helmet and heavy black goggles—the easiest of his many disguises to remove. He loathed this constant masquerade. The hats. Wigs in all shapes and colors. Even false noses. But he detested more the consequences of not wearing them. Fans pointing, grabbing, chasing, dozens of legs and arms threatening to squeeze and trample the very life out of him in their relentless pursuit.

Hey now, boy, don't cry. Be a good soldier, that's right. It's all over now. Everybody's gone. It's okay. Here, use my handkerchief. . . .

He was a scared eight-year-old belting out R&B tunes at Saturday afternoon concerts. Week after week he watched in choking horror as the teen audience went berserk, bouncing up and down, hysterical, until finally charging the stage—desperate to get at him, surrounding him in white loafers and striped knee socks, demanding a part of him, yanking off his tiny bow tie, swiping his red silk handkerchief. Once they even got his shoes.

Victor always saved him.

Parting the frenzied crowd. Hoisting up little Roland. Bundling him tightly in his arms. Safe. Secure. Loved. Victor was the father and mother Roland Williams never knew.

Victor Zahmedahn. The most sought-after manager of musical talent of the late sixties. He had discovered Roland quite by accident. The boy had landed his first television commercial. Victor happened to be on the set, a courtesy to a songstress client. He planned a fast exit. All of a sudden this scrawny six-year-old Latino kid—his name then was Rolando—belted out the first few lines of the burger jingle.

Victor Zahmedahn knew what he heard—the clarion call of solid gold.

He went to work.

The kid, he quickly learned, had been adopted by his foster parents. Freddie and Mary Mae Williams. A fat, beer-guzzling garbage collector and his complaining wife. They had filed for the adoption only a few weeks after Roland did his first radio ad. Maybe they cared for him, after a fashion. That was an open question. But there was no disputing that Roland's earnings swiftly moved the Williamses from a flat in the Crenshaw district to a charming four-bedroom Spanish stucco in Beverly Hills. The only appreciation Freddie and Mary Mae showed their new son was to beat and ill-feed him—when he wasn't working.

Victor hired a big legal gunslinger. He found out about the physical abuse. The lawyer built a masterful case showing that the Williamses were greedy moneygrubbers. Utmost discretion was exercised. It was all handled out of open court, out of the newspapers. Victor wanted a clean slate for his new protege. The Williamses were silenced with five thousand dollars a month. A bargain. In the deftly arranged settlement, Victor won legal guardianship, with complete control over Roland's financial and personal affairs.

He became the boy's manager. And much more. He was Roland's protector. His taskmaster. His savior. Victor devoted his considerable talents to cultivating and molding this precious human vessel, this musical instrument of such exquisite rarity.

To masterminding the Roland Williams mystique.

In the beginning, Victor would watch his little discovery for hours on end, considering his potential from every angle. "You look like the Third World poster child," he teased the boy. "Look how skinny you are. Like a beanpole. But those eyes! The whole world could get lost in those green eyes!"

He lopped the final vowel from his ward's first name. Rolando became simply Roland. "We'll keep the adopted name, we'll keep Williams," Victor proclaimed. "With that voice and those exotic looks, boy, you're going to need a name that's as nonthreatening and familiar as the kid's next door."

Nonetheless, as Roland's talent began to be recognized, a unique strategy was at the heart of his rapidly growing popularity. Avoidance of the media. Let them report the numbers on the charts. Make up wildly improbable stories about Roland's personal history, if that's what the fans demanded. Fight to pop a flashbulb at him as he ducked out of frame.

In the media's zealous pursuit, an enigma was created. A persona nobody knew, but everybody wanted to know. An untouchable mind and body to go along with the ethereal voice and virtuoso guitar work. The Roland Williams mystique.

Victor created it. He had to.

The boy would have been eaten alive if thrown to the press. Performing was one thing—onstage Roland was magic, sheer magic.

Transformed by his music. Transported to another world, his own private world. He became *the* Roland Williams.

Offstage, with strangers, he was somebody else. Insecure. Sometimes unable to speak. Occasionally he stuttered.

It was the most uncanny mix of overwhelming talent and lack of self-confidence, of stage mastery and personal terror that Victor had ever seen. But he had managed to capitalize on it, to turn liability to asset—to make Roland Williams a star in spite of himself.

Roland drank in the utter privacy of the starkly beautiful canyon land. His ranch was the only place on earth where he felt at ease with his strangely circumscribed life, his reclusive existence, as one of the world's most famous faces. Here he could wander for hours over his acres and acres and feel at peace, at one with himself, gloriously alone. It was at this ranch that he reached his creative peaks. Almost all his best lyrics had been born here.

If the songs he composed—many of them celebrations of the down-trodden and the ordinary, working men and women and families, common folks who withstood backbreaking burdens to find dignity in simple lives and honest pleasures—if these songs seemed at odds with the fabulous riches he had accumulated, well, so be it. The riches that fame brought enabled him to buy this ranch, but that didn't mean he had forgotten what it feels like to be hurting, scared, alone. He remembered, all right. Before Victor. When his own mother, his *mamita,* went away.

"How's it goin', Lucinda love?" Roland held out a sugar cube. The Arabian addax, a relative of the antelope with long, curving horns, tested unsteady legs to nip gratefully at the sweet lump. "Where's that vixen daughter of yours?"

He looked around for the fragile two-month-old which Lucinda had stoically delivered as Roland stood by on a rainy December night. "Oh, there you are," he called to the youngster, which had emerged from behind a manzanita tree. *"Mamita* takin' good care of you?"

If Victor were still alive . . .

Roland knew what Victor would have said. A TV interview? Don't. Don't take the chance. Don't risk it.

He didn't want to. Roland was scared. Petrified. What if he made a total damn fool of himself in front of a worldwide TV audience?

But he had to do it. Had to go through with it. He had given his word. Christine DuRand. At noon. He had promised.

"I still can't believe we got him," Christine called out as soon as she heard the door open.

"Not only have we got him, honeybunch," cooed Maggie as she lumbered over to the makeup table, "but I've got something *on* him!"

"Something that will stretch the interview further than five minutes, I hope. Research can't come up with anything." Christine turned from the mirror to face her assistant and stifled a laugh.

Maggie was wearing that red-and-white-striped pinafore-caftan again—the one that made her look like a Red Cross tent.

Quickly Christine returned her gaze to the mirror and began to scrutinize the crease of gray shadow above her eyes. As usual, she was not quite satisfied with her own work, but too impatient for a lengthy session in the makeup department.

"So whatcha got on Williams, Sherlock?"

"Oh, I did some sniffing around." And a lot of other things which would shock the hell out of you, sweetie.

"Atta girl, Rafferty. I knew you'd come through. Juicy stuff?"

"Better than juicy. Sexy. Heavvvvy duty."

Maggie plopped down on a nearby couch and waited. She was enjoying herself. Baiting Christine was always such a hoot. She got so damn impatient, so intense.

"Okay, Mag. Give. What did you find out?"

Christine strained to control herself. She was used to Maggie's "catch me, squeeze it out of me" games by now. But this morning it took all her will power to hold back.

Patience. Maggie's info would make the interview. It always did.

What a find Maggie Rafferty was. She was "connected" in Hollywood. Not in the sense that she was important, but on a much more visceral level. It was her town. She'd grown up here. Knew the famous pals of her film-director father as "Uncle Freddie" and "Uncle Barry." Played doctor with other neighborhood kids, who were now studio insiders.

They fed her delicious tidbits while she made the rounds at "in" restaurants like Spago, Morton's, The Hard Rock Café. Or got her hair done at Ménage à Trois. Or grocery-shopped at Jurgensen's. Or stopped for a midnight hot dog at Pink's. Wherever she went, Maggie was working the crowd.

Whatever else Maggie did to gather her goodies, Christine wasn't entirely sure. The woman's appetites seemed to know no bounds. All that mattered, though, was that she delivered. And the goods were usually first-rate.

Like Rod Steiger's dalliance with suicide. "Just ask him about it. His daughter says he'll talk."

Steiger had. At length. Reviewing the way he'd planned to do himself in, and the reasons why he hadn't. The interview ran eight minutes—more air time than Christine had ever been given for a single piece. Even Irving Taubman, the network president, let word filter down that it was "fascinating television."

When Christine got her own show she immediately plucked Maggie from the research department to be her assistant—with a healthy expense account. She deserved it. Over the last six months Maggie had supplied dozens of leads on big stars: Liz Taylor, Rod Stewart, Racquel Welch.

And now Roland Williams.

"Maggie!" Christine almost yelled, visibly agitated now. "I've got to be at Lightning Records in less than two hours. Let's have it."

"In a sec," Maggie murmured, pulling two small slips of pink paper from a gigantic pocket. "Before I forget, you've got a couple of messages here."

"Screw the messages. What about Williams?"

"My, my. Aren't we uptight this morning? With all the hot rides Blair's been giving you, it must be time for your sixty-thousand-mile checkup."

Christine frowned. She detested Maggie's casual and often downright sleazy references to her personal life, but had learned that overreacting merely egged her on.

"Hmm. Call here from a doctor. Dr. Michaels. Did the rabbit die?"

"Never heard of him," snapped Christine.

"Oh, wait. Long distance. Six twelve area code. Where's that?"

"Minneapolis." Christine snatched the slip from Maggie's hand. "Kent Michaels? It's been more than ten years. He's married now. Why in the world would he be calling me?"

"Sugarbuns, you're a glamour girl. With her own TV show. In Hollywood. And you don't understand why an old beau from the hometown gets the hots when he sees you on the tube? Probably wants to give you a free physical."

"He's a surgeon, Mag. Cardiac specialist."

"Mhmmmmm. Speaking of heartthrobs, our favorite, Ballsy Blair, left two messages for you before nine A.M. Shirley says he sounded ticked off. You two have a bad night?"

Christine sighed. "We *didn't* have a night, that's the problem. By the time Denny Bracken called back to confirm the interview, it was too late to drive out to Malibu."

"Kiddo, when it comes to a gorgeous sex machine like Mr. M, it is never too late. But if you're not up for it anymore, let ol' Mag have the next dance. Hell, I'd wallow through a mudslide on the Pacific Coast Highway to climb into his bed."

Christine laughed in spite of herself. "He'd probably get off on that. Now when are you going to cut this infantile routine of yours and give me the poop on Williams?"

"Okay . . . okay." Maggie smiled at Christine. "Fasten your seat belt."

"I'll take my chances," said Christine, crossing her arms.

"First off, Mr. Songbird is truly into cooking. He—"

"*Cooking!*" Christine cut her off. "Who gives a damn about cooking? We're not going to be at his home. There won't be a chance for any B-roll of him stirring up rice and beans in his solid-gold caldron or—"

"I *know* that." Maggie pouted. "It isn't that he cooks, girl. It's *who* he cooks for."

Now we're getting somewhere. . . .

"Mr. Superstar. Mr. Top of the Charts. That's five charts in one week. Mr. Oh-So-Private and Almost Excruciatingly Shy—"

"Maggie, cough it up, for Godsakes—"

"Mr. Roland Williams keeps a hot and sexy companion. In the guest house behind his splashy little bungalow in Bel-Air. Hans filled me in, hon. And after I turned on my, ahem, irresistible charm, he told me lots more."

I can imagine. . . . "That's still pretty lame," Christine said. "These days a good-looking twenty-four-year-old recording star with a live-in girlfriend won't even shock small-town Baptists."

"Precious face, trust Maggie. Who said anything about a *girl*friend?"

Christine's mouth dropped open.

"Isn't that *too* much?" Maggie was in heaven. Shocking Christine was better than three-way sex blindfolded. Almost.

"Hans swears that for the past several months Williams has been this close to—are you ready? *Burton Ratchford.* Can you believe it?"

Christine could not.

Roland Williams. Idolized by a legion of teenage girls from Portland to Pensacola. A singer whose sexual magnetism had spawned near-riots during his concerts.

This man was gay? And his lover was the country's chief fund-raiser for the Democratic Party?

— CHAPTER —

Two

They were naked. By the light of the fire reflected in their eyes, as the slender, well-muscled, light-skinned man gently moved to enter his golden-skinned lover from the rear, they looked like two magnificent beasts, joined in the half-light, forming a new synthesis of being. The younger man emitted a high keening sound, a trill that seemed at the edge of human hearing, a lament from deep in the subconscious . . . a lament that these two could never mate in any but this animal, carnal way.

Finally, the fair-skinned man cried out—it was a cry of pure joy— and the lament of his lover stopped. And with the flood of pleasure came contentment and sleep.

Now the flames of the fireplace were reflected in a hundred small beads of sweat on their entwined and still forms.

Roland tossed the last bits of dried apple and banana to the chattering monkeys and stood up, happening to glance down at his khaki shorts. He laughed softly and shook his head. The bulge at his crotch was absurdly obvious—the way it always was when he thought about being with Burton.

A glance at his Rolex watch. Nine-thirty. Less than three hours until he had to face Christine DuRand—and her camera. How could he manage it? Sit there like Sunday dinner, like helpless prey, while a reporter fired question after question at him? He had seen this DuRand's show. She was tough. She went for the jugular.

"It'll be a cinch, Ro," Burton had said. "Easy as roller skating. You'll zip right through it."

Roland didn't think so. He wasn't sure the words would come. Christ, maybe he'd start to stutter. Walking quickly back toward the adobe house, the parched sand and stone crunching noisily underfoot, he became more determined with each step to phone Burton. Make him listen to reason this time.

Cancel the whole thing.

"It's your wife," came the announcement from the short, scruffy woman with the irritating voice. She was wearing an Army green surplus jumpsuit.

Looks like she used the damn thing as a sleeping bag. . . .

Burton Ratchford glanced up from his well-organized desk to scowl at Sally Hansen. He didn't like interruptions—especially by the likes of this unkempt, impertinent young woman. His "assistant." Had he known she came with the job, he might have reconsidered.

Not really, of course. He was merely learning quickly that the political jungle was as abuzz with annoying insects as his old jungle, the high-powered world of the entertainment lawyer.

"Tell her I'll call back," he muttered, burying himself again in the handwritten lists in front of him. Tentative schedules for Roland Williams's Democratic fund-raising concerts.

The voice again. "I've already told her that twice this morning. Didn't you see the messages when you came in?" I'm here to help raise big bucks for the party, asshole. Not to help you play hide-and-seek with the wife. . . . "Okay," Burton shot back at her, yanking the phone receiver off the hook so fast he sent a heavy brass paperweight clanging to the floor.

"June!" It was more a command than a greeting. "How are you?"

He didn't need to ask. He had the picture. His wife of twenty-one years, sitting in the sunny breakfast room of their sprawling San Fernando Valley home. Drinking weak coffee laced with strong Jack Daniel's. Kids already off to school. Rosa, the housekeeper, busy tidying up. Nothing to do until eleven-thirty, when three other bored Encino housewives would join her for a go at what they called tennis.

He had walked out on her almost a year ago. But she phoned every day, usually at about this time—always to complain about something.

Burton deftly shifted the phone to the "June" position, the receiver cradled on his shoulder, just far enough away from his ear to buffer her self-pitying soliloquy.

"God knows how I'm surviving, Burton. Debbie has to get braces. She's very upset. She refuses to go in for the fitting. Jonathan is probably going to flunk calculus. And David. David has decided he is old enough to date. And a *shikse* tramp yet. Camille something. He asked her to the movies on Saturday night. She's a *junior,* Burton—from that all-girls Catholic school, Saint whatever-it-is, in Studio City. I've seen this one in action. At a party at the Bronfmans' a couple weeks ago. Dancing and thrusting her snatch at our David. It was disgusting. I don't think he should be allowed to go, Burton. Do you? Burton? Burton, are you listening to me?"

"Wha . . . yes, of course I'm listening."

"Well, do you think he should go?"

"Why not?"

"Why not? Why shouldn't your thirteen-year-old son go out with an older woman who'll probably rape him? Burton, you used to be the most conservative father in our neighborhood. And now you don't care how your own son loses his virginity? What's happened to you?"

Plenty . . .

Burton Ratchford had been the son every mother dreams of. The smartest kid in Hebrew school back in the tidy stucco-and-brick homes of the Borough Park section of Brooklyn. State wrestling champion in high school, but he got to Yale on an academic scholarship. Graduated Phi Beta Kappa. Went on to Yale law school and made the *Review.* Hired out of college by a prestigious New York law firm specializing in entertainment law, he finally decided to move out West where the *real* celebrities were. There he went on to make millions for his clients. And for himself.

With blond, fair-skinned good looks and a slender build, he was adored by women. Contrary to popular belief, he bedded few. But he married well. June Richman. Sole heir to the Richman scrap-metal fortune after her parents died in a freak private jet crash. She was nineteen. He was twenty-eight. They were wed seven months later.

Now he was forty-nine and just coming to terms with his homosexuality.

He'd fought it for years. God, but the crotch doesn't lie, does it? It may horrify, but it hardens nonetheless . . . as it had some years ago, at the sight of his sturdily built teenage nephew Bobby, crouched over the football at that family picnic. The boy wasn't queer. Neither, Burton told himself, was he. Blot it out. . . .

Charlie, the mailroom boy at one of the studios. Burton was so sure his glances weren't obvious. But why, then, did the boy slip him the note? *"Anytime."*

There had been others. All sublimated. All repressed. It couldn't be. He wouldn't allow it.

But eventually he did. Late one windy November night in San Francisco, after a maddeningly long and grueling video session for one of Ratchford's newest accounts. He wandered off in search of a relaxing midnight supper, a fine bottle of wine.

He found both. And Marvin. His waiter at the snug North Beach restaurant. Marvin fancied himself a singer. He tried to prove that later as Burton sipped cognac in Marvin's cramped walk-up.

The kid was no Sinatra, but what the hell? After such a rotten day, Burton was feeling too good, the cognac was doing its job too well.

Go with it.

When Marvin began fondling him, Burton watched in amazed silence. Before long, a huge smile crossed his face and he was moaning with pleasure. Incredible. Marvin's lips. Marvin's tongue. Just how it felt best. In the way no woman could know, and never had, to Burton. He fell asleep, spent, in Marvin's arms, luxuriating in the sensuous stickiness of sex. And release—at last he had tasted the forbidden. He had known another man.

In the harsh slant of morning light, entirely different emotions overwhelmed him. Fear. Hoping to God this no-talent fag wouldn't pop up in L.A. to embarrass him. Then anger. Guilt. Remorse.

Burton slipped quietly out of the apartment vowing, Never again. Knowing even then that the vow was empty and useless. He broke it many times. Always out of town, with a stranger. The possibility of being found out ate at him, but each new partner only increased his appetite.

Then the AIDS epidemic struck. That sent him running to a series of doctors—on the sly, of course—until finally he was reassured that he hadn't been infected. Still, the threat of contracting the disease, of dying an ignominious, shameful death, drove him back into safer sexual terrain. He swore off gay sex for two whole years. Until Roland Williams. They'd met at the Shrine Auditorium the night Roland had swept the Grammys, surpassing even Michael Jackson's record by winning ten of the coveted awards.

Reporters weren't allowed backstage, but somehow two camera crews had managed to corner Roland. On his way out, Burton had noticed the two-way, rapid-fire interrogation and Roland's extreme discomfort. Instinctively, he stepped in.

"Sorry, Mr. Williams is late for the NARAS party at the Bonaventure. That will be all for now, thank you."

"Hey, who are you anyway?" demanded a surly interviewer, shoving a microphone under Burton's chin as he guided Roland away.

"I'm his attorney," Burton answered sharply.

That wasn't true, then or later. But it was the beginning of a relationship that went far beyond that of a lawyer to his client.

"Burton? Burton! Jeezus. Are you reading a book? I said what about Sunday dinner? Will you be here?"

He suppressed a groan. "Yes. Of course, June. You know I've never missed."

He hadn't. Leaving his lucrative practice to go to work for the Democrats had meant a pay cut of nearly half a million a year. It was a daring gamble. But if . . . if he could help to unseat Sullivan, the Republican incumbent . . . if a Democrat was in the White House again come January . . .

To Burton it was perfectly clear. He'd have his pick of a choice job in Washington. Maybe even Cabinet level. He had his eye on Commerce. Or Interior. Hell, why not?

Divorcing June in the meantime was out of the question. He just couldn't afford it.

And staying with Roland Williams was an absolute necessity.

He needed Roland. More than for sex. He needed him for the fundraising concerts. As many as possible. That magic voice of his could reap beaucoup bucks for the Democratic candidate for President. And do wonderful things for Burton.

Who knows? Maybe in ten, fifteen years—Burton Ratchford, first Jewish President of the United States . . .

It had a nice ring.

Irving Taubman hurried out of the Four Seasons and made his way toward Lexington Avenue, a fat H. Upmann cigar jutting out beneath his neatly trimmed mustache, the tingle of the after-lunch brandy coating his tongue. He adjusted the soft felt fedora on his nearly bald head and finished buttoning his navy-blue Chesterfield. Pulling on fur-lined leather gloves, he checked his Piaget watch.

Fifteen minutes. That's all it would take to reach the massive steel-and-glass high-rise overlooking the East River. International Network headquarters. He'd be there at the stroke of two. No need to take a taxi. Filthy inside, all of them. And the drivers. My God. They never shut up. Irving despised wasting time, and people who wasted his. Far better to take a brisk walk. It cleared the mind.

He hustled across Lexington against a red light. A sleek gray limousine swerved to miss him, almost sideswiping a bus.

Irving smiled. It was good to be back in New York.

Here a short walk could be a challenge. Play a little dodg'em with traffic. Enrage a few cabbies. So much more fun than Los Angeles, where nobody walked anywhere. Those who did got tickets for jaywalking.

His first week with the network, Irving was crossing Rodeo Drive in Beverly Hills and got the first jaywalking ticket of his life. Such embarrassment. A stupid cop stopping you on the street. Worse, it had cost him. A hundred and seventy bucks—because he hadn't bothered to pay the original thirteen-dollar fine. The memory still rankled.

But nothing could dampen the man's spirits today. March seventh. The network's monthly board meeting. His fourth anniversary as president. An extremely profitable six months behind him. And ahead? Perhaps chairman of the board.

Irving smiled again. I'm fifty-eight. Dollinger is seventy-six. The old fart has to retire soon. And when he does, who else steps in but his handpicked president? The power. The money—two million a year at least when you added in bonuses, stock options, all the other perks. Enough, thank God, to finally dump Blanche. The freedom—

that's what it's really all about. Freedom to wallow in tender young pussy to my cock's content.

The final rung up the corporate ladder looked easy. A lead-pipe cinch.

When the network had stolen Taubman away from Home Box Office four years ago, he'd been given a mandate: Lower the budget, raise the ratings. He'd done both, faster than anyone had expected. Irving Taubman knew his job. He knew damn well what IN was selling. Magical puffs of smoke. Evanescent, ever-shifting smoke. Hot today. Gone tomorrow. That's show biz, that's how he ran the network. His management philosophy was equally simple and to the point. He'd learned it growing up in Miami, watching his father run the extravagant nightclub in the Deauville Hotel. It could be expressed in seven little words: "What have you done for me lately?"

No one at IN messed with Irving. He was rock-solid. And today he would stun them all. He let out a harsh laugh. They ought to crown me king.

First Avenue. Five more minutes. Snowflakes tickled his jowls. Wind whipped around the exposed flesh of his naked ears. Irving sucked on the Upmann and tramped forward, his size thirteens leaving huge cookie-cutter tracks in the thin crust of snow. Under his breath, he rehearsed his speech.

"All of you are aware how well our latest celebrity-interview format, *The DuRand Report,* is faring. Well, I'm here to tell you that since I ordered it on the air only six months ago, it has pushed us over the hump. The strong ratings numbers have literally made us Number One. The Number One network—nationally and internationally. I don't have to tell you what this means in terms of advertising revenue."

A round of applause is certain here. Wait about ten seconds.

"And our future looks even rosier—"

Pause a bit. Let them hang expectantly. Clear the throat. Shuffle papers. Then give it to them.

"Now for that little surprise I've been promising. The television gods are smiling upon us, gentlemen. I have arranged for an exclusive—I repeat, exclusive—interview. With none other than Great Britain's Princess Diana! It will air in three segments on *The DuRand Report.* Each one carefully slotted into a key ratings period. In short, get ready for the television coup of the decade. . . ."

Stop here for a slight smile. Not smug. But confident. Powerful.

"And if that doesn't give IN a lock on Number One, I don't know what will!"

Irving's heart pounded an excited crescendo as he reached the stark high-rise.

Great stuff. And there's no way the board will ever be the wiser. So DuRand lined up the Shy Di interview herself—so what? These guys don't know videotape from film, f'crissakes.

Inside the enormous marble-floored lobby, Irving handed his hat to a thin, slightly hunched-over man who stood anxiously waiting there.

"Afternoon, Jeremy. Brisk one today!"

"Oh, yes, sir. You're right about that, sir," stammered Taubman's New York assistant, brushing droplets of moisture off the hat.

They walked to the elevator in single file—the rich country squire and his manservant. The network president and his sycophant.

At the third floor, Irving stepped out onto a thick green carpet. A shapely number wearing a red knit dress took his coat.

"Thank you, Miss, ahh—"

"Oh, Linda, Mr. Taubman. I'm new." She giggled.

Irving had an impulsive urge to pinch her rounded red knit bottom. But he controlled himself admirably. One of his hard and fast rules: Never dip your wick into the secretarial pool. The other female executives, producers, on-air talent—all fair game. Supposedly bright enough to know what they were getting into. But receptionists and secretaries, no way. Too low on the totem pole. Too indiscreet. Trouble.

Marching toward the boardroom, Irving took a slim gold pen and pad from his inside pocket. "Call Pearce," he wrote.

I'll deserve a little reward after this meeting. And nobody lines up special deliveries like Rexy baby. Can't imagine anything better than that last one. She couldn't have been more than twenty. Nice, clean. And what tits! Loved the white cape and garter belt. And the best thing is . . .

He opened the solid walnut doors. . . . I'm charging these tootsies to you guys.

Irving smiled a warm greeting to R. F. Dollinger and the eleven other somberly suited men seated around the rectangular table.

"Can I help you, miss?"

Tashi Qwan stared longingly at the huge chunks of pâté. The *pasta* al pesto. The dozens of cheeses—from French Brie to Canadian Cheddar to Swiss Jarlsberg. Fruit from New Zealand, Israel, Mexico.

"No. Just admiring," she said, turning away from the sales clerk.

Tashi was very hungry. She'd had nothing to eat since yesterday afternoon's tea. Opening her soft leather Gucci bag, she took out the London *Daily Mail* classified section once again. For forty-five minutes she'd been wandering around Knightsbridge, trying to summon up courage.

To the clerks at Harrods, where the sight of such gastronomic bounty had beckoned Tashi like a desert mirage, she looked much like any other discriminating, rich customer.

It wasn't merely the designer clothes—from the Giorgio Armani suit to the Charles Jourdan shoes. Tashi was strikingly tall and slim, with the air of elegance and sophistication that accompanies fine breeding. A porcelain china-doll face, a delicate mix of Chinese and English. Intelligent, calming almond-brown eyes. A fashion model perhaps. Or a rich businessman's wife. The mistress of an Arab sheik.

She was none of these.

Tashi Qwan was a struggling student. Broke. Unemployed. And quite desperate to make as much money as possible in a hurry.

She read the ad for the sixth time that morning.

EXCITING CAREER OPPORTUNITY. ATTRAC-
TIVE WOMEN, 18–45. FLEXIBLE HOURS.
POSSIBLE 1,500 POUNDS/WK. LANGUAGES
A BIG PLUS. SOME MODELING PREFER-
ABLE, BUT NOT ESSENTIAL. APPLY IN
PERSON. 180 ESSEX CT., ROOM 203.
10 A.M.–2 P.M. THIS WEEK ONLY.

It sounded too good to be true. There had to be a catch. But fifteen hundred pounds a week! She could enroll at the Royal College of Veterinary Science after all, if only she could earn that kind of money.

She'd been searching for a job as an interpreter. All those years of study that Daddy had insisted upon—she was fluent in English, Chinese, French, Italian, and German—would finally pay off. Get her out of this jam. But she'd had no luck. Even at the European Economic Council, where she knew the chief of personnel.

"It isn't that you aren't qualified, my dear," he'd said, peering out over his bifocals. "It's all that gobbledygook to do with your birthplace. Oh, I know you're a British subject—but born in Hong Kong, you see. And living here just over six weeks. It would take me months to clear you. And right now we have nothing available anyway. Frightfully sorry."

They were all sorry. But none as sorry as Tashi Qwan, nineteen years old and alone in London.

She was the illegitimate daughter of an affluent British career diplomat—Reginald Hutchins. He had been stationed in Hong Kong when he fell wildly in love with her mother, Sasheena Qwan. Tashi was the product of their passion.

Not until she was ten was she permitted to meet her father. Sasheena never forgave Hutchins for reneging on his pledge to leave his wife. She relented in answer to his repeated entreaties to see his daughter only after he established a generous trust fund for Tashi and promised to finance her education.

Hutchins loved his daughter enormously. He called her his crowning achievement, his proudest accomplishment. They met in Hong Kong or other exotic locales like Bali or the Portuguese island of Madeira at least once a year. They booked into the world's best hotels—Hotel du Cap on the French Riviera, the Royal Danieli in Venice, the Sacher in Vienna. Wherever they were together, Hutchins never failed to marvel at his daughter's maturing beauty and mind.

She wanted desperately to become a veterinarian. Hutchins insisted that she study near him, in London. Delighted, she agreed. He outfitted her with a new wardrobe in Paris, saw to it that she settled into a charming flat in Sloane Square and spent as much time with her in those first heady days as his schedule permitted.

But their hours together were stolen.

Constance Hutchins had known nothing of Tashi. At least, not until three weeks ago, after Hutchins's sudden and untimely death. He fell from his polo pony and suffered a fatal stroke.

Tashi found out that evening, watching the BBC news.

Her father, best friend, adviser, confidant, benefactor—all gone. Constance Hutchins, who discovered Tashi through letters and ledger records her husband had kept through the years, cut off the girl's money within the week.

Tashi knew she'd never see a shilling of the million-pound trust fund. Or the quarter-million in cash and securities he'd set aside for her education. Constance Hutchins had the power in this town, and Tashi had none. Constance was contesting the will, and it was all over.

She gets the money . . . you lose.

Tashi was forced to move from the posh flat to a small boarding-

41

house in South Kensington. Forced to sell off most of her new clothes for food and rent.

Now she was down to practically nothing.

Even returning to Hong Kong was not an option. She didn't have the plane fare. She owed her solicitors a great deal of money. If she threw herself on her mother's mercy, her dream of veterinary school would be sacrificed to the unappealing prospect of endless dreary days in Sasheena's restaurant.

Tashi felt a stab of pain in her lower abdomen—a hunger pang. She tucked the newspaper back into her handbag and left Harrods in a brisk walk. Heading toward Essex Court. Gnawing on her bottom lip.

You have to do it. Have to apply for that job, whatever it is. There won't be any packages from heaven. Daddy can't help you now. . . .

From his glassed-in solarium, Roland stared blankly out over the lush greenery and tiled roofs of Bel-Air and Beverly Hills.

"Burton, I can't do it, I just can't," he slurred into the phone.

"What do you mean, you can't? I thought it was all set!" Burton pushed himself away from his desk. "Where the hell are you?" *Jesus, it's eleven-thirty. He has to be at Lightning in half an hour. . . .*

"At home," Roland whimpered.

"Where at home? Roland, are you stoned?"

Roland took a long drag from the fat roach and slithered closer to the soothing hot jet of water, nearly dropping the phone into the steaming Jacuzzi.

"Mhmmmmmmmmmmm."

"Listen to me, Ro. You stay right there, hear? It's too late to make it by noon. I'll get the interview moved back. I'm coming over there now. Roland? Stop smoking that goddamned thing. Get yourself together!"

Burton slammed down the receiver and quickly dialed the publicity offices of Laurence & Ferber.

Mamita, Mamita! Don' go! Me go, too!

The toddler began to wail, two tiny hands outstretched toward the tall, graceful woman.

"Shhhhh, *querido mío,*" came the caress of the husky voice. "Your *mamita* is here. . . ."

Roland slumped sideways, slipping down into the hundred-plus degrees of churning water. The bubbles tickled his nostrils. He jerked his head up. Eyes open. Awake, momentarily.

That dream again. Christ, am I ever going to shake that damn dream?

It happened nearly every time he smoked a joint. The same faint memories, pieced together into one vivid scene. Over and over again.

"My, my, Inés—how fancy you be!"

"Coulda been a model, that Inés. Class written all over her. Loads of it."

"Oughta be able to catch a millionaire looking like that, *mija!*"

Mamita is leaning over him, all dressed up, stroking his cheek. He's on the bare linoleum floor. Three other women are there. Her girlfriends, whistling at *Mamita,* teasing her.

Now she stoops to give him a kiss. Her breath smells of sweet wine.

He squints, trying to see exactly what she looks like. But her features are blurred, like a picture out of focus.

He reaches for her. She backs away. He begins to cry.

And she's gone. . . .

When he was younger, he would wake up sobbing, his small shoulders rising and falling helplessly. And there Victor would be, comforting him. Urging him gently back to sleep.

These days the dream just made him angry. Angry that he had been abandoned, stuck in foster homes until finally adopted when he was five. Angry at a mother who could do such a thing, who could care so little for a son who needed her so much.

She wasn't a mother to me. If it hadn't been for Victor, I'd probably be pumping gas, or collecting garbage, like Freddie Williams.

If it hadn't been for Victor . . .

He dozed again, his chin slowly sinking into the hot, soporific water.

"Dr. Michaels, call twenty-three, please . . . Dr. Michaels, twenty-three . . ."

Good God, what now?

Within the past half hour Kent Michaels had been paged seven times. Nuisance calls, all of them—nothing an intern couldn't have handled.

And he was exhausted. Six hours of bypass surgery, and enough stress to test the will of Gandhi. Then his nightly rounds of the post-op wards, highlighted by forty-five minutes of hand-holding with an octogenarian millionaire. An eccentric collector of fine art. A friend of the family. And worst of all, too painfully reminiscent of his own dad's final weeks, last September.

It had not been one of Kent Michaels's better days.

Given the time to think about it, Kent probably wouldn't have been able to remember a really good day. Not in the past year.

"Emotionally you're under a state of siege, Kent," his analyst, Paul Silver, had counseled. "Everybody's shooting at you from different directions. You're feeling deserted and frustrated. All your defenses are down. Best thing you can do now is stay in your foxhole. Just carry on one day at a time. Tough it out. Wait for things to change. They will. You'll see."

Not soon enough.

Kent yanked at the receiver on the wall phone near the nurses' station and dialed twenty-three.

"Dr. Michaels here."

"Did you miss me?"

Aw, shit.

"Darlene. How are you?"

Darlene Swenson. Best body on the nursing staff of the University of Minnesota Hospital. And the most calculating brain.

"Rested, Doctor. And relaxed. And very horny. When are you coming over?"

"It's a total zoo here, as usual. And you know me—Dr. Workaholic. How was the, uh . . . trip?" Michaels, you idiot. Don't ask. Cut it short.

"Jamaica? Wonderful, soothing, and dull. Wish you'd been there."

"I could do with a vacation, all right."

"So why not enjoy mine vicariously? Come on over later, I'll fix you a rum drink that will make you see swaying palms and a turquoise sunset. Then I'll pour sand in your shorts, and we can be in our own private beach cove. How's that for an offer you can't refuse?"

"Sorry, just can't tonight, Darlene. Really beat. Maybe a rain check?"

"Hey, you have been at the hospital too long. Take a look outside, Doctor. It's winter. You must mean a snow check. How about Saturday?"

"I might have to go to Mayo over the weekend."

44

"Okay. Let's talk tomorrow afternoon. I've got a surprise for you here you won't believe."

He hung up, sneaking a furtive glance at the two nurses standing nearby. Did they overhear? Figure it out?

Christ. Who cares? Everyone knows Swenson's hot on my tail. Should never have gotten started with her. Or half the women I've slept with recently.

A womanizer. That's what he'd become. On the surface anyway. And it bothered him. He wasn't one of these doctor studs who felt compelled to conquer body after body. "Promiscuous" was one word Kent had never applied to himself. Now apparently others did.

He could see it in their eyes. The way they sized up Kent Michaels's newfound, newly divorced lifestyle in a glance: Ah, here's the good-looking surgeon, on the make. Six-foot-two jock with the kind of body women fantasize about. Golden-blond hair. Mesmeric blue eyes. A hunk. Independently wealthy to boot. Watch out, girls . . . this lucky guy has it all.

Kent didn't feel lucky. Not anymore. Even though luck had been his birthright, some might say.

He'd been born to wealth and accepted it without hesitation, without guilt, without apology. He had taken advantage of every opportunity it could offer. He'd also worked hard. All-American running back at Northwestern, where he was summa cum laude. Everyone figured he'd turn pro, then eventually take over the family business. Oil. Grandpa Michaels had wisely listened to the advice of his close friend John D. Rockefeller.

But Kent did things his way. He went straight into medical school. Now he was quickly earning himself a statewide reputation as a cardiac surgeon and professor of cardiology at the University of Minnesota.

That's the way life fell into place for Kent Michaels. He had never questioned it—until last year.

First his father died. It was slow and agonizing. Then came his breakup with Lucia, the dynamic, attractive, always-in-charge assistant dictrict attorney he'd married five years earlier. Not her fault. Not his. Blame it on hopelessly conflicting lifestyles. He zigged when she zagged. The sex went first. Soon they were like two boarders in the same house.

Splitting up was his idea. She got almost everything—including the lovely house in Prospect Park.

Kent got his freedom. And a jump backward in time: another chance to dive into new beds. Without responsibility, without com-

45

mitment, without a joint bank account. Kent Michaels was on his own again. Available. Ready.

Or so he had imagined it.

Reality was something else again. It wasn't long into his new life that Kent made a puzzling discovery. He didn't much like it. Oh, he could go through the motions. But he wasn't really participating. The encounters left him feeling . . . well, sort of lost, empty, adrift.

He'd sampled a variety of women. A beautiful English professor he'd met in the campus swimming pool. A stylish French international banker who lived in New York. A number of nurses on the staff. But something was missing. A vital part of Kent Michaels was in the OFF position. And he didn't know how to get it back on. It had been that way for months.

Lonely. Yes. Even though his professional life brought him into constant contact with stimulating people, Kent felt closed off. Isolated. Guarded. There was no one he really wanted to communicate with. He realized that since the divorce he'd slowly slipped into the role of confirmed recluse—working more hours than he ever had before, spending what time he had for himself alone in his stark luxury condominium, dating only when he felt compelled to satisfy a physical urge for the warmth of another body next to his. And lately he felt less and less compelled.

"All systems are temporarily down, I guess," he'd joked with Silver, the analyst, last fall. Now it was almost spring. Kent's outlook had not improved.

In the past, whenever his spirits sagged, work had been his cure-all, recharging him, at least momentarily. Making him feel useful, needed—sometimes omnipotent. Performing delicate cardiac surgery was, after all, like breathing life into another human being. He could do that.

He could still do that. But it seemed he had used up whatever storehouse of psychic rewards the operating room had once held for him. At the hospital Kent put it on automatic and got through the day.

And at the end of this particular day a dull migraine was eating its way across his forehead. Kent had recently marked the passage of his thirty-fifth birthday. Right now he felt fifty. Finishing rounds, Kent rode the elevator down to the second floor. Reaching his office, he shoved open the door to the fir-paneled waiting room.

"Oh, Dr. Michaels. Your friend Jim Bennett with the police department phoned again. He said it wasn't necessary to call back unless you'd heard something," said Betty, his secretary, with an inquisitive look.

"Okay, thanks. Did, ahhh, Miss DuRand return the call?"

Betty's eyes widened. "No. She didn't. Would you like me to place it again?"

"Nah, don't bother. Maybe tomorrow. Goodnight."

"Get some rest, Doctor. You look awful."

Kent sat in his silver Porsche, waiting for a full blast from the heater. Snowy ten-degree nights like this used to energize him, make him feel alert and alive. Tonight he just felt cold, depleted, tired.

And, in an odd inexplicable way, worried. About Cathleen Rand.

Why would the FBI be interested in *her?* But that's what Bennett said, and he swore his sources at the bureau were solid. "Plead the Fifth Amendment if they contact you," he'd joked. "I know a good bail bondsman."

Can't imagine her getting in big trouble. Hell, maybe the personality changed with the name. Wonder if she ever married? Jesus, it's been a long time. Seems like an eternity since she wrote me that Dear John letter. Cathleen . . . Christine.

He put the Porsche into gear and roared across the icy parking lot on automatic pilot, oblivious to the winter hazards.

He was thinking he might try phoning Christine again when he got home.

In the dream-state fog of marijuana smoke and swirling Jacuzzi steam, Roland's mind continued to drift and float.

Sixteenth birthday.

They'd had a wonderful dinner at Scandia, he and Victor, seated at Victor's favorite booth in the Garden Room. After dinner, Victor ordered a bottle of Dom Perignon and allowed Roland a few sips to celebrate. His sixteenth year. Their eighth together. His third platinum album. It was an occasion to remember.

In the limousine on the way home, Victor slowly slid his fine bony fingers to the boy's leg, stroking the sinewy muscle and the contours of his thigh. At first Roland hardly noticed. He was sunk deeply into the smooth leather seat, arms outstretched above the seat back, feet dangling over the jump seat in front of him.

Victor's touch became more insistent. He pushed the button that sent up the glass partition separating them from the driver.

Roland sat up, dazedly, as if he had just been awakened.

"What's wrong, Victor?" His voice betrayed his puzzlement and confusion.

"Nothing, son. Not a thing," said Victor, caressing Roland's face as a mother might a child's. "Roland, you know how much I care for you?"

"Mmm-hmmm," said Roland, letting his eyes close.

"Well, it's just that you were never old enough to truly understand before. And now you are."

Roland felt a hand. He opened his eyes to see that he was being bathed in a gaze of passion. It scared him.

He wasn't afraid of Victor. He knew Victor would never hurt him. Victor was a friend forever.

That was it. He was afraid to risk their friendship. He didn't want to stop singing and recording, didn't want to lose Victor's sure-handed guidance, didn't want to wind up back in a foster home, unwanted, unloved. He tried to make light of Victor's advances. Tried changing the subject. Victor knew what Roland was going through. He'd expected it. The boy was a virgin. He needed time.

Victor had time. Several nights later Roland walked from his bedroom up the circular stairs to Victor's room. He intended only to say goodnight, to try explaining his feelings since the birthday dinner.

"Come in, Roland," said Victor. "I've been waiting for you."

"I . . . I, uh . . ."

"Hush. Come here, son. Come sit by me."

Roland saw that tears had clouded Victor's eyes and his lower lip trembled slightly. He threw his arms around the dear man. He could smell floral cologne.

"Victor—"

"Shhhhhhh."

They kissed. And when Roland saw how happy this made Victor, he wasn't afraid anymore. They kissed again. And again. Soon Roland found himself sharing Victor's bed, feeling the elder man's arousal, his desire so long repressed. Soon he was sharing Victor's passion.

Morning arrived before he returned to his own room—a morning quite unlike any other. Roland felt splendid.

And he continued to feel that way after their lovemaking. To the day of Victor's death, five years later, at the age of fifty-eight. An acute attack of angina.

Victor left everything to Roland. His estate, his 10 percent of Lightning Records. A fleet of classic cars. Roland didn't care. He had been abandoned again. First his mother, and now Victor.

He had loved Victor so very much. But now he was alone in the huge, lonely house, hearing only his own footsteps on the gleaming hardwood floors. And doubting. Doubting everything. Himself. His strength. Even what he and Victor had had together . . .

"What the hell—Ro! What're you trying to do? Drown? Jesus, c'mon outta there!"

"M'okay—"

"Yeah, yeah, you're okay, all right. Look at you. If this isn't the most unprofessional, childish stunt I've ever seen—"

"M'okay, I said!"

Roland was attempting to stand in the swirling Jacuzzi, but his legs were rubber. Burton had him under the armpits and was tugging furiously, his own clothes soaked through. Finally he managed to drag Roland out onto the tiled floor. He let him drop with a thud.

"Uhhhh—" groaned Roland, as his head bumped against the floor.

"I don't believe this. Honest to Christ." Burton grabbed a hose used to water the solarium plants and began showering Roland with ice-cold water.

"Hey!"

"Get up, you son of a bitch!"

"Stop it!"

"I said, get up! You're gonna go through with this. For once, you're gonna act like a man."

Three

The vigilant maitre d' caught them out of the corner of his eye. They were rounding the corner of the Beverly Hills Hotel lobby and walking toward him. The tall, voluptuous redhead, wearing the tailored off-white Ungaro suit today. Very chic. She was with a paunchy middle-aged man dressed in black, as usual. But they were early. By half an hour at least.

"Hurry up," he said, clicking his fingers at the busboy. "Prepare the table for Miss Crosse." Thank goodness the party at her favorite banquette had just left.

He checked his watch. Only twelve-ten. Maybe Miss Crosse finished taping her television show early. But wasn't it live? The maitre d' didn't know. What he did know was that Jewel Crosse, the most powerful gossip maven in the country, didn't like to be kept waiting. Especially not in the Polo Lounge, where she and her producer, Howard Ruskin, lunched nearly every day.

He shot an anxious glance back toward the busboy, then relaxed. The final spoon was being set. Ahhhh . . .

"Miss Crosse, so nice to see you. Right this way."

Trailing after him, Jewel scanned her surroundings as only a true professional can. Imperceptibly. Adeptly. In just those few seconds she gauged precisely the luminosity of the room, its star power.

Sean Connery at table three. With his wife, Micheline. Smart lady. Talked him into doing yet another 007. Pity he's married, though. Such a sexy Scotsman. Never forget our last interview in his room at the Century Plaza. He didn't wear his rug. Or his shoes.

Dudley Moore over there on the right. With a breathtaking blonde, of course. Uncanny how such a short fellow, with a club foot yet, could beat the odds and wind up a Hollywood sex symbol.

Shirley MacLaine with—who's that, her manager? At that small table next to the bar? Well, it *is* perfect for eavesdropping.

But banquette number one, tucked into the corner opposite the bar, with a clear view of the entrance to the Polo Lounge, was the best for Jewel's purposes—to see and be seen.

A Jewel Crosse entrance never went unnoticed. And now, as she glided in behind the pink tablecloth onto the dark-green cushy seat, making room for Ruskin, Jewel felt a dozen or so sets of eyes scrutinize her. The ones from out of town. Tourists and deal makers. Looking over coffeecups, peering out from behind tinted glasses, glancing up discreetly from conversations. All curious about the woman who popped onto the TV screen for half an hour each morning, chatting with the stars and offering juicy Hollywood gossip.

Was Jewel Crosse as heavily made up as she appeared on TV? Yes. Was her short, stiff hairdo really that brassy shade of red? Yes. Were her breasts actually as large as—yes. Definitely. Jewel had knockers men couldn't resist. They were perfectly proportioned considering her five-foot-nine, slim-waisted body. Rumors regarding her melonlike mammaries rivaled stories about Ronald Reagan's hair. Did he or didn't he dye it? Did she or didn't she have implants?

There was no disputing that Jewel made the most of her assets. With specially designed clothes and lingerie that made men want to lunge. Many had, and many had been chosen to receive her favors. Those, that is, who could do Jewel Crosse the most good.

"Wine today, madame?"

Jewel nodded to the waiter.

"And tequila, sir?"

"Yeah. Uh, make it a double," Howard decided, removing his dark sunglasses with a swooping gesture and planting them in the inside pocket of his double-knit black jacket.

Black was Howard's good-luck color—had been ever since the day he got his first directing job. A dog-food commercial in his hometown,

Milwaukee. Twenty degrees at high noon. Snow four feet deep. He'd been hired as assistant director, but by some freak accident his boss tripped over a child's wagon hidden in a snowdrift and broke his leg. Howard, wearing a black ski outfit that day, took over.

The advertising agency liked his commercial so much, they asked him to direct many more. Eventually he moved to Los Angeles and began producing shows.

Just how the child's wagon got into the snowdrift was never investigated. But from that day onward, Howard Ruskin never wore anything but black.

Today, his black silk shirt was open at the collar, with two gold chains dangling on a hairy chest. Black double-knit beltless pants. And a yellow silk pocket scarf (a dash of color on accessories was acceptable).

The drinks arrived. They sipped at them thirstily.

"A double today, Howard. What's this, a celebration?"

"Ah, Jewel, honey, we got it so good, the two of us, know what I mean?" He smiled at her fawningly.

Jewel adjusted her skirt, crossed her slim, shapely legs, and examined her long red nails. Quite sure she wasn't ready for what was coming next. Howard Ruskin was an average producer and an okay lay. But it had been almost a year. She was ready to move on. Unfortunately, the network brass liked Howard. He'd be there forever. As long as she was, too, it paid to be, well, nice.

"I just can't believe it," he continued. He was massaging her thigh now. "We're so good together in bed. I just can't get enough. Our little, ah, afternoon delights upstairs here after lunch. Perfect, know what I mean? And, hey, know the best part, honey?" He finished the tequila, signaling the waiter for another.

I'm just dying to hear, you booze-addled sot.

"The best part is, since we've been making it, it's even better for me when I'm with the ol' lady."

Jewel stared at him, not believing what she had heard. She glanced around to see if anyone was listening.

"Yeah, yeah," Howard said, nodding exuberantly. "When I'm with Alice I fantasize about you and your gorgeous bod!"

Jewel stifled her outrage. Julie Andrews was passing by. Jewel smiled in greeting, then turned and said stiffly, "Howard, really. I don't think this is the place to go on about us. Or Alice."

How can I bear another minute with him? Why don't I tell him to take a flying leap?

She knew why.

Ever since that smelly Greyhound bus had deposited her, an under-privileged teenager from a broken home in Santa Cruz, on Hollywood Boulevard twenty-five years ago, Jewel had instinctively and single-mindedly screwed her way up the Hollywood media ladder. To the creaking of bedsprings, her status continued to rise—from junior writer to having her own morning national television show, *Crosse Covers Hollywood*. Now two million viewers watched her daily interviews and show-business commentaries. Not bad.

But not good enough. Jewel wanted to ascend higher still. She wanted more. More than four A.M. wakeup calls and nine A.M. deadlines. More than screwing Howard Ruskin. Much, much more.

"A call for you, Miss Crosse," said the pretty young female page. She placed the phone next to Jewel's wineglass.

Jewel reached for the receiver, glad for any distraction from Howard. "Yes?" Her voice was cool, queenly. "Oh, Bruce," she said, warming instantly for her longtime assistant. "What's doing?"

"Nothing you're going to like, sugar," Bruce sighed, indulging in a dramatic pause to observe his angular face in the heart-shaped mirror over his desk. He smoothed the pastel T-shirt over his inverted stomach, yanked out an unruly eyebrow, and, with a flourish, placed it in the wastebasket.

"What do you mean?" Jewel demanded.

"Well, 'member your old, ahem, pal from your days at the International Network? I speak of none other than Miss Christine DuRand."

Pal . . . I should have that little Midwestern twat's job. I satisfied enough of Irving Taubman's kinky whims to be running the network myself by now.

"What about her?"

"Miss DuRand, it seems, has set up an exclusive with Roland Williams."

"I don't *believe* it!" Jewel gasped. "She never beats me out of an exclusive. Remember when I got Al Pacino? Meryl Streep? Williams must be desperate for publicity all of a sudden. Who's his flack?"

"Laurence and Ferber. Denny Bracken."

"*That* putz?" she whispered loudly. That putz who has the hots for me? "When's the interview?"

"Tomorrow. Four P.M. Postponed from today at noon. Should I call Brack—?"

"No," she replied curtly. "I'll handle him." She hung up, then motioned the waiter over to pull the table out.

"I have to use the john, Howard. Christine DuRand has an exclusive with Roland Williams tomorrow. While I'm gone, why don't you make a few calls and find out why the hell she got it instead of me?"

Jewel fluttered out of the Polo Lounge, breasts bobbing, a trail of Giorgio perfume wafting in her wake. The elevator door was standing open and ready, and she marched inside and pushed 2. The room she and Howard usually shared was on the second floor, and she was anxious to reach it. The call to Laurence & Ferber required privacy.

Denny Bracken, you little runt. Jewel has what you've been panting after. . . .

"Okay, Chicki, you set?" asked the ruggedly handsome man, slipping the crash helmet on the curvaceous brunette's head. He caressed the curls spilling out over her light-blue racing jacket and gave her his well-practiced lascivious look.

"Now just remember, when we hit the reservoir, we switch seats. Go ahead, get in."

She opened the door of the special-formula Lamborghini and strapped herself in. He backed up three paces, then charged the car and made a careening, one-handed leap over the open top. He overshot the driver's seat. Grazing his tailbone on the stick shift, he landed heavily in his co-star's lap.

The toupee went flying. The silver satin jacket ripped. The brunette started to giggle.

The director yelled, "Cut! You okay, Jason?"

Jason Kramer, middle-aged romantic leading man, big box-office draw, million-bucks-up-front movie star, was not okay. Not even close.

"Yeah, yeah. Sure. I'm fine. Let's go. Let's take it again," he said unconvincingly, struggling off the brunette.

"No way," interrupted the costumer. "That's four jackets you've gone through tonight. I'm fresh out. And it's seven o'clock. Can't get any more till tomorrow."

The director turned to his producer with eyebrows arched into question marks.

Blair Montgomery dug his Nike tennis shoe further into the Bel-Air dirt. Christ, this estate is running me five thou a day. And Kramer keeps botching his lines, screwing up the simplest stunts. At this rate, *Crackup* is going to cost me more than *Mean Machine* and *Speedway 500* did together.

He looked up at the director and with his index finger made a slicing motion across his throat.

"That's a wrap," barked the director. "Three o'clock tomorrow afternoon. Same location."

"Fuck it, Tom," Blair started in on the slightly built young man next to him. "If we have to supply Kramer with drugs and keep him up to his crotch in bimbos, let's emphasize the sex, shall we? He can't handle the coke. Never could."

"I know, I know," replied Blair's assistant defensively. "But Rubin says any deal has to include—"

"Screw that manager of Kramer's. Tell him his balding matinee idol already has us half a million over budget. One more day like this and I'm gonna scrap the film, feed Kramer's drug problem to the press, and collect the insurance money."

"Blair?" came the low feminine voice.

Tom Schmidt breathed a sigh of relief.

As Blair swung around, his scowl was immediately replaced by a warm and easy grin.

"*Christine!* How'd you find me?"

"We reporters know a number of location managers, and some of them are even our friends," she said, smiling back at him.

He glanced approvingly over her outfit, a loose-fitting Sonia Rykiel knit coat, wide-legged pants, and silk blouse.

"Well, great timing. I've got a big surprise for you, sweetheart. Buy you a drink? Come on over to the trailer."

He took her hand, leading her through the maze of technicians scurrying to pack away huge Panavision cameras, cranes, dollies, lighting gear, and props. Two storage trucks wheeled in to load up two identical Lamborghinis.

"Will you look at this place?" Blair made a sweeping gesture, indicating the acres of manicured grounds, gardens, marble statues, two pools, and four guest houses. "Willie scouted around for months trying to come up with an estate like this one, where we could—are you ready? Drop a pickup truck from a cargo plane. No kidding. The truck's going to land in the pool over there."

"Must be costing you a mint, Mr. Montgomery." Christine laughed, looking up at him.

"Bet your sweet ass. Not even including rebuilding the pool. You know, it boggles the mind, the stuff you have to come up with to sell tickets these days. Over the past few years—that's, say, four films maybe

—we've wrecked hundreds of cars, gone over bridges, walls, through buildings. Only thing *left* is an airborne assault!" Those sexy laugh lines around his eyes suddenly disappeared. "Uh, Christine," he said with exaggerated seriousness. "This is off the record, of course."

Christine didn't reply. As if I'd be interested in using anything about car crashes versus pickups plopping into pools! Sometimes Blair takes himself a tad too seriously. Check that. Many times.

Blair opened the door of the luxurious motor home and guided Christine up the stairs. Collapsing into a baby-soft brown leather chair, she watched him pour large goblets of chilled white wine.

"A Mendocino County Gewurztraminer. You're gonna love it," he grinned, toasting her.

"Mmmm. It is nice," she had to admit. She started to relax, kicking off the open-toed pumps and wiggling her toes. "So what's the occasion. The big surprise?"

Blair winked at her and drained his wineglass. "I know you'll be amazed to hear this, Chris. But I've actually maneuvered it. Shooting *Crackup* and all. I've been able to arrange my schedule so I can take next week off."

Christine waited.

"Don't you see? I can join you in London while you're over there for the Princess Di interview."

Christine shifted in her chair, which made a squeaking sound. She took a sip of wine and tried to smile.

"But, Blair," she said, cupping the goblet in two hands as she stared down into the wine, "you know I'm going to be very busy over there. The Roland Williams interview has been postponed until tomorrow afternon. So now I'll have only four days in England to accomplish everything."

"And four nights," he interrupted, grazing her cheek with his hand as he sat down across from her.

She looked up at him. The calculatedly casual suede jacket, Halston striped shirt, cashmere sweater, dark-brown corduroy slacks. His wavy dark-brown hair. Sun-burnished skin. The laugh lines waiting for that slow, easy smile.

It is tempting . . . what fun to do London with Blair. Lunch at San Lorenzo, dinner at Waltons, dancing at private clubs like Anabel's and Tramps, gambling at those posh casinos. Maybe I could even take a couple of extra days and . . .

"I thought you might be able to get away for a few days afterwards. We could fly over to France. See Nice, Cannes. Or we could spend a very romantic, private weekend at this marvelous chateau. What's the name of it? We were on location there last year. D'Esclimont. That's it. Chateau d'Esclimont. Outside Paris. Overlooks a gorgeous lake, has a moat, very secluded. It's like a storybook castle."

Hold it. Time out. You can't, Christine. Be realistic. You're going to need your strength and all your rest when you're over there. You'll have to concentrate. Look your best. Do your best. No time, no time for frivolity. Just tell him.

"Blair," she began, slowly, softly. "I'd like very much for you to be over there with me. But this is . . . well, it's my shot, you know. Probably the most important interview of my career so far. I worked forever setting it up." She stopped and met his eyes. "Look. I may be paranoid about this. But I just can't plan to do anything but work once I get there." She squeezed his hand.

He stood up abruptly. Poured himself more wine.

"So that's it? You've got work to do, so I'm out of the picture? What am I, a convenience? I thought we were a team, that we had a relationship. Or maybe I'm wrong. Maybe you're onto someone else. Someone new. Like the guy you were with last night."

Christine felt her face getting hot. Why should I defend myself? I've done nothing wrong. *He's* acting like the child, putting me on the defensive.

She set the wine goblet down so hard, it almost shattered on the marble-topped table.

"Blair, don't be ridiculous. You know very well where I was last night. At home. You phoned me there at nine o'clock, and I explained that I was waiting for a call from Denny Bracken, confirming the Williams interview. Why are you accusing me of sleeping with someone else? You know better."

"Do I?" he said archly, giving her a hard look from the bar.

"Yes, you do, damn it," she challenged, getting up and swinging her chocolate-brown bag over her shoulder. She took a step toward the door and looked back. "We've been through this too many times before. These childish fits of jealousy. I don't understand them. And, frankly, sometimes I wonder if the relationship is worth having to replay these stupid little scenes again and again."

She left, slamming the door. Briskly she walked toward her car, feeling the chill March air cool her face, the wet grass moistening her toes. A little off balance from the wine, a little shaken. But relieved, somehow. Glad to have spoken her mind. To have wiped the slate clean. How I hate these silly love games. Whatever happened to trust?

"Chris. Christine, baby. Wait."

She kept walking.

He caught up and took her arm, turning her around. He tried to pull her toward him.

"Blair, don't. It won't work. I really can't settle for this kind of behavior. Your doubts."

"I know, angel face. Please, I just got carried away. I'm sorry, Chrissie. It's the day. The pressure. Kramer mucking up the film. All that. It caught up with me. And I turned it all on you." He wrapped his long muscular arms around her shoulders. Her face pressed up against the cashmere sweater. It was warm and comforting.

She dropped her handbag and put her arms around his waist.

"Besides," he said gently, kissing the top of her head, "I was really looking forward to getting away with you. We really need to escape for a while, you know? Get a new perspective. Have some fun away from the business."

"I know we do," she said. "Oh, I wish you could understand, Blair. London. Princess Di. It may be vacation for you, but I can't take time out. Taubman is counting on making three shows out of this single trip. I've got to interview everybody in London who knows her and is willing to talk to me. Plus standups all over the city. I—"

"You worry too much. You have an advance crew over there setting things up right now. They'll handle all those details. Once you're in England, you'll find more time than you thought. Now I'm not going to push it any further."

He put his hand under her chin, lifted her face up and started to kiss her. She drew back a little at first, then met his lips. Hugging him more tightly, she felt his strong chest against her, his tautness pushing into her.

She was back to where she'd started. To the reason she'd come here tonight, going to the trouble of tracking down the movie location and driving from the studio in heavy traffic. You need this man, Christine. Despite the games. Despite his tantrums. He rounds out your life. Don't wreck it.

"Dinner?" he asked, as they walked to her car.

"Yes. I'm starving."

"How about Chinois? I'll follow you to Santa Monica. And," he smiled, opening the door for her, "while you're driving, think about the restaurants in London you'd like me to take you to."

"Blair, we—" she started to protest.

He put a finger to her lips, cutting her off. "I said I wasn't going to push it. And I'm not. I'll get my own suite at the Connaught. If you find time for some nightlife, I'll be there. Simple as that. No pressure, no hassles."

She started her car, looking up at him, smiling a little. Saying nothing. Men. They always get what they want.

"Oh, and by the way, I happened to speak with Nigel Dempster this morning. Told him we'd be coming over there. A mention in his *Daily Mail* column can't hurt. Everybody in London reads it. Might do us both some good."

Roland stood at the Art Nouveau bar like a mannequin in a store window.

His mind was thick with cobwebs, still caught in the marijuana haze he'd dissolved into that afternoon. Still reeling from being dragged from the warm, comforting Jacuzzi. Burton screaming at him. The smack of icy water.

He shivered anew at the thought.

Nursing a wine spritzer, Roland swept an unsteady glance across the Touch Club. A striking melange of black and white, etched glass and mirrors, mahogany and brass, marble floors. A private enclave for the monied, the powerful, the show-business set which preferred intimate touch dancing to gyrating disco antics. A small crowd. Sedate. Usually.

Tonight it was standing room only for Lightning Records' annual fiscal-year-end party. After-tax earnings had topped off at slightly more than 20 percent. And, it seemed, the entire staff of three hundred and every stockholder were determinedly celebrating.

Roland didn't feel like joining in. He didn't want to be there. But Burton had insisted.

"So you hate crowds, Ro, but you're a major stockholder," he had said. "Lightning has been good to you. And to me, too—I've made a bundle as their outside counsel. We'll have a couple of drinks. Shake a few hands. Pay our dues, right?"

"What about photographers? The paparazzi will—"

"Forget about the press. Bracken has that under control. He knows the rules. No reporters or cameras at functions you attend." Burton had smiled warmly at this point. "Relax," he said. "Try enjoying yourself for a change. You're getting yourself all worked up—blowing everything out of proportion because of this DuRand interview.

That's not till tomorrow afternoon now, and it'll be a snap anyway. Tonight is ours."

Ours. He glumly surveyed this overcrowded madhouse of sweaty, inebriated party-goers and ordered another spritzer.

A year ago, before Burton, Roland made the briefest of cameo appearances at this same event. "Arrive at the climax, leave before the denouement." He could still hear Victor saying it. And, as usual, it was the best advice. With long experience, Roland had the routine down: the art of getting in and out of a typical Hollywood gathering in under forty-five minutes. Sometimes under twenty-five. One drink. Two appetizers, at most. A brief chat with the guest of honor, a nod to the presiding publicist. Then split.

He'd been at the Touch Club bar an hour and a half already. It was time to escape.

Turning around, his eyes swept the room and finally caught a glimpse of Burton. He was about fifty people away, circulating through the elegant dining room, looking like a forties movie idol in that pin-striped, double-breasted suit. The silver-blond hair, clearly delineated bone structure, the strong, even arrogant jawline, the slender, muscled body.

Roland felt his mouth draw back into a smug smile. He's mine. Hands off. He flushed with pride and then started to relax. Maybe another half hour. Then I'll pry him out of here. We'll go home and get some sleep. Together.

Zzzzzzt, click, Zzzzzzt, click, came the unsettling noise off to the left.

A splash, no, two, now three splashes of light.

The surprising glare of flashbulbs blazed in Roland's eyes. Goddamn. Who has the fucking camera?

He strained to see past the dance of iridescent polka dots and finally recognized the outline of a man even taller than he, about six feet six, painfully lean, with the sharp features of a ferret. As the dots cleared, Roland's suspicions were confirmed by the single streak of white on the left side of the intruder's head of slicked black hair. An impeccably tailored suit hung on him like a shroud.

That freeloading sleazebag. Who the hell invited him?

"Jacques." The authoritative voice hailed the unwanted guest from behind. "Good of you to join us." It was Burton, who stepped in between them, a human buffer.

"Jacques Laffont, you know Roland Williams, Lightning's Number One recording artist. Roland, you certainly know Jacques, Hollywood's famed chronicler of the stars."

Oh, yes. Roland knew. The entire show-business community knew about Laffont. He claimed to be French royalty, a count or marquis, Roland could never remember which. The lineage was probably as genuine as the skunk stripe on his head. But the man was someone to be reckoned with nonetheless.

Everyone read *Inside Hollywood,* the newest, and least orthodox, of the town's daily entertainment trade papers. Often its headlines grossly oversold the accompanying text. Facts were frequently at some remove from reality. But it was aggressive. *Inside Hollywood* scooped its more established rivals, *Variety* and *The Hollywood Reporter,* with awe-inspiring regularity.

The town's decision makers reached for it along with their morning Maalox—earlier if they had something to hide or were anticipating disaster.

Jacques Laffont's bitchy column documented the activities of the standard cast of preeners who showed up for Hollywood's endless soirees, art gallery and restaurant openings, and movie premieres. His chief rival was *The Hollywood Reporter*'s George Christy. In fact, many accused Laffont of trying to ape Christy's widely read column, "The Great Life." Not to his face, however. No one ever criticized Laffont to his face.

His own column was called "The Fast Lane." Of course Laffont did his best to make certain that life's lane was more congested and less comfortable for those in his disfavor. And Hollywood, meek as usual in the face of anyone with the power to affect careers, went out of its way to show its appreciation of his services. With an occasional case of Laurent Perrier champagne, say, delivered discreetly to Laffont's home. Or half a dozen shirts from Bijan, perhaps.

"Yes, charming. Charming to make your acquaintance," Laffont was saying in tones of professional condescension. His rheumy eyes wandered approvingly over Roland's cream-colored silk suit and black shirt, settling finally on the russet silk tie.

"Mmmm, *très délicieux*," he pronounced. And waited.

Now it was Roland's turn to say, "You like it? It's from Battaglia. Next time you're in the neighborhood, drop by there and pick up one. Tell them to put it on my account."

From stories he had heard, there would soon follow an anxious phone call from the manager at Battaglia. "Excuse me, Mr. Williams, but Mr. Laffont is here looking at neckwear."

Yes, fine, fine. Bill me.

"And he has this, ah, slight problem."

Yes?

"You see, he can't make up his mind among *four* neckties. He assures us you won't mind."

Sure, why not? At one hundred dollars each.

Roland stared back at Laffont. He didn't care. He wasn't taking the bait.

Laffont's eyes hardened, and he was frowning. "Surprising," he intoned through his nose, "that you're the only Lightning artist here tonight, isn't it?"

"Very astute of you, Jacques," Burton interjected, smiling at the petulant columnist. "Actually this party is strictly for Lightning's staff, investors, and board of directors. What you may not know is, Roland here is the only artist who owns a major portion of company stock."

Laffont managed a tight little response of minor amusement. "So what do you think about Burton here turning his back on Hollywood to work for the Democrats?" he said to Roland, still eyeing the tie. "Or are you sympathetic to the party yourself?"

"Jacques, Jacques, great taseeyaaa!"

Saved by the bellow of publicist Denny Bracken.

They all looked down. Bracken stood only five feet six inches—not even that without lifts in his shoes. But he was effective, especially in the music business. That had been his game for more than twenty years, and he knew all the players. He pitted them against each other like chess pieces, as only a cunning and powerful Hollywood PR man can.

Denny was dressed in customary style—dark-green gabardine slacks, red-checked V-neck sweater, pale-yellow shirt and a bright-green bow tie. He looked like a TV color test pattern gone berserk.

"So, Jacques, how ya been? Didja get a drink? Listen, I got the chairman of the board over here, dyin' to meetcha. Roland, Burton, if you'd excuse us . . ."

Laffont was gently but firmly guided away by his elbow.

Roland felt overwhelming relief. "Where was Bracken earlier?" he asked Burton.

"Got me. I guess he gave Laffont an exclusive on this one. I'm sure Bracken stipulated that you were not to be a target. But the sour old queen always wants to run the show." He squeezed Roland's arm briefly. "I'll take care of it."

Denny had steered Laffont toward the buffet table, a groaning board of delicacies dominated by a huge ice sculpture, a sparkling centerpiece in the shape of an elaborate monogram—LR.

"You goin' to the reception at the Academy for Spielberg tonight, Jacques?" Denny asked, watching the columnist dip fussily into the vast array of food.

"But of course," Jacques sputtered through a mouthful of caviar. "Redford's supposed to show."

"Need a lift?"

Jacques Laffont didn't drive. Didn't have a license. The word around town was it had been revoked after the California Highway Patrol nailed him for drunk driving on several occasions. Laffont's story was that driving wasted his time and energy. "A dissipation of the creative spirit," as he was fond of declaring. If publicists needed him badly enough, transportation would be arranged. It always was.

"Delighted," said Laffont. "When are you leaving?"

"Pretty soon," Denny answered, looking at his watch. "But enjoy. We don't have to rush. I have a limo tonight."

Jacques's wildly untamed eyebrows arched in pleasure. Bracken should be good for dinner afterward. Dudley Moore's 72 Market Street in Venice would be nice.

"Just one thing, we gotta make a quick stop on the way. Pickin' up Jewel Crosse." Denny was thinking about Jewel's phone call and what could come of it. That tall, exquisitely-stacked body of hers . . .

Laffont stopped gnawing on a lobster claw and grunted. "If that woman is tagging along, count me out. I'd rather *crawl* the two miles."

He disposed of the chewed claw in an ashtray, spun on his Gucci heels and glided off with the air of a prima ballerina forsaking her leading man.

"Denny." It was Burton, who had suddenly materialized at Bracken's side. "Nice going with Laffont." He looked around furtively, making sure no one was eavesdropping.

Together they walked through ornate etched-glass doors to the disco and sank into a low leather couch next to a palm tree.

"Yeah. Guess I did okay. Never know with that bird." Denny sipped from his piña colada. "He's weird."

"Best of all, Roland doesn't suspect a thing. When do you think the photo will run in Laffont's column? Any chance of next week?"

"Don't know. Lemme check with him tomorrow. I'll send him a case of wine or somethin' in the mornin'. Try to work it out."

Burton murmured his assent. "Good. It would be terrific timing if the DuRand interview ran around the same time Laffont uses the photo. With a couple of paragraphs about Roland, right? Not just a caption. Tell Laffont about the new video for *Razzle Dazzle*. The international concert tour coming up. Then promise him you'll have an exclusive announcement. Just for him. You know, about the fund-raisers, very shortly."

"Well, now, I'm not sure I can swing all that. I can't—"

"Can't? What do you mean, can't?" Suddenly, without warning, Burton's voice had become a strident whisper. "What the hell *else* have you got to do for Roland?" he demanded. "All these years as his publicist, and how hard have you worked? I'll tell you. Not hard. Not hard at all. Keeping the press away. Fending off reporters and cameras. Big deal."

Bracken stiffened but said nothing.

Burton refused to let up. "You've been on easy street," he snapped. "Three thousand a month for doing nothing. Now's your chance to prove it's been worth it. Call me tomorrow."

Burton pushed himself up out of the couch and went to find Roland. Stupid-assed flack, he thought. Jesus, what you have to go through to make these publicity *shlemiels* move their fat butts . . .

"What kind of a restaurant is this anyway?" grumbled the distin-guished-looking man stroking his salt-and-pepper beard. "Cauliflower soup with pumpkin chunks. Sweetbreads and sauerkraut marinated in Pernod. What's wrong with steak and potatoes? We should have gone to the Cock and Bull."

"Come on, Dad," coaxed Maggie Rafferty, determined not to argue with her father on his birthday. "This is a celebration and Nickels is the hottest spot in town. Look, Donald Sutherland is sitting over there. And Linda Evans at the corner table."

"I can see stars at the studio. Don't have to eat next to them. Espe-cially lime-and-garlic soup. Who in the hell concocts these atrocities?"

"Nicholas Yusorovic. The owner and the chef. It's Yugo-American cuisine, Dad. All natural ingredients. I'm sure there's something here you'll enjoy. Why don't I order for us both?"

"Oh, no. My dear, I don't want to chance living like you. High off the hog—and still looking like one, I might add. Thought you were going to exercise classes," he said, frowning.

"I am." Maggie bit her lower lip and stared down at the freshly starched light-blue napkin.

Why is it always like this? He never gives me a chance. Always criti-cizing. Complaining. When my grades weren't good enough in high school. When I refused to attend law school.

Instead she'd chosen the University of Southern California's School of Cinema and TV. Hoping the genius of alumni like George Lucas would rub off. Hoping someday she'd be a powerful, successful Hollywood director like them. And like her father, Billy Rafferty.

"It's still a man's town. You'll never make it," he'd yelled at her the day she applied to USC. He had not let up since.

In the five years she had been out of school, Maggie had worked on several low-budget films as a production assistant. Menial tasks and thankless hours. Going for coffee. Unpacking costumes. Driving around remote location shoots in Arizona and Mexico in search of gas stations and motels.

Billy Rafferty wasn't pleased with his daughter's "indentured servitude," but he never offered to put her on one of his films. And Maggie didn't expect it.

The International Network job paid more. And the expense account allowed Maggie the pleasure of being able to treat tonight. She'd hoped that would make a difference somehow.

Billy Rafferty's sixty-sixth birthday. He didn't look more than fifty, sitting there, square-shouldered, in his habitual navy-blue blazer with the Rafferty crest. Gray flannel slacks. Blue pin-striped shirt. He was always dressed impeccably. Fastidiously groomed. Wealthy. And single.

But Billy Rafferty would never remarry. When Maggie's mother died of leukemia nineteen years earlier, he withdrew from the Hollywood social scene. Since then he had attended only the premieres and parties necessary to "do business." He seldom dated. The man worked as if there were a mission to fulfill, a promise to keep. While governesses attended to plump little Maggie, his career flourished. Three Oscars and five nominations. Billy Rafferty had the right to be proud of his record. His only regret was that he didn't have a son.

"Excuse me, Mr. Rafferty. Madame." The thick accent came from behind Billy.

Maggie looked up to see muscular forearms and a bulging chest under a white apron, then the handsome Slavic face.

"I just wanted to shake hand of such a wonderful filmmaker. I see all your pictures. *Nameless Faces* . . . mummahh." He kissed his fingers. "Pure artistry."

"I, well. Thank you, uh . . . Nick."

"Nicholas. Nickels for short." He smiled broadly. "We fix the two of you something special today?"

"Ya gotta good steak back there?"

65

"Certainly, sir. And for the lady?" Hmmm, pretty face. But what a body. My God.

"The Szechuan sautéed breast of pheasant with pistachio-nut stuffing sounds righteous," Maggie said, not taking her eyes off him.

"So be it. Again, excuse interruption. And enjoy."

"Nice young man," Billy said a few moments later, as he adjusted his red silk pocket handkerchief. "There, now, you see, do you think you could ever attract an enterprising, spirited guy like that, looking like you do? What about a fat farm? The Oaks at Ojai. Rancho La Puerta in Baja. Maggie, *do* something with yourself!"

"Do something?" Maggie shot back. "What do you mean? I'm supporting myself. I'm making damn good contacts in this town. I'm copping exclusive info for an international television show. I'm even going to London next week. To interview Princess Diana. And no thanks to you for any of it." Damn. Can't you ever hold your tongue, girl? Oh, what the hell? He always does it. Always needles me into an outburst.

"Princess Di, huh?" Billy's bushy black-and-white eyebrows shot up. "How'd you nail that one down?"

"Christine did it. She knows Di's hairdresser. It took two years of phone calls and gifts to him to pull it off. Apparently he convinced Diana that she needs to start molding her own image. And what better place than the hottest interview show in the world?" She sounded proud and excited at the prospect.

"So. DuRand gets all the glory. What'll you get out of it?"

"Christ, can't I do anything right? I don't want to be on camera. I like what I do. And I'll be making contacts in London. That's what this business is all about, isn't it? Contacts?"

"And talent," he said curtly, watching Maggie reach for the sourdough rolls.

"I have that." She looked up and took a defiant bite into the roll.

For several moments neither spoke.

"So, how's it going with *Precipice?*" she finally asked, attempting to shift the mood.

"Great," Billy grinned, blue eyes twinkling. "We're half a million under budget. Looping right now. Editing starts next week."

"The trades sure are making a big deal about this one. Your first time out as writer, producer, and director."

Billy took a long and reflective sip of his Guinness stout. "Maggie, what's this I hear about you sharing that flophouse with some faggot?"

She slammed the roll on the table. This time her temper could not be contained. "Hermosa Beach is a fine area. It is not a flophouse. Paul Livingston is a highly educated, gifted choreographer, and besides, what business is it of yours who I live with?"

Billy narrowed his eyes and looked straight at his daughter, her cheeks flushed crimson. *"Someone* has to think of the family name."

"Oh, is that it? The family name?"

Heads turned. Conversations stopped.

"You know when I'll start thinking about the family name? When you start treating me like family!"

Maggie stood up, yanked her multicolored Mexican tapestry bag off the floor and stormed out of Nickels' restaurant.

Four

"It's four-ten in the P.M. on KKGO, your jazz sta—"

Christine flicked off the car radio. She didn't need to be reminded that she was already late for the Williams interview. Ten minutes late.

It was the phone call from England which had thrown her off schedule. Marc Azar. Her hairdresser at Saks in Beverly Hills for years. Now he worked for the Princess of Wales.

Shouldn't have gabbed on and on like that. But I had to, didn't I? Good old Marc. He really did manage to orchestrate my interview with Princess Di. God, I still can't believe it. Next week I'll be with her at Highgrove.

Believe it . . . but stop thinking about it. One interview at a time. Concentrate on Williams.

Traffic along Sunset Boulevard slowed to a crawl. Lightning Records was now less than a mile away, but it would be half past four at least by the time Christine arrived and managed to connect with her crew. Ordinarily, showing up half an hour late was perfectly acceptable. It gave the crew just enough time to set up. She'd arrive for the final lighting adjustments. A short chat with the celebrity. Then right into the interview. Today she wanted more time. Nothing must go wrong. The interview was too important, and setting it up had been too much of an ordeal.

At a red light, Christine scanned her list of questions for Williams, wishing the car's air conditioner wasn't on the fritz. It was hot. What began as a mild, overcast morning had quickly turned into a scorcher of an afternoon. She struggled out of her blue linen jacket. The peach silk blouse stuck to her back. Tiny pinpoints of perspiration stood out on her forehead, threatening to moisten her bangs and free them to their natural kinks.

If only I didn't have to go through Bracken on this, she thought, pulling away from the light. He's such a suck-up artist. She still remembered her first encounter with the man, shortly after *The DuRand Report* began to air. She had asked Maggie to phone Bracken about covering a Lightning party. He turned Maggie down—rudely.

The following day she called Bracken herself. Usually, even if cameras were barred, the publicist was gracious enough to invite her to the affair. Together Christine and Maggie would work the room, often leaving with several scoops and promises of interviews for future shows.

But Denny Bracken was not the type to give anything away.

"What's your name again?" he'd growled after listening for about thirty seconds. "Christine DuRand? Well, here's the story . . . Chrissie. I don't care if you're Ayn Rand, and you've won three Emmys. No reporters at Lightning parties. Company policy. Period. Got it?"

And he'd hung up. Before Christine could protest that she knew both *People* and *20/20* would be there.

Despite Bracken's nastiness, Christine kept calling. He was the best music publicist in town. Handled all the big names. And occasionally he came through for her. But never with Roland Williams.

"Strictly off-limits," was his standard response.

Nothing had worked. But then this week Bracken called her. Christine still wasn't sure why. Of course, it didn't hurt that *The DuRand Report* had placed in the top ten in the WorldWide Ratings for four months running.

Maybe a case of a flack finally getting smart. Maybe Williams is getting insecure. Who knows?

Bracken's offer of Williams had come as a surprise, but the gift had strings attached. "Listen, Chrissie, I got great footage of Roland. Him receiving his platinum for the video of *Moonshadows*," he'd begun. "You realize that this is the first video to go triple platinum, don'tcha? At twenty-nine ninety-five a clip! Some record, huh? *Record,* get it?"

After a burst of nervous laughter, he'd promised Christine an exclusive on the material.

Sure. Exclusive to me and three other shows, Christine had thought.

"Sounds good, Denny. How much time do I have for the interview?"

"How's 'bout five minutes? You can be all set up at Lightning and we'll bring Roland in for a coupla questions. Bambo, you got yourselves a nice little exclusive package."

No way, Mr. Snake Oil. My ratings are worth more than five minutes. It'll take at least ten to warm Williams up. If I can warm him up.

"Gee, Denny. Twenty minutes sounds much better. You know how interviews go. It takes that long to establish real rapport. And we want to make this a *very* special report."

Bracken didn't bite. "No can do, sweetie. You know what you've got here? Roland Williams. Hottest recording artist on the planet. Sells more than any other artist, any country. That's Springsteen, Jackson, and Prince put together. The man doesn't have time, sugar. Five minutes or nothin'."

"I guess it's nothing, then," Christine replied firmly. Hoping she was making the right move, her hands tightened on the phone receiver.

"Hokay. If that's the way ya want it. Sorry, Chrissie. You lost out this time." And with his usual unceremonious style, he'd hung up.

An hour later, he called back. With a new proposition. Ten minutes.

Christine held her ground, knowing her high ratings were her edge. Her best bargaining chip. She went for broke, giving him until the day before she left for London to schedule the interview. Shortly after eight-thirty that night he called her at home. He'd spent three hours convincing Williams to do it, he said. But his client would agree to fifteen minutes and no more.

Christine pushed again. Twenty minutes. Bracken said no again. Then called back after midnight to say yes. Only if she promised to use the platinum video footage. And only if she restricted her questions to Roland's career and asked nothing personal.

Christine had won.

Disguising my inquiries as career questions shouldn't be difficult, she thought, taking a sharp right into the Lightning parking lot and waiting for the massive steel gate to swing open. Fund-raising concerts for the Democrats? If that isn't an important career decision, what is? And Williams's relationship with the party's finance chairman. Isn't that bound to affect his career?

Bracken may be unscrupulous. But he doesn't have the *chutzpah* to

70

stop the interview with the camera rolling if I happen to stray a little. I'll find a way.

Arthur, the uniformed chauffeur, placed the two large Vuitton bags and briefcase in the master bedroom suite. Surveying these surroundings, he chuckled softly.

Guy like Rex Pearce making it in here? Looks like something out of a fairy tale.

His eyes swept over the carved and painted bed, canopied in light-green satin. The antique coverlet. Nineteenth-century armoire and Louis XV armchairs. The bleached hardwood floors and huge Oriental rug.

Arthur had been up in Mr. Pearce and Miss Davis's Fifth Avenue penthouse lots of times. But this was his first gander at the bedroom.

The rest of this place is bad enough, he chuckled. Like a damn museum. That big case of little glass bunnies, them seals and giraffes, in the living room. Huge rugs hanging on the walls! Great big paintings that look like my five-year-old was let loose with her crayons. And all them old chairs and chests, ready to fall apart any second . . .

Arthur returned to the foyer, where Miss Davis was turning on the lights. Strangest fixtures he'd ever seen, hanging off the walls like that.

They were hand-blown Venetian glass sconces.

"Will that be all, ma'am?"

"Yes, Arthur. Thank you. Goodnight."

It was good to be home.

Diedra Davis removed her Black Willow mink, kicked off the uncomfortable high heels, and walked slowly to the living room, being careful not to slip on the wide-board oak floors, polished to their usual high gloss.

Ahhhh. Something new. She examined the ebony table from France. Slid her hand over the large Henry Moore sculpture, wondering when Rex would stop. His appetite for expensive possessions seemed insatiable. The mirrored case was packed with Steuben and Baccarat glass figures, the walls heavy with tapestries, Mirós and Picassos, the room crowded with rare antiques.

Rex. She shook her head in amusement. He's like the poor boy who suddenly gets handed several million. Can't spend it fast enough. Doesn't matter what doesn't go with what.

Diedra preferred understatement. Open spaces. Pastels. Clean lines.

Little to distract from their spectacular view across Fifth Avenue. She looked down now across Central Park to the clear, calming reservoir barely visible in the gray mist of early evening. To the left, the Metropolitan Museum of Art, that stately temple of culture, knowledge, sophistication.

It was almost the same view, Diedra reminded herself, that Jacqueline Bouvier Kennedy Onassis once had. Even now she found it hard to believe that she lived near the building once occupied by the former First Lady.

She drank in Manhattan at twilight. The limousines and taxis jockeying for position on Fifth. Fashionable pedestrians scurrying off to the theater, Tavern on the Green for dinner, the Plaza's Oak Bar for a drink. It seemed a lifetime away from her struggling days.

Okay, sister. Watcha doin' here so late at night? Past your bedtime, ain't it?

Cops. They were all the same. Sometimes a free fuck would shut them up. Most times it didn't. "Tell you what, babe. I'm going to put you to bed. Why don't you move that sweet ass of yours over to the car. On the double, hear?" Busted. Again and again. At least it meant a place to sleep unless too many girls were crammed in the same cell. Next night, back out on the street again. All made up. Miniskirt up to there. A sixteen-year-old pro. Fifty bucks a john.

Now she earned half a million a year. Tax free.

And all because of Rex Pearce. Her business partner, her lover, her man. She'd be glad to see him after these long days on the road. She'd missed his outrageous sense of humor and his large, warm body encircling hers as they slept. But he'd been called to Toronto for a couple of days, unexpectedly. Just as well. She could use time alone.

The three weeks had been rough. London. Paris. Rome. One of her quarterly trips. Endless interviews with out-of-work models, actresses, teachers. Even a few housewives. All with reasons of their own, not all of them financial, for answering her discreet ad in the classifieds.

After making her selections, she spent hours cross-checking. Doctors' reports for diseases, of course. But also former employers and personal references. No one suspected. Diedra could run the personnel department for the Fortune Five Hundred. If anything, she was even more meticulous, even more careful than an ordinary business would be. She needed the best. She needed mental stability. Absolute dependability. Total trustworthiness. Unfailing discretion.

Diedra helped Rex run the most lucrative international syndicate of call girls in the world. High-class girls. Intelligent. Well dressed. Professional. Expensive.

Men from Singapore to Alaska paid anywhere from five hundred to five thousand dollars a night for their services. Diedra couldn't afford to take on a girl who might be trouble.

The syndicate had been her idea. Ten years ago, not long after she'd met Rex, in Las Vegas. She was waitressing in a casino, newly arrived from Los Angeles—one of her many attempts to stop whoring. For several nights she noticed the boyish-faced middle-aged man. Her instincts told her when a man was interested. She noticed that his eyes followed her fishnet stockings whenever she approached his blackjack table.

Then he reached out and pinched her. Hard.

"Honey, you got the longest legs and the cutest little bubble butt I've ever seen," he announced. Like she should be grateful for the news.

"Well, mister," Diedra hissed back at him, raising his double vodka in the air with a quick, graceful movement, "you sure haven't seen much then, have you?"

And she dumped the vodka over his head.

The casino fired her, but Rex tracked her down. He apologized and offered her a job. Counting cash. Drug money. In New York.

Her alternatives were limited. She accepted.

Once in Manhattan, Diedra couldn't believe her luck. She moved in with Rex. The largest apartment she'd ever seen. And he seemed genuinely to care for her.

In bed he was a complete surprise. She'd expected him to be rough and demanding, like when he was working, dealing with the incorrigible sorts their business attracted. But, amazingly, Rex was the most tender lover she'd ever known, concentrating more on her pleasure, it often seemed, than his own. Cuddling, kissing, coaxing her into ecstasy.

Rex called her his Costa Rican refugee. He loved watching her long angular body. Touching her creamy cocoa skin. Looking into her deeply set eyes, green flecked with gold. "Like tigers' eyes," he'd whisper as they made love.

He dressed her in designer clothes. Showed her off in elegant restaurants like Lutèce and the Russian Tea Room. Took her dancing at El Morocco. Introduced her to the art world. Guided her patiently through galleries and museums.

Diedra opened up to him. Told him more about her past than she'd ever admitted to anyone. About arriving in this country as a skinny little girl from the tiny Costa Rican village of San Ignacia with her mother and father. Her father's death in a senseless bar fight. Her growing up in the teeming *barrio* of East Los Angeles while her mother scraped and struggled to keep them fed and clothed on a maid's wages. The parade of men who slept with, but never married, her mother. The one, a brash Brazilian nightclub singer named Jorge Cima who believed in *candomblé*—voodoo—and chanted terrifying oaths in a tongue she didn't understand when he'd raped and impregnated her at fourteen.

Against her mother's angry threats, she'd had her baby, a boy. When she and her child had no place to live, no means of feeding themselves, it was Cima who then put Diedra to work on Sunset Boulevard. Soon, however, he was raging at her to give up her baby. One afternoon, he simply grabbed up the child and returned hours later—alone.

Diedra cried for days, refused to eat, refused to work, until Cima beat her mercilessly and left her in an alley for dead.

She was battered and broken, but not dead.

Not yet sixteen, but ripe as a mature woman, Diedra began working the streets on her own, always on the watch for Cima or any other pimp who wanted to claim her. And she did well, sometimes earning as much as a thousand dollars a night. When she was arrested, she gave false names. After several months on her own, she had the cash she needed. She put it in the hands of the right people, who brought her baby back.

Now she had something to live for. Hope. She began taking clerical courses, planning for the future. A legitimate job, especially with a company in which she could eventually advance beyond the secretarial pool, was her goal. A chance for the two of them to escape from the tiny apartment they shared in the *barrio*.

She was terrified the day Cima reappeared. He was drunk, raving out of his head. He had finally found her, he roared, because he wanted her back.

And then he noticed the child, napping on the bed.

Cima's face contorted in a terrible rage. He rushed at the sleeping child, but before he had taken three steps, he fell heavily to the linoleum floor, a broad kitchen knife between his shoulder blades.

Diedra's girlfriends helped her dispose of the body, but she had to leave town in a hurry. And her three-year-old was entrusted to the temporary care of her best friend, Violet.

Two weeks later Violet was arrested for a parole violation and the child taken from her.

Diedra was beside herself with fear and guilt. Yet she saw no recourse. She couldn't go to the police or the county authorities. She had to face the awful realization that she'd never see her child again.

The loss haunted her. She felt tremendous regret, a gnawing emptiness. She now lost all ambition to change her life. So she just went on. Working the streets. Numb and alone, for years.

Then Rex. Someone who she could trust. And love. And talk to. She did that, sometimes for hours on end.

But he rarely spoke of his own past. "Better you don't know, baby," he said. "Less you have to worry about should somebody ask."

She knew that he was Canadian. And had worked somewhere abroad, when he was much younger, as a mercenary.

What Rex used to do hardly seemed to matter. They were happy together. If he was not totally faithful, Rex was at least discreet. She knew he loved her.

And respected her. For the way she'd wholeheartedly gone after what she wanted. Berlitz classes in French, German, Italian. Making connections in major cities around the world. Visiting them all at least twice a year. Running her classified ads. Screening and training the girls herself.

Rex was proud of his woman. And well he should be, she thought. She had come a long way. She had discarded the losing hand she was dealt and had come up with a royal flush. She had reinvented herself.

Diedra sat lightly on the long hand-painted silk couch, reached for the sleek malachite cigarette box, and put a Players between her soft lips. I've built this syndicate into a multimillion-dollar business. Got him out of that drug-run game and away from that scum he was dealing with. Now it's just the two of us and our dependable, loyal IBM personal computer. She stood and walked slowly to the bedroom, trailing blue cigarette smoke. Shuffling through her briefcase, she removed three thick files.

Ummmm. Fifty-eight new ladies. Priceless, each one of you.

Diedra padded down the hallway to her office, her tired feet luxuriating with each deep step into the thick carpet.

It was her favorite room. Uncluttered. Modern geometric furniture in white. Soft pink walls. Clean hardwood floors with a large rectangular rug in a pale lavender.

She placed the three files next to the computer. Tomorrow she would rise early to feed it all the necessary information. Cross-referencing each girl, so that in seconds she could find a five-foot-six-inch redhead in Australia. A honey blond in Paris. A stunning brunette who spoke German and French in Rome.

Most of them were "A" girls. For anything goes. Others were "S"— some restrictions. And a handful were classified as "V." The virgins.

Diedra lit up another Players and smiled. She had picked up a few new virgins on this trip. The agency still got calls for them. From gays in the closet, mainly. The ones who just needed a showy date to allay suspicion. And sometimes the older gentlemen, she reminded herself. Guys who can't get it up anymore, but get off on being near an attractive young thing who's clean-looking and innocent.

Yes. Must be ready to satisfy all appetites in this business.

She turned out the lights and headed toward the bedroom. There she slipped out of the still unwrinkled knit celadon suit, reached for a red satin robe trimmed in marabou, and stepped into white satin mules.

Opening a small Queen Anne chest which had been conveniently converted into a miniature liquor cabinet, she poured herself a glass of Chambord. The classic rich black raspberry potion went down easily.

She raised the liqueur-coated glass high in the air. "Here's to you, Diedra," she said aloud. "Welcome home, honey. There ain't no place like it on earth."

The shiny '76 El Dorado convertible glided down Wilshire Boulevard through the heart of Beverly Hills. Top down. Doing fifty miles an hour. Like a large boat. A canary-yellow boat, rudderless, absolutely out of control. Nearly nudging the back bumpers of chic little foreign numbers foolish enough to block the way.

Within twenty seconds the El Dorado changed lanes three times. Made an illegal left turn onto Beverly Drive. Cut off a red Jaguar, a Gray Line tour van. And grazed the designer-jeaned behinds of a middle-aged couple walking their freshly shampooed Pekingese.

Brakes screeched. The couple shrieked. The dog yapped.

The man behind the wheel of the vintage Cadillac continued his telephone conversation. "Jewel, sweetheart, quit with the 'what ifs.' I told you. I got it all worked out. Don't worry your pretty little head about anything. Tonight, okay? Nice quiet dinner. L'Orangerie. I'll fill you in on all the details. Bye, beautiful."

Denny Bracken hung up the receiver on his car phone and gave himself a reassuring wink in the rearview mirror. Yessiree, Jewel baby. Dyn-oh-mite Denny's your man. He's gonna get you an interview with Mr. Roland Williams. Make you shine. Shine! Be grateful, sugar, be grateful.

Reeling onto Santa Monica Boulevard, toward Hollywood, he reached for the electric razor in the glove compartment. Plugging it into the cigarette lighter, he started shaving wide swaths across his cheeks and jowls, oblivious to the curious looks he was drawing from inside other cars. Denny Bracken had his own way of blotting out the world.

Shouldn't be too tough convincing Roland to do another interview after he gets through with DuRand, he thought. Kid just needs a little warmin' up. He's bright. He'll get the hang of it.

Doing Jewel's show'll be a snap. Five minutes in the studio, that's it. National, too. And she gets pretty high numbers. Ratchford will love it.

That guy. Fuckin' pain in the ass. Makes workin' with Williams a real bitch. But what the hell. I can handle it.

Denny Bracken had been handling Roland Williams's publicity for the past twelve years—ever since the talented young singer signed with Laurence & Ferber, the largest celebrity public relations firm in the world, with offices in Hollywood, New York, and London.

Denny had to admit Ratchford was right, though. Representing Williams had been pretty easy. A trip down the gold-and-platinum road. A publicist's dream. The kid didn't really need print or TV to sell his songs. He didn't want publicity. And he didn't sound off like some of his other clients, alienating fans.

Plenty of Bracken's charges gave him head pains. He bailed them out of jail. Supplied them with drugs when they needed to be up. Cloistered them in hospitals for the "chemically dependent" when they crashed. But handling Roland Williams had been like sipping a tall Kahlua and cream. Smooth. Mellow. Sweet.

All Bracken had to do was keep the thirsty media wolves at bay. Simple stuff. Slap some hands, hang up a few phones, be a hard-ass. No problem. Burton Ratchford changed all that. Stepped in and took over. Started snapping his fingers at Roland's publicist.

"Denny, we've got to give Roland's image a goose. Maybe a poster. More concerts. Especially in Europe. And TV. How about a satellite interview? Reporters at a couple hundred stations, say, hooked up to Roland here in a studio."

Ratchford had settled for *The DuRand Report* and an extensive international concert tour, promoting Roland's newest album, *Razzle Dazzle,* and accompanying video.

Then those *meshuggeneh* political fund-raisers. Christ, all of a sudden I'm working for the Democrats. . . .

Denny made a fast right into Lightning's parking lot and slammed on the brakes. The massive seven-foot metal gate was closed.

"Full alert today, huh, Tony?" he called to the guard who buzzed him through.

"S'right, Mr. Bracken. Always total security when Mr. Williams is expected. Should be along any minute now, I guess."

Tony put a finger to the beak of his cap as the Cadillac lurched by, passing rows of Rolls-Royces, Porsches, a Clenèt, five limousines and even a few lowly Mercedeses. Advertisements on wheels of the label's success. Lightning was, so to speak, on a roll. Its headquarters was truly one of the most palatial corporate settings in Southern California. The straight, clean lines of the enormous marble-clad structure always reminded Denny of a space-age museum. Or a fortress. Yes, a high-tech fortress.

He hurried toward the double black-tinted glass doors, a jerky little bounce to his gait, one hand smoothing his red-and-gold argyle sweater.

Can't tap dance my way through this one. . . .

He checked the large gold wall clock in the lobby. Four-thirty P.M.

The kid will be paralyzed at first. Gonna have to help him along. Make him comfortable. But one cassette is all DuRand gets. Pushy broad. Insisting on twenty minutes. Giving me that London bullshit.

He fingered the stopwatch in his pocket. "Bambo!" Denny yelped out loud. Like he'd discovered something important.

The two secretaries on the other side of the elevator eyed him with curiosity.

He grinned. At nothing in particular. An insular grin, full of deception and self-satisfaction.

He had it. A way to stretch this interview even further. Make it, make her—Christine DuRand—work for him.

After her report airs, get hold of the original cassette. Take the good stuff she didn't use. Coupla quick soundbites. Close-ups. Without her in 'em. Add some of the *Razzle Dazzle* video. A few stills of Roland at his ranch. Bambo. A nice three-minute package to send TV stations everywhere. Bambo. Double Roland's exposure. Just like that.

He stopped at two immense bronze doors. Flipping open a small metal box built into the wall, he punched up a code. A distant buzz. The doors clicked open automatically. Denny entered the magnificent conference room. It was dominated by a long, rectangular table made of a single solid slab of opalescent glass.

Crew's almost set up. Where the hell's DuRand?

"Hi, guys." Denny extended his short, sweatered arm to the T-shirted camera and video operator, then darted over to the couch where the field director, Stu Graham, sat in Roland's camera position waiting for the lights to be adjusted.

"Stuey, gladtaseeya. Nice jacket. Ralph Lauren?"

Stu nodded.

Denny chattered on, making small talk, killing time. But his mind was on Stu's—and Christine's—boss, Irving Taubman.

Wonder how he'll take my asking for the Williams interview cassette. Probably he'll put up a little fuss. Journalistic integrity or some shit like that. I'll talk 'im into it. Remind him what a coup he already has. And if he plays stubborn, well, then, I guess I'll just have to put on a little pressure. . . .

The huge doors opened. Denny spun around.

"Chrissie, howyadoin'?"

He was a cyclonic blur at her side before Christine could even get past the doorway. He held out both arms in greeting, then deftly grazed puckered lips past the side of her face, never touching her. The Hollywood kiss.

"I'm fine, Denny. Sorry I'm a little late."

"S'okay, kid," he purred, resting his arm on her shoulder. "Crew's about set up. Roland should be here any sec. Perfect timing. Glad we could work things out."

Maggie trudged up the North 400 block of Fairfax Avenue, her size ten spike-heeled sandals clip-clopping on the sidewalk. The march of a determined woman.

She knew these three short blocks above Beverly Boulevard as well as any in Los Angeles. They were, as far as she was concerned, a gastronomic paradise. Small family-owned bakeries, open-air produce markets, kosher butchers, delis, tiny grocery stores redolent of honeyed Middle-Eastern pastries and feta cheese. A cluster of authentic Mom-

and-Pop restaurants, each offering its own ethnic speciality.

Maggie had eaten her way up and down this stretch of Fairfax. Falafel in pita bread at the Tel Aviv Café, roast goose with *nockerl* at the Budapest, "seven precious vegetables" at Yung Hwa. Followed, of course, by cheesecake at Canter's, across the street.

The cavernous twenty-four-hour Jewish deli was one of her secret late-night haunts. Often, ravenous after a night of intelligence gathering during which she'd been unable to face yet another caterer's mound of steak tartare and cold pasta salad, she'd squeeze herself into one of the vinyl-covered booths. Half a strawberry cheesecake would disappear in fifteen minutes or less. Between bites she peeked out from behind a *People* or one of the trades to make sure no one was watching—if no one saw, the calories didn't really count.

But food was not Maggie's mission today. More like revenge. Pride. Ego. And, yes, feminine curiosity also pushed her forward. To 444 North. The Original Fairfax Yugoslavian Restaurant.

She paused at the spotless glass door, unable to see through the stiffly starched white curtains.

What if he isn't there?

I'll leave. No. I'll wait.

What if he doesn't recognize me?

I'll leave. No. I'll refresh his memory. Turn on the charm.

What if he tells me to fuck off?

I'll leave. Then I'll definitely leave.

She took a deep breath, tossed back the unruly mane of long chestnut hair, raised her chin high—go for your sleekest look, girl. She shoved open the door.

Over there. In the last booth on the left, close to the kitchen. Nickels Yusorovic was here, all right. And alone.

Though he cooked for hundreds daily at his own restaurant, Nickels himself ate only one meal a day. Often he took it here, in the late afternoon. Early enough to avoid a crowd, and to enjoy the company of the owners—his friends Sreten and Ziva Mijailovic. Their smiling eyes, quick laughter, and the spicy aromas wafting from their kitchen never failed to remind Nickels of Kragujevac, the Serbian village where he'd spent the first thirteen years of his life.

Ziva cooked lusty, satisfying meals—plates overflowing with succulent *cevapcici,* kabobs made from mixed ground veal and beef. Or her delicious *burek,* feathery filo dough stuffed with cheese or veal.

This afternoon he had chosen the *sarma*—a heap of these steaming cabbage rolls stuffed with meat and rice sat before him, awash in their savory sauce.

As Maggie blustered through the door, Nickels had just speared the last of the egg dumpling that accompanied the *sarma*. She was glad there were so few people in the restaurant. Without hesitating, she marched back to his booth directly under the permanent gaze of a stuffed pheasant, poised high on the wall to her left.

"*Zdravo kako ste,*" she announced with an air of triumph, like a schoolchild who has just won the regional spelling bee against all odds.

"*Gospodr koja je otisla,*" he shot back, regarding her with intense brown eyes.

"I, ahhh, didn't get that far," she said, helpless, feeling foolish that she hadn't anticipated a reply.

"Why did you get as far as you went? Learning to say 'How are you?' in Serbo-Croatian—who taught you that?"

"Your pastry chef, Ivan." She sat down across from him.

"So Ivan gave you language lessons?" He fingered his dark, wiry mustache and eyed her quizzically. "Why's that?"

"Because I asked him to," she replied matter-of-factly. "He's, ahh, best friends with my roommate. Paul Livingston."

"Oh. I see. Best friends," he said, chuckling. "Is that what you call it in this country? And did he tell you to find me here?" There was a hint of condescension in his voice.

She nodded, noticing then the strong, square hands.

"And so," he said, taking a long sip from the glass of pale but pungent Niksic beer. "Here I am. You are going to apologize now?"

"Apologize? For what?" she said, startled.

"For jumping up and leaving my restaurant. Causing such a fuss. Disturbing my guests. That is what I said to you when you came in. *Gospodr koja je otisla*—'The lady who runs away.'" He was frowning, but the eyes danced.

Is he amused or angry? Playing with me, or interested?

"Actually," she began calmly, inventing as she went along, "I had to leave that particular evening because of an emergency at the studio. I—"

"Studio?" His eyes widened. "A lady executive we have here then?"

"Sort of." She twisted a large sapphire ring on her finger and tried to sound nonchalant. "I work for the International Network. Producing pieces for *The DuRand Report*. Always tracking down leads.

81

Never know when I'll jump up and go." She laughed nervously.

"Or when you show up and sit down." He half smiled.

They were interrupted by a sorrowful voice. "Nickels, my friend, I have bad news," said the man suddenly towering over them. He was their tall, rosy-cheeked host, dressed rather formally in gray flannels, a black wool jacket, white shirt, and bright-red bow tie. Known to friends as Lucky, this time he apparently was not.

"I've tried all my contacts. All over town," Sreten Mijailovic continued, placing a small demitasse cup of thick, dark Yugoslavian coffee before him. "And nowhere can I get for you the goat cheese. I am sorry about this."

"It's okay, my friend. My thanks to you for trying. Oh, excuse me. This is Miss Rafferty. Perhaps she would like to try some of Ziva's *torta od cafe moka?*" He looked at Maggie.

"Oh, no, I couldn't," she protested. Whatever he was offering, she was determined to do the ladylike thing and refuse it.

"Yes. Yes. You must try," urged the gracious owner, disappearing back into the kitchen.

"Sretan, some Proček, too," Nickels called after him. Then to Maggie, he said, "It's a special dessert wine from my country. You will have some."

"I really shouldn't . . . I . . ."

"But you will," he said firmly, knowing he was wrong to forcefeed this woman. Such a beautiful face, he thought. Classic bone structure, really. Fifty pounds less, she'd be stunning.

Maggie wanted to regain control of the conversation before an entire meal appeared. "You're trying to find goat cheese?" she asked.

Nickels sighed and brought the tiny cup of steaming brew to his lips. The coffee was sweet, thick, almost mudlike in its consistency.

"Yes. Goat cheese. Can you believe? I'm in a—what you call it—quandum?"

"Quandary?"

"Yes. A quandary over cheese. That is my fate today. A silly way for grown man to spend his time, no? Tracking down goats." He laughed softly.

"What's it for?"

"What is everything for these days? Rich people. Some fancy-shmansy movie people who are giving private party tomorrow night. For the wonderful actress from France. Simone Signoret. You know her work?"

Maggie nodded.

"Magnificent. I tip my chef's hat to her. It is her I try to please. So these people, they say Mlle. Signoret loves the *chèvrefeuille*. A soft goat cheese that ripens, like Brie. Can I get? And can I prepare for her as appetizer the baked *chèvre frais*—the fresh goat cheese? They tell me this only four hours ago. I tell them no problem. I can get."

"But you can't get?"

"No. Not so far. I call all over. My usual supplier, in northern California, can't do such an order on so short notice. Too late for my friends in France to deliver. Goat cheese, you know, they worship it in France. But here? Where can you find goats in America?"

"I think I might know." Maggie reached for her large handbag and got up. "Where's the phone?"

He gestured to the back and turned to watch her disappear into the kitchen.

That green silk dress—all wrong for her. Too blousy. She looks like Austrian drapery. What she needs is . . . listen to yourself, Nickels. You don't even know the woman and you try to change her. Remember Anna? Don't you ever learn? He sat there, thinking about his childhood sweetheart, Anna Jarkovic. And the day she'd arrived in America, ten years ago. Wearing that paisley babushka and the dark-blue dress. He'd sent for her. He was eighteen then, waiting tables at Ma Maison. Ready to support a wife and family.

She tried, God knows. They both did. But Anna didn't like her new home. Particularly not the "loose-living people" who populated Southern California. She'd cloistered herself in their tiny West Hollywood apartment. Sewing. Cooking. Refusing to socialize with the "strangers" Nickels called his friends. Finally she went back home.

The divorce was swift and simple. For Nickels, the emotional aftermath was not. He felt a failure. Wanting only her. Needing her, he thought, an emotional anchor to keep him securely moored to reality. Four years ago word came to him that she'd remarried.

Maggie bounded back to the booth just as Lucky was delivering thick slices of cake to the table.

"Done!" she announced dramatically, sliding into the booth.

"Done?" he asked, astonished.

"That's right. Done. You've got your goat connection." Smiling with satisfaction, she handed him a napkin with a phone number scrawled on it.

"That's Sadie Kendall's number. Up north. Near San Luis Obispo. She's got more than a hundred goats running around a farm up there. All spilling out milk for the kind of expensive cheese you want. She makes it herself. Call her by six tonight, and you'll have what you need by tomorrow morning."

Nickels grinned widely and got up quickly, almost spilling the open bottle of Proček. Taking her face in both his hands, he kissed her loudly on both cheeks.

"Maggie," he said, "you are a—a wonder. That's what you are. So now I see why you have important job at the network that makes you run away from dinners late at night."

He sat back down and took a large bite of the cake, motioning for her to try some. *"Torta od cafe moka,"* he said. "Mocha cake. Delicious. Try."

Maggie hesitated, then took a dainty taste of the frosting.

My God, real buttercream. And all those walnuts! She felt like shoveling the entire gooey mess into her mouth in a single swift motion.

"How you know this Sadie?"

"I don't. My roommate Paul went to school with her." Struggling for control, she put down her fork.

"This roommate Paul seems to know everyone."

"Close to it." She kept staring at the cake.

"Well," he said, raising his glass. "Here is toast to roommate Paul, who made it possible for you to speak my language. And for me to get goat cheese."

They clinked glasses.

"And tomorrow night, after you finish your work, you come to my restaurant. This time stay for dinner. As my guest. Sample some of Sadie's cheese." He winked at her.

Maggie smiled in agreement and took another sip of wine.

Christine felt the blazing hot 650 Omni lights beating down on her back. And the awful dampness all over her body. Trickles of sweat trailed to the nape of her neck, dampening the waistline of her skirt, moistening her pantyhose to that uncomfortable stickiness she detested.

There she sat. On the royal-blue velvet couch in Lightning Records' conference room. Across from the hottest recording star in the world. Camera rolling. Denny Bracken's stopwatch ticking away.

Five minutes. She'd been trying to interview Roland Williams for a full five minutes. And was getting nowhere.

From the moment he'd entered the room, tall and fit in tight

84

French jeans, a black shirt trimmed in silver, and dark sunglasses, she'd sensed trouble.

Not the kind she'd had with Robert Mitchum a few months earlier when she'd asked why he didn't do television commercials. "To get paid for it, do commercials?" he'd snarled back, clutching a tall glass of gin.

"A lot of actors do that," she'd countered determinedly.

Mitchum leaned over so close she could smell his boozy breath. He placed a hand near his crotch and jerked it up and down in an unmistakable manner. "A lot of actors do that, too. I'd rather go out and rob a fuckin' bank."

That part of the interview was unusable. Mitchum's answers were peppered with four-letter words, too many to bleep. And he'd known exactly what he was doing. It was called giving a reporter a hard time.

Williams was doing the same thing now, in a different way. First he insisted on wearing the sunglasses. It took coaxing from Bracken to get them off.

Christine had expected him to be shy, withdrawn—nothing she hadn't dealt with before. Over the years she'd warmed up some of the coolest subjects in show business.

But Williams was a total surprise. Beneath the cool and magnetic exterior, there was something so delicate about him. He seemed on guard, waiting for her attack even before they were introduced.

"Hello, so nice to meet you," she had said. Friendly. Open. He said nothing. He merely nodded. Christine was baffled. In all her experience interviewing celebrities, nothing close to this had ever happened before.

It got worse. The camera began rolling. Bob Luther, her cameraman, said, "Okay, you've got speed, Christine. Take it."

"Roland," she said, smiling at him, "we've all heard so much about how you got started in the music business. But never directly from you. What was it like? How did you begin?"

"That's a long story," he replied, closing the subject.

Christine wasn't alarmed yet. Sometimes it took a few questions to get the words flowing, the usable answers. What did surprise her— no, shocked her—was his voice. That multimillion-dollar musical instrument. Those gloriously flowing tones. When he spoke, Roland Williams sounded like an old lady with a bad throat. Such a tiny soft voice he was barely audible. It was almost ludicrous.

Randy Worth, the soundman, turned white. In a panic, he cranked up Roland's microphone level.

Christine didn't react. She kept smiling at Roland, warmly. Knowing that anything might throw him off and possibly ruin the entire interview. Try another marshmallow question.

"How do you feel when you sing and play your guitar, Roland? What is it that goes through your mind?"

"It feels good."

"But other than good. How else does it feel? What does it do to you? For you?" Please say something. I'm counting on this for at least a ten-minute segment. So is Irving Taubman.

"Can't say really. Can't describe it." He stared blankly past Christine's left shoulder.

Now, I know you're not dumb. So either you're terribly shy or you're playing with me. . . .

She went on. Still working on the warm-ups. Puffy, inoffensive questions to bolster the star's confidence. Make him feel comfortable. At home. Candid.

"Congratulations on your platinum for the *Moonshadows* video."

"Thanks." He was staring at the sheet of paper on her lap.

Is he trying to read my questions upside down? She struggled to regain eye contact, knowing how crucial it was to the success of the interview.

Christine rarely referred to her written questions. Too risky. It threatened the rapport. Broke the concentration. Nothing was worse than having a celebrity think you weren't really interested in what he had to say.

If only he'd say something *interesting*.

"How many platinums do you have now?" She was groping.

"Let's see, fourteen, I guess." He looked at his hands.

"I know you've received numerous awards. But do you know exactly how many, over the years?" she said softly, coaxingly.

I can't believe it. This is like talking to a eight-year-old. The man is twenty-four and an international star!

"Gee. Ahh. A lot of them. I don't remember exactly."

"Success, though, at such a young age. How has that affected you?"

Look at me. Please, will you look up at me?

"Started young." He continued staring down.

It's like he's afraid of me. I'm trying to be as nice as I can. But he's so frightened. No wonder he's low profile. He can't talk! Christine felt that familiar tightening at the base of her chest. Signaling that her body was tensing.

"You did start at a young age," she said, circling back for another try. "How difficult was that?"

"Sometimes it was tough." His eyes flickered up.

She caught them and held them with her own. Experience had taught her to persist in this quiet, nonthreatening way. Conveying to him that she cared. Whatever traumas he'd gone through, he could tell her. All about them. Tell Christine. It's okay. Tell me. . . .

"Tell me what you mean—tough?"

"Well, growing up onstage and all. I . . ." He stopped.

Christine sat perfectly still, saying nothing. Just looking at him. Sympathetically. As Don Winston, her news director at Channel 8, had once told her, "Sometimes, Chris, the best reporter response is no response. No matter how long you have to wait after a question, don't say a word. Put the person on the spot. Just wait."

She waited. For what seemed like half an hour.

Finally, he spoke. Very slowly. "I, ahh, had trouble when I was younger with all that attention. You know. I was always afraid of the fans coming at me. Reaching for me. Like hundreds of spiders trying to get me. And all I wanted to do was run . . . escape." He was still looking at her.

Hallelujah! Maybe we have something here after all.

"And how do you handle fame these days?" she followed up.

"Well, I still keep pretty much to myself. But mostly I enjoy my work, you know? I love writing music and hearing the notes I've put together on the guitar. I love singing. And when I'm up onstage, I'm my most alive. When I'm not working, it's, like, I get pretty down and out."

"Tell me about being down and out, Roland." Don't stop. Please don't stop.

He did stop, shifting his green-gold eyes off to the right. She could see him mentally checking himself. Afraid again, afraid to give too much away.

Then he murmured, "Oh, just a little blue, that's all."

"I know you had a very good manager when you started out—Victor Zahmedahn." Christine said it quickly to change the subject, trying desperately not to lose that hint of rapport.

"Yeah." He was still looking away.

"What kind of influence did he have on your career?"

Again nothing. For long seconds. He looked at his watch. Then over at Denny Bracken. Stalling. Deciding how to answer her.

"He was the strongest influence on my career . . . and my life . . . that I've ever known. The man molded me. He worked so hard with me and helped me believe in myself. . . . If it hadn't been for Victor, I wouldn't be here talking to you today."

Good for you, Roland. Your fans will love it. A few more answers like that and I've got a piece.

"Roland, I'm curious about something. And I'm sure your fans are, too. Why is it that you haven't done more interviews?"

"Didn't want to."

"But why?"

"Just scared, I guess." He shrugged. And smiled. For the first time, he smiled at her. A sensual smile, sexy even. Something usually reserved for performances. Or, she imagined, personal relationships.

Christine found it mesmeric. "You were scared of wha—"

"—That," he cut her off, pointing to the camera and chuckling.

"Yet you stand up and entertain thousands of people onstage."

"It's different when I'm up there. Up there, I'm not me, I'm someone else. I step into another world. I'm transformed somehow." He said the words slowly. Carefully. Like he was admitting something to himself for the first time. "I can do anything when I'm performing . . . go on for hours . . . never get tired. It's like . . . like I'm superhuman."

"Do you think you are superhuman sometimes?"

"No," he said sharply, as if trying to retract the words just spoken. "No, I'm just a singer."

"A singer who's done more than okay." She laughed a little.

He picked it up. Nodded. Chuckled softly. She saw his shoulders drop ever so slightly. He was relaxing.

Now, Christine. Do it now. You couldn't have more than eight minutes left, and Bracken is guarding every second.

"I understand you're going to be doing some concerts soon, Roland. Fund-raisers. For the Democratic Party. You haven't done that before. Why now?"

The reaction was instantaneous. A shudder ran through his body. The growing sense of ease was gone, vanished. "Ahhh," he stammered, shifting a little and tugging on his jacket. "Ahhh, well, yes, I am. But I'm not sure just what I'll be doing yet, so I'd really rather not comment on that right now." His voice trailed off.

Denny Bracken looked up from his stopwatch. Mouth open. Face reddening. The bitch wasn't supposed to ask anything like that. How the *hell* did she find out about the fund-raisers anyway?

"But this is a major step in your career," Christine went on evenly. "In your image, the way people perceive you. You've given that some thought, I'm sure."

His forehead was sprouting small beads of perspiration. "Yes . . . wah . . . w-well, not too much. I . . . me . . . me . . . mean, it doesn't ree . . . ree . . . really have to d . . . d . . . do with my image. . . ."

He's stuttering. My God, he's stuttering. But I have to go on. "It doesn't? Raising money, lots and lots of it, for the Democrats during a Presidential election year? If this sudden political activism doesn't have anything to do with your image, why did you decide to do it?"

"It's, ummm, it's per . . . per . . . sonal . . . and I'd rather not—"

"—I understand that Burton Ratchford, the former entertainment lawyer and now finance chairman for the Democratic Party, has something—"

That was as far as she got. Roland was already on his feet, pure terror on his face. Before Bracken or anyone else could say a word, he was gone. Running from the room. Blindly. Snapping off the microphone cord.

Randy jumped up to retrieve it just as Williams disappeared down the hall.

"You bitch!" Denny Bracken was screaming back at Christine as he raced after his client. "You cheap-shot no-talent bitch. You'll be sorry for this one, DuRand. I'm going to pull your plug in this town!"

Five

Irving Taubman gently replaced the silver-plated telephone receiver in its cradle. And began counting to one hundred. Slowly.
Mouthing the numbers as he went along.

He stood, staring down at his sleek glass-and-chrome desk, and then
began pacing his Los Angeles office, stopping briefly at the austere
Louise Nevelson sculpture, the murky blue-and-gray Frank Stella
mural. Moving on to the large window that overlooked a serene
Japanese-style garden in an interior courtyard below.

Ninety-eight . . . ninety-nine . . . one hundred. He watched the
miniature waterfall send a continuous stream of water cascading over
a bed of pebbles and Oriental flora. Concentrating on his heartbeat.
Keeping his breathing even. Keeping himself in check.

He'd get to the bottom of this, he vowed. His way. Methodically.
Calmly. Efficiently.

"Mr. Taubman?"

Finally, she's here. It took her long enough. He turned to face the
network's newest star.

Christine was holding a videotape cassette in one hand, a small pink
telephone message slip in the other.

"I'm sorry, but your secretary has already left, and I found this note to see you when I got back from my interview with—"

"Yes, my dear." He motioned for her to sit on the chrome-and-leather chair across from his desk.

"We've really got something with Roland Williams," she enthused, tapping lightly on the cassette box before placing it on the small side table next to her. "A scoop. Would you like to see it?" She watched his face for signs of approval, but saw only an implacable mask.

"Not right now, Christine," he said, sitting down. He folded his hands, elbows on the desk, leaning toward her. Expectantly, as if waiting to be told something important.

"Okay. But before you do look at it, I have to explain something. You see, Roland—"

"Christine," he said, cutting her off again. His voice was still soft and even. "There seems to be a problem with London."

She gave him a quizzical look. "Problem? What do you mean—a problem?" Could she have misunderstood him? Everything was set over there. Her flight was tomorrow.

"I don't know," he replied, watching her closely.

"Neither do I. What kind of a problem could there be? The interview was confirmed more than a month ago. We've been cleared by several royal departments and Princess Diana's personal aides."

"That's what I thought, too," he said, pausing. "Tell me, when was the last time you spoke with your connection at the palace?"

Christine was beginning to feel distinctly uncomfortable. This seems like an interrogation. What is Taubman getting at, anyway?

"Just this afternoon. And he said everything was fine. In fact, he'd already met with our advance field director, John Lacey. They were planning the sit-down interview for Tuesday afternoon." She sounded positive and emphatic, but now in her mind she was replaying the conversation with Marc, trying to remember if there was anything at all that might have hinted at a snag.

"Well, apparently the Buckingham Palace press office has come across something they don't like the smell of. A security snafu of some sort. They sent word through the British Consulate here that everything has been tabled."

"Tabled? For how long?" she gasped.

"Indefinitely." He picked up an expensive Italian glass paperweight and turned it over in his hand. "Until they say so, we're left hanging."

"But I don't understand. . . ."

"Neither do I," he countered. "That's all we know so far. All we

91

can hope is that they clear this thing up in a great big hurry." He looked at her sharply. "We've already sunk a bundle into this. Not to mention the publicity campaign just launched. I *want* this interview, Christine."

Come on, tell me, his eyes seemed to be saying. Tell me what this is all about.

She stared at him in disbelief. Her hands were cold and clammy.

"I hate to think," he continued, "of the catcalls from the columnists and the rest of the industry if we have to cancel the damn thing just because of a stupid security-clearance screw-up." He was still looking directly at her.

"Mr. Taubman," she managed, "I . . ." Her voice trailed off. Neither spoke for several long moments.

"By the way," he said finally, with an air of affected nonchalance, "I don't have to worry about you, do I?"

She looked at him, stunned, her jaw agape.

"You know—there's nothing in your past, say, that could be the reason for this? You understand it's a question I have to ask."

For a few seconds her voice deserted her. When it finally returned, she said as calmly as possible, "Good God, you know my background. I grew up in Minnesota. Went to Northwestern University. Did television commercials in New York. I was an editor of *Celebrity* magazine before I joined KQV's news department. And I've been here at IN since 1980."

"Christine, my dear," he replied, "we are not discussing your resumé. What we are focusing on at the moment is your personal life. Now, is there anything in that life which the British might find offensive?"

"No—no!" she shouted at him, bolting up from the chair. "I have nothing to be ashamed of. And you know very well how hard I worked setting up this interview. It took me two years. Two whole years. It's the biggest coup your network has ever had!"

"Now, Christine, wait—"

"No, *you* wait, Mr. Taubman. I'll be damned if I'll stand here and listen to your insinuations that I might be to blame." She took two steps toward him and leaned over the desk. "I can assure you, *I* am not the problem."

With that, Christine turned quickly and marched out, leaving Irving Taubman sitting in his large black leather chair, still holding the glass paperweight.

As soon as she slammed the door, she was sorry. But he didn't come after her. And she was determined not to go back and apologize. She refused to give him the satisfaction.

It's not my fault, she told herself, returning to her own office. Probably some minuscule detail. A paperwork error. How dare that pompous ass accuse me of mucking things up. Damn, I wish I could reach Marc now and find out what's happening. But he said he'd be in Paris for the weekend. I won't be able to call him until Monday.

Christine stayed in her office just long enough to pick up her briefcase and gather messages. Blair had called from San Francisco. There until Sunday. Would call her in London. Sure. Hmmm. Kent Michaels called again? Left his home number this time. How odd.

Still fuming, Christine turned out the lights, closed the door and headed for the parking lot. It wasn't until she stepped on the accelerator and bolted toward Sunset that she remembered. The Williams tape. It was still sitting on that side table. Across from Irving Taubman's desk.

"Nice place you got here, Jewel," said Denny Bracken, peering around the luxury condominium. Not sure he meant what he said.

The decor was unmistakably feminine, no doubt about that. But overdone even for Denny's taste—all white with lace tablecloths, flounces, pink ribbons, taffeta draperies. What my mother would have kissed off as "froufrou," he decided. Very impractical.

"Ya know," he continued, examining a slender ivory cigarette case, "this reminds me a little of one of the rooms in Barbra Streisand's house. Kinda fantasy-like."

"Really?" Jewel replied, unimpressed, moving over to the bar. "What'll it be, Denny?"

A trip to the bedroom would be nice. I'd like to rip that black lace number right off your long, tall, voluptuous body.

"Oh, Scotch, please. A double. I need it."

He walked over to join her, idly flipping his car keys up into the air and catching them, a habit he'd had since Hamilton High School. It was considered cool in the fifties, but for Denny the gesture had never lost its charm—especially when he wanted to charm a lady.

"Here you are."

He took the crystal tumbler, pausing to gaze boldly down the low V neckline of Jewel's dress.

"Come, let's sit down," she suggested, gliding over to a small love seat hand-embroidered with hearts and cupids.

"You look really great, Jewel," he said, sinking down into the soft cushions.

"Thank you." She crossed long, shapely legs. The slit skirt crept up higher. "Now, Denny, before we go off to dinner, can you just give me an eensy clue about my interview with Roland?"

"Sweetheart," he said, drinking in her Chloë perfume, "I've gotta surprise for you. You're gonna get somethin' even better than Roland Williams."

She smiled seductively. *What the fuck does that mean? Is he trying to weasel out of his promise?*

"Jewel, baby," he continued, skimming a hand down her thigh to her knee. "How'd you like to have Christine DuRand's job?"

Four A.M. Irving Taubman rolled over and reached for the Gaviscon next to the bed. Peeling open the small silver packet, he popped two chalky-sweet tablets into his mouth and chewed rapidly.

That's six antacids in less than three hours. Wish to Christ they'd do something. He had been trying to sleep since one A.M., but the gnawing pain in his stomach wouldn't let up. *Never should've had the pepper steak at Chasen's. I knew better, but what the hell. My own kid's birthday party. Still can't believe he's fourteen already. Next he'll be begging for the car keys. He's turning into a goddamn California cliché. Surf, screw, and drive.*

But Taubman was suffering from more than overindulgence. Every time he closed his eyes, he could see the members of the International Network's board. All staring at him in stony silence. Old Dollinger himself taunting. *"So, Irving, when are we going to see this marvelous three-part interview with Princess Diana? You know, the one you've already hyped all over the world. The one that's supposed to make us top banana in the whole jungle?"*

He turned over on his right side. He could feel the vodka, the champagne, all that rich food, and the strong espresso sloshing inside him.

No use. Can't sleep. Gotta get up.

He flicked on the bed light. Tying the maroon velvet robe around his thick waist and slipping into matching slippers, he tiptoed out into the hallway. There he stopped briefly to punch up a code on the small alarm panel, disarming the motion detector.

God forbid it should go off and Blanche wakes up. She'd be blasting the hell out of the place with her .38 before the police could get here.

At his wife's closed bedroom door he listened for the familiar sound. There. Something between a cough and a buzz saw. Just as he'd remembered it. Her mouth open. White cream slathered over her face and neck. Streaked blond hair wound around those stupid-looking sponge rollers.

They'd slept in separate rooms for the last five years. It was an amicable arrangement, one of the minor adjustments they'd made to enable them to go on living together without killing each other.

Irving made his way to the family room and plopped down in front of the huge Advent screen. Using the television's remote control, he began flipping from channel to channel. It was the four A.M. time warp. A bombardment of famous faces miraculously young again. Cary Grant, Jimmy Stewart, Bette Davis, Donald O'Connor. Nothing but old movies. Who in the hell programs this crap? On his own network the overnight-news anchors were droning on about some obscure world crisis. Talking heads.

He turned the television off, pushed himself up out of the chair, and was about to go to the kitchen in search of more Gaviscon when he noticed his briefcase. It was sitting next to the new Vespa motorbike from which Josh, eyes bright with excitement, had ripped off the wrapping paper before dinner. Opening the briefcase, he took out the small square cassette box. What the hell, might as well look at it. Have to by Monday, anyway.

Irving shoved the cassette into the tape deck, fast-forwarding until the familiar face of Roland Williams filled the large screen. He watched the full seventeen minutes, enrapt. Then he rewound the final five minutes and played it once again.

My God. We've got ourselves a major story here. Williams doing fund-raisers for the Democrats. He could finance their whole campaign! The Republicans will go ape shit. That DuRand doesn't miss a trick. If only I could trust her. Something's fishy about the London deal. But I'll keep working on her, get her to come clean.

Carefully he put the cassette back in the box and placed it in his briefcase, then locked it. We'd better get this on the air fast. Before some columnist or the wire services scoop us.

Irving walked back to his bedroom carrying the briefcase. His head was aswirl with ideas, the gnawing pains forgotten. What drama. That exit. Roland Williams leaping up and running away just because he'd been asked about his political leanings. Astonishing. Great TV.

No wonder that twerp Bracken has been leaving messages for me all over the place. That's one publicist who's got his dick caught in a vise grip. And I'm going to have the pleasure of making him squirm. . . .

The sky was streaked in reddish dawn over the dark Pacific as the two oddly matched men emerged from the cedar-sided A-frame. The short one skittered to keep up with the taller blond man, who charged forward along the shoreline with an anxious gait.

Burton Ratchford had insisted on this early-morning rendezvous. Somewhere private, he'd told Denny Bracken. Safe. Where their meeting would go undetected. He was deeply concerned about the leak. There must be one. How else could Christine DuRand have known about the fund-raisers? And her question about Roland's association with him—how much did she know?

The two moved quickly on the beach, the brisk wind burnishing their cheeks crimson. Their tennis shoes left bold imprints in the cold, wet sand of perhaps the most expensive waterfront property on the West Coast. The Malibu Colony. An exclusive enclave off Pacific Coast Highway, a private preserve for the rich and famous who treasured privacy at any price. Johnny Carson, Dyan Cannon, Ryan O'Neal, and many, many more. They all had homes here.

So did one of Denny Bracken's clients, a rock star who was conveniently on tour. Arranging a pass to get by the security guards had taken some intricate maneuvering. But Denny knew where the house key was hidden. He also knew this Malibu meeting place would suit Ratchford's oversize ego.

Six A.M. wasn't Denny's finest hour, however. He clipped along at Burton's heels, a soggy paper cup of coffee clutched in one hand. The beige liquid sloshed back and forth in the cup, slopping over onto the wrist of his crew-neck sweater.

"So how's Roland doing?" Denny asked, puffing.

"Better now. At least he was sleeping when I left. But last night was impossible. Stormed into the house after that interview and refused to calm down. Throwing things. In a total rage. Finally he went into the bedroom, locked the door and turned up the stereo. Danced himself into a state of exhaustion."

"That right?" Denny wondered why Ratchford had decided to confide these personal details.

"He's scared, Denny. Keeps saying he won't do the fund-raisers. He's petrified that DuRand will air the interview. Put the word out about his . . . ahh . . . his relationship with me."

Oh, I get it, Denny said to himself. Ratchford wants to make sure I know what's goin' on between them. So I'll see how damaging that DuRand thing could be. What does he think, I just fell off a pumpkin truck or something?

"Nah, Burton," Denny replied with confidence. "That won't happen. That interview will not air."

"I assured Roland it wouldn't. That you had everything under control." He glanced back over his shoulder at Bracken, then stopped to allow him to catch up.

"You know, Denny," Burton said gravely, "it's imperative that a way be found to derail that woman. I mean, strip her of everything."

"She's a bitch, all right," Denny agreed.

"Not just her job," Burton continued. "Her reputation. Her credibility. So that anything she might say about Roland will be laughed off all over the country. Have you hired that private detective?"

"Yeah. Marty Jasper. Old pal of mine. Does a lot of celebrity divorce work. The guy's relentless. And he's been tailin' DuRand since last night."

"Anything so far?"

"Well, no. But I—"

"But what?" Burton cut him off. "Suppose your pal Jasper doesn't come up with anything substantial. Suppose she's clean. What then?"

"No way," Denny said, running out of breath. They had started walking again, and Burton was taking such large strides that Denny was nearly jogging. "Listen, this guy is connected. Especially in show business. DuRand has been in television around L.A. for five or six years now. Had to have fucked an unscrupulous actor or two. Or maybe she's into girls. Even better. Don't worry. We'll get somethin' on her, and then we'll nail her ass to the wall. She'll never work on TV again. Anywhere."

"Yes, but what if they go with Roland's interview on Monday? Before you've had a chance to—"

"Can't. I told you. DuRand leaves for London today. Her Monday show is in the can. They won't even think about Roland till she gets back."

Burton still wasn't satisfied. "What if Taubman decides it's so hot that they edit it into Monday's show?"

"Listen, Burton, you're getting carried away here. Leave Taubman to me. The interview will not air."

"You've talked to him?"

"Well, no. Not yet. But if he doesn't get back to me over the weekend, come Monday, nine A.M., I'll be sitting on his desk waitin' for him."

"Why should he cooperate with you?"

"Simple. Let's just say I know something about ol' Irv that I shouldn't."

Burton stopped again, abruptly. He looked down at Denny, scrutinizing him with an intensity that made Bracken self-conscious.

"Okay," Burton said urgently. "But what about the fund-raisers? We weren't going to announce Roland's involvement for a couple of weeks. By now half the International Network staff is probably aware of it. By Monday, if not sooner, the rumors will be on the street. How can we stop that?"

"Why stop it?" Denny countered. "We'll confirm it. And do one of our favorite columnists a favor to boot. Tomorrow I'll call Army Archerd over at *Variety*. Give him a scoop. Tell him all about Roland's new political inclinations. And the fund-raisers—when do they start?"

"Late this month. San Francisco."

"How many all together?"

"That depends on his tour schedule. For now we can say six, safely."

"All right. Roland Williams skedded for six fund-raisers. Supporting his newfound favorite party. Army will love it. Probably lead with it on Monday. The wire services pick it up by noon. Bambo. We got a hot national story. DuRand's been de-scooped."

"Okay. Okay." Burton began walking again, at a slower, more thoughtful pace. The sun was visible now. Its rays were tenderly bathing the multimillion-dollar sandy front yards, casting them in a yellowish light.

Ahead Denny could make out several colorful flags snapping in the breeze, each one mounted, he knew, on a separate parapet. Marking the house—or castle—of television's favorite villain, J.R. Eccentric guy, that Larry Hagman. Sure knows how to call attention to himself. Hear that he entertains on Sundays. Has a bunch of people over, but refuses to speak. Savin' his voice, or his sanity, or something. Bizarre. Really bizarre, Denny thought.

"There is one more thing," Burton said.

"Yeah?" Denny was startled. *Christ, I thought we'd covered everything. But with this guy—never.*

"What we need is. We need a . . ."

Denny looked up at Burton uncomfortably. *This sudden preoccupation with choice of words could be trouble. Holy shit, what now?*

"Denny, what we must procure," Burton said, back on track now, in control again, "is a woman."

"A wha—?"

"A woman." Burton turned to face his short companion. "A gorgeous woman. For Roland. In other words, Denny, a front. A beard. Get it?"

Jesus, the guy is serious. . . .

"Yeah, sure," Denny said, nodding.

"Look, Denny," Burton continued, "and here I am being bare-assed honest with you. You must know my reasoning. It is of utmost importance that no one suspects Roland. Especially just how his life relates to mine. So starting with this upcoming international tour, you are to see that he travels everywhere with this mysterious new friend. Make her from some faraway place, maybe. Feed the press a line about her noble lineage or some such shit. Do whatever you have to do. I want you to make it look like Roland Williams is crazy in love—hell, even thinking of marriage. I don't care what it costs. Neither does Roland."

It was a cleansing rush. At the same time soothing and exhilarating. As Christine hoisted her slender body out of the chilly chlorinated water, she could understand comparisons doctors made between strenuous exercise and drugs.

According to some sports physiologists, she'd read recently, the neurochemical high produced by certain types of exercise—swimming or long-distance running, to name two—are nearly indistinguishable from the high obtained from opium or heroin.

Toweling off now, Christine couldn't imagine feeling better, though she'd never tried either drug. She'd extended her usual forty laps to seventy-two. A whole mile. And her lithe and shapely limbs felt liquid, as if she were still floating. The headache she'd woken up with no longer throbbed behind her ears.

Enveloping herself in the warmth of a powder-blue fleece robe, she sat down on a cushioned chaise longue, thankful, as always, for this peaceful poolside hideaway in the heart of West Hollywood. Christine had lived in the Andalusia for three years. A charming, old-fashioned Spanish-style structure built in 1927, its white stucco exterior, in the right sunlight, seemed to sparkle before your eyes. The Andalusia was located just a block south of Sunset, but it remained totally untouched by the bizarre and often seamy crowd that prowled the Strip. Like a proud Spanish citadel, it sat secure, sturdy, and amazingly quiet.

Christine's apartment, with its high beamed ceilings, rich hardwood floors, simple but sturdy stucco walls, and awesomely large tiered brick fireplace, provided her with a sense of ease and peace. It offered much needed calm at the end of marathon days on the job.

But this pool—this magnificent pool, the pride of some meticulous laborer who'd arranged each colorful Spanish tile with an eye toward perfection—this was her safe place. Her respite. Total escape, which she needed often. Particularly on this overcast Saturday morning.

Christine had not slept well. Lying in bed, she'd replayed the conversation with Taubman again and again. Searching her mind for reasons why the Princess Di interview could conceivably have been called off. Desperately hoping it might still take place. Wishing she hadn't been so hotheaded, so quick to walk out on her boss.

And what about Roland Williams? She'd done a fine job. Taubman would see that, even without an explanation as to why Williams had run off. Even if the London trip never happened, the Williams interview would redeem her, reaffirm in Taubman's mind her professionalism. If she kept doing work like that—and she would—he couldn't afford to fire her. He'd have to overlook an occasional display of emotion.

But Williams himself? Her mind wandered uncomfortably back to him. She thought about Roland Williams the star. The man. The complicated, sensitive person he must be inside. And the pain she had seemingly caused him.

There was something about this tall, catlike, green-eyed and handsome singer—a softness that ran counter to the usual Latin machismo. A fragility. That smile of his, when it finally broke through. Both sensual and friendly. Radiating, she sensed, a remarkable capacity for warmth, caring—for love. His music wrapped ordinary men and women in a cloak of homage and protection, but what safety did it offer him?

Had she wounded him, this rare and delicate superstar who had hidden behind security guards for so many years? She had taken a shot. Yes, she had. Fired at him. Drawn blood. And he had run.

The thought was unsettling. Granted, it was her job. To examine relentlessly, to ask the tough questions. If she didn't, she would soon be off the air—and someone else would just as quickly replace her.

Christine loved the challenge of interviewing celebrities. Especially the bright ones. The cat-and-mouse play of it. The game of wits she often found herself caught up in. That was the charge for her. The bigger the star, the rougher the terrain. Bringing back a scoop and a powerful, dramatic interview like the one with Williams was the zenith. As good as it got. The brass ring.

But the satisfaction was seldom total. Often it was accompanied by less pleasant sensations. Like the aftertaste of guilt Christine now had concerning Roland Williams.

She was on her way up the two flights of tile-and-stone stairs that led to her apartment, ready to make coffee and get on with the day, when she heard her phone ringing. Realizing she'd forgotten to flick on the answering machine, Christine quickened her pace. Her thongs flapped noisily as she hurried inside and grabbed the receiver just before the caller gave up.

"Hello?" She hoped it would be Irving Taubman, calling to say London was back on.

"Cathleen?" said a husky, masculine voice. "Sorry, I can't get used to calling you Christine. It's Kent. Did I wake you?"

"No. No," she assured him, carrying the phone over to glass doors which led to the balcony and peering down at the bursts of brilliantly colored flowers in the courtyard below. "It's good to hear your voice, Kent. How are you?"

"Great. Just fine. Had one heck of a time catching up with you, though. Thanks for leaving your home number with my service last night."

"Sure. Sorry I couldn't get back to you sooner." So why the call, Kent? It's been ten years.

"I've caught your show a few times in the doctors' lounge. Never home at that time, it seems. You look great, Cathleen. Prettier than ever."

She waited. "Thanks. That's nice of you to say."

"I guess you must like it out there. The job and all . . ."

"The job. The weather. The fact you can exercise year round out-doors. It is wonderful. And I do like it, yes. Very much so. Now tell me, how are you doing at the hospital? I understand you're chief cardiac surgeon now. Mother keeps me posted." She was glad she recalled that paragraph from one of Sarah Rand's weekly epistles from Minneapolis.

"She does, huh?" He sounded pleased. "Yes. I was promoted just last year. And it's pretty demanding. A lot more pressure. Longer hours. But, well, you know, I always liked that."

"Yes, you did," she said, remembering. Thinking about Kent Michaels, the college football hero. Towering over her in his freshly laundered football uniform. His hands, manicured but still rugged-looking, around her waist. His lips on hers. He was so strong and good-looking and achingly alive in those halcyon days. But someone else's now.

"So how's married life?" she asked, trying to sound nonchalant. "Any offspring yet, Doctor?"

"No. And none on the horizon, I'm afraid. Lucia and I split up about three months ago. Our divorce will be final in June."

"Oh." She was surprised. "I guess Mom missed that."

"Well, we kept it very low key. Out of the papers and all. So the word hasn't really spread too far yet."

"It must be difficult for you. I'm sorry, Kent. I—"

"Don't be. The marriage lasted five years. That's saying something in itself these days. Now I'm just another statistic. We all wind up that way sooner or later anyhow." He chuckled. A low, self-deprecating sound. Resigned. Bittersweet.

"I guess so."

Neither of them knew what to say next.

Kent finally broke the silence. "Cathleen, is everything all right?" he fumbled, not sure how to say what he had to. "I mean, is anything going on out there? Any trouble you might be having?"

"Trouble?" She was startled. What's he getting at? There's plenty I could unload today, but not on someone I haven't seen or heard from in years. "No. Nothing out of the ordinary, considering the television business. What do you mean exactly, Kent? Why do you ask?"

"I—well—you see, a couple of days ago, I got a call from a pal of mine. He's with the Minneapolis Police. Nice guy. And he, ahhh . . ."

He what? What in the world, she wondered anxiously, does someone from the MPD have to do with me?

"He works in investigations," Kent continued. "And it seems that his department has been contacted by the FBI . . . about you. Apparently they're putting together a backgrounder on you. Just routine stuff, he assured me. Nothing to worry about." He waited for her to say something. "Cathleen?"

What is he talking about? The FBI? Is this a joke?

"Kent, are you serious?" she asked. Hoping he'd say, Hey, just kidding. Gotcha. April Fool's a couple of weeks early. But something told her he wouldn't. Some sense of foreboding made her realize Kent Michaels had never been more serious.

"Cathleen, I wouldn't have called if I didn't think this was important." His tone was soothing. Gentle. "I have no idea why the FBI is on your case. But the fact is they are. And I thought you should know about it."

Christine dragged the long extension cord over to a couch and sat down. "I don't understand," was all she could manage. "Why would they be investigating me? It doesn't make any sense."

"I know. I'm sure it's nothing to worry about. My friend says it might be just a follow-up on a case regarding someone you know. Do you have a friend who's gotten into some trouble with the law recently?"

Blair? His movie? That actor—Jason Kramer. A bona fide druggie. Always high on coke, heroin . . . who knows what . . . maybe . . .

"Oh, Cathleen?" He made an effort to sound offhanded, but succeeded only in betraying his anxiousness. "One name did come up during our conversation. He said the bureau had specifically asked about that guy you used to go with in New York. What's his name? Jacobs?"

"Steven?" she whispered. "Steven Jacobs?"

"Yeah. That's it. Stockbroker or something. On Wall Street, isn't he?"

"He was. Now he runs a major conglomerate. Plastics, steel, cement."

"Well, the bureau was curious about him. How long you'd dated him. If you'd lived together. What the status of the relationship is now. I told him I had no idea."

How would you? He's the man I left you for. My God. No, it couldn't be. Not Steven. So much time has gone by. How could anything he's done be used against me?

"Kent, I don't know how to thank you for calling me. You can understand, it's a little unsettling to hear about all this." The headache was back, pounding against the base of her neck. Her hands were shaking. She felt weak.

"I can imagine how you must feel, Cathleen. But please don't let this throw you. I'm certain it isn't worth getting worked up about. My pal says this kind of follow-through goes on all the time. Doesn't mean anything."

She said nothing. Her mind raced. Fitting pieces of the cockeyed puzzle together. London canceled. Taubman blaming her. The FBI. Questions about Steven. She couldn't see it clearly yet. There were still pieces missing. But already she didn't like what she saw.

Slapping ten dollars on the counter, Denny Bracken slid his wallet, two gold chains, and a diamond pinky ring into the safety-deposit box. A balding attendant handed him a towel, toga, and slippers. Denny headed for the locker room.

He was already fifteen minutes late for this clandestine meeting at the Pico-Burnside Baths, one of the last old-style bathhouses in Los Angeles. He didn't care. His tardiness was carefully calculated.

Serves Taubman right.

Denny found his locker and let his pants drop to the cement floor, thinking about his telephone conversation with Taubman earlier that day.

The louse. Almost hangs up on me when I finally reach him at home. Treats me like some two-bit *shlemiel*. But when I mentioned the two magic words *Rex Pearce*, he sure snapped out of it, couldn't wait to meet me here after that.

He can wait just a little longer, Denny decided, coaxing the light cotton toga down over his head. Let him sweat.

He slammed the locker door, chuckling out loud now. Amused by his pun. Sweat! That's rich.

This all-male bastion was, of course, a temple of sweat. The regulars, mostly septuagenarian Jews who grazed here daily on hot wooden benches in the Russian Room or the Eucalyptus Room, came to sweat buckets. Sweat—in Yiddish, *shvitz*—was the object of the place.

The Pico-Burnside was one of Denny's favorite haunts. Rock stars showed up now and then to *shvitz* their way through hangovers. Dodger manager Tommy Lasorda was a regular when his team was in town. But Denny normally frequented the baths to escape from his world of famous faces. He came here to relax. He loved sparring with the geriatric "tough guys" who treated the place like their own college fraternity. Arguing about Israel one minute, the daily double at Hollywood Park the next. Swapping bawdy stories about big-bosomed broads. Kidding each other about putting on the pounds while downing huge bowls of cold borsht and plates of gefilte fish.

Walking down the corridor now, he paused outside the Russian Room and peeked through the small window, checking the action. It was pretty busy for a Sunday afternoon. Off to one side a group of naked men in their sixties and seventies were splayed out on benches, looking like fat sea lions sunning themselves as they cooked in the hundred-sixty-degree heat. Eyes closed. Mouths open. Huge bellies heaving upward. Each awaiting his turn, Denny knew, for a *plaitza*.

A *plaitza* was better than a rubdown. Better than a mud bath. When the *parchik* worked you over, applying the eucalyptus leaves to your skin, letting the plant's rich oil penetrate into your pores, it was one of the best feelings in the world. Relaxing and soothing and stimulating your muscles, all at the same time.

Denny watched for a moment as the deft *parchik,* a guy named Manny, rustled the soapy leaf over a pale belly. And heard the inevitable low groan of pleasure from the happy recipient. There was nothing like a good *plaitza*. Denny would be back for one himself, right after he took care of business.

Heading toward the Eucalyptus Room, he reviewed his plan. He was deep in thought and thus oblivious to the muffled guffaws coming from two men approaching him. They'd never seen anyone quite so short in a toga. The billowing white garment reached down to Denny's ankles, and he looked ludicrous, like a miscast angel who had strayed from the school Christmas pageant.

The steam inside the Eucalyptus Room was dense. Clouds of hot, fragrant fog surrounded him. Sweat started oozing from his pores.

"Taubman?"

"Over here, on the right," came the irritated voice.

Denny padded blindly in the direction of the voice, feeling his way with his hands. After about five steps he collided with something wet and fleshy.

"Ouch. *Shmuck!*" the voice yelped in pain.

"Oops. Sorry. That you, Irving?"

"Who'd you expect, the Pope? I've been here half an hour, dripping like a leaky faucet. And he asks if it's me. Who else?"

Denny sat down beside Taubman, his toga hanging out over the moist bench. "Are we alone?" He squinted into the steam, searching for other towels or togas.

"How the hell should I know? Forgot to bring my fog lights."

"Gotta be sure. Stop breathing for a minute," Denny commanded in a low voice. Listening for signs of other life, and hearing none, he proceeded. "Okay. I think it's clear. Wouldn't matter anyway. The guys here could care less about show biz. They'd rather boast about who had his first *plaitza* in Kiev." He laughed.

"Cut the crap, Bracken. It feels like Miami one hundred times over in here. Let's talk."

"Right. We got plenty to talk about, Irv."

"Irving. I particularly like the *-ing*. Nobody calls me Irv."

"Not even Rex Pearce?" Denny shot back. It wasn't the way he'd planned to open the subject. But Taubman was such a putz.

"All right. What about Rex Pearce? And what the fuck does it have to do with me?" His was a studied tone, approximating boredom.

"A lot of that, Irv-*ing*. A lot of just that. I'm talkin' fucking, Irv-*ing*." It was time to lay down his winning hand and grab the pot. "Y'see, I know all about the little, shall we say, surreptitious rendezvous you've been enjoyin' the past several years, compliments of our mutual pal, Rexy baby. All those bimbos you've been ballin' from Geneva to Hong Kong. Not to mention the lays at the Carlyle every time you go to New York on business."

"So what? What's that prove?" Taubman sounded edgy but defiant.

"I also happen to know," Denny went on, ignoring the interruption, "that you are in the habit of chargin' the sweet young things you take advantage of to the network. Now, I could be wrong, but somehow I feel sure your superior, R. F. Dollinger, a strict Baptist as I recall, would be shocked to hear that you're shellin' out the network's hard cash to get your rocks off, so to speak."

"You can't prove a thing," challenged Taubman.

"Oh, but I can. F'instance, I know all the company names our buddy Rex uses as fronts. I pay those fake companies, too. For services rendered to my hornier clients, y'know? Sunny Productions. Coast Restaurants. I know 'em all. And I'll bet it wouldn't be tough to find those names on your expense accounts. I'll bet Dollinger could find 'em. In minutes. And wouldn't he be thrilled with the scintillating details of your five-hundred-buck screws."

Denny knew he had him, but couldn't resist playing it to the hilt. "All those special requirements of yours, Irv-*ing*," he continued.

" 'Nice girls' only. But you settle for reasonably clean. And the disguises. Gotta give you credit there. What imagination! The long white cape. Nippleless black bra. Lacy garter belt. Oh, and no panties. Dollinger would probably get a hard-on just hearin' about how your cuties dress up. And your wife, Blanche—just think how she'd take the news."

"Okay, okay!" Taubman stopped him. Then he lowered his voice to a gruff whisper. "What do you want?"

"Atta boy, Irv-*ing*. I knew you'd come around to my way of seein' things. What do I want? It's pretty simple, really. Just three things."

"Go ahead—what are they?" Taubman felt faint from the heat. The relentless steam was choking him. He could hardly breathe.

"First, I want the master tape of the Roland Williams interview.

"Second, I want a written pledge that you have destroyed all the copies. And that the interview will never air. Your star reporter got a little carried away on that one. She was out for blood. Turned my client inside out. He still hasn't recovered. By the way, Irv-*ing*, Christine DuRand is persona non grata at Laurence and Ferber. Not one of our clients—and you know we have a stable of celebs matched by no other public-relations firm—not one of 'em will ever agree to an interview with Ms. DuRand again. Our executive board has voted to shut her out of Hollywood." Denny smiled and licked away the salty drops of water that dribbled from his upper lip.

"But," Taubman gasped, "that is against Publicist Guild rules. You're playing with fire, Bracken. Wait'll the trades get ahold of this. It isn't ethical."

"Maybe not. But it's the way I do business. Besides, who's gonna tip off the trades? Certainly not you, Irv-*ing*. You've got too much at stake here," Denny said smugly. He was holding the whole deck. Taubman didn't have a chance.

"And third?"

"Ah, yes. Third, I want you to fire DuRand. Monday morning, she's through."

"Is that all?" said Taubman sarcastically, sure that it must be.

"Glad you asked. Because that's not quite it. Just one more thing. I have a fabulous suggestion for DuRand's replacement. Real talented lady who used to work for you, in fact."

"Yeah? Who?"

"Jewel Crosse."

• • •

A barrage of popping flashbulbs greeted Jewel Crosse as she stepped daintily from the sleek white limousine at the entrance to Jimmy's restaurant in Beverly Hills.

Click, *zzzt,* pop . . . click, *zzzt,* pop.

"This way, Jewel."

"Over here, Miss Crosse."

"Could you turn your head a little to the right, please?"

"My, my," whispered the slender, fashionably dressed man climbing out after her. "The paparazzi are out in full force tonight. There must be at least fifty of them here."

Jewel grunted, her smile frozen in place, her mind intent upon making certain she gave the photographers a three-quarters from the left. Her best angle. Smoothing the tight-fitting aubergine silk dress over her ample curves, Jewel glanced down briefly. She noted with satisfaction that her top buttons were splayed open, showing off to best advantage as much of her Rubensesque bosom as she could get away with.

"Excuse me, sir. Can we get the spelling of your name, please?" The request came in a high-pitched voice from a disheveled-looking fat man with a Nikon strapped around his neck.

"This is my assistant, Bruce Stenson. Nothing personal," Jewel quickly interceded. It wasn't often the Hollywood press gave her this much attention, and she didn't want to find herself in the *National Enquirer* next week having an affair with Bruce.

Though she adored the attention, Jewel was wary as she plunged into the elegant, dimly lighted lobby of Jimmy's. So many photographers spending so much time on her could mean only one thing. The gala cocktail party inside—one of the hundreds she was obliged to attend—was a bust. Too many celebrity no-shows.

As soon as she and Bruce rounded the corner, her instincts were confirmed. The private party room was crowded—with all the wrong people. Publicists, studio executives, newspaper columnists, television reviewers, and the usual smattering of freeloaders stood elbow to elbow. Some were propping up the light-blue wall paneling; others jammed together near the bar in front of a mural—a French artist's impression of the Malabar Coast, an exotic array of shrines, temples, and natives that covered the entire wall. An engaging piece of artwork, but rather incongruous, Jewel thought. Not that it mattered. At soirees such as these, few paid attention to anything other than the celebrity count, the always lavish display of food and the freely flowing drinks.

"Looks like a real fanny-bumper," joked Bruce, straightening the pink pocket handkerchief in his Perry Ellis jacket.

"Yes. All the wrong fannies," Jewel scowled, promptly sitting down at a small, round table off to the side. "Get me a Campari and soda, will you, sweetie?" she said, crossing her lovely legs.

She was ready now to hold court.

Jewel had long passed the point where she actually had to "work" a party. These days there was no reason for her to waste her time circulating. Bruce could do that. The important players made it a point to come over to her.

If the party was really a dud, often all Jewel did was nod and shake hands for a short time, then leave. Tonight—a welcome-to-Hollywood party for television's latest beefcake turned actor—looked like it might be worth half an hour.

"Jewel, Jewel, my dee-ah," came the glaringly affected British accent from overhead. It was Archibald Webster, a publicist with a completely bald head and a walrus mustache. Everyone knew the old boy had come from somewhere in Iowa, but an extended holiday in Shakespeare's homeland years ago had made its permanent alteration upon him—he'd returned home sounding like a London vaudeville comic. In its inimitable fashion, Hollywood had accepted the dreadful accent, as it did most affectations, graciously. Archie Webster was simply playing a part, a familiar enough phenomenon locally.

Webster turned back briefly to yank on the elbow of a good-looking sandy-haired young man. Deferring to the publicist's firmness, the young man abruptly abandoned the two people he'd been speaking with—and now stood in the queenly presence of Jewel Crosse.

"Jewel, dah–ling, I'd like you to meet our guest of honor, Neal Burgess. Neal, Jewel is one of Hollywood's most important television personalities. Surely you've seen her show?"

"Ahhh. Sure. Sure, I have." The young actor shifted uncomfortably, looking down at Jewel. "Watch it every night."

Webster's already tight smile tightened.

"That's odd," Jewel mused, staring back at television's newest hunk. "I'm on in the morning." Her eyes traveled from Neal's large brown eyes to his chest, to his crotch. "You must stay up all night."

"Jewel, dee–ah. Forgive Neal's confusion," Webster put in. "I'm sure you understand. Just moving to Hollywood, a new series and all that. He is the star, you know. Keeps him very busy indeed. Neal, why don't you tell Jewel about *Speed?*"

"Yes," Jewel agreed, blinking up at the obviously ill-at-ease actor. "I'd like that. Come now. Sit down." She patted the elegantly carved chair beside her. "And fill me in. He'll be just fine, Archie. We'll have a nice chat. You go and enjoy the party."

The queen had spoken. Uncertain of what else to do, Webster adhered to protocol. He wandered off in search of a much-needed double martini.

"So," Jewel began, as Neal sat down. "How did an All-American football player from Michigan State get all the way to Hollywood?" Screw the rest of the party, she said to herself. This is the best-looking body I've seen since Tom Selleck debuted in *Magnum, P.I.*

"It happened pretty fast, actually," he started, his voice tinged with nervousness. "The producers of the series, ahh, *Speed,* that is . . . it's about a motorcycle racer, see? They were looking for an unknown. And, well, a girl I used to date back home in Charlevoix, she works out here modeling and acting now. And she told her agent about me. And the next thing you know, they fly me out here to test for the part. So, well, I got it," he said with finality, raising both hands up at once and slopping his drink over his white silk shirt. "Darn!"

"There's a waiter. Get some cold water and a towel," Jewel commanded.

"Oh, it's okay. Just ginger ale." He smiled at her while trying to brush the wetness off his chest.

"Really? You don't drink?"

"Not much, ma'am. Can't handle the stuff. Besides, I come from a pretty strict family." He grinned. Large, perfectly even teeth gleamed at her.

Jewel was intrigued. Nothing excited her more than a young body, strong and firm. Especially if the body was attached to such a gorgeous, rugged-looking face. The idea of seducing this naive jock from the Midwest was becoming more and more appealing. And considering her steady diet of après-lunch sex with Howard Ruskin, Jewel decided she owed herself one. The party was definitely shaping up.

"Your Campari, Jewel. Sorry I took so long," Bruce apologized, placing the glass in Jewel's hand. He took a slow sidelong glance at Neal. "Oh!" he exclaimed, sticking out a delicate hand. "We haven't met. I'm Bruce."

Neal shook it, squeezing Bruce's fingers together.

"My, my, you really are a football player, aren't you?" Bruce tittered. He started to sit down next to this unexpected surprise.

"Bruce," Jewel interceded, "Neal and I were having a little private talk. Why don't you go over to the buffet table and check out the action? See who's hanging around the shrimp bowl."

"Oh, all right," Bruce said sulkily. "Back in a few minutes." He gave Neal a short wave before vanishing into the crowd.

"So, what kind of a deal do you have, Neal? What's firm?" As she asked the question, Jewel draped an arm casually over the back of his chair.

"Pardon, ma'am?"

"First, please don't call me ma'am. You sound like a cowboy. Firm. That means, how many weeks are you guaranteed on this show?"

"Oh, I get it," he chuckled. "Thirteen. I mean, they're starting with five. And if we do good in the ratings, well, then—"

"—Then you do the rest. Are you any good?"

"Huh?" he asked, confused.

"Are you good? A good actor? Do you have any experience?"

"A little. In high school I was the lead in the senior class play. And I did a television commercial for a department store back in Michigan. That's about it," he said with uncertainty.

"What about a coach? I mean an acting coach. Are they providing you with one?"

"Yeah. Yeah. I have what they call a dialogue coach. We go over the lines together every day. He's a big help."

"Neal," Jewel said softly, leaning close to him, letting her breasts cascade forward as she spoke. "You need a lot more than five episodes on a new series to make it in this town. Suppose the series doesn't go? What then?"

"Well, I have an agent and he says—"

"Says." She stopped him. "Agents say a lot of things. But few of them deliver. Especially when the client is a new guy on the block."

Jewel shifted in her chair and slid her hand under the tablecloth, placing it nonchalantly on his knee.

Neal reflexively jerked back his leg.

"Relax," she soothed. "No one can see. Now, what you need is some good publicity. Spread your name around this town. Plaster the streets with billboards. Talk to all the columnists. And get yourself a nice long interview on a highly rated television show."

"I'm sure you're right, ma'am, er, Miss Crosse . . ."

"Jewel will do."

"Jewel. I know you know what you're talking about. But I've got a publicist and a manager already, and I figure they'll take care of all that."

"They're supposed to. But, Neal, if you want to be a star, you can't rely on others. You're going to have to make a big push yourself. And I can help you do that." Her hand crept up his leg.

"You can?" he said, astonished. Then he looked around guiltily to see whether anyone else had noticed what was going on under the tablecloth. He could smell Jewel's strong perfume, and it made him feel slightly intoxicated.

"I can," she assured him, smiling seductively. "A twenty-minute profile of you on my show. It's the highest rated celebrity interview show in the country," she lied. "We'll sit down together and do a very positive interview. Football player headed for overnight stardom, that sort of thing. I'll get some footage of you playing ball. Some behind-the-scenes on *Speed*. Neal," she announced, squeezing his meaty thigh, "I can make you look like the greatest thing since Gable."

"Gee," he enthused, hardly distracted by the squeeze. "That's great. That's just great. How can I thank you, Jewel?"

"We'll talk about that, Neal. Maybe later tonight. Where are you staying?"

"The Beverly Wilshire. It's just a few blocks from here. A real short—"

"I *know* where it is. Why don't you give me the key?"

"What?"

"The key. Your room key, Neal. If you give it to me I can meet you there after this party. And we can talk some more."

"Well, I don't know . . . I . . ."

"You know how important Archie says I am, don't you?"

Neal looked around in quiet desperation. Where was Archie now?

"Don't you?" she insisted.

"Ummm. Yes. Yes."

"Then?"

Neal reached into his tweed jacket.

"Quickly, under here," Jewel said, opening the hand on his leg and accepting the key. "There, that wasn't difficult, was it? I think you're going to do very well in this town, Neal."

He nodded at her blankly.

Jewel stood up. "Ten o'clock, Neal. I'll order champagne. Be prompt. Or all the bubbles will be gone."

• • •

"Yes?" The deep, ominous voice echoed from the huge rock.

Maggie leaned out the car window and shouted into the speaker embedded smack in the center of the craggy mass of stone. "Maggie Rafferty, with a guest. Here for the screening."

There was a brief pause.

"Okay, Ms. Rafferty, you can pull right up the hill."

The electronic gate swung open and the tan BMW surged forward up the steep, winding driveway.

"This'll be fun, girl," urged Maggie. "Get your mind off London."

"That would be a blessing," sighed Christine, still wondering why, in her present mood, she'd agreed to attend this weekly Sunday night screening at the Playboy Mansion. It wasn't as if she were curious about the place.

Although she'd never been invited as a guest, Christine had covered plenty of charity functions and done several interviews with Hugh Hefner at the immaculately manicured country estate. Maggie wasn't exactly a mansion regular, either. But occasionally she managed to have her name added to the Sunday night list of Hollywood VIPs and a handful of others who sank into large, comfortable brown leather couches just outside of Hefner's downstairs office to watch a not-yet-released movie. For her the major attraction wasn't the film, but the chance for intimate chats with James Caan, Carol Connors, Buck Henry, and other Hefner favorites.

"You know," Maggie said, pulling up to the picturesque circular driveway, "I would kill for an invitation to Hef's annual New Year's Eve party. Everybody wears pajamas, just like him. Isn't that a hoot?"

"I'm sure you'll manage to wangle an invitation to the next one," Christine said as a valet opened her car door. Her friend's constant effervescence cheered Christine. Maggie never seemed to run out of energy. Or optimism.

"So how're you doing, girl?" Maggie asked in a motherly way as they approached the massive carved wood front door.

"I'm fine, Mag," Christine assured. "Really. But after the movie you have to fill me in on this man you're gaga over. Nickels. I want the details," she kidded.

"*All* of them?" said Maggie, stifling a giggle.

"Shhhh . . . I think we're late. The movie's started."

They tiptoed into the large darkened room and sat down quietly.

It was a silly movie. A science fiction–horror spectacular, replete with gory space mayhem. Maggie was fascinated.

"A friend of mine did the makeup on this one," she whispered, nudging Christine. "Ever seen the way they put those bloody masks together? We ought to do a behind-the-scenes piece on it. Real visual."

Christine nodded, averting her eyes as a brilliant but deadly laser beam sliced through the innards of a hapless space-shuttle passenger, splattering what she knew was only a thin red dye all over the screen, but turning her stomach nonetheless.

My God, this is disgusting. Why do people actually pay to see such dreck?

She tried to get comfortable. Shifted in her seat. Folded and unfolded her hands, crossed her arms, recrossed her legs. It was no use. Her mind would not rest. It kept going back to Steven Jacobs.

"Mag, I'm going to the loo," she said, excusing herself.

But Christine did not go near the small guest bathroom off the high-ceilinged entrance hall. Instead, she found a telephone and dialed the number in New York that she had called repeatedly since yesterday morning. Her reportorial instincts made her want to get to the bottom of whatever was threatening her—the crazy FBI business, the delay in the London trip—and fast.

"Mr. Jacobs's line." The voice sounded distant and indistinct.

"This is Christine DuRand again. Has he called in yet? Has he gotten my message?"

For a moment there was only static. "I have your message right here, Miss DuRand," the voice said now. "I told you, he's out of the country."

"I know, but hasn't he called?"

"Not yet, Miss DuRand. As soon as he does, I'll give him your message. It's marked 'Urgent,' as you requested. Goodnight, Miss DuRand."

The line went dead, and for a long moment Christine stared at the phone receiver, until she finally replaced it in its cradle, turned and walked across the enormous entrance hall. Her heels clicked loudly on the stone floor. She knew she didn't want to see any more of the movie. Impulsively she took a sharp left, opened one of the glass doors overlooking the mansion's sprawling backyard and slipped out into the darkness.

Moist night air filled her lungs, refreshing her. She took several deep breaths and zipped up her fawn Ultra Suede jacket against the chill, thankful she'd worn slacks and a cozy angora sweater.

Slowly she walked along the pathway toward the poolside bar and sat down on one of the high stools near the entry to the grotto. A facsimile of a subterranean pond, lush with potted greenery and always supplied with stacks of thick plush towels, the grotto was part of the fantasy life of the mansion. A perfect setting for an orgy or a private tête-a-tête, but even better for Hef's visitors to examine in wide-eyed wonder. On this damp winter evening the grotto did not echo with squealing, raucous laughter or with the splashing of unclad bodies. It was utterly calm, thoroughly peaceful. Christine stared distractedly at nothing in particular, ignoring the lavish surroundings.

She was thinking about another fantasy residence on another large, meticulously landscaped estate.

It was the summer of her first year in New York. She was still Cathleen Rand then. She was weekending at what looked like an enormous Normandy castle, complete with tower, moat, and thirty acres of lawn and flower gardens.

The castle sat incongruously fifty yards off Long Island Sound. Clear blue water lapped against smooth white sand, enhancing the fairy-tale setting and reminding Cathleen of visions of what the world held in store for those who dared to venture forth. She had, in fact, only recently arrived in New York. Barely twenty-one, fresh from college. And never had she seen anything so overwhelmingly opulent.

The occasion was a wedding. Cathleen and about twenty-five others from various pockets of the country had settled into the guest wings. The rooms compared favorably with the finest European hotels, each one featuring eighteenth-century French furniture, a private bath with heated towel racks and bidet, and a direct line to the kitchen for liquid refreshment or late-night snacks.

The bride, Julie Norton, a breathtaking five-foot-ten-inch beauty from Tuscaloosa, had, for the past two months, been Cathleen's roommate.

"Now, sugar, you've just gotta come," she had drawled sweetly when Cathleen hesitated. "Ah just know you'll have the bes' time. All of Hank's friends'll be in from Dallas and everywhere. All those good-lookin' men. All that money. I'll be sure to toss you the bouquet."

Julie had struck oil. Hank, her megabucks Texan, owned dozens of wells. Granted, he wasn't exactly a dreamboat. Fifty-three years old, with a stomach that stuck out like a water balloon, and a half-dozen thin strands of painstakingly combed hair under his ten-gallon hat. But Hank was wild for Julie. He had purchased this "lil' ole house" so his bride could be comfortable while pursuing her acting career in Manhattan.

The wedding was glorious. Julie's six sisters were bridesmaids, decked out like Scarlett O'Haras. The bride's train of imported antique lace measured twenty-six yards, and twenty-six white doves were released into the rafters. "One for every year mah lil' girl has made this earth a better place by bein' here," Hank gushed to one and all. Outside, a magnificent fountain of cherubs spewed Louis Roederer Crystal.

After the ceremony three hundred people sat down at beautifully set tables on the sprawling back lawn to enjoy a ten-course dinner. Julie's favorites were served—cold pike pâté, boned stuffed duck, spinach crepes, and chicken cannelloni with cream sauce.

Halfway through the meal, too full even to sample the intermezzo sorbet, Cathleen excused herself. Escaping the noisy crowd, she made her way down a slight incline to the water's edge. There she stood, wondering at the large colonial and Tudor homes across the bay. Wondering how having so much money changed people. Julie, it seemed, was already changing.

After a few minutes, glad for these stolen moments alone, Cathleen decided to rehearse some of her lines for an audition on Monday morning.

" 'And have you mercy too!' " she began, remembering that her acting coach had stressed visualization. Seeing herself as the helpless Desdemona. " 'I never did offend you in my life; never loved Cassio. But with such general warranty of heaven as I might love; I never gave him token.' "

" 'By heaven I saw my handkerchief in's hand . . .' " The voice from behind her was resonant and male.

"Wha—?" Cathleen turned around, stunned.

"I'd go on," said the intruder. "But since we haven't been introduced, I hesitate to call you a perjured woman."

She struggled to recover her aplomb. "Are you an actor?" she asked. How else could he have been able to spout Othello's lines on the spot?

"Afraid not," he replied, taking a couple of steps closer toward her. "I'm in the money business. Stocks. Steven Jacobs." He held out his hand. "I'm Hank's investment manager."

She shook his hand firmly. "Cathleen Rand. Julie's roommate. Uh, make that former roommate."

"Actress?" he asked, admiring her pink chiffon dress.

"Not yet."

"What are you auditioning for?"

"An off-Broadway production. They've asked me back twice now," she said proudly.

He was silent for a long moment. He looked at her with such intensity that Cathleen felt self-conscious. As though she should check herself in a mirror, make sure there was no spinach caught in her teeth.

Later he would tell her he had never been so taken by a woman. It had scared him. He was married. Not happily. But married. For ten years. And comfortable in the luxurious apartment on Park Avenue with his wife, Suzanne, and their two children.

"Do you think," he asked haltingly, looking out over the bay, "that Gatsby could really see the green light from here?"

"I guess so," she replied quickly, trying to think of something intelligent to say. To let him know she'd read F. Scott Fitzgerald's classic, too. "I mean, it's not all that far, is it? But somehow I always thought that light was more in Gatsby's imagination than an actual fixture on Daisy's dock."

He looked at her again, smiling, his arrogant dark eyes crinkling at the corners.

The water was now cast in the golden-red glow of the setting sun. "So we beat on, boats against the current, borne back ceaselessly into the past," he said, softly, evenly. As though he'd repeated the same passage many times before.

"You've memorized all of *The Great Gatsby?*" she asked, intrigued now by this melancholy stranger.

"Naw, not the whole thing. I just remember certain parts that mean something, reflect my own feelings about life."

"And *Othello?*"

He smiled again and ran a hand back through his light brown hair. "My memory is a little unusual."

"Photographic?"

"Something like that. Yes." He paused for a moment as if deciding what to say next. "Do you need a ride back to town?"

"Oh, no. Julie's lent me her car for the week. And I have to get up early. So I'm leaving soon."

"So am I. We'll follow you. Make sure you get home safely."

She looked at him, confused.

"My chauffeur and I. Whenever you're ready."

Cathleen Rand was not ready for Steven Jacobs to walk into her life. When they met she'd just about talked herself into returning to

Minneapolis if she didn't get that off-Broadway part. Giving up on New York. Her money was running out. The tiny walkup she shared with Julie cost her three hundred and fifty dollars a month. And now she had to find a new roommate. Modeling jobs were scarce. The prospect of landing a Broadway role looked slim. She couldn't even get an agent until she got an Equity acting job.

Most of all, though, she missed Kent. She longed to feel his arms around her again. Wanted to know she was safe. Loved. At home. They were already engaged. But she'd insisted on trying her luck in New York, and he'd gone along with it.

"For a year, sweetheart," he'd said. "You should go for a year. You'll always be sorry if you don't. But remember I'm here waiting for you. I'm going to love you for the rest of your life, Cathleen. Cathleen Michaels. Sounds kind of classy, huh?"

He'd kissed her long and hard that morning at the airport six months ago. And now she wanted to go back. She would marry Kent. Have his children. Start her grown-up life.

Part of her wanted that. Another part told her to stay in New York, despite the obstacles. To work as a Kelly Girl. Substitute-teach in high school. Babysit. Do anything to pay the bills and keep on studying acting. Keep on auditioning. That part of her wasn't willing to let go, not yet. Every time she was ready to pack her bags, it warned her: Don't leave. Don't give up. Give it a little more time.

Steven Jacobs stepped in at exactly the right moment to provide that time.

"I never date married men," she'd told him when he saw her to her door that night after the wedding. The fact was, she'd never been approached by a married man before, but her Roman Catholic up-bringing was enough to impel her to turn down his proposal immediately.

As antiquated as it seemed sometimes, even to her, she was saving herself for her wedding night with Kent Michaels. She was still a virgin. Cathleen didn't need an aggressive, married, Jewish financial wizard in her life. Especially when she also found him so physically unappealing.

Steven was slightly built. Five feet eleven. He had a rounded, soulful face and a prominent nose. He always dressed impeccably in made-to-order pin-striped suits, Sulka shirts, and conservative neckties. Most women found the overall package quite attractive. But Cathleen did not.

It was Steven's intelligence. His drive. His insatiable hunger to learn about everything from interior design to jet engines. And his great love of the theater. All of this fascinated Cathleen. She bent the rules and went out with him.

"But only for lunch. And I'll meet you at the restaurant," she'd warned him.

Their lunches grew longer and more frequent. Eventually he started picking her up at her apartment. Within a month they were seeing each other four or five nights a week.

By that time Steven had moved from Park Avenue to a furnished apartment in the East Sixties. He told Cathleen that he was a free man now, that he was negotiating with Suzanne's lawyer about the divorce.

He'd cast a Svengali spell over Cathleen. Drawing her into his world. Explaining to her the intricacies of the proxy fight he was waging to take over a plastics conglomerate, taking her to the floor of the New York Stock Exchange.

They saw all the new Broadway shows, often partying afterwards at Sardi's with the cast, producers, and director.

She was introduced to his favorite restaurants. Elaine's on the Upper East Side and "21," where she could gawk at the likes of Ethel Kennedy and her brother-in-law Ted. La Côte Basque, where the after-dessert petits fours were irresistible.

It was during their second dinner at La Côte Basque that he tried to teach her how to eat European style, with the fork held in the left hand. Cathleen was incensed. Insulted. She threatened to walk out of the restaurant.

"Suit yourself," he told her coolly, slipping a morsel of sole amandine into his mouth. "But believe me, in some circles eating like this is very important. You'll thank me someday."

Her education hadn't stopped there. It was Steven who also taught her how to shop wisely. "Quality, not quantity, Cathleen," he'd lecture as they roamed through Saks. "Don't buy two cheap dresses. One more expensive black linen sheath will last you five years. Just change the accessories."

But Steven changed far more than her table manners and shopping habits. He transformed her entire way of life. Helped her get a theatrical agent. Encouraged her to enroll in classes for voice, tap, and ballet. Sent her to auditions and modeling go-sees in his limousine.

By November she had landed three network-television commercials, an off-Broadway show, and an audition for the Actors Studio, a rare break for an inexperienced actress. She suspected Steven had pulled some strings to make it possible. But he denied it.

Whenever she was tired of sitting in unruly high-school classrooms to collect forty-three dollars a day, or depressed by reading for hundreds of commercials and seldom landing one, or was suffering the sting of rejection from yet another Broadway audition—Steven was there.

"Princess, you must not give up on your goals. Remember, if you shoot for a star, you get a chorus girl. Shoot for a chorus girl, you get nothing. Keep on shootin', princess. You'll make it to the top."

She didn't make it back to Minneapolis that Christmas. Instead, she wrote Kent a long letter, breaking their engagement. She tried to explain that she cared for him but needed more time in New York. To learn. To grow. "I'm changing so much," she'd ended the letter, "sometimes I don't recognize myself."

Steven Jacobs helped to complete the metamorphosis.

"I've got an idea that will make you the star you really are," he'd announced over German pancakes during a holiday brunch.

"What's that?" she joked. "You're going to buy a theater for me?"

"No, dum-dum," he joked back. "I'm going to revamp that Plain Jane Midwestern image. How does Christine DuRand sound?"

"Who's she? A fashion consultant? Or a voice coach?" she asked warily. She was always leery of Steven's suggestions.

"Neither," he said, neatly folding his napkin before blotting powdered sugar on his upper lip. "She's you, princess. Welcome to Manhattan, Miss DuRand."

So Christine DuRand it was.

A few weeks past her twenty-second birthday, Steven threw an elaborate party upstairs at "21" to celebrate her first Broadway role, a small part in a Michael Bennett musical. He gave her a delicate diamond heart on a silver chain to commemorate the occasion.

That night he wore a dark-blue tuxedo with a light-blue shirt and red bow tie. For the first time, Christine found herself thinking how sexy Steven looked. Watching him across the room talking to Julie and Hank, she thought about how lucky she was. And how much she cared for this eccentric, driven yet sensitive man named Steven Jacobs.

Without even realizing it, she had fallen in love with him.

It didn't matter now that he was eleven years her senior. Or that he was married. He looked young, and the divorce was in progress. She was much wiser than she'd been six months before. And she wanted Steven in a way she'd never wanted Kent. The way, she thought, a woman wants a man.

After the party, when he suggested they go back to his apartment, she didn't object, as she had in the past. She knew it was time. He had been patient with her. Guiding her. Teaching her. Making her feel secure. Loved. Now she would be his.

Steven was gentle, aware that he was her first lover. Careful to spend a long time on foreplay. He moved his fingers lightly over her nipples. Down to the softness between her legs. Probing gently to find her clitoris. Massaging it tenderly for long, exquisite moments. Then bringing his mouth down to the spot which aroused her most. Only after she was totally relaxed, wet, ready for him, did he enter her. Pushing slowly. Moving in small, loving thrusts and pulling out just before he came in a long, ecstatic rush.

Finally, Christine DuRand was his.

Although Christine never had an orgasm with Steven, knowing he was satisfied made her feel content. Complete. And she knew he loved her. Why else would he keep talking about marriage?

"We'll have a huge wedding, princess. At Hank's place on Long Island if you like. He's offered. Of course, it'll take about a year for the divorce to be final. But we'll have fun. You'll see."

And they did. Although Christine insisted on keeping her own apartment and working whenever she got a commercial or acting job, she spent most of her time traveling with Steven. They went everywhere. The Orient, Europe, Hawaii, the Caribbean. Even Alaska. They were business trips for him, mainly. But there was always time out to luxuriate in the world's most splendid playgrounds.

It was during that trip to Rio de Janeiro, Christine remembered now, pacing alongside Hugh Hefner's pool, that she first suspected Steven was more than an investment manager.

He'd returned to their suite at the Rio Palace Hotel very late one night. Christine had been frightened. Steven always called if he wouldn't be joining her for dinner. She was afraid he'd been in an accident and was lying helpless somewhere.

It turned out she was half right. Steven was grotesquely bruised and bleeding from the nose when he pounded on the door of the suite. As Christine opened it, he extended the open palm of one hand; on it rested a tooth, one of his front uppers. He limped over to the bed and collapsed on it.

"Don't call a doctor. I'll be all right," he instructed. Then he passed out.

Christine did what she could to clean up his face and stop the nosebleed. She applied cold compresses to his badly cut and bruised eyes.

The next morning Steven hired two bodyguards and announced that they'd be staying at the Rio Palace until his face healed.

Christine swam, read three novels, and tried not to press Steven for an explanation of what had happened, thinking he would tell her in time.

When he didn't, she finally confronted him.

"Just a little accident, princess," he'd reassured her, examining his gap-toothed smile in a hand mirror. "I'll be back to normal by the weekend. Then we'll go home. Don't you worry."

That was more than she could bear. "How can I help but worry?" she'd exploded, slamming down a volume of Tennessee Williams plays. "A bodyguard follows me everywhere. I can't go to the bathroom without feeling I'm under surveillance. You're all beaten up. You won't let me call a doctor or a dentist. And this place," she sobbed, "it seems like we've been here a month already. Hiding out. What do you expect me to do, enjoy it?"

"Christine, princess, please don't cry. Don't." Steven sat down next to her on the bed and gently ran a hand over her thick curls. "I'm sorry. I can't say anything more. Believe me, you're better off. Accept it and forget about what happened."

He waited for her sobs to diminish, then added firmly, "Now, the subject is closed. I never want to hear you bring it up again."

Christine seethed with anger and confusion, but said nothing. She thought about leaving him. She wondered if her own life might be in danger.

Then she began to think about the other times. Those long trips to Las Vegas. He always went there alone, phoning her every day but never leaving a number.

And what about that exchange at Heathrow Airport? Steven had stepped out of their chauffeured Daimler and handed a brown leather briefcase to a man she didn't get a good look at. Then he'd returned with a different case. It was covered in a sort of tweedy material, she recalled.

Little things. But they were beginning to add up. And Christine was becoming more and more frightened.

Once back in New York, however, she was confronted by another dilemma. Christine discovered she was pregnant. At first she was happy. Despite their current difficulties, she was still very much in love with Steven. And they'd already decided to have children after they got married.

But the divorce was holding them up. The arduous process had stretched from one year to two. Initially, Christine was understanding. She listened sympathetically to Steven's complaints about Suzanne's financial demands. And her fight to win sole custody of the children.

But now she was expecting his child.

"I want to be married by the time I start to show," she told him, minutes after her gynecologist had confirmed the pregnancy.

"Princess, I'd love that. But considering the circumstances with Suzanne at the moment, don't you think it would be more prudent if we—"

"No!" she shouted, stamping her foot. "No. No. No. I want my baby to have a father. If you won't marry me, I won't have the baby!"

She was hysterical. Crying. Screaming. Saying things she'd never imagined she could.

An abortion? What if her parents found out? It was a mortal sin! She'd burn in hell. How could she? Why wouldn't he marry her? It wasn't fair.

Steven managed to calm her down that afternoon by promising to ask his lawyer about a quickie Mexican divorce.

But by the next day, when he reported apologetically that the at-torney had said a Mexican divorce was out of the question, Christine had done some checking of her own. A trip to the Hall of Public Records had yielded a crushing discovery. Steven Jacobs (a.k.a. Seth Jacobsen) had never filed for divorce from Suzanne Erlich Jacobs.

"Never," she confronted him quite calmly. "You never signed a paper. Never filed. All this time you've been lying to me. Promising me. And now I'm having your child. Why, Steven, why? I thought you loved me."

He pleaded that he did. That he worshiped her. Adored her. Wanted her for his wife.

Christine didn't listen. That night she flew to Los Angeles, where she stayed with her best friend from college, a nurse at a clinic in East Los Angeles. A week later she had the abortion there.

Steven did not give up. In fact, he was relentless. He wrote long letters urging her to move back to New York. Twice he flew out to California. Christine refused to see him. Whenever he called, she hung up the phone.

In the years since, thoughts of Steven Jacobs came less and less often. Her career had assumed primary importance in her life.

The many happy times they'd spent together . . . the influence he'd had over her . . . what she'd done to their child—all of it was now only a vague shadow, tucked somewhere deep in her memory.

If it hadn't been for Kent Michaels's phone call, that's where Steven might have stayed. Locked away and all but forgotten. But tonight, in the lonely darkness behind the Playboy Mansion—so still she could hear herself breathe—Christine felt salty tears glistening down her cheeks, leaving tiny tracks in the rosy blush she'd dusted on carelessly and without enthusiasm.

They were tears she wasn't ready to face. Tears from the past, which made her suddenly fearful about the future.

— CHAPTER —
Six

"Ah, so! Wha' pree ladee doing, work so hard so erlee?"

Diedra Davis spun around from her computer and let out a shriek of laughter.

There was Rex, in that "authentic" antique kimono. The wizened owner of the small shop in Osaka had sworn that it was a treasure of the Koyun Dynasty. And a bargain at three thousand dollars.

Not long after that, Diedra checked and discovered there had been no Koyun Dynasty. She had discreetly kept this from her mate.

Now, with the imposter kimono of faded dusty-rose silk wrapped around his ample frame, his hair askew and face bristly with gray unshaven whiskers, Rex Pearce looked as absurd as he sounded. In one hand he clutched his habitual eye-opener, a bullshot.

"Ah, yes. Good morning. Mr. Chan, isn't it?"

Diedra would humor him. "I do think your accent is a bit off, though, baby. That is a Japanese garment. And, tell me, what time was it I felt your huge presence fall into bed this morning?"

"Ah, that be tree." He held up three fingers. "Tree o'clock, beyoo-ful ladee. Sorry I wake you up." Rex grinned.

Diedra stood up and held out her arms. "Welcome home," she said, laughing. Slipping her hands under the silk robe, she felt his body bend to her as she pressed her fingers against his hairy back.

"So," Rex went on, reluctant to abandon his script. "You want to play with my chopstick?" He whisked the kimono open briefly, giving her a quick flash.

She took the bullshot from his hand and took a gulp of the beef bouillon and vodka. "Rex, you are one sick puppy," she teased. "Too bad you're such a good pimp."

Rex grunted. "How'd you do this trip, sugarbuns?" He was running his hand back and forth over her bottom.

"Good. Better than good." She turned around and hit a button on the computer. "Look at that."

A parade of women's names, arranged alphabetically and including vital statistics, ages, addresses, experience, and classification began moving up the screen.

"Almost sixty new ones, babe," she said exuberantly. "We're rich."

"Honey pie, we've been rich. Now we're gettin' filthy rich."

He kissed her on the back of her neck and wrapped his arms around her waist. They both watched Diedra's new enlistees float up and out of frame.

"Hold it a sec," Rex said.

She pushed the space bar, freezing the names on the screen.

"Just remembered," he said. "Find any virgins this time?"

Diedra turned to face him again, crossing her arms over her yellow cashmere sweater and giving him a wan smile. "Why? You ain't satisfied with what you got here anymore?"

"Who you kiddin', tiger? I'm nobody's fool," he replied, winking at her. "Why go out for hamburger when you've got steak at home?"

"Paul Newman said that. I want to know what Rex Pearce says."

"Paul and I see eye to eye. They're my sentiments exactly."

"Seems to me," she murmured so softly it was barely audible, "you been spreadin' your sentiments around lately."

A licentious smile spread across his lips. "Hmmm? My beauty out of sorts this morning? Needs a little lovin' with ol' Rex?" He pulled her close for a long, wet kiss. "That's just for starters."

"It'll do for starters," she said, brightening, feeling his hard protrusion beneath the kimono.

"Honey tongue," he said, "before I get too horny to carry on a decent business conversation, let's take a look at your new flock of virgins."

"Can't it wait?" she asked seductively.

"This will take just a minute, angel face. And you are going to be tickled pink. We've got an order you won't believe."

Diedra took a Players from the carved ivory cigarette box on her desk and lit up.

"I only got three Vs this time," she said, exhaling a blue cloud of smoke. "Seems like the species is damn near extinct. What are we looking for? Maybe we got somebody on file already."

"No. It should be a brand-new girl. Fresh. Unaffected. Clean. And a stunner."

"Who you want, Miss America? I was in Europe, remember?"

"That's important. She should be sort of mysterious. Enigmatic. We're better off with a foreigner. Come on, punch up the Vs on your magic screen, woman."

"Okay, okay," she said, growing impatient. "But you gonna tell me who this girl is for? Or we gonna play guessing games?"

Rex sat down on the edge of an S-shaped white plastic chair, nearly tipping it over. "Whoops!"

He was enjoying the little frenzy Diedra was working herself into. She was a great broad, but too impatient. He had to bait her once in a while. Nothing serious. Just let her know who was boss.

"So?" she demanded, putting her hands to her hips.

"Babe, I love it when you get worked up." He smiled at her. "Gets me up, too, if you know what I mean." He chuckled lightly.

She sat down and began typing on the computer keyboard, ignoring him.

"All right. My God. Go away for a few weeks, and you lose your sense of humor."

"Hardly," she said stiffly.

"Hey—it's no secret who's asking for this girl. I was just having a little fun."

She kept typing.

"Dee? Do you want to know, or what?"

She nodded.

"Well, you won't believe it. Remember when we were in Cannes last spring? That guy from Hollywood I introduced you to over at the Carlton Hotel? Runty guy. Couldn't be more than five seven."

Diedra slowly turned around to face Rex. She remembered. "You mean that slippery little creep who kept ordering double Scotches? The one you got so drunk with I had to have the manager help me get you up to the room? How could I forget that jerk? A flack, isn't he? Backus . . . Bracker . . . Bracken, that it?"

"Right you are, sweetstuff. Denny Bracken. God, you sure have a memory." He saluted her with his glass.

"Skip the shmaltz," she said, still slightly miffed. "So it's Bracken who wants this virgin? What for? He's gay?"

"No. Not him. I'm certain about that. I hear the little squirt is a human dipstick. Doesn't pay for it, either. Probably uses the old 'I can make you a star' line."

"So just who are we servicing?"

"Bracken. I mean, he's our contact. We've been supplying his clients for years, see. A lot of the older guys in the recording business. The ones who've run out of groupies to screw."

"I get it," Diedra said. "This virgin's for some old fart who can't warble it up anymore."

Rex laughed. "Not even close! Now this is the part that will shock the hell out of you. Ready?"

"Have been for half an hour now," she said, feigning a yawn.

"Okay. Just off the top of your head, who's the most successful, the sexiest male recording star you can think of?"

"In the States?"

"Anywhere. The whole world. That's how big this guy is."

She stared at him blankly.

"Don't tell me you can't guess?" he said. "It's Roland Williams!"

Diedra was stunned, rendered momentarily mute by the news.

"You heard right, babe. The guy makes millions singing and shaking his ass. Little girls massage themselves to sleep listening to his records. Women come in their panties at the sound of his voice. The guy is Mr. Superstud on his videos. But in real life he's a fag. A peter puffer! And the word is getting around—that's why Bracken needs us. He wants a foxy-looking woman to travel with Williams on his concert tour next month. I told him it'd cost ten grand a week. And he agreed. Baby, we're going to be more than filthy rich, we're going to be—"

Before Rex could finish the sentence, Diedra whirled around to face the computer. Mechanically she punched up "V."

"What's the matter? Ain't that the best news you've heard all day? I mean, this is the biggest job we've ever had."

"I know. Of course I'm excited," she said in an oddly empty tone of voice. Her hands were shaking. Her flesh felt simultaneously hot and cold as she leaned close to the screen and scrutinized the three names that materialized:

> Gina Alberto—Rome
> Leslie Musante—Paris
> Tashi Qwan—London

"I—I just want to make sure we have someone," Diedra mumbled. "Someone suitable."

Jewel Crosse was not asleep when her dainty bedside telephone ting-a-linged. It was two-thirty in the morning. She was lying there, still seething with rage, beneath the frilly pink comforter on her four-poster bed. Hands and face slathered with a thick avocado-based night cream. A black satin beauty mask encasing her icy-blue eyes in darkness. Three thicknesses of Charmin wrapped around and carefully clipped onto her stiff coiffure. It was Jewel's normal bedtime look—when she slept alone.

Promptly at 10 P.M. she had slipped the key into the door to Suite 609 at the Beverly Wilshire Hotel. Full of anticipation over her tryst with the lean and muscular football-player-turned-actor. It had been some time since Jewel had treated herself to such temptingly taut flesh. The allure of stretching this rendezvous into a long-term affair was most appealing.

Patiently she sat there until ten-twenty, assuming that the prolonged festivities at Jimmy's were responsible for Neal Burgess's delay.

At ten-thirty she phoned the restaurant's owner, Jimmy Murphy, who informed her that the party was long over. "Since nine o'clock, at least, Miss Crosse," he assured Jewel in his melodious, vaguely Irish accent.

She immediately ordered an extravagant dinner for two from room service. Complete with chilled Dom Perignon. Thirty-five minutes later, when the feast arrived, she signed Neal's name to the bill, adding a generous fifty-dollar tip.

She didn't touch a morsel. Not the ruby-red filet mignon. Not the golden broccoli soufflé. Not even the creamy chocolate mousse. Instead she stalked the room like a wounded lioness, downing glasses of champagne, checking and rechecking her watch, throwing off sparks of an anger which burned white-hot.

At eleven-thirty she abandoned the suite, slamming the door loudly behind her. Teetering down the hall into an elevator and out through the ornate lobby, she fell into her waiting limousine—and began plotting revenge.

Several suitable scenarios for his comeuppance had flashed before her masked eyes. Neal Burgess falling off his motorcycle, splintering one of his brawny legs and maybe an arm, too . . . Neal Burgess getting high on two glasses of wine at a party and puking all over the executive producer of his television series. Run the item as a humorous reader at the end of the show. Leave her viewers laughing at the dumb jerk . . . Neal Burgess being busted for drugs. Improbable. But who could predict what Hollywood might do to the bumbling All-American?

Jewel had time. Wherever he went, whatever he did—she'd know. She had the town wired. She'd see to it that young Mr. Burgess got what he deserved. One false move, Neal honey, and bang, you're dead!

The phone jingled irritatingly for the third time.

"Hang on, for crissakes," Jewel complained as she groped blindly for it, smearing the greenish-gray emulsion on her pink satin sheets.

"Yuck!" Her hand squished onto the pearly-pink receiver.

"Jewel? That you?" The male bark was insistent, anxious.

"Of course it's me. Who the hell is this and how the fuck did you get my private number?"

"Whaddaya mean? It's Denny. Denny Bracken. You gave it to me yourself," he shot back, offended.

"Not to be used as a wake-up service. Or didn't you know it was the middle of the night? I hope this is very important, Denny."

"You betcher sweet bippee it is, Jewel doll," he enthused. "Now hop outta the sack and grab your notebook. I've got your lead story for this morning's show, and I'm comin' over right now to dictate it in person."

There was always a line at Nate 'n Al's.

Up front, near the glass cases of smoked fish, creamed herring, pans of salads, puddings, and pickles, a throng of customers waited impatiently for tables, trying to keep the pungent deli smells from driving them crazy with hunger.

Billy Rafferty never queued up. The privilege he enjoyed was afforded only to those dozen or so top Hollywood deal makers who'd been treating the noisy and popular Beverly Hills delicatessen like home since it opened in 1945.

Breakfast, seven-thirty sharp, at Nate 'n Al's, arguably the best delicatessen in Southern California, was one of Billy's rituals. A daily indulgence. He rose promptly at six, put in a vigorous half hour of simultaneously lifting hand weights and pedaling an exercycle, quickly showered and dressed. Then he briskly walked the twenty blocks to the landmark on Beverly Drive.

Any other Monday morning he'd have been in a chipper mood, anticipating the satisfying crunch of his *latkes,* the large and crispy potato pancakes he always ordered on the first day of the week. But this morning Billy wasn't hungry. He would order, but he really didn't feel like eating.

He charged now through the back entrance like a miniature bullet train. The Hollywood trade papers were clutched tightly in his hand. Billy was in a mood to run over just about anything in his path this morning. The letter that arrived by messenger last night had sent him into a blind rage. As he whisked past the kitchen, nostrils flaring at the smell of sizzling kippers, Billy gave the head cook a tight little nod. He paused at the back of the busy restaurant beneath a suspended case of cooling melons and grapefruits. A flurry of busboys and middle-aged waitresses loaded down with heavy platters of steaming omelets, pink lox and freshly baked bagels rushed past him.

Billy's troubled eyes roamed the crowded booths. He scanned the crush of customers waiting up front. Dan Campbell, his attorney, was nowhere to be seen.

Catching the attention of the hostess, Billy stealthily held up two fingers. She gave him a knowing look and gestured toward the front. Billy managed a smile of appreciation. Then, with the nonchalance of someone just returning from the rest room, he strolled up the aisle, nodding to several other regulars, and slipped into a large banquette near the cash register.

Damn lawyers, he thought darkly. They're all the same. He looked up to see Campbell pushing his way toward him through the throng.

"Billy," said the lanky, graying man in greeting, maneuvering himself behind the freshly cleaned table. "How do you always manage to make me feel I should go back home and have my suit pressed?"

Campbell settled into the brown leatherette seat, plunked down a suitcase-sized briefcase, and picked up the laminated menu. "Haven't been here in ages. What's good?"

"Everything, Dan," Billy replied with a cordiality he didn't feel. "It's the only place for breakfast in Los Angeles."

"Ah. Blueberry blintzes. Great. And some decaf. Already past my caffeine limit today," the lawyer said, checking his watch.

"It's seven forty-five, Dan. We have forty-five minutes," said Billy curtly. Then he ordered for both of them.

Daniel R. Campbell was the senior partner of Campbell, Dalton, and Taylor, a large and well-regarded law firm situated in downtown Los Angeles. He had been Billy's attorney for the past fifteen years. And he'd always done a fine job. But there were two things Billy disliked about Dan. First, he never failed to look disheveled, even when wearing the most expensive tailor-made suit. Second, Dan was consistently late.

"Here it is," Billy grumbled, handing over the stiff piece of parchment paper.

"Hmmm." Dan inspected the letterhead and skimmed the five short paragraphs. Then he reread the whole thing more carefully.

"Anything to worry about?"

"I'm afraid so," said the attorney, refolding the letter.

"What do you mean?" Billy exploded. "They're full of crap! *Precipice* is mine! My project. I wrote it. *Longhand,* for crissakes. For two years I wrote it and rewrote it. I—"

"Billy, Billy. Calm down," Dan soothed. "I know you wrote the screenplay. The studio knows you wrote it. No one is questioning your integrity. But what we've got here"—he tapped the letter on the table—"is Max Groffsky, one of the most clever entertainment attorneys in the city, claiming that his client wrote *Precipice*. And asking for compensation."

"Compensation? I'll give him compensation. I'll hire somebody to break his legs," Billy growled.

"Now don't talk foolishly. Groffsky, Hall, and O'Keefe specialize in these plagiarism cases. And they have a reputation for extracting rather large settlements. They're stickup artists."

"They're rotten liars, the lot of them," Billy roared. "We should just take the friggin' thing"—he tried to pry the letter from Dan's hand—"and tear it up."

Deftly the attorney moved the letter out of his frantic client's reach.

"Now get hold of yourself, Billy," Dan ordered, "and try to look at this situation objectively. Because this is your first time out as writer, producer, and director, *Precipice* has probably gotten more advance ink than any other movie this year. Everybody knows it's a spy thriller about a research scientist, set in the aeronautics industry. We probably should have expected something like this. With the kind of budget you have on this film, you're a natural target, a sitting duck."

"Yeah, for some two-bit shmuck like this Leonard Rybar," Billy fumed. "The guy probably teaches writing at some second-rate college and—"

"Rybar," Dan broke in, "must have something, Billy. Otherwise a slick operator like Groffsky wouldn't be representing him."

"What? What the hell could he possibly have?"

The waitress, startled by Billy's outburst, almost dropped the plate of blintzes in the lawyer's lap.

"Billy," Dan said, "look. Stop getting so worked up. You asked for my opinion. What I can tell you is that this letter has the markings of something that could develop into a legal nightmare. But Max Groffsky has not filed a lawsuit. All he is asking for right now is some willingness on your behalf to enter into a discussion about compensating Rybar."

"For what? For what?" Billy shoved his plate of untouched *latkes* away angrily.

"That's what I would like to find out. With your blessing. I'm telling you, Billy," the lawyer continued, looking steadily at the agitated older man, "it looks like we've got to play this one out. See what they've got."

"Shit. That's what they've got. They're full of it."

"I am only too certain that you are correct. But these cases are becoming trickier and trickier, Billy. That's why we can't afford to take a chance. We really have to find out what Rybar has before we can dismiss this letter."

Billy was silent. His face was beet red.

"What I suggest," Dan went on calmly, "is that I meet with Groffsky and see what kind of evidence this Leonard Rybar has." He put a hand on his client's bony shoulder in an avuncular fashion. "Billy," he said, "unfortunately I have to tell you something else."

"What now?"

"I don't want to upset you further, God knows. But it has been my experience in these cases that if the plaintiff has anything at all which might stand up in court, it's cheaper in the long run to pay him off."

Her head throbbed. Behind the sunglasses her eyes were red and puffy. Her mouth was parched. And her stomach was in a state of pitiable confusion: Hungry one moment, nauseous the next.

Christine had felt this way since waking up thirty-five minutes earlier. Now, fully dressed but without makeup, she unlocked the door of her office at the International Network.

"What a dumb move," she chastised herself for the umpteenth time that morning. She should never have taken those sleeping pills.

After she'd gotten home from the Playboy Mansion, still distraught over the Steven Jacobs business, Christine knew rest would not come easily. Sleep would have to be coaxed.

First she took a long, hot bubble bath in her shiny black enamel tub. Slowly rubbed rose-scented lotion over her body. Slipped into a soft blue satin nightgown. Poured herself a glass of chilled white wine and held on to the bottle. With her free hand, she chose a volume of John Keats's poetry from her bookshelf. Snuggling under the covers, she planned to read herself to sleep.

It didn't work. By two in the morning she was still wide awake. Seeing Keats's words. Thinking Steven Jacobs's lines. And wanting desperately to talk with him, find out if he knew what the hell was going on, why her life had suddenly taken this distressing turn. Her sobs grew in their force with each sip of wine.

In the midst of a flood of tears, Christine decided enough was enough. She had to do something.

It was then that she remembered the tiny bottle of sleeping pills in her medicine cabinet. Her internist had prescribed them when she first started doing her own show and was having trouble relaxing.

"But I never take drugs," Christine had protested.

"Trust me," the doctor urged. "Taken occasionally there is nothing in these that can harm you. And you need your rest, young lady."

Christine had the prescription filled, but resisted taking the small white tablets. The plastic bottle had rested for months on the top shelf. In case of emergency, she'd told herself.

And this sleepless, vastly unsettling, angst-ridden night, Christine decided, was it.

The label read, "Take as directed." Christine thought she remembered the doctor telling her to take two, and that's what she did.

The combination of the wine and sedative did the trick, too well. Within minutes she was plunged into deep sleep. So far under that she never heard her clock radio alarm. Sometime later the disturbing dissonance of a new rock band called, appropriately enough, The Crash, finally jolted Christine awake. She came to in a fog, lethargic and groggy, unsure what day it was or what she should be doing.

When the fog lifted slightly, she checked the clock and groaned. It was 9:45 A.M. She was already late.

Why hadn't anyone called? She found the Princess phone on the floor next to her reading chair where she'd taken it to try Steven Jacobs's answering service one more time. Just when was lost in the night's haze of alcohol and tears, but she remembered she'd finally decided against making the call.

The phone was off the hook. Damn.

Ten excruciating jumping jacks, two cups of black coffee, and a brisk shower later, Christine was climbing into the first suit she found hanging in her closet. She forced her feet into plain black leather pumps and rushed off to work.

Now, looking up numbly from her cluttered desk, she noticed three message slips which had apparently been slipped under the door sometime earlier that morning. Retrieving them, she recognized the fastidious penmanship of Norma Scott in Irving Taubman's office.

As Christine was focusing on their content, the phone made a tremendous clanging noise. She lunged for the receiver.

"Yes?"

"Is Ms. DuRand there yet?" asked a clipped voice.

"This is Christine."

"Oh!" the voice said, flustered. "Ms. DuRand, this is Norma, Mr. Taubman's executive secretary." She stressed the word "executive."

"Mmmm."

"Mr. Taubman has been waiting to speak with you since quite early this morning. I'll tell him you're on your way up."

What could it be now?

Christine stepped over to her makeup mirror and inspected her pale, tired face. Oh, God, why this morning? I look like the lead in a horror film.

Hastily she dusted a tawny blush over her cheeks and applied a thick, dark-brown mascara. Finally she smoothed on an iced mauve lipstick.

Turning, she looked longingly at the coffeepot near Maggie's desk. She briefly considered taking the time to boil water for a much-needed cup of her favorite Columbian blend.

But then the phone clanged again, sending Christine scurrying out of the office.

"Go right in," chirped Norma Scott. "He's been waiting for you."

Christine gazed back expressionlessly at the middle-aged woman. Norma had a pinched face and wore big, round glasses. Christine had never trusted her.

Norma's owlish eyes followed Christine until she disappeared into Irving Taubman's office.

"Close the door," commanded Taubman as he pushed himself up from his unnaturally tidy desk. He glared at Christine. He looked to her like an outraged bull ready to charge, but Irving was holding himself firmly in check. He had already counted to one hundred. Six times.

"Well?" he said expectantly.

Well what? Christine thought of shooting back. But today she was operating in slow motion. She stood silently for a few seconds until she remembered her last visit here. Irving Taubman, she realized, wanted an apology.

Christine took a halting step forward, trying to ignore the pounding in her head.

"Mr. Taubman," she began, "I'm really very sorry about my behavior here last Friday. It's just that—"

"Last Friday?" he shouted. Then he caught himself. "Last Friday, my dear young woman," he said evenly, "is *history*. What about this morning?"

Christine stared at him blankly.

"I don't understand." She felt like a naughty schoolgirl who had missed the first half of class. "What happened this morning?"

"You don't know?" Taubman said too loudly.

It cannot be, he fumed. My shiny new star. My little ratings dynamo. The best entertainment reporter on my staff, and she *doesn't know!*

Irving stared hard at Christine. Amazing. Something about her manner, the way she stood there, uneasily shifting her weight, arms folded across her red blouse, her face a forlorn picture of confusion. Either Christine DuRand was a very good actress . . . or she really didn't have a clue.

"So you didn't see, or even hear about, the lead story on Jewel Crosse's show this morning?"

"No," Christine said without hesitation. "What was it about?"

Irving stepped over to his elaborate tape deck and shoved a cassette into the machine.

"Let me remind you," he said, "that Jewel goes live in New York at six A.M. our time. So what you're about to see has been public knowledge for about five hours now."

In seconds the screen changed from bright color bars to a close-up on Jewel Crosse. She was smiling priggishly and angled three-quarters from the left, as usual.

"You know," Jewel's video image began, "I always like to save some startling entertainment-industry news for the end of my show, after my daily celebrity interview. But this morning, friends, I have something which I feel compelled to share immediately. In fact, I've been privy to this exclusive information only for a very short time myself."

Christine looked over at Taubman, who was staring at the screen, transfixed.

"It involves the International Network," Jewel was saying. "Of course, you all know about the much ballyhooed interview with England's Princess Diana which the network has been promoting with a vengeance. Well, it seems that—" up pops a photo of Christine, a most unflattering pose, over Jewel's right shoulder—"Christine Du-Rand, when she was known as Cathleen Rand, had more than a casual flirtation with the underworld. And now Buckingham Palace has found out about it."

Christine felt herself sinking.

"Naturally, the Royal Family is aghast. The skeleton in DuRand's closet is Steven Jacobs, a New York investment manager implicated in London a few years ago in an international racketeering caper."

Sinking . . .

"DuRand, it seems, was his traveling companion at the time. In fact, she and Jacobs were *this* close for four years. And that's enough to scare off anyone. Especially the Princess of Wales. . . ."

The sinking sensation was replaced by a new wave of nausea, which Christine struggled to keep from giving in to.

"Meantime, back in Hollywood, the infamous DuRand . . ."

Oh, God. How could there be more?

". . . has outraged many with her unorthodox methods. Only last Friday she so infuriated music superstar Roland Williams during an

137

interview session that he fled the room! Word has it that we won't be seeing *that* story on the air either.

"These days, you just never know what you will be seeing on the International Network. . . . And now for that intriguing interview with Shirley Mac—"

Irving Taubman hit the off button so hard he thought he'd injured his index finger.

"So!" he said, flexing the finger uncomfortably. "What do you have to say about our complication in London now? How could you sit here, in this very office, swearing that you knew nothing? That you weren't the problem. Did you think this could stay your little secret forever?"

Christine wondered if she'd be able to form the words, any words, in her own defense.

"Haven't you anything to say for yourself?" he demanded.

"But—" she finally sputtered. "I didn't know. I had no idea that—"

"You didn't know that this guy was mixed up with the Mafia? What, you were blindfolded the whole time? With earplugs yet? I'm sorry, Christine. I'm a very tolerant man, but I find that too hard to swallow."

"Mr. Taubman," she pleaded, collapsing onto the shiny black leather couch, shaking her head. "It's *not* what you think. I didn't know. And I certainly had no idea that Steven's dealings in London were responsible for . . . for this." She hid her head in her hands and her shoulders began to rise and fall.

Irving poured a glass of water from the black metal decanter on his desk and took it over to Christine.

"Here," he said gruffly.

Christine sipped gratefully, thankful for the cooling rush of liquid down her throat.

"Now here is my suggestion, Christine," he said, sitting down beside her. "You've been under a great deal of pressure. More than you know, perhaps. And what you need right now is some time. Time to relax. Be alone. Think things through. I want you to take a week off. Two weeks if you like. Don't worry about anything here. We'll talk when you come back."

"But I can't possibly take time off now. What about the Oscars? They're coming up in—"

"Plenty of time yet, my dear." He sounded as if he wanted to close the subject.

Christine cleared her throat and swallowed hard. "Mr. Taubman?"

"Yes?" he said solicitously.

"Then what about the Roland Williams interview? When are we going to air it?"

"I told you, Christine," he said, "I don't want you to worry about work right now. You need time. A rest."

"But it's an excellent interview," she protested, looking directly at him, her gaze defiant. "And we should run it soon. Before the word gets out about Williams doing concerts for the—"

"Christine, Christine. Not now," he said, a slight edge rising in his voice. "We'll discuss it all when you get back."

He smiled at her, but Christine was studying his eyes, looking for a sign. She found it. They were hard, unyielding. They flashed with a glint that sent a shiver through her body.

She stood up. "In that case, Mr. Taubman," she said, calling upon every measure of strength within her, "I won't be coming back at all. I quit."

Slowly and with great difficulty, Tashi Qwan trudged up the uneven wooden steps toward her tiny flat. She was wearing heavy rubber galoshes, which made her long, slim feet look gigantic. It was awkward and hazardous trying to angle them onto the steep and narrow steps winding up to her room.

She was lugging a large paper sack of groceries. There was a gaping tear in the sack where the rain had soaked through. Struggling to keep her balance, leaning with one hand on the crumbling plaster of the dark and stained wall, she clutched the groceries close to her makeshift raincoat with the other.

The coat was merely a large green plastic garbage bag with three holes snipped out. Consequently the girl's slender arms and the bottom half of her corduroy dress were drenched.

A sudden crack of thunder shook the house, and Tashi shuddered. The clinging wetness of her clothing brought goose bumps to her flesh.

The single light bulb swaying on its cord above her doorway fluttered briefly, then went out, submerging her in murky blackness.

"Oh, no!" she moaned, leaning against the wall, resting the sack on her bony hip and praying for the electricity to be restored.

It was all too much to bear. The day had been miserable, the worst since she'd moved to this flat in South Kensington. Actually, it was the attic of a Victorian terrace house, newly converted in slipshod fashion by the strange couple who owned the place. They'd acted as if they were doing Tashi a favor the morning she'd arrived to inquire about it.

" 'At'll be it fer ya then?" asked the skinny pockmarked mistress of the house, idly scratching her behind in a most unladylike manner.

"What? What do you mean?" Tashi had stammered, looking around at the cramped and airless accommodations. The water closet was so small she'd practically have to slip in sideways. The steep slant of the ceiling would force her to crouch in places to avoid bumping her head.

" 'At it, then?" the woman inquired again, pointing to the small suitcase Tashi was holding. " 'At all ya got?"

Tashi nodded an ashamed yes. All her lovely designer suits and dresses had long since been sold. She'd needed the money for food.

"Well, then, girlie, you've gotcherself a 'ome," announced the woman. " 'Sagood thing yer not one of 'em fancy dressers, 'cause as ya can see, ya got no closets 'ere, girlie." Then she launched into an attack of laughter, doubling over at the waist. Soon she began to hiccup.

"Oh, it's nothin'," said pockface's husband, Jeb, when Tashi looked sympathically at the woman. "Always workin' 'erself up like that. Went on fer six days once. Back in seventy-nine. What a time we 'ad of it. 'Ad to take 'er to 'orspital. All 'em doctors frettin'. Didn't do a lick of good. But once I got 'er back 'ere, I snuck up on her late that night, in the dark, see."

Jeb took a couple of steps, moving like a prowler up to no good. Then he brought his right hand back in slow motion.

"An' I slapped 'er upside the earlobe so 'ard some blood came gushin' out. 'Ad a bad earache for 'bout a month. But sure as 'ell cured 'em 'iccups." Jeb smiled proudly, placing his big thumbs inside his red suspenders and pushing his arms out.

She stayed as far away from the Hackers—for that was the landlord couple's improbable name—as she could. They were a rancorous pair, perpetually feuding with each other.

These days Tashi had problems enough of her own. It was hard enough, before dawn each workday, climbing out of a warm bed into the icy dark of her flat. Hard enough leaving for work by six A.M. and not returning until five that evening, drained and weary to the bone.

140

After giving up on finding work as an interpreter, nearly penniless and without a wardrobe for an office or even a waitressing job, she'd taken a job in Sloane's Fish Market, not far from her flat. At seventy pounds a week, it was the best she could find.

Mr. Sloane, a kind and elderly man with a huge handlebar mustache, was fond of Tashi. Liked her spirit. She'd told him about her plan to attend veterinary school, and he'd encouraged her.

"Workin' 'ere for two years, savin' your pennies, and you'll be able to start classes. And I'll let you come in part time when you need extra money," he'd promised, smiling at her with gold-capped teeth.

Tashi's dexterity with a fish knife amazed old man Sloane. He couldn't get over how swiftly this slip of a girl could cut her way through a mountain of trout, salmon, or eel, slicing, deboning, and beheading faster than anyone he'd ever trained.

What the fatherly fishmonger did not know, of course, was that Tashi's deftness was a direct consequence of many years spent in humbling labor at her mother's restaurant in Hong Kong. Tashi never discussed her family with her employer, though she was often struck by the irony of her situation. Here she was, an educated young woman who had learned to speak five languages under the guidance of her wealthy and socially prominent English father, and the best job she could find in London was wielding a fish knife. No better than she would have been doing back home.

But Tashi was young, attractive, full of enthusiasm. And she was willing to be patient. Willing to work her way through veterinary school. If only she could keep her spirits high and remain optimistic.

At present, in the blackened, choking stairway, that seemed a monumental task. With the stench of her dank and fish-scented clothing flaring in her nostrils, Tashi longed to be inside her small room. To peel off the fetid dress. Wash her weary body of the day's toil. Just as she was about to kneel down and attempt crawling up the narrow passageway, the light bulb flickered. Several times it flashed, only to die again. Finally it steadied, then glowed brilliantly.

Tashi maneuvered herself up the steps more quickly than ever before. Unlocking the door, she yanked on the string hanging from the overhead light, overjoyed for once to be safe inside her Lilliputian quarters.

Carelessly she dumped the sack on the sagging single bed. A tin of canned meat tumbled out, and two lemons spilled over the side and made quick little thuds on the wooden floor.

Tashi ripped off the garbage-bag raincoat, tugged off the heavy, wet galoshes, unzipped and slipped out of the foul-smelling dress.

She was collecting the lemons off the floor when she noticed the yellow envelope near the door. It was damp and tread-marked from her boots.

Tashi picked it up, examining the name and address visible through the cellophane window in the left-hand corner.

A cable for me?

She was certain there had been a mistake.

No one knew she was living here except Sasheena Qwan. And Tashi phoned her mother every two weeks to assure the concerned woman that she was doing very well as an interpreter. That she'd begin school within a year.

But the cable address read:

> MS. TASHI QWAN
> 113 SOUTH BAILEY ST.
> SOUTH KENSINGTON
> LONDON SK1Z 6RL, ENGLAND

Being careful not to rip the damp paper, Tashi opened the envelope and read the brief message.

> SEAT BOOKED ON PAN AM FLIGHT #41 TO
> N.Y.   TOMORROW 3 P.M.   EXTENDED
> TRAVEL ASSIGNMENT.   CONTACT SOONEST.
> D. DAVIS

Tashi let out a whoop and bounced the lemons off the low-slung ceiling. Pulling on a pair of worn jeans and a heavy sweatshirt, she grabbed a handful of change and ran out of the flat in search of the closest pay telephone.

Smiling bravely as she marched quickly through the corridors, Christine left the network immediately after the disastrous meeting with Irving Taubman. Into the lobby and out the main doors. Exchanging "Good mornings" and "How are you's" with technicians and secretaries along the way. Pretending nothing unusual had happened. As if she hadn't just walked away from one of the most coveted positions in the television industry.

In the blindingly white light of the parking lot she found herself staggered by the most absurdly simple question: Where do I go now? She didn't want to go home. It was the middle of the day. Working people didn't go home in the middle of the day. They were in their offices, their factories, their stores, their studios . . . but Christine didn't have anyplace to go, not anymore.

Her mind reeled. Her legs were unsteady. She felt as if she were drunk again. Where the hell do I go? What do I do?

Sliding behind the wheel of her car, she did the only thing she could think of. She drove. Just drove. Aimlessly at first, until she realized she was headed in the direction of the beach. At Pacific Coast Highway, she headed north. Toward Malibu. Heading toward Blair's. Driving on automatic.

But when she got to the turnoff to the Colony guard gate and Blair's beach house, she kept on driving. He wasn't home, she knew that, but Shanu would be. And Christine didn't feel like having to face anyone, not even Blair's houseboy.

The coastal scenery above Malibu was gorgeous, and the day itself was travel-brochure perfect. Clear and crisp. Blue cloudless sky, vast foam-flecked Pacific lapping against a seemingly endless fringe of golden sand. Traffic was light, and at times Christine felt as though she were all alone on the twisting, winding highway. Its effect on her was hypnotic. Reassurance that the world could still be a beautiful place.

She tried not to think. She tried not to think about anything. She saw the sea gulls swooping on rocky outcroppings, and the starkly white sails of Hobie Cats knifing through the water, and the occasional smokestack of a huge freighter far off in the distant horizon.

So many lives. So many separate existences, all being lived and played out at the same time, in the same gigantic theater. She smiled. Somehow the reminder that she was but a tiny part of it all gave her momentary peace.

But the sudden encroachment of civilization roused her from this welcome calm. The highway signs said she was entering the city limits of Ventura. My God, have I come this far? She looked at her watch. Three-thirty.

As quickly as it had materialized, the illusion was broken. Her feeling of well-being evaporated. She was back in the world of harsh reality.

Christine had not yet allowed herself to release the emotion pent up inside her. She continued to steel herself against that, but now she began to focus on what she had just done and why she had done it.

A few hours ago she was absolutely certain that quitting—turning her back on a network which was not totally in her corner—was the only course of action open to her. Her instincts had told her that Taubman planned to fire her as soon as he could find a replacement. Now she wondered. Had pride blinded her? Should she have accepted Taubman's offer of a few weeks off to consider her situation?

And where the hell was Steven? Why wasn't he returning her calls? Now more than ever, she had to reach him somehow. Her entire career could hang in the balance.

Christine guided her Mercedes off the highway and soon pulled up in front of a large seafood restaurant. The parking lot was nearly deserted, but a sign in the window said OPEN/ABIERTO. She went inside and found a pay phone. Dialing the number from memory, she waited impatiently as it rang several times.

"Come on, come on," she said anxiously.

"Mr. Jacobs's line."

"This is Christine Du—"

"—Yes, yes, Miss DuRand. Mr. Jacobs has been attempting to reach you all afternoon."

"He has? Oh, Christ. Well, what did he—is there a message for me?" Now she was distressed that she had taken the drive. She should have been near the phone.

"Where are you? Are you at home?"

"No, I—I'm heading home now," she said. "Tell me the message."

"Mr. Jacobs said, 'Be home by seven-thirty, your time, and await contact from him.'"

Christine's voice became tinged with irritation she could not conceal. "Await contact? What the hell does that mean? Is he going to call at seven-thirty or what?"

"That is the message, Miss DuRand. Goodbye."

The drive back was not restful in the least. To save time, Christine got on the 101 freeway, but rush hour was already underway and traffic slowed to a maddening pace. And when a fender bender just past the Los Angeles County line brought all lanes to a stop-and-go crawl, she thought she might lose her mind completely.

Escape presented itself in the form of the Topanga Canyon exit. Then she headed east on Ventura Boulevard. It had loads of traffic lights, but at least cars were moving. By the time she reached the turnoff in Studio City that would take her through Laurel Canyon

144

and into West Hollywood, it was a few minutes past seven. If she was lucky, she could still make it home in time.

The tension of the snarled traffic had shot her nerves completely. She was drained, exhausted. And angry. How dare Steven leave me a message that sounded like an ultimatum! How dare he come back to haunt my life like this!

Christine finally pulled her Mercedes up in front of the Andalusia. She was visibly shaking. Her hands vibrated nervously as she jerked the key out of the ignition, got out, and locked the door. It was seven thirty-one.

Head down, Christine rapidly traversed the tiled courtyard. Her head had begun to ache. Her stomach fluttered out of control. She loathed this sense of helplessness, of not being in charge of her own life, her own fate. She was thinking about Steven Jacobs. Whatever he has to say, it'd better be good. . . . She was thinking about Taubman. Maybe I should call him, tell him I've reconsidered. No. I can't. I won't. But . . .

Hurrying up the steps leading to her apartment, Christine was oblivious to everything but her troubled thoughts.

And then she nearly screamed. Grabbing for the handrail to catch herself, she found herself staring into the face of a ghost.

"Hello, princess," he said tenderly, holding out his arms as he walked down three steps to greet her.

Dressed in a perfectly tailored dark-blue suit, pin-striped shirt, and solid silk tie, he smiled down at her quizzically, as if he couldn't quite formulate the correct words to say next. Looking so much like he had that evening all those years ago on Long Island.

"I heard about it, Christine," he said simply, pulling her toward him.

"Yes." It was all Christine could manage. Her knees buckled slightly, but he held onto her. It was as if she were walking through someone else's bad dream. Playing out a part. Going through the motions until the clock radio jarred her awake.

"Come on, princess."

The sound of Steven's voice broke her spell. She started to revive.

"Let's go inside," he said. "I have only a few more minutes."

Christine handed him the keys and followed him into her apartment.

Inside, Steven scanned the living room with the expert eye of an antique dealer at an estate sale, noting the value of each table and chair, every small sculpture, the hand-loomed Mexican rug. He missed nothing. Stepping over to the fireplace he plucked a brushed gold picture frame off the mantel and examined the photograph. It was a shot of Blair and Christine, he in a tuxedo, she in a stunning strapless evening gown. It had been taken at the Emmy Awards the previous fall. They looked very much in love.

Christine sank down into the plump cushions on her couch, still too shaken to say anything that would make sense. And too angry to trust herself. And yet she had to say something.

"Steven—"

He held up a hand to cut her off. "I was in Singapore when I got the word about Crosse. And I have to be in Zurich by tomorrow. But I had to lay over in L.A. long enough to make you understand why all this backfired . . . on you."

Steven placed his hands behind his back. "Before I begin to explain things . . ." Like a goddamn college professor, Christine marveled to herself. He looks like he's about to address a group of freshmen on the first day of school.

"Steven—" she tried again.

"No. No. Let me go on, princess," he insisted. "I know you're hurting now. I wouldn't be here if I didn't feel that I could make it better somehow. Just hear me out."

Christine looked away from him, fixing her gaze on the grain in the hardwood floor near her feet.

"First," he continued, "I want to tell you how proud I am of you. You've done it, Christine. All by yourself. The little girl from Minneapolis. With no help from me or anyone else. I know. And I know how hard it's been for you. Working your way up. But now you have it, princess. You're a bona fide star. And nobody can take that away from you. Nobody."

Christine looked up at Steven as if she could see through him. As if he weren't really there.

Steven walked over and sat down next to her. He reached for her hand. She pulled it away.

He paused to fix in his mind the image of the girl—the woman—who sat beside him. Her bright eyes, now clouded in pain. Her uncombed curls cascading around her face, still unspoiled by the ravages of time and a demanding profession. So far from what she was when he'd first met her. So far yet from the woman she wanted to be.

Not a day passed that he hadn't thought about her. He'd followed her television career with the same keen urgency he'd felt when she was knocking herself out at audition after audition on Broadway. He always knew she had the drive and determination to go after what she wanted and get it. Now, when she had succeeded, he was responsible for bringing her down.

"Princess, you know you're the only woman I ever loved. I would do anything not to hurt you. I tried. I tried to shield you. Thinking if you didn't know, you'd be protected. And I was scared, too. Scared that if you ever found out, you'd leave me. I didn't think I could bear that." His voice cracked ever so slightly. For an instant she thought she might actually witness something she hadn't ever before—Steven Jacobs's tears. But no tears came.

"Why didn't you warn me, at least? Once I moved here, why didn't you—?"

"Shhhhhh." He put his index finger over her lips. "You kept hanging up the phone, remember? And I had no idea you'd ever become implicated in any of my business involvements. That trouble in London was nothing major."

"Jewel Crosse certainly made it sound like something major," Christine answered angrily.

"All right. On paper, yes, it looks bad. And Crosse must have some powerful snoops over there in England. Because when this all blew up in seventy-nine, I was granted immunity from prosecution. The deal was, my role in the whole thing was kept under wraps. Fleet Street never got a whiff of it."

"And neither did I."

"No. You didn't. You were there but I made sure you knew nothing. God, it was what—seven years ago? You remember when we stayed at the Connaught?

"Of course. And I remember the mysterious briefcase exchange at the airport, too. What an idiot I was."

Steven's dark eyes caught hers and fought to hold them.

"During that trip I was desperately trying to gain control of a British steel company," he went on. "Stowell, Limited. It was worth about seven hundred and fifty million. I had a fairly large percentage of the proxies in my back pocket, but to win I needed more leverage. So—and I'm telling you this because you should know, not because I'm proud of it—so I arranged for some stockholders to be paid off to vote my way."

He sat back, and, despite himself, a flicker of satisfaction passed over his face. Christine saw it, and her stomach twisted more tightly into knots. "And your Mafia buddies took care of it, right?" she shot back. "The same thugs who beat you up in Rio?"

Steven's body stiffened. His face flushed. "You know, Christine, you're not making this any easier. You're a big girl. You should realize by now that not everybody is as honest as he or she might like to be. You're a rarity, sweetheart," he said, his voice softening. "A precious gem. A true straight arrow. It's all up front with you. That's why I fell in love with you. I knew you were decent. I knew I could trust you."

Christine mumbled her reply, but it was loud enough for Steven to hear. "I wish I could say the same," she said.

"I don't blame you for being angry. You have a right," he continued. "But I had my dream. I still have it. Just like Jay Gatsby. But I'll get there my own way. In my own style. And so, princess, will you."

There was a sharp knock at the door. Christine's shoulders shook.

"It's all right. You remember Shaeffer, my driver, don't you?" Steven stood up and checked his watch. "Be right down!" he yelled toward the door.

Turning back to Christine, he caught her eyes again.

"Look, sweetheart. I wanted you to hear this firsthand, that's all. The truth is, that bitch came pretty close. But she blew everything out of proportion."

Christine felt the world caving in on her now. Jewel Crosse was right, and there was nothing even Steven could do to undo the damage.

"Maybe," he started slowly, "what you need is a few days alone. My yacht is in the Caribbean, Antigua, I think. If you like, I'll send the plane for you and—"

"No," Christine said adamantly. "No, thank you, Steven."

"All right. I understand. But, princess, I just want you to know this. I'm on your side. And I can be a pretty powerful guy when I set my mind to it. Anything you want or need, sweetheart, it's yours. That's a promise."

Christine couldn't hold back any longer. "Don't you think you've done enough already?" she asked, not hiding the bitterness. "Well, don't you?"

Steven sighed deeply and stood, towering over her. "What you're going through right now, I know it's my fault. But I also know you're still a star. You're going to push yourself up over this hurdle and be in the race again. Better than ever. And someday I'm going to make it up to you. There will come a time and a need. Trust me. You can do that now."

He was walking toward the door, but he stopped and turned toward her once again. "Sorry for mucking things up, princess."

She said nothing.

"I love you, Christine," he said then. "Remember that."

Seven

When Roland saw the hunter-green Rolls-Royce appear on the television monitor, he made a spur-of-the-moment decision. Setting aside a book on Australian wildlife, he slipped out of his robe and slid between the sleek satin sheets on his custom-made hand-carved sandalwood bed. He clicked off the reading light, plunging the bedroom into darkness.

By the time the third security guard had waved Burton on, up the steep driveway and into the Rolls's berth in the enormous eight-car garage, Roland's eyes were determinedly closed. But his heart was pounding. He could feel it booming away just below his Adam's apple.

Roland didn't want another scene. Over the past few days the quarrels with Burton had been virtually nonstop.

In the aftermath of the Christine DuRand interview, Roland had refused to discuss the Democratic fund-raising concerts that Burton was planning. And he wouldn't even look at the itinerary for his imminent international tour.

Since that horribly upsetting Friday afternoon, he had cloistered himself up here in his sprawling hilltop home, canceling all business except for a taping session for the video of his new single, "Hungerin'." And he'd even walked out of that session early, leaving a crew of thirty and four Lightning executives stupefied.

Roland Williams was a professional to the core. This kind of behavior from him was unprecedented and totally baffling.

He heard the bedroom door click open and Burton's muffled footsteps on the white shag carpeting. Then, as Burton's eyes adjusted to the darkness, for a long moment there was nothing. All Roland could hear were the violent thumpings of his own heart. He couldn't stand it. He sat up. He flicked the bedside switch that controlled the overhead track fixtures, flooding the room in a blaze of light.

The blinding brightness gave Burton a start.

"I thought you were asleep," he said finally. He was at the foot of the bed, briefcase in hand.

"Couldn't," Roland murmured, crossing his arms across his chest. "You're late."

"I know, Ro. Sorry," Burton said, placing his briefcase carefully on a white lacquered table. "Couldn't be helped. Some of the higher-ups from D.C. were in. The meeting went on longer than I'd anticipated. I thought—"

"I thought," Roland interrupted, "tonight was supposed to be ours. Dinner at ten, remember? You didn't call. I didn't hear from you. What am I supposed to—"

"Roland—" Burton's voice was defensive now—"I said I was sorry. Look," he continued, tugging at the knot of his plum tie, "when I started this fund-raising gig, we both knew there would be times like this. Some unavoidable late nights. I can't help it."

He tossed the tie down onto the table matter-of-factly and stepped into the closet.

"I had a video session tonight," Roland yelled from the bed. "And left it early, just to come home and fix the spinach lasagna you love."

Burton didn't respond. He took a long time to hang up his suit. Then he slipped on a dark terry-cloth robe and walked slowly over toward Roland, a smile fixed on his face.

"Did you hear about the DuRand bitch? She was fired today. Right after the Jewel Crosse report." He put a hand on Roland's cheek. "Just like I promised."

Roland said nothing.

"She can't hurt you now," Burton went on. "No one will believe anything she says anymore. And besides, she won't have anyplace to say it. The woman is persona non grata in the business."

Roland ignored this update, too. "You could have called," he said petulantly.

Burton glared at his lover, a wave of anger rushing over him. The anger had been building for some time. He felt like screaming. Like grabbing Roland by the shoulders and shaking him and shaking him until . . . until what? Burton caught himself. He would not succumb to his own inner rage. Without a word, he turned away from Roland, disappeared into the bathroom and closed the door firmly.

Burton took a long look at himself in the bathroom mirror. His eyes were bloodshot and rimmed with dark circles. His skin was pale. His mind was racing, a jumble of numbers, actual and projected, dollars and cents, concert dates, grosses, and his own ambitions for them.

What Burton Ratchford needed, he decided, was a good night's sleep. What he needed even more was the full cooperation of Roland Williams. He couldn't permit another fight.

Roland's defiant behavior of late had taken Burton by surprise. He had always been in control of the relationship, the dominant partner, the man in charge. But now he was unhorsed, stymied—uncertain how to deal with his recalcitrant lover. Burton realized now how much it was really Roland who held the reins. Without Roland he could not reach his destination. The first fund-raiser—in San Francisco—was less than a week away. Then the international tour was to begin.

Burton had spent endless hours juggling dates, times, and locations to arrive at an all-inclusive schedule. Over the next six months Roland would tour through the Orient, Europe, Australia, and New Zealand. But he would also return to the States several times to raise money for the Democrats—for Burton.

All Burton needed now was Roland's signature on each performance agreement. The contracts were in his briefcase.

When he returned to the bedroom, the lights were out.

Roland turned away from Burton, onto his side.

"Ro?"

Burton slipped into bed. "Ro," he said softly, rubbing the back of Roland's neck gently, "would you like a massage?"

Roland stared into the darkness and made no reply.

"Come on. Roll over on your stomach. You've had a tough few days, and we really haven't had much time together. Let me work that tension away. Ro?"

Still offering no response, Roland shifted silently onto his stomach. Burton smiled to himself. He had his chance now.

Smoothly and with an expert touch, he began kneading the young man's supple back, gradually increasing the speed and pressure.

He worked wordlessly. He was communicating through his fingertips now. He was telling Roland that everything was okay, that it was still good between them, that the feelings remained strong, intact. And as a distinct rush of excitement charged down his arms, past his hands and into Roland's flesh, Burton knew that Roland would believe him. Would surrender to him. The power was Burton's again. His hands roamed up and down Roland's long, lean frame, manipulating the firm muscles of the shoulders, calf and thigh, squeezing and pulling and pressing until Roland could no longer suppress a groan of pleasure.

Finally, using his fingertips like feathers, Burton ran them across the soles of Roland's feet and upward toward the backs of his knees.

"Stop that," Roland protested. "Burton, stop . . ."

But Burton continued the light, feathery touch up Roland's legs and into the crevice of his buttocks. Then he shifted onto his knees, leaned over his lover and began using his tongue. Slowly, tantalizingly, he ran it up the small of Roland's warm and silky back.

"You know what that does to me," Roland cried weakly, clearly on that threshold where his nerve endings vibrated between a pulsating, mind-bending pleasure and a sensation so electrifying it hurt. "Quit it, Burton . . . don't."

Burton's tongue moved mercilessly up Roland's spine.

Unable to withstand more, writhing with delight, Roland turned and grabbed his tormentor by his powerful arms.

"All right . . . all right!" he gasped, eyes filling with tears. "I'm sorry I got mad. I'll *do* the damn concerts. Anything you say. But no more interviews. Not ever. You hear me?"

"Ummmmmmmm," Burton murmured, too distracted to discuss ultimatums.

"I don't get," Nickels Yusorovic called to Maggie across a massive pyramid of organically grown beefsteak tomatoes. "Why you quit, just because this Christine quits? It does not make sense."

"I told you," Maggie said, examining one of the plump red fruits and placing it carefully in a large brown paper bag, "there's no reason to stay on." They were on a date of sorts—an early-morning marketing expedition for Nickels' restaurant at the Central Market in downtown L.A.

"What?" he questioned, moving on to a large crate of mushrooms. "Nothing else you can do there? What about another show? It's a big place, no? This network?"

"It's a big place, yes," said Maggie. "But aside from *The DuRand Report,* nothing interests me there. And now they'll just hire a whole new regime to come in and replace our show. No, thanks."

"But giving up such an important job," Nickels argued, motioning for the produce merchant to tag the mushroom crate with his name, "is not a smart thing, uh?"

"Listen," Maggie replied, slightly exasperated, "I wouldn't have offered my services down here in no man's land in the middle of the night just to hover over the carrots and cauliflowers if I knew you were going to interrogate me like this."

"Interrogate? Listen to this woman. I ask a few questions and all of sudden I am . . . like, a, ah . . . heavy. Maggie, I just am concerned for you. What, I ask myself, will you do now?"

"Nickels," she replied, "it's just the way Hollywood works. You're riding high one day. Down the next. So I quit a good job. Most likely it would have turned into a rotten job. I'd be working for someone I didn't like. My next project is building Christine's ego back up and then finding another show for the two of us. Now, can we move on to another subject?"

Maggie walked past Nickels toward the green beans. "You want some of these?"

"Yes. Ten pounds. Make sure they snap."

"All green beans snap."

"You know TV, but I know green beans. Look. I show you." He picked up a long, thin bean and broke it in the middle. "You hear that puny little *pfft?* Now this," he said, breaking another, more rounded bean, "is a bean who snaps."

"Yessir!" Maggie saluted and clicked her heels.

Nickels scowled but his eyes danced brightly. He began to scrutinize a mound of Flame Tokay grapes as big as walnuts.

"So," he continued probing, "you have seen your boss and explained to her that you have done this thing of great altruistic?"

"Altruism," Maggie corrected him lightly. "No. Haven't been able to track her down. She's not answering her phone."

"What?" said Nickels in mock surprise, swallowing a fat reddish purple grape, seeds and all. "This great detective Maggie Rafferty, who finds out all secrets of the stars? Who even finds goat cheese in San Luis Obispo? She can't find her own boss?"

"Christine is more a friend than a boss," Maggie sniffed. "She's probably out in Malibu with her man. I know the number, but there are times when one does not disturb, if you know what I mean."

"Oh, yes. I do know," he assured Maggie, baring strong, white teeth at her.

"Say, did you notice?" Maggie had abandoned the beans and was walking toward Nickels. As she drew close, she slid her hands inside her stretch jeans to show how much extra room there was. "I lost weight."

"How much?" he politely inquired, a bit embarrassed that he hadn't noticed—but on a body like Maggie's anything under a twenty-five-pound loss would be almost imperceptible.

"Ten. Ten big ones. And by next week it'll be fifteen," she said enthusiastically.

"How do you do this?" he asked. "Lose this weight so quickly?"

"Not that quickly," she said, returning to the green beans. "But I do it mainly at an elegant torture chamber in Beverly Hills that passes for an exercise salon. Under the tutelage of a sadist named Brad Larson."

"So these workouts, they pay off."

"Yeah. I guess so. I just wish I could speed up the process."

"Maybe I help."

"How? Put me on your steam table between lunch and dinner?"

"No, no," Nickels said. "This is better. You come to my restaurant in the afternoons, and I will show how to fix the most delicious dishes which will melt in your mouth and melt off pounds, too." He beamed at her, proud of the way he'd handled the words.

"When do we start?"

"Tomorrow," he said with a promising wink.

It was a dazzling morning in Malibu. A brilliant shaft of sunlight bounced off the mirrored wall across from the commodious king-sized bed. Christine woke to the thunderous surge of waves crashing on the beach, feeling more relaxed than she had in days.

Last night in Blair's arms she'd been swept away into a sea of pleasure. Endless lovemaking. Both of them insatiable. Twice they'd drifted off, exhausted, into sleep—and twice they'd awakened again, hungry for each other.

She stretched like a languorous cat, too satisfied to move. With the stream of white sunlight bathing her in its warm glow, Christine's body felt liquid. Pliant. Sensuous. The heavy scent of sex—an aromatic mixture of herself and Blair—permeated the air.

Finally she sat up, slowly raised her arms over her head and yawned.

Maybe Blair will come back to bed after his run on the beach. Maybe we could . . . oh, stop. You're not a boy-crazy teenager.

Out in the hallway an antique grandfather's clock, a family heirloom of Blair's, began to mark the hours. Christine counted nine chimes.

Too late. He'll hardly have time to dress if he still wants to make it to the *Crackup* location by ten. Come on, DuRand, let's get the body moving.

Reluctantly, she climbed out of bed, her mind clinging to the memory of Blair's hands caressing her breasts. The magnificent pressure of his body on top of hers. Of him inside her. Stepping into the shower, Christine felt a twinge, a titillating quiver between her legs. She wanted Blair again. Wanted to feel him coming, exploding deep inside her.

This overwhelming lustfulness astonished her. But once the hot, needlelike jets of water began spilling over her shoulders and down her back, once she'd lathered up in sudsy jasmine-scented soap and the residue of the long hedonistic hours with Blair began swirling down the drain, she saw things more clearly.

The truth was, she needed the distraction. Nothing else demanded her time. There were no deadlines to meet. It was an alien, unsettling feeling. Christine was accustomed to packing each day until it overflowed with activity. Every minute had counted. She was always striving to be more productive.

Now she had nothing to produce. No show to get on the air. No interviews to bone up for. No publicists to call. No editing sessions to supervise. Christine knew she was suffering from a severe, if temporary, case of insecurity. At this time in her life it was vitally important to have a man like Blair Montgomery.

Toweling off and snuggling into a long velour robe, Christine smiled as she remembered his reassurances of last night.

"Stay here for a few days," he'd said without a moment's hesitation. "Hide out. Swim. Rest. Stay a week. Two if you like."

They were grilling chicken breasts over the open pit in Blair's rustic kitchen. He was slathering spaghetti sauce onto each plump morsel, a culinary secret he'd gleaned at a recent party at the John Forsythes'.

"But Christine, honey," Blair added firmly as he tossed the pastry brush, thick with the sticky red sauce, into the sink, "first thing tomorrow morning you gotta phone Irving Taubman. Tell him you want your job back."

Christine looked at Blair in shock.

"Honey, the guy's human. And he's been in the business forever. He knows you creative types flare up like firecrackers every once in a while, and then regret it. I've dealt with guys like Taubman. Believe me, he'll take you back."

"But—I don't—"

"You don't what?" he interrupted. Taking her by the shoulders, his eyes met hers with a look so penetrating that for a moment Christine wanted to pull away.

"So you lost your temper. So what? Just because that snoop Crosse happened to dredge up something out of the archives and spit it out all over the tube, you're going to walk away from the network? Wrong move, Christine. *Think* about it."

Christine was thinking about it now as she stood in front of the mirror, running a hand through her damp hair and maneuvering the blow-dryer with the other.

What have I got to lose by calling Taubman? My self-respect, for one thing. Not that there's a hell of a lot of that left, anyway. I'd better talk to Maggie first. No. No. This is my decision. I'm the one on the line here. Oh, Christ, I don't know. Maybe I should get out of this rotten business all together. Go into another field. Public relations. Or producing. Some safe spot where I can put on a few years and some extra pounds and still be able to do what I do and enjoy it. Oh, screw . . . I'd like to disappear for six months. Then come back with a whole new career. Hmmm . . . leave Los Angeles? Move to another city. Chicago? Too cold. Miami? Too boring. Dallas? Seattle?

Quit dreaming, Christine. Hollywood is the only place for you. Either you find another job in television or call Irving Taubman and ask forgiveness.

But if he takes you back, what then? Ha! Can you trust any television executive? Isn't that why you quit? Because if you didn't . . . if you took the time off Taubman was suggesting . . . he would have replaced you quicker than he can scan a Nielsen report. The day you came back, he would have booted you out so fast . . . forget it. Just leave things as they are for a while. Figure out what you want to do. Meanwhile, this isn't too shabby. . . .

Christine unplugged the dryer thinking things weren't really that bad. You'll survive it. Just hold on.

The moment she stepped out of the bathroom, she heard a hard rap at the bedroom door.

"No need to knock. You own the place," she said, laughing, expecting to see the door swing open and Blair standing there, panting and drenched with sweat from his run.

Instead Christine found herself looking down at Shanu, the diminutive Chinese houseboy, perfectly attired as usual in a black suit, starched white shirt, and black bow tie.

He was standing stiffly at attention, holding a large silver tray with a pot of coffee, two fresh croissants, a tiny dish of orange marmalade, a dainty china cup, silverware, and a white linen napkin—all artistically arranged around a black cordless telephone.

"Mista Mongumly kaw faw yoo," the houseboy announced, nodding toward the phone.

"You mean he's on the line? This one here?" she asked, picking up the phone. Shanu set the tray on a round glass table and vanished.

"Blair?"

"Hiyah, Chris. How's it goin'?" His voice was buoyant and determinedly so.

"Fine. Wonderful. I just showered and thanks to Shanu I'm about to have breakfast. Then I think in a little while I'll take a swim." She sat down on the bed and poured herself a cup of the houseboy's steaming brew.

"Great."

She waited for more, but when there was only silence on the line, she asked, "Where are you? I thought you were out on the beach."

"Ahh . . . no. I had to get up very early. A breakfast meeting at the Beverly Hills Hotel. I'm in my office now. I, ah, just read the trades."

Again there was a silence.

"So?" she replied. Why does he sound so strained? It's like, what's wrong with this picture? What's wrong with this conversation?

"Chris," he sighed, "I thought you told me yesterday you quit the network."

"I did." She stood up, placing the coffeecup on a cane sidetable. "Who says I didn't?"

"The trades. There's a big page one story in each of them, with Taubman saying he canned you because of your past."

"Blair, that's ridi—"

"Now, I know you weren't quite yourself yesterday. But there's a big difference between quitting and being fired in this business."

Christine could feel her face growing hot.

"Of course I quit!" she yelled into the phone. "What do you think I am, some kind of dimwit? I knew exactly what I was doing yesterday. It was my only option. But I was *not* fired. And you have no right to insinuate that—"

"Okay, okay. Calm down. I believe you. I just thought you should know about this." His voice had turned icy.

"And what am I supposed to do about it?" Christine shot back. "Call Taubman and ask for a retraction?"

Christine felt like she was burning up. The cozy velour robe now felt heavy and damp with sweat. She ripped it off and stood there naked, fuming.

"Christine?"

"What?"

"I, um, hate to tell you this over the phone, babe. But I was, ah, glancing over my calendar here. And it seems that my brother from Salt Lake City asked me a few months back if he and his two teenagers could camp out at my place for a couple of weeks. And I, ah . . . well . . . forgot that . . ."

"So, when are they coming?" Christine asked coolly.

"They're due in tonight. Jeez, I just don't know how I could have overlooked this. Lucky it was written down here. Otherwise, I—"

"Yeah. Right."

"I'm really sorry about this, Chris. I know I said you could stay for a few days, but—"

"A week, Blair. You said a week. 'Two weeks if you want, Christine.' But that was last night, wasn't it? Before you . . ."

Christine had to stop because her voice cracked. She sat back down on the bed, took a deep breath and swallowed hard. Blair's silence was enough to tell her she was not wrong. He was dumping her. Like a spoiled sack of potatoes. Off the air, end the affair. Just like that.

"Blair, I understand perfectly," she began again, enunciating slowly. She wanted to let him know that she knew exactly what he was doing. "I'll be out of here within the hour. And you won't hear from me again."

She got up, walked resolutely across the room and placed the cordless phone on the silver tray, disconnecting the call. She was still naked. But Christine DuRand didn't know whether she felt hot or cold.

"It's glorious. Just beautiful," Tashi gasped, staring back at her multiple reflections in the four-way mirror.

She twisted her body slightly to get another perspective on the crimson charmeuse sheath; it was strapless and reached to her ankles. Over that she wore a long tunic in brilliantly beaded blue-and-white mousseline. Of all the dresses, suits, and gowns Tashi had tried on this afternoon, this was her favorite.

"What do you think, Miss Davis?" She turned anxiously to face her new employer.

"Please call me Diedra, Tashi. You needn't be so formal," the older woman reminded the girl for the third time that day. Then she stepped back appraisingly. "Ummhmm," Diedra murmured in approval. "This one's perfect for the concert in San Francisco on Saturday. Real patriotic. The Democrats will pledge allegiance to you, honey." She chuckled.

"I just love it," Tashi gushed. "It's so . . . so bright."

Now she did a full circle turn in front of the mirror, watching the sparkling red, white, and blue reflections dance back at her.

"But it's still understated," Deidra pointed out. "Not too flashy. That's important for your image. You're going to be watched very closely, honey, and photographed constantly. What we want is style, class, and a touch of fun."

"I'm having a great deal of that already," Tashi said, laughing as she slipped back into the dressing room.

Yes. But I wonder for how long. This is going to be a lot harder on you than you know, Diedra thought, looking around in search of the saleswoman. She unfastened the silver clasp of her taupe handbag. Her fingers located the thick wad of folded one-hundred-dollar bills.

She'd told Denny Bracken it would take seventy-five thousand dollars to outfit Tashi. And in less than four hours she had spent more than fifty thousand—not a difficult task in Beverly Hills.

Outside, the limousine driver was rearranging a trunkful of colorful bags and boxes. Suits from Lanvin and St. Laurent Rive Gauche. Shoes from Bally and Andrea Carrano. Gowns from Charles Gallay,

Giorgio, and the magnificent designer boutiques in the opulent Rodeo Collection. Casual clothes from Caritta and Theodore. Bags from Gucci. Necklaces, bracelets, and accent pins from Fred and Cartier.

"Yes, madame?"

The saleswoman was short, with thinning hair dyed an outrageous carroty orange. She wore a simple black dress, but five heavy gold chains hung around her creased neck and a pair of turquoise-and-gold rings encircled bony fingers. Heavy gold circles hung from her ears. And she wore a large gold bracelet on each freckled wrist.

Welcome to California, thought Diedra with amusement. My God, the people here are so gold-conscious. Why don't they just hammer the stuff into helmets and wear them out to lunch?

"We'll take the Fabrice," Diedra announced. She held out sixty-five crisp hundreds. "Cash."

"Certainly, madame," replied the gilded salesclerk, giving the statuesque tawny-skinned woman a quick onceover as she accepted the money.

It wasn't often customers paid cash. Even the big stars and most affluent studio executives' wives used checks, credit cards, or their house accounts. The last cash customer she'd waited on was an Arab sheik. He had a dreadful body odor and four aides to carry his money in leather briefcases. It was a bit unsettling.

But the clerk was baffled by Diedra. Perfectly groomed, in a white Chanel suit. She looked foreign, exotic. And mysterious. Why on earth was she wearing that huge-brimmed padre's hat? With a veil yet.

There was a reason. Not that Lena or Millie or any of the other girls Diedra had worked the streets with more than a decade ago was likely to be strutting up Rodeo Drive in stiletto heels. But you never knew. One of the nearby hotels had been a hooker's haven years back and Diedra wasn't about to take a chance.

She turned to face the mirror, adjusted the veil under her chin, and silently congratulated herself. She had been right about Tashi Qwan after all.

That morning in the tiny lobby of L'Ermitage, where they were staying, Diedra hardly recognized Tashi. It was their first meeting since London. The young woman Diedra remembered interviewing was impeccably dressed and beautifully coiffed. Whatever had happened?

Diedra learned of Tashi's reversals as she guided the girl on a fairy-tale voyage through Beverly Hills. The Cinderella transformation began with a shapely blunt haircut at Vidal Sassoon. Then came the shopping spree. It went swiftly. Tashi was a perfect size six and looked stunning in almost everything she tried on.

"I can't believe this is really happening to me," Tashi had squealed with delight several times that afternoon.

Denny Bracken wanted a show-stopper on Roland Williams's arm, and that's just what he was going to get.

Still, Diedra worried about how the lovely young woman would hold up under the pressure. In her own gowns and jewels Tashi would look worldly and sophisticated, but underneath, Diedra knew, she was a naive and vulnerable nineteen-year-old. More highly educated than most. Well traveled. Very bright. But unprepared nonetheless for what lay ahead.

"Ready to go," called Tashi, startling Diedra as she stepped briskly out of the dressing room.

"This way." Diedra smiled, heading for the exit.

"We aren't going to any more stores, are we?" Tashi asked lightly. "You must be exhausted. And I already have so many new clothes, I won't be able to decide what to wear!"

"Oh, yes, you will, honey," Diedra assured her. "Next we do your wardrobe charts. We're going to sit down and make lists of all your outfits, how to accessorize them, and when to wear them."

"Miss Davis . . . Diedra?" Tashi said hesitantly, as they settled into the comfortable tan leather seats of the limousine put at their disposal by the hotel. "We haven't really talked about just what I'll be doing on this tour with Roland—"

"Hush, honey. Just a moment," Diedra warned, cutting her off. She pressed a button, sending up the glass partition separating them from the driver. "Now we have privacy." She nodded toward the partition.

Tashi returned the nod to show that she understood and waited for Deidra to continue.

"As I told you earlier, Tashi, you'll be traveling all over the world with Roland. And you're going to be introduced as his fiancée. You won't have to talk to reporters, so you needn't worry about making up any stories. Mr. Bracken, Roland's public relations representative, will give the press a statement about your relationship. Just stick with that information and you'll be safe. We'll be discussing all this in detail with Mr. Bracken over dinner tonight."

Tashi's eyes were still clouded in confusion. "Yes," she persisted, "but I'm just wondering why you chose me or . . . anyone, for that matter. A star like Roland Williams . . ." Her voice trailed off as she struggled to find the right words. "Doesn't he already have a girl-friend? What I mean is . . . will I be interfering with anything . . . any . . . ?"

"Honey," Diedra said softly, covering the young woman's hand with her own in a maternal gesture. She looked across at this delicate china doll in her brand-new clothes—a pair of beige gabardine slacks and a furry angora sweater. Was it possible the girl was that sheltered?

"Roland doesn't have a girlfriend. He has a boyfriend."

Diedra felt Tashi's body tense. "I'm sorry. I thought you under-stood. You're here to . . . well, basically to mislead the columnists and photographers who stalk him. To make them think he's in love with a woman."

"Oh," was all Tashi could manage. For the first time that day she was unhappy.

Maggie was out of breath.

"Which way to cardiac intensive?" she panted to the first nurse she saw.

"Up to six and turn left. It's room 6036," the nurse said quickly as Maggie whisked by. Then she turned to call out, "Family members only."

Maggie didn't hear her.

Her mind was busy replaying the message she'd heard on her an-swering machine just half an hour ago. "Maggie, this is Dan Camp-bell," the foreboding voice had begun. "I hope you get home and hear this soon. Your father is at Cedars in cardiac intensive care. He had a heart attack at the studio this afternoon. I'm sorry about letting you know this way, but I didn't . . ."

That was all Maggie bothered to listen to. Within seconds she was in her BMW, speeding north on the San Diego Freeway in a state of shock—and guilt.

I walked out in a huff the last time we saw each other, as usual. That dinner at Nickels', his birthday . . . oh, shit! How could he have a heart attack? He's never sick! Never misses a day of work! And he's in great shape. Always exercising. There must be some mistake. Maybe it was just gas pains . . . something he ate. But what if—no! You sonuvabitch, you better not die on me!

She stepped out into the wide corridor on the sixth floor of Cedars-Sinai Medical Center. Then she rushed through a maze of doctors and nurses toward the tall, lanky man in the wrinkled suit.

Dan Campbell was leaning up against the wall next to room 6036.

"Have you seen him?" Maggie asked anxiously.

"Yes. For a few minutes," Dan nodded. "He's all right, Maggie. But they're running diagnostic tests. And the chief cardiologist says a by-pass might be indicated. I hope you don't mind, but in your absence I sort of took the place of family."

"No, 'course not . . ." Maggie had started to open the door.

"Oh, she's his daughter," the lawyer said to an imperious-looking black nurse walking briskly toward them.

The nurse made a notation on her clipboard and gave Maggie a half smile.

"Thanks, Dan," Maggie said, squeezing the man's arm and walking into the ward.

There were eight beds. Each was partitioned off for privacy. Billy Rafferty was in the second bed on the right. His eyes were closed. There were tubes running up into his nose and needles sticking in each arm, connected to more tubes.

Maggie felt queasy. Her ears started to ring. She was afraid she might be sick to her stomach.

Uneasily she sat down on the chair beside the bed and bent her head forward, hunching over and resting her elbows on her thighs.

That helped. When she sat up again, Maggie felt less lightheaded. She could see her father's bony chest rising and falling with regularity under the cotton hospital gown.

Thank you, God, she thought. Thank you for this. I really would have missed the old bastard.

She stood up slowly, reached for Billy's limp hand and took it in her own. He felt tepid, lukewarm, as if the blood was barely circulating. Maggie shivered, looking down at the usually fiery, cantankerous old man, now so still and small and helpless lying there. He was really all she had. And at that moment she felt a surge of overwhelming love and responsibility. Maggie knew how much her father had always meant to her.

"Time's up, dear."

She felt the nurse touch her shoulder gently. "He'll probably sleep through the night. Why don't you come back early tomorrow, around ten? You should be able to speak with the doctor then."

Dan Campbell was still outside the door when Maggie stepped into the corridor.

"Come on, Dan," she said, taking his arm. "I'll buy you a drink across the street and you can tell me what happened."

Sitting in Kathy Gallagher's restaurant on Third Street, Maggie sipped a Diet Cola as Dan enumerated with customary efficiency the events at the studio earlier that day.

"He seemed fine, Maggie," the lawyer began. "I met him during the lunch break of a looping session. We had some business to discuss. That was, let's see, around two-thirty. By the time I got back to my office, quarter to five or so, there was a call from Billy's secretary. She said he'd been rehearsing one of the actors through some lines when all of a sudden he got this terrible pain in one arm. The next thing they knew he'd collapsed."

"Why did Carol call you? I'm his daughter, for crissakes."

He took a sip of his Dewar's and soda. "Take it easy. She did call you, but got your machine and didn't want to leave an upsetting message. So she called me then. That's what old family lawyers are for. Besides, it's Billy who's lying in that bed, not you or me. It's him we've got to be thinking about."

Maggie sighed. She felt guilty again. Damn, why do things between me and that man always get so tangled up in knots?

"I don't understand it," she said now, shaking her head back and forth. "He seemed so healthy, always had energy to spare."

"And a great deal of pressure to go with it," Dan reminded her.

"Yes, but he's always been under pressure. It's self-inflicted. Dad just isn't happy unless he's charged up about a project. The more hurdles the better."

"Well," Dan said, pausing for a moment, deciding how to tell his client's daughter about Billy's current predicament. "Lately, Maggie, he's been pretty riled up about something over which he has no control."

"What's that?" Maggie gave the attorney a sharp, intense look. "What do you mean?"

He pursed his lips and waited before answering. "I hate to admit this," he said finally. "But I guess there's no getting around it. I've been thinking about it all afternoon and evening. You see, Maggie, that business your father and I discussed this afternoon may have . . . hell, it may have pushed him over the brink. Billy's being threatened with a lawsuit—for plagiarism."

Maggie stared back at Dan, incredulous. Her father was one of the few trustworthy, incorruptible men in his profession. He still went to mass and took communion every Sunday. There was no way on earth he would steal someone else's story. He was too damn proud.

"For *Precipice?*" she asked.

Dan nodded.

"That is ridiculous. Who's the writer?"

The lawyer hesitated. "This is a breach of client confidentiality," he said weakly.

"Fuck that!" Maggie exploded. "I want to know who's out to kill my father!"

Dan looked around to see if anyone was eavesdropping, then leaned closer. "A guy named Leonard Rybar," he said quietly. "Works for Jet Stream Labs in Palmdale. He's an electrician on the maintenance crew there. That's the odd part." Dan pressed his hands against his forehead, like he was trying to fit pieces of a complicated puzzle together.

"Why?"

"Because you'd think someone claiming to have written *Precipice*—you know, a complicated kind of plot about a research scientist in the aeronautics industry who sells defense secrets to the Russians—you'd think the guy would be higher up. A scientist himself or an engineer or something."

"So he's a smart electrician trying to swindle a buck."

"Fifteen million bucks," Dan corrected her.

"How strong is his case? What's he got?"

"His case," Dan paused briefly, "is as strong as his attorney. Max Groffsky."

"Oh, my God," she said in disgust. "That scum."

"But a ruthless one, a smart one, Maggie. Groffsky has won plenty of these cases."

"I know, I know," said Maggie sharply. "And every one of them out of court."

"That's right," Dan said, frankly impressed by Maggie's familiarity with Groffsky. "And that's how we're hoping to play this one."

"But what's Rybar offering for evidence? Have you seen anything?"

"Yes. I did. Just this morning. It was my second meeting with Groffsky. He showed me Rybar's script. It's called *Bargaining Chip*. And it was registered with the Writers Guild in 1980. I have to tell you, Maggie, I looked it over pretty thoroughly while sitting there in Groffsky's office. And it scared the hell out of me. I'm not a screenwriter, but it certainly looks like *Precipice* in the rough."

Maggie said nothing.

"Also," Dan continued, "Rybar sent registered copies of his script to Universal, MGM, and your father's studio. Groffsky showed me the rejection notices from story editors at all three studios."

The natural flush in Maggie's rounded cheeks had gradually faded. Her hands were clenched around the glass of Cola. She felt as cold as the crushed ice within it.

"So what do you know about Rybar?" she asked finally.

"Not much yet. He's forty-nine. Lives in a small condo on Michillinda in Pasadena. Not married. I have a couple of my assistants checking further. But no matter how you slice it, the evidence looks fairly substantial. And, as I told your father, in cases like this it pays to settle out of court. Otherwise Billy could find himself caught up in a nightmare of legal battles and negative publicity. He doesn't need that, especially not now."

"Dan," Maggie said evenly, looking squarely into the lawyer's tired hazel eyes, "what my father needs is his integrity and the respect of his colleagues. You know damn well he won't give up without a fight, even in court. So you go ahead and let Groffsky sue."

"But, Maggie—"

She held up her hand, refusing to listen. "Now," she said, pausing dramatically, "we have a great deal of work to do, Dan. There's gotta be a way to prove that this sleazeball's script is a fake. And that the sonuvabitch is lying through his goddamn teeth."

Eight

Sarah Rand was adding the final swirls of fluffy white meringue to a coconut cream pie. "Did you ever manage to get through to your friend Maggie last night, dear?" she asked.

"Sure did," replied Christine, sipping her second cup of coffee. She was still in her robe and enjoying the extra warmth from the gas stove as her mother completed her morning baking. The overpowering aroma of newly made cracked-wheat bread and chocolate-chip cookies filled the room with well-being, security, a sense of place. It reminded Christine of all the other Friday mornings she'd spent in this cozy kitchen, sitting here at the round oak table, wrapped in the warmth of her mother's unvarying routine and unchanging love.

"And how's Maggie?" asked Sarah, carefully sliding the pie into the oven.

"Fine. She's doing some free-lance field directing for the National TV News Syndicate. But her father just had a bypass. So she was a bit distracted when we talked."

"Oh, what a shame," Sarah said sympathetically. "I'll have to remember him in my prayers."

"He's doing quite well so far," Christine continued, ignoring her mother's instinctive turning to prayer. It was a sore point between them.

She'd never told her parents that she had, however briefly, carried Steven Jacobs's baby. At the time, Christine told herself that mentioning the abortion to her mother, especially, would be enough to give Sarah a nervous breakdown. Her mother's devotion to Roman Catholicism was absolute. For Christine the abortion marked more than the end of her love affair with Steven; it also led to her abandonment of the faith of her childhood.

Not of God. She still felt strongly about a supreme being. But she refused to attend mass anymore, to participate in the ritual. To give lip service to something she no longer felt a part of. Considering the church's unbending position on premarital sex and birth control—and, of course, abortion—it just seemed too hypocritical.

Sarah poured herself a mug of steaming hot coffee and joined Christine at the table.

"I was wondering," she began casually, as if the thought had just now crossed her mind. Christine looked up from the newspaper she'd been scanning. "When are you going to get together with Kent?"

Christine was hardly in the mood to socialize. The past five days at her parents' home had been soothing, familiar. She was trying to restructure her goals and rebuild her ego. It was a safe place to lick her wounds.

Although she knew it should not have surprised her, the way Blair ended their relationship still weighed heavily on her. His timing had been exquisite. Bravo! Great theater! But a rotten way to treat someone in real life. Christine felt used and tired and unprepared to deal with anything outside the red-brick walls of this three-bedroom sanctuary in South Minneapolis.

"I don't know when I'll see him, Mom," Christine finally answered. "He's very busy at the hospital, you know."

"But he has called several times, dear," Sarah persisted. "It's rather rude not to see him, don't you think?"

A deep frown furrowed Sarah's still pretty, pixieish face. She'd never understood why her daughter jilted Kent. And she had never liked Steven Jacobs. Not just because he wasn't Catholic, although in truth that was a factor. She didn't trust a man who traveled in limousines and private planes—a man who showered extravagance even on her, sending expensive perfumes, scarves, and sweaters at Christmastime. "He acts like it's his holiday, for goodness' sake," she'd complained. Sarah had always suspected Steven would never divorce, never marry her daughter. She couldn't have been happier when the affair was finally over.

"Sure smells good in here, Mama!" boomed the deep, throaty voice. Christine was spared further discussion on the subject of Kent Michaels, at least for now, by the entrance of her father, Ted Rand, who had shrugged off his dark-blue parka, dropped it on a plastic mat in the laundry room, and walked into the kitchen.

"Don't know if the driveway is getting bigger or I'm just getting older," he announced, blue eyes twinkling as he joined them at the table.

Christine laughed. Then she reached over and planted a loud smacking kiss on her father's wet and windburned cheek. He'd been making the same joke about shoveling snow off the drive forever.

"That's my little girl," Ted said, grinning as always.

Things hadn't changed much at 131 Oakwood Drive since Christine left for New York ten years ago. Sarah had redecorated, replacing the hodgepodge in the living and dining rooms with sturdy, comfortable, Colonial-style furniture. Ted had finally given in to his wife and installed a remote-control opener on the garage door.

Christine's room remained the same: a colorful patchwork quilt neatly arranged on her single bed, her stuffed animals lined up against the pillow, college sweaters and sweatshirts folded in the bureau drawers. Hanging in the closet were her Pendleton skirts and wool slacks, covered with plastic bags. Christine's first kindergarten drawing, a scribble in crayon, had been laminated, framed, and placed on display in the center of a blush-pink wall. It was, after all, their little girl's room.

Christine was an only child. And she had arrived late in her parents' lives, an unexpected gift. They'd finished building the house just before she was born.

Ted was retired now. For forty years he'd been a foreman at Minnesota Mining and Manufacturing. But he and Sarah had no plans to migrate to Floridian warmth, as many senior citizens did. South Minneapolis was their home. The neighborhood was still lined with stately maples and was relatively safe. All their close friends were nearby.

Ted enjoyed ice fishing in the winter. Sarah was involved with several church groups. And they both liked kicking up their heels on Saturday night with their square-dancing club. Life was full for Sarah and Ted Rand. The only cloud over their contentment these days was their daughter. It was clear that she was overwrought and terribly unhappy.

Christine's visit had come as a surprise. When she'd phoned from the airport in Los Angeles to tell them she was on her way, Sarah heard the hurt in her daughter's voice. It sounded as though she'd been crying. And when they met Christine at the airline gate, it was apparent to Sarah that she had not been eating well. She was pale, thin, worn-out.

Sarah Rand could never fathom where her daughter's drive came from. All the fuss about a career and all the difficult times she'd seen Christine go through, trying to prove herself, getting hurt, going back at it again—it just didn't seem worth it.

Maybe this time, Sarah hoped, would be a blessing in disguise. Maybe this time, here at home, Christine would realize life was more than tracking down movie stars and being on network television.

"Your mother says you got a call from Edward Sorenson over at KMPT. What'd he have to say?" Ted asked now.

"Oh, not much. Just wanted to know how I was doing," Christine said. She was being evasive about the phone call late yesterday afternoon from her old high-school pal. Eddie was news director at a local television station now. And he had called to offer her a job reviewing plays and films on his nightly ten o'clock news.

"That right? Thought he might have been interested in you—for a job, I mean," Ted slyly persisted, watching his daughter closely.

Christine couldn't help smiling guiltily. Ted Rand didn't miss much. His mind worked like a precise machine, his humor was razor-edged, and he had an uncanny ability to get what he went after. If overwhelming ambition was genetically imposed, she often thought, hers had come directly from this man.

"Okay, Dad," she relented. "You're right. Eddie did ask me to do some work over there. But I'm not sure. I'm just not ready to make any decisions right now."

"That's all right, Cathleen. We understand," Ted said softly, placing his rough, ruddy hand on his daughter's. "You just take your time, honey. Get back on your feet. You know we both love having you here at home."

Ted was interrupted by a short clang from the telephone in the hallway.

"I'll get it," Christine said, standing up quickly, thankful for the minor distraction.

"Hello?"

"Miss DuRand?" questioned the nasal, masculine voice.

Immediately, Christine was sorry she'd answered the phone.

"Christine? This is Clete Bofay at *USA Today* in New York. Sorry if I got you out of bed. But I wanted to get your reaction . . ."

Reaction to what? she thought. Something about his voice implied that this was not good news. She considered not saying anything, just hanging up.

"You've heard, haven't you, that the International Network has hired Jewel Crosse to, ah, well, to replace you?"

Christine felt a hot piercing pressure in her throat. As if someone were trying to choke her. She tried to compose herself. It was a routine reaction call. Standard fare in the news business. As a reporter, she had asked similar questions countless times:

"How did you feel when you lost the part?"

"When the series was canceled, what was your reaction?"

"What's it like being replaced by another actress?"

Now, this time, the tables were turned. It didn't matter that the question was routine, that this Bofay person was only doing his job. She felt like crawling into a hole and hiding.

"Miss DuRand? Christine? Are you still there?"

"Y–yes . . . I mean, no, I hadn't heard," she said, fighting to keep her voice from breaking. "When did this happen?"

"It came over the wire early this morning. I had a heck of a time tracking you down. Thought for sure you'd know by now. Well, anyway, now that you do know, how do you feel about it?"

How do I feel? Oh, swell. Just wonderful. Best news I've had in months, you idiot. What the hell do you expect me to say?

"Listen, I'm afraid I have no comment on this," she almost whispered.

"By the way," he pursued, "I have it on very good authority that Crosse will be making close to a million a year. That's considerably more than you were getting, isn't it?"

More? It's double! That slimy back-biting bitch!

"I'm sorry," she said as steadily as possible. "There is nothing I have to say."

Gently Christine replaced the receiver, reached for the jack and disconnected the telephone.

By six o'clock Tashi looked ravishing. The afternoon had been devoted to falling in love with San Francisco, and it was about four when she'd returned to her room at the Huntington to begin the painstaking task of readying herself for the big moment. Finally, wriggling into the

172

red-white-and-blue Fabrice, she was ready. Ready for Roland Williams. Ready to go on display.

The fund-raising concert was sold out, of course. Arriving by limousine, Tashi was ushered past thousands of curious eyes, her beauty and style remarked upon, wondered at, envied and admired, as she glided past and claimed her seat. It was in the front row—the space reserved for those very important people in the superstar's life. Now, all of a sudden, she was part of that privileged group.

Tashi had long been a fan of Roland's, but she never dreamed she'd be attending one of his concerts. Not like this. Not sitting there so close. She was transfixed. She could not take her eyes away from him.

Roland loped on stage to thunderous applause wearing a bright-red jumpsuit festooned with sparkling beads and glittery braiding, waving his electric guitar above his head. His green-gold eyes blazed, his teeth gleamed white against his golden skin. Across his temples was stretched a banana-yellow bandana. He moved like a fantasy creature—so rhythmic, so fluid that he seemed weightless, untethered by gravity, able to leap and swirl and glide in midair.

He tortured the guitar with an agonizing explosion of sound, his opening salvo, chaotic, beckoning, irresistible. The crowd leaped to its feet, screaming back its own welcome. Roland whirled and dipped, still showing no mercy to the guitar, and then just as suddenly the cacophony stopped.

And now came the voice. Roland's voice was a miracle. Melodious, ethereal one moment, harsh and demanding the next. With apparent effortlessness he merrily led his audience up and down his tonal range like the Pied Piper, enticing and enchanting his listeners into distant lands of heart and soul, moving within seconds from tenderness to anger, loneliness to love.

It was as if he were living the music, breathing the lyrics. Rocketing into the highest emotional stratosphere and taking everyone along for the ride with him.

The audience gave Roland a four-minute standing ovation, hooting and shouting for his return, begging for more, unwilling to let go of the high he had put them on. Tashi watched Denny Bracken time it on his stopwatch.

Roland walked slowly back onstage, and the auditorium nearly rocked off its foundation. Flowers pelted him, and ecstatic fans crushed to the front and tried to reach for his hand, his leg, anything to prove that he was made of flesh and bone and not ghostly smoke.

He held up both arms as a signal for quiet.

"Thank you very, very much," he whispered into the microphone. "You make me feel loved."

At that the cheers started up again, until he calmed them once more.

"I would like to do one more number now," he continued. "It's kinda special to me—my very first hit, a long time ago when I was not yet a man. I hope you remember it. I dedicate it to all of you here tonight who have ever lost someone you love. . . ."

An unearthly quiet now settled across the packed hall. Roland removed his guitar, took hold of the microphone and lilted the bittersweet ballad into the air.

> *All my days I spent with you,*
> *Opened up my world, you see,*
> *Never doubted you'd be there for me.*
>
> *Looking back it seems so clear*
> *Love was there when you were near;*
> *Then you left me all alone again.*
>
> *Oh, the pain you put me through,*
> *How I tried to cling to you;*
>
> *But you closed your world to me*
> *All alone, my destiny.*
>
> Amor, amor no quiero,
> No quiero mas amar.
> *Love I do not want,*
> *I do not want to love anymore. . . .*

Afterward, while waves of applause still washed over the now empty stage, Denny Bracken hustled Tashi backstage, where a throng of reporters, photographers, and TV camera crews awaited. During a brief photo session, Denny circulated a one-page press release introducing Tashi as she stood stiffly next to a heavily perspiring Roland. She smiled radiantly for the cameras. But inside she was feeling very differently.

Roland had yet to say a single word to her. Not all evening. Not even a hello when Denny introduced them back at the hotel. In fact, he hadn't even looked directly at her. When she reached out to shake his hand, he did not take it.

At first she dismissed his behavior on the grounds that he was simply keyed up before his performance. After all, Denny had told her he was introducing several new numbers, some of them including fireworks, which could be dangerous. And that, she assumed, was enough to put even a superstar on edge.

But as the evening progressed, Roland's demeanor remained icily distant. By the time they arrived at a party in his honor at the resplendent home of a socially prominent supporter of Democratic causes in Sausalito, just over the Golden Gate Bridge from the city, Tashi was confused and worried. It was as if he didn't want her there at all.

"You must be very tired," she whispered meekly to Roland as they stood in a reception line together, greeting guests. She glanced sideways at him, searching his face for answers.

"M'okay," he murmured between handshakes.

He wasn't okay. Far from it. Though outwardly he appeared to be calm and in control, inside he was furious. Seething.

He would never ever, he had promised himself, forgive Burton. Pulling a stunt like this. Matching him up with a woman. A woman, for crissakes! Ridiculous. And the way Burton had announced it all, so nonchalantly, just an hour before the concert. Breaking the news offhandedly as he slipped into his tuxedo jacket.

"Ro, remember that surprise I mentioned a couple of weeks back? The guarantee that we'll have no more problems with rumors about us?"

"Yeah, guess so," Roland said, although in truth his memory of it was vague. So much had happened since that trying time of the Du-Rand interview that he had almost discounted the possibility of a backlash.

"Well, you're about to meet her."

"Meet who? A female attack dog? Is that what you've lined up?" Roland said, chuckling, from the bathroom. He was standing at the mirror, carefully arranging his dark locks over his bandana.

"Not quite, Ro," Burton replied, coming up behind Roland and kissing him lightly on the back of his neck. "What I've arranged is a companion for you, a decoy. To mislead the press."

Roland whirled around to face Burton. "What the fuck are you talking about?"

"A female companion," Burton continued, ignoring Roland's outburst. "She's a beautiful Eurasian girl who—and you'll like this—aspires to become a veterinarian. I'm sure you'll hit it off fine. We're going to introduce her in every city as your fiancée."

Roland's eyes blazed. "I'm not going anywhere with any woman!" he said angrily. "And where the hell do you come off, arranging something like that? Take your little surprise and shove it, man. Send the tramp back home. I'm traveling alone!"

The hotter Roland became, the more calm and coolly persuasive Burton was. Finally, he got Roland to agree to go through with the plan, at least for this one night.

"But that's it. No more!" Roland declared.

"Just give her a chance, Ro, that's all I ask," said Burton.

Then the doorbell rang, and the awkward introductions were made. Roland was thoroughly rude to the girl.

Watching the two of them now at the party, Burton saw that Roland and Tashi were still not making any progress. Though they stood side by side, they could have been hundreds of miles apart. They didn't touch. Didn't speak to each other. Their eyes never met.

Burton accepted two glasses of freshly poured Piper Sonoma sparkling wine from a waiter and moved toward the ill-at-ease couple.

"Why not take a break, you two?" Burton suggested cheerily, handing each a long-stemmed glass. "Almost everyone is here by now. Great place, huh?"

He practically herded them over to a magnificent wall-sized window view of the bay. "Nice of Henry Klabin and his wife to extend their hospitality, wasn't it? He's a multimillionaire. Made it all in the Silicon Valley. Notice all the security?" Burton gestured toward three large men hovering near the entrance. "More of them are circulating in here. Now that's what I call a private party!" He laughed, too loudly. The hard stare from his lover told Burton all he needed to know.

"Excuse me, gentlemen . . . Miss Qwan. Herbert Montague."

The middle-aged man who'd come up to them was jowly and had a large potbelly. He looked like a disheveled penguin in his rented tuxedo. His hand thrust out in Roland's direction.

Roland shook it rapidly and mumbled a brief hello.

"Sorry to interrupt, Mr. Williams. But I just had to tell you how overwhelmed I was with your performance. It was truly spectacular," the man enthused. "Magnificent."

"Glad you liked it," Roland replied curtly. He turned back to Burton, hoping the man would leave them alone.

But Montague did not take the hint. "Guess you made a bundle tonight," he persisted. "Keep that up, and you'll drive the Republicans right out of business!" He laughed at his own remark, a big-bellied laugh that boomed through the crowded room.

"From your mouth to God's ears," Burton said, amused by this odd character and relieved to have the burden of making conversation lifted temporarily from him.

"Say," Montague asked now, "just how many of these concerts do you think you'll have to do to put the Democrats over the top?" He took a step closer to Roland.

"Well," Roland hesitated, looking down at his glass, "can't say, really. Larger houses in some cities, you know."

"Who's your favorite candidate?"

"Oh, I don't know right now," Roland answered, becoming increasingly uncomfortable under this questioning.

"Come on," the portly man urged. "I'll bet you're a Senator Whittaker supporter. He's a big friend of show business and the arts. Minorities, too. And I'll bet—"

"Hold on there, my friend," Burton said firmly, cutting Montague off. "Roland isn't committed to any particular candidate yet. Our job during the—"

Burton felt a fierce tug at his jacket sleeve and stopped in midsentence. Turning his head, he saw Tashi leaning toward him, as if desperately wanting to say something. For an instant their eyes met. Hers had the look of a frightened animal.

"What?" Burton said when he heard what she whispered.

Montague blanched, spun around quickly and loped toward the exit.

Burton took off after him. Just as the fleeing guest reached the front door, two security guards tackled him, wrestling him to the floor.

"You mean he was taping me?" Roland said to Tashi in amazement after she hurriedly repeated to him what she had told Burton.

She nodded.

"But how did you—?"

"What did I tell you, Roland," Burton said delightedly as he rejoined them. "Not only is she beautiful, she's savvy as well. The shmuck's a reporter for that sleazy syndicated radio show *Let's Hear It.* You know, it's like the *National Enquirer.*" He turned to face Tashi. "If your keen eyes hadn't caught it, my dear, Montague would be blasting his exclusive interview from here to Bora Bora. What the hell tipped you off?"

"The microphone," Tashi said softly. "A tiny pinhead hidden just below the carnation on his lapel. A businessman I once worked for as an interpreter in Hong Kong often used a similar device during meetings."

"Amazing," said Burton.

177

An uneasy silence settled over the three of them.

Then Roland turned to Tashi, his eyes taking her in for the first time. He saw an exquisitely contoured, delicately sensitive face and intelligent almond-brown eyes. And for a moment, a fleeting instant, he bathed her in a warm and appreciative stare.

Roland Williams didn't have to say anything. That one brief look of approval was enough.

"Can't you move this thing any faster?" complained Jewel from the back of her sleek, white limousine. "It's already twelve forty-five."

"Sorry, Miss Crosse. Nothin' much I can do."

Jewel Crosse's regular chauffeur had had the bad taste to become ill, and the nervous young man in the driver's seat was called at the last minute that morning. What he didn't know was that half a dozen other relief drivers had turned this same assignment down. Most anyone who wheeled a stretch Cadillac around Hollywood knew that a day with Jewel Crosse was enough to give you ulcers or at least a severe case of gastritis.

"I just don't understand it. Tom always gets me to the Bistro Garden in fifteen minutes."

"Doin' the very best I can, Miss Crosse."

They were ensnared in lunch-hour traffic on Wilshire Boulevard. It was impossible to move a fraction faster. Ahead, an endless bumper-to-bumper stream of Rolls-Royces, Jaguars, Mercedeses, and lesser conveyances formed a solid ribbon of automotive machinery up the boulevard. Cañon Drive, their turnoff, was ten or more long minutes away.

"Dumb-assed juvenile delinquent," Jewel grumbled to herself. Stupid kid should cut his hair, at least. He looks like a leftover hippie.

Frustrated, she sent up the glass partition between them. She was wearing a favorite suit today, a beautifully tailored Givenchy in a delicate shade of pink. In combination with her flaming red hair and heavily made-up face, she looked like a new flavor at Baskin-Robbins. On her left lapel was an imposing solid-gold pin in the shape of a fiery sun—a gift from Irving Taubman welcoming her back to the network. "To remind you how brightly you will shine on your new show, Jewel," as he'd put it.

At first glance the pin, which had a gaudy, glitzy heaviness about it, looked like a Christmas cookie spray-painted gold. But Jewel wore it everywhere. It had become something of a trademark for her. She was convinced it brought her good luck.

She hoped it would work for her with Jacques Laffont.

Jewel could barely tolerate the sight of the trade-paper gossip columnist. Few people genuinely liked him, but most eventually found themselves sucking up to Laffont for one reason or another. Today was Jewel's turn. Lunch had been her idea, and for a very good reason.

Neal Burgess.

His television series, *Speed,* was quickly ascending in the ratings. The former football player was becoming one of those Hollywood catch phrases which was often heard but seldom deserved—an overnight success. Each time Jewel saw his good-looking rugged face on the cover of another national magazine she became more determined to carry out her revenge. All she needed was information.

Since that humiliating evening at the Beverly Wilshire, Jewel had been combing the city in search of dirt on the rising star. For weeks she'd contacted everyone she could think of who might be willing to dump on young Burgess. Money was offered—a fee, large or small, depending on the informant. But so far not a smidgen of scandal, not even a hint.

Now she was desperate. Jacques Laffont was a last resort.

Laffont attended all the A-list parties. He eavesdropped on some of the juiciest and most important conversations in town. Rumor had it that he'd once had a studio chief's phone tapped to check out a story.

What Hollywood read each morning in Jacques Laffont's column was not only breezy and scintillating. Usually, it was at least partially based on fact.

Jewel sank back more deeply into her seat, lost in thought, simmering in her own bitter juices.

Jacques Laffont checked his Cartier tank watch and grunted. His luncheon date, he noted, was exactly twenty minutes late. Laffont had made his grand entrance at the Bistro Garden at twelve-thirty sharp. Promptness was a habit. Why be rude when you aren't picking up the tab? Jacques Laffont never picked up the tab. It was unthinkable to him, spending his own money on food. Expense-account eating in Hollywood was a minor art form. Publicists charged off meals to clients. Clients—producers, directors, actors, studio executives—wrote them off to their companies or personal corporations. A daily blizzard of credit-card charge slips swirled and fell in snowy heaps at the feet of "celebrity" restaurateurs throughout the city. An influential show-business writer like Laffont always had invitations for lunch and dinner. He could count on at least four lavishly catered parties or premieres a week. And breakfast? Laffont rarely ate breakfast.

He surveyed his surroundings from the comfortable banquette. He was seated inside, facing the garden patio, amused as always by the spectacle of the famous and would-be famous who gathered here to lunch beneath the California sunshine.

At a large circular table Jacques spotted Kenny Rogers's wife, Marianne, in animated conversation with a handful of other Hollywood wives. Oh, there's Olivia Newton-John. And Linda Evans—*Dynasty* must be on hiatus. But, my . . . is that . . . ? Yes, by God, Jessica Lange. I've never seen her in a restaurant. Didn't know she was tame enough to be trusted with a knife and fork.

Laffont chuckled and fussily smoothed over his white Calvin Klein jacket, aware that he, too, was on display. In fact, he reveled in that. So far, five out-of-work actresses had stopped by to graze his cheek with a kiss and say how well he looked, each hoping her obeisance would be rewarded by a mention in his column.

His second glass of Laurent Perrier was empty. He held his glass aloft and nodded, bringing a passing waiter to an abrupt stop.

"Another, sir?"

"Please."

Might as well enjoy myself. Can't begin to imagine what that rattlesnake of the airwaves wants. But she wants something. I don't think we've passed more than five words between us in ten years' time.

Laffont checked his watch again. Almost half an hour late? No excuse for that. She'll have one, though, I'm sure. Let's see . . . she's probably been sucking off Taubman under his desk. Or that third layer of makeup took an extra hour. Or maybe it was the spray shellac she uses on her bulletproof hairdo.

Jacques Laffont smiled smugly and raised his fresh glass of champagne. "Here's to you, bitch."

Christine was not looking forward to seeing Kent Michaels. She knew he would be curious about what had happened back in Los Angeles. He'd ask the inevitable questions about Steven Jacobs and the FBI. He'd want to know whether she really quit her job or was fired. She wasn't ready to face his interrogation, well-meaning though it might be. And she didn't see why she should have to.

Kent was an old boyfriend, no more, no less. Her long-ago love for him had been a girl's, not a woman's. So much time had passed since then. So many things had happened. They were virtual strangers now.

Christine had been home just under two weeks. Already she was beginning to feel better about herself. And she knew this was not the time to open up to someone else. Especially to an old fiancé, newly divorced.

But Kent kept calling. By the third time he asked her out, she'd run out of excuses. Not to accept, she told herself, would be glaringly impolite. And Sarah Rand, who was always within earshot of the telephone, had already begun to make an issue out of her daughter's bad manners.

A Thursday lunch was agreed upon, at Interlachen, Kent's country club. On the appointed day she slept late, hurriedly showered, did her hair, and applied the barest minimum of makeup. Then she pulled on a warm red cable-stitch sweater, slipped into a pair of heavy dark-gray woolen slacks, and shrugged into her blue fox coat.

The instant she walked into the country club dining room, Christine wished she'd spent more time putting herself together. Kent was already waiting for her at a corner table, his back to the expansive windows which overlooked the gently rolling golf course. His face was bronzed, handsome as ever, and in stark contrast to his ivory sweater. Outside, snow was lightly falling, adding to the endless blanket of dazzling whiteness. Against this wonderfully scenic backdrop, he looked like a model in a billboard ad.

Christine had forgotten how very attractive Kent was. And when he stood up to take her hand, how tall.

"My," she said, a bit nervously, "you're certainly looking fit, Doctor."

"Just back from Aspen. Some long overdue R and R. Guess you can relate to that." He flashed her a quick grin.

"Yes. I guess." She forced a smile as they sat down.

For a split second, she was caught by his pale-blue eyes. His look was full of warmth, and it made her feel even more uneasy. She looked away briefly at the sun-glazed snow. This is going to be a brief lunch, she reminded herself. An hour and a half. No more.

"I ordered some OJ for you," he said, motioning to the tall frothy glass of freshly squeezed juice. "Remembered you used to like it."

"Thanks," she said, picking up the glass. And as she did so, he raised his in a toast. "But I think I'd like a little vodka in it," she added.

"Oh?" He seemed surprised.

"You don't mind, do you?"

Recovering quickly, Kent signaled to the waiter. "Of course not.

You're a big girl now." After the waiter placed the drink in front of Christine, Kent lifted his glass once again. "Welcome home, Cath . . . sorry, Christine," he said.

"Thanks." It came out awkwardly.

And then, as though he'd anticipated this initial hurdle, he added quickly, "Let's just forget our recent histories, okay? We've got a lot of old times to relive."

And remarkably, within a few minutes, Christine felt her initial defensiveness evaporate. They dredged up memories of everything from high-school pals to college football games to their most disastrous and embarrassing moments together. As they ordered, munching on sesame-seed breadsticks, Christine caught herself marveling at how much she was beginning to enjoy herself.

"Remember the time I fell and broke my ankle on the skating pond?" she asked with a girlish giggle.

"Do I? I'm the one who had to carry you home—with your skates on." He gave her an impertinent look. "I'd say you were maybe fifteen pounds heavier then."

"Probably," she agreed.

"Uh, by the way," he said teasingly, "there's something I've been meaning to ask you. About that purple sweater I gave you one year for Christmas. The one with the flowers all over it . . ."

Christine burst out laughing. "I hated it! I always figured your mother had picked it out. Your taste was never that bad."

"You're right. It wasn't. She did. I confess."

"I don't think I ever even wore it."

He pretended to look hurt. "I noticed."

As the lunch went on, Christine began to realize there was a great deal she'd forgotten, or maybe never knew, about Kent Michaels.

His dedication to his profession, for one thing. When he talked about performing surgery, the awesome task of working inside the human heart, the tremendous challenge of replacing valves with man-made substitutes of metal and plastic, or stitching patches over nature's mistakes in the heart wall, his face took on a look of intensity, concern, determination.

"Have you ever operated on a child?" she wanted to know.

He seemed pleased that she'd asked. "Yes. About eight weeks ago. A six-year-old girl. Her heart was completely worn-out, enlarged to twice normal size by struggling for so long to compensate for a grave congenital weakness. A transplant was her only hope. Thank heaven, recent advances in drugs to combat the body's rejection of a donor heart made the operation an option with a decent chance of success. It was virtually impossible to find a donor. But we did—in time. And the operation went well. I don't think I've ever gotten more satisfaction from anything I've done than when I looked into that little girl's big brown eyes the day after we opened her up."

Kent, it was plain to see, was doing just what he'd always wanted to do, fought to do. His decision to study medicine had come as a rude shock to his family. He'd been raised from boyhood to become a lawyer, like his father and grandfather. In the fullness of time, he was expected to assume control of the family oil empire.

But when Kent returned from a summer vacation in Europe, a headstrong nineteen, he announced his decision to become a cardiac surgeon. War broke out in the Michaels family. His father threatened disinheritance. His mother begged Kent to reconsider. Instead of knuckling under, he left home and was prepared to work his way through the rest of college and into medical school. Eventually his father bowed to what appeared to be the inevitable and sent him off to Baylor, to the college of medicine run by famed heart surgeon Dr. Michael DeBakey in Houston. Kent returned home to fulfill his residency at the University of Minnesota hospital and was quickly offered a staff position.

Christine had always encouraged Kent to follow his dream of becoming a doctor. She had believed he had the makings of a good one. He'd excelled in school, graduating with top honors. He had a charismatic kind of charm that won people's confidence. And she imagined his natural grace and agility had some bearing on his success as a surgeon.

What she hadn't ever fully appreciated, perhaps until now, was what she had had in him as a person. Indeed, what they'd had in each other. When they were going together so many years ago, they were both too young, too inexperienced.

My God, this is the first normal, down-to-earth man I've seen socially in years, she thought, as Kent continued talking about his work. It's all up front with him. No games. No ulterior motives. He's just out there doing what he does.

Whoa now, hold it, she thought, resting her silverware beside the half-eaten cheese omelet on her plate. It's hardly the time or place for thoughts of the future with Kent Michaels. He lives too far away, a world apart. And he's been through changes, a lot of them. So have you. Besides, who says he's even interested?

"Hey," Kent was saying now, as he finished off the steak sandwich in front of him, "enough about me. How about your visit home? Aren't you glad to be back in the bosom of the good old Midwest for a while?"

"It's a change. And I needed it," was all she replied.

Kent shook his head. "I really don't understand how anybody can live in California. I spent a little time in Palm Springs last year. Jesus, what a drag. Everyone walks around like they're in a coma. And Los Angeles—the smog's so thick you can't see the mountains. Can you imagine what that air does to your body?"

"There are advantages," Christine countered lightly.

"I suppose," he relented. "I guess I just can't see why anybody would want to leave Minnesota. We've got everything right here. Clean, beautiful lakes, good shopping, great restaurants. Culture, too. Excellent museums, the Guthrie Theater . . ."

"You sound like a commercial."

"Maybe," he said, taking a final sip of coffee while glancing at his watch. "And I'm afraid I have to take my act over to the hospital now. Rounds this afternoon. Surgery at five."

Two hours had vanished. Despite herself, Christine felt disappointed that their lunch was at an end.

Outside, clutching her coat as he hailed the valet to retrieve their cars, she felt the need to say something to let him know she was sorry to see him go. "I really enjoyed today," she offered. She was afraid it came out sounding too tame.

He smiled down at her. "I'm glad," he said. "I wish I had more time. . . ." He seemed to be hesitating. "But Saturday—Saturday afternoon let's take a drive to Forest Lake. Remember? I just built a new cottage up there, not far from Mom and Dad's. You'll like it."

He'd brushed her cheek with his lips and was driving off in his Porsche before she even had a chance to accept.

Billy Rafferty's fists were clenched when the wide door to his hospital room whooshed open. His mind was spewing obscenities. And his heart was pumping much too fast for a man who'd just undergone a coronary bypass.

"Hi, Pops. How're we doing today?" asked his daughter, closing the door behind her.

Billy glowered at her. "Maggie, for Godsakes, will you quit with the 'we' business? You sound like one of the constipated nurses they've got patrolling around here."

"My, my, we're in a bit of a snit this afternoon, aren't we?" Maggie teased as she eased into the chair next to his bed.

Since his hospitalization, she had made it a point to visit Billy twice a day. Usually she also managed to smuggle in a treat from Nate 'n Al's. This afternoon's was a lean corned beef on rye sandwich and four huge kosher pickles. Unsliced, the way her father preferred them. But he barely seemed to notice the white paper bag she placed in front of him.

"Snit?" he growled. "I'll give you a snit." Reaching for the trade papers scattered on the bed, he said, "Didn't you see this?" He shook *The Hollywood Reporter* at her furiously. "Go ahead. Read it. 'Rafferty sued for plagiarism.' Fifteen million that liar is trying to steal from me. Bastard. And can you imagine the legal fees? After this case Campbell will be set for life. He'll never have to work again. I'll probably lose the house, so—"

"Dad," Maggie cut in.

"Damn it, Mag—"

"Just hold on, will you? I already read the trades. And you can bluster on all you want. But let's talk like grownups for a minute. You knew this would happen—Dan told you. You had a choice, and you decided to take Groffsky on. So the trades have a splashy story. So what?"

"That goddamn Jewel Crosse has already blasted it all over the world, too," Billy ranted on. "Six people called to tell me. One from Paris."

Maggie shook her head in sympathy. "Someday I'm going to nail that broad."

"I'll supply the hammer," Billy agreed, his face red with the exertion of his tirade.

"Dad, calm down. Remember your blood pressure. You'll get through it and you'll win. This kind of stuff happens all the time."

"Not to me it doesn't." Billy gave his daughter one of his "what do *you* know" glares and sighed. His life seemed on a collision course. Here he was in this sterile hospital where they brought in sawdust for food three times a day. And his room looked like a damn mortuary.

There were flowers everywhere. Long-stemmed roses in large glass vases. Tulip plants with colored foil wrappers. Huge arrangements of gladiolus, dahlias and birds of paradise. Exotic orchids. No matter which way he turned, Billy was surrounded by a sweeping splash of color.

He thought he must singlehandedly be keeping all the posh flower shops in Beverly Hills in business this month. Not that he believed for a moment that any of the senders of these elaborate floral tributes cared whether he lived or died. He figured they were just scared, or guilty. Scared that if he pulled through, he wouldn't ask them to work on his next picture. Guilty because they hadn't taken time to drop by and see how he was doing.

Billy had never spent ten lonelier days. And he'd learned a very good lesson. Never count your friends on more than three fingers. His only visitors had been Dan Campbell, his longtime secretary Carol Flanagan, and his daughter.

Maggie pushed herself up out of the chair and crossed the room to examine the cards on the morning's flower delivery. She was wearing a bright-yellow cotton suit which was already severely wrinkled in the back. Earlier in the week Maggie had announced she'd lost twenty pounds. He couldn't tell the difference.

"Dad," she said now, walking back to his bedside, "I've got an idea about the case. But I need your cooperation to proceed."

"I told you once," Billy bristled back at her. "No. I don't want you involved in this. It's my problem. You tend to your own. By the way, did you find a job yet?"

"You know I'm free-lancing." Maggie struggled to smile back at him. She had promised herself she would not lose her temper while Billy was in the hospital. "Don't worry, I won't be hitting you up for a loan."

She tried to steer the conversation back to the course she had plotted. "Listen, Dad, I know Dan is doing his best to investigate Rybar. But I think we have to go further than that. I—"

"Maggie, I warned you—"

"All I want to do," she said, raising her voice and overriding him, "is to go through your 1979 and 1980 files. Look, Dad, you can't afford to overlook a clue. Maybe I'll find it."

"No, young lady. No. And that is final."

"Okay, you win," she lied. "I'll butt out."

"Good," said Billy with an air of finality. "And you'd better start right now. Dr. Matloff will be here to check my new plumbing any second."

Maggie bent over and planted a wet kiss on her father's brow. "Behave yourself, you old grouch. See you later this afternoon. I love you."

As Billy Rafferty watched his daughter leave, a smile forced its way onto his lips. When he reached for the white paper bag from Nate 'n Al's, small drops of moisture glistened at the corners of his eyes.

"Jacques, do have some dessert," Jewel urged as she rearranged the large napkin over her pink linen skirt.

For Jewel the lunch had been an endurance contest. Laffont had ordered two appetizers, wolfed down a generous plateful of bratwurst and German potato salad, and had gone through nearly a bottle of champagne.

Picking languidly at her seafood salad, she'd tried several times to shift the conversation in a direction that would lead to Neal Burgess. Each time Laffont had leap-frogged to an entirely different subject, almost as if he were intentionally evading her. Dessert would give her more time. He had to order something.

"The soufflé, Monsieur Laffont?" suggested the waiter. "The chocolate or the raspberry perhaps?"

Laffont pursed his lips in deliberation, as if the decision were of the gravest import.

"Oh, do have something, Jacques," Jewel coaxed again. "We can afford to be a little wicked."

He placed an elbow on the table and cupped his chin in his hand. "I do love the soufflé . . . but the chocolate mousse is so good, too."

"Have both! Jacques, please have both. Why should you have to choose?" Jewel hoped her revulsion was well concealed. It'll be a wonder if he can even stand up.

"Wellllll," Laffont said, "all right. The mousse and the soufflé. Make it raspberry. And"—he lifted his glasses off his nose slightly to make direct eye contact with the waiter—"some extra whipped cream on the side."

Jewel relaxed. She had half an hour more, at least. And walking into the restaurant at that moment was her opportunity for a perfect segue.

"Umm," she said casually. "Look who's here."

Laffont grunted. "Pierce Brosnan," he said without glancing up.

"Amazing, isn't it," Jewel went blithely on, "how far he's come since *Remington Steele* debuted on television? A few years ago nobody knew his name. Now he's an international star. You never can tell, can you, Jacques, just who's going to hit?"

"Maybe you can't, dear, but I knew right away he'd make it big."

His eyes lifted now to follow Brosnan as the maitre d' led the handsome actor to a table in the garden. "A gentleman among gentlemen, that young man. Like the early Cary Grant . . ."

"Your mousse, sir." The waiter placed a small stemmed glass of chocolate mousse in front of Laffont and topped it with a peak of whipped cream. He put the bowl of white, frothy cream on the table, next to Jewel's coffeecup. "The soufflé will take a few minutes more."

"Looks fabulous, Jacques. Go ahead," Jewel enthused, watching in dismay.

Laffont slid his tongue across a rounded spoonful of gooey mousse and whipped cream. His eyes ascended heavenward. "Speaking of Brosnan," Jewel said now, determined not to waste this opportunity, "it makes you wonder, doesn't it, how long this television beef-cake trend can last? Selleck was the first, of course."

"Marvelous chap," Laffont managed between bitefuls. "I interviewed him at his home in Hawaii once. Bright man. He'll go far."

Jewel looked over at Laffont, who seemed lost in some private reverie, his spoon poised in midair. "It does make you curious, though," Jewel persisted, trying to snap him out of it. "Doesn't it? What actor will be next, I mean. I'd say perhaps that young fellow in the new series, *Speed*. What's his name? Plays a motorcyclist."

Laffont spooned up another glob of mousse and turned to Jewel, looking at her blankly as he swallowed.

"Surely you know who I mean. Oh, what is his name?" She continued to feign memory loss. "It begins with an N. Nick? Ned? Neal! That's it, Neal. Neal . . . Burgess."

"Yes?" deadpanned Laffont. "What about him?"

"Well . . ." Jewel said, clearing her throat.

The soufflé arrived. All dialogue lapsed while they both watched the waiter break open its crusty top with a spoon, releasing a tiny cloud of raspberry-scented steam.

"I'll add the whipped cream. Just set the soufflé here," Laffont commanded. The waiter dutifully did as he was told.

"Whoo, I must rest a moment," Laffont announced, pressing his hands lightly on his swollen stomach. He glanced down quickly to see if all the buttons on his beige silk shirt were still fastened.

Jewel seized this chance to pick up the thread of conversation once again. "Off the record, Jacques," she said in her most gossipy tone, "you know what they're saying about Burgess, don't you?" If he had anything on the guy, she was certain he'd spit it out now. Jacques Laffont wasn't about to let her tell him anything.

Laffont sat there thoughtfully for several moments. Then he straightened up and took a deep swallow of champagne.

"You mean that he's got a bad coke habit, that he's dealing to support it?" he said finally, lifting his eyeglasses and turning to gaze directly at Jewel. "I thought everybody knew that."

"Everybody does, everybody does," Jewel exulted. "I heard that ages ago." Her mind was reeling with her triumph, and all she wanted to do now was escape from this unctuous old glutton. She knew, however, that she must press for details, specifics, hard fact. Hearsay was not enough.

Now, she thought. Make it plausible. Give him more bait. Let him hook himself. "My information is, he's being supplied by some girl he met, a Spanish actress. . . ."

"Afraid not," Laffont said imperiously, raising his coffeecup for the busboy to refill it. "My sources tell me he—"

He halted in mid-sentence as his elbow came back down toward the table and struck a glancing blow against the bowl next to Jewel's cup.

Black coffee sloshed out, splashing down her blouse and onto her skirt. A whoosh of whipped cream followed a split second later. The bowl landed in her lap, upside down.

"How terrible, Jewel," Laffont said mildly, as three waiters raced to her aid. "Sorry."

"Sorry!" she yelped, aghast. Puffs of whipped cream and ugly dark splotches of coffee now peppered her once lovely pink suit. Another large airy blob of the cream rested just above her eyes, on her short fiery red bangs.

"Can I do anything?" Laffont offered, watching the waiters daub Jewel feverishly with water-soaked napkins.

The noisy restaurant had come to a sudden stillness. Aside from muffled titters of laughter, there wasn't a sound.

"No," Jewel said angrily. "There is nothing you can do. You've already done it, Jacques. Maybe I should have ordered a tablecloth for my suit."

Laffont sniggered. "Perhaps for your face, darling," he said as he got up to leave. "It would be such an improvement."

Jacques Laffont strode unsteadily out of the Bistro Garden, a look of profound satisfaction on his face.

"Sweet Jesus," said Maggie, shivering as she brushed snow from her mint-green down jacket. "Now I know what 'colder than a witch's tit' really means—except I don't know which tit is colder! It is *freezing* out there."

"Below freezing," Christine corrected her apple-cheeked friend. "Thirty below with the wind-chill factor. Welcome to balmy Minneapolis." She plopped Maggie's duffle bag onto the dresser of the guest bedroom and sat down on the bed.

"Couldn't you have picked summer or fall or spring to run back home and hide? For the sake of my delicate system, that would have been a whole hell of a lot easier." Maggie joined Christine on the bed. Her smile, at least, was warm as toast. And as welcome on this arctic morning.

"I'm just so glad you're here, Mag. But what a surprise. Why didn't you call? At least I could have picked you up from the airport."

"No way." Maggie shook her head defiantly. "This is a sneak attack, girl. Wasn't about to let you be armed and ready with a million reasons why you've decided to stay in suspended animation here at the North Pole. My mission is 'home delivery,' boss lady. Yours—right back to Tinsel Town where you belong."

Christine cast her eyes downward.

"Come on, kiddo. What's wrong?" chided Maggie gently. "Still in the dumper?"

"Mag, I'm just not sure I'm ready to handle it back there yet," she said slowly, sadly. "I mean, I want to, God knows I want to—but it seems so—so futile. What am I going to do, anyway? I don't even know if I'll be able to find another television job."

"Hey, it's Mag you're talkin' to, child. President of your fan club. Of course you'll find another job. You've got a firm base back in L.A., Christine. A lot of people there still have great respect for your work, despite the London flap." She reached over and lifted Christine's chin to look directly in her eyes. "And I'm one of 'em."

"But you're my friend."

"Damn straight I am! Too bad *I* can't hire you!"

The outburst of laughter from Maggie was so infectious that, despite herself, Christine couldn't help but join in. Before long the two of them were reduced to whimpers and tears, unable to stop laughing. Christine leaned over to embrace her friend in a ferocious bear hug.

Still in the grip of Christine's arms, Maggie continued with the script she had rehearsed dozens of times on the long flight in from the Coast. "What about Don Winston over at Channel 8? I'll bet he'd give you your old job in a minute."

"I don't know, Mag—"

190

" 'Course he would! They've got some dumb blond Dora Dildo over there now. She's terrible, really awful! Winston would be a fool not to take you back. Call him at least, girl. It would be a start."

"Maybe," Christine murmured halfheartedly, releasing her hold on Maggie and leaning back on the bed. She stared at the ceiling, seeing nothing.

"Listen, sweetie, you know as well as I do that Hollywood has a memory about five minutes long. They don't care if you were Hitler as long as you can deliver the goods. By the way"—she paused, selecting her words carefully— "I know you've always landed your own TV jobs. But maybe now is the time to get a powerful agent working on your side. You know, just for a little extra juice."

"Yeah, sure." Christine laughed sardonically. "I'm certain William Morris would sign me immediately. They might be able to get me a role in a movie—as a gun moll. Maggie, don't you see? I'm going to have to start all over again. None of the good agencies would touch me now."

"I wouldn't be so sure," Maggie said firmly.

"Well, I am. I feel lousy enough. I refuse to go begging at a talent agency."

"Okay, okay," Maggie relented. "But just remember, you're the crackerjack reporter who won the Emmy two years ago. And you're the one who has the best reputation in Hollywood for celebrity interviews. And you're the one *Newsweek* predicted would be the next Barbara Walters. And you're the one who singlehandedly sat there putting her own pieces together when the tape editors went on strike—"

"That was only for a couple of days," Christine protested. "Some of the other reporters did the same."

"Not as well as you did it, Miss Humble Pie. Listen to me, Christine." Now Maggie took her friend's hands in her own. "You're too damn hard on yourself. You always have been. No matter what you accomplish, you never take time to pat yourself on the back. Well, hell's bells, girl, now's the time. Don't sit here sniffling. You're a dynamite interviewer who can do anything she damn well pleases in that town full of phonies and hacks! Just come back home and get rollin', honey!"

Christine was almost in tears. She wanted so very much to believe what Maggie was saying, but she was afraid, still too afraid.

"Okay, so maybe it'll take a few months to find a new slot," Maggie went on softly, draping her arm around Christine's shoulders. "But you're a survivor, Christine. And you can't let me down now. You're my inspiration, for crissakes. Just get up off your tired little tush and do it. I'll be there to pick you up if you fall."

She winked and gave Christine a little grin. "Even though we both know you won't."

Christine managed a weak smile in return. She wanted to change the subject. "How's Jewel Crosse?" Seldom did Maggie pass up a chance to rail on at Jewel.

Maggie took the question as a positive signal. At least Christine was interested enough to be curious about the latest gossip.

"You mean the motor-mouthed maven of the airwaves?" Maggie said with disgust. "She's the same bitch we always knew she was. Nobody on the staff at the network can stand her. And I hear she's constantly kvetching at Taubman—that is, when she's not fucking him."

"You're joking," Christine said, sitting straight up.

"My dear," Maggie continued in her most affected tone, "would I jest about a subject as revolting as the Divine Miss C? You bet your sweet ass she's jumping into the sack with ol' Irv—or maybe onto the floor, it's more her style—every chance she gets. I got the inside poop. One of the cleaning ladies made the mistake of walking into Taubman's office late one night, and there was Jewel humping the chief on his couch."

"Unbelievable." Christine was grinning now. It was a genuine grin, no doubt about it.

"Believe it, honey. Jewel is no dummy. She's got her act down pat. Sleeps with the guy closest to the top and writes her own ticket. She did the same with that wimp Howard Ruskin—her former producer. Ever meet that wonderful piece of work?"

Christine nodded, chuckling now. "The greasy guy who always wears black," she said, remembering. "I can't imagine anyone making it with Ruskin—even Jewel."

"Think of it this way, sweetie—they deserved each other." Maggie let out another whoop of laughter. "Gotta admit, though," she continued, "even Taubman's better than Ruskin. I mean that old goat Irv can probably at least get it up! Think of the hours it must have taken Ms. Pulchritude to do the job with Ruskin. Probably used a forklift!"

God, I love this woman, Christine was thinking. What would I do without her?

"So what's she snared Taubman into doing?" Christine asked.

"Stockpiling her wardrobe, for starters. By three thousand bucks—that's three big ones a month poor little big boobs is stealing from the network. She claims she spends a thou a month just on shoes!"

"Shoes?" Christine repeated, taken aback. "You never see her feet on camera. Maggie, I didn't even have a wardrobe allowance. God, she's such a horror."

"Honey, you know what they say. What goes around, comes around. Jewel Crosse will get hers. You can count on it."

"Let's hope so," Christine replied. A look of inspiration crossed her brow. "Mag," she said, "maybe we should make sure she gets hers."

Maggie hooted. "Now you're talkin'! What'll we do? Mow her down on Sunset Boulevard with that perilous vehicle you wheel around town?"

Christine shook her head. "No, I'm serious. That bitch has gone too far on her own venomous steam. We've got to trip her up somehow."

Maggie was exultant. I've got her, she thought. She's hooked. I *knew* she couldn't get Hollywood out of her blood.

"What about insects?" she said, playing along. "Insects and rodents? That guy who supplied all the roaches, rats, and whatever for *Indiana Jones and the Temple of Doom?* How 'bout we get him to dump a barrelful of gnawing squirming critters in Jewel's dressing room. And—"

"Uh-uh," Christine interrupted, laughing. "They wouldn't go near her. She'd scare them to death."

"Yeah, really. We'll get brave ones," Maggie said. "I can see the headline in *Variety* now. BUGS BITE CROSSE AS SHE BITES DUST."

They both laughed until tears once more streamed down their cheeks. Christine fell back on the pillow, weak and out of breath.

"Got another idea," said Maggie finally. "How's this? We slap her favorite hairspray label on a can of roach killer, leave it on her dressing table and let her blast herself away."

"Tempting, very tempting," Christine agreed. "But still not quite right."

"I could leak the word to Taubman that she's got herpes."

"Maggie, now that's totally useless. Taubman has probably had it already for—"

"Christine—" Maggie's tone was serious now. "Forget about Jewel for now. It's you I'm worried about."

Christine was about to protest.

"No, let me finish. You look tired. And you've lost five pounds at least. Girl, you've got to shake yourself out of this self-imposed depression. Licking your wounds for a few days is one thing. Locking yourself up here is another. Can't you see it's time to come on back where you belong?"

"Maggie, your coming all the way out here means more to me than I can ever say. But it's no use. I'm not ready. And I've been home less than ten days anyway. I just don't see why—"

Maggie held up a hand, refusing to listen any further. "Now, please, Christine, hear me out one last time. I've got to get back by tomorrow night to check in with my sweet, even-tempered father and—"

"Oh, God," Christine blurted. "I'm so sorry. I haven't even asked how Billy is."

"He's fine. Hangin' in. He's a tough old geezer. Still at Cedars."

"And the lawsuit?"

"Unchanged. But I'm working on it. Spending a lot of time going through his private files—without his blessing, of course. I borrowed the key from his secretary and had a duplicate made."

"Naughty girl, as usual. Any clues?"

"Not yet. What a huge pain in the butt that whole business is."

"And how about Nickels? Things still hot between you two?"

"Never hot enough for me. But I do see him most every day. We're still in the 'just friends' stage. He probably won't realize I'm female till I knock off about a hundred more pounds."

"Maggie," Christine sympathized.

"*Hey,* it's all right. I'm down twenty-five already. And that's another reason why you better get your little buns back to town, Ms. DuRand. Because I'm still sweating it out with brawny Brad Larson—and you're going to have to make good on that trip to Hawaii soon."

Christine smiled. "I never go back on a promise," she said. "Twenty-five more pounds and the Kahala Hilton is yours."

"That shouldn't be too hard. I've sold my soul to the National TV News Syndicate for the next couple of weeks, and you know how fast they bang out stories. The slam-bam, thank-you-ma'am news. Should shake about fifteen pounds off the old bod, at the very least. I'm even covering the Academy Awards for them."

"At the Dorothy Chandler Pavilion?"

"Yeah, backstage. Then on to some 'fun' parties afterwards."

"God, what a zoo. I don't envy you that one, Mag," Christine said, remembering all too well what a hectic nightmare the Oscars could be. But this would also be the first Academy Awards ceremony she had not covered in years. And secretly she knew she'd miss the excitement

194

of that special evening. Just one more reason she couldn't face going back to Los Angeles—not yet.

"So," said Maggie with an air of finality, "we'll fly back together tomorrow afternoon. I've already made your reservation."

Christine regarded her dear friend and sighed. "You don't give up, do you? I guess that's why I hired you. Anyway, even if I wanted to— which I don't—I can't. I have a date tomorrow."

Maggie's eyes widened. "My, my—a date? With who? Oh, of course. Now maybe all this is making some sense. How is the good doctor?"

"Kent? He's fine," Christine said evasively.

"That's it? Fine? Just how fine is he? And how closely have you two gotten reacquainted?"

"Not close at all, I'm afraid. Just one lunch."

"Are you interested?"

"Umm," Christine stalled. "Yes and no."

"C'mon, Christine, are you interested—yes or no?"

"Yes. I guess so. But he lives here, Mag, and seems perfectly content to stay here the rest of his life."

"So you have a commuter relationship. Look at Phil Donahue and Marlo Thomas. They did it for years."

"That was Chicago and New York. We're talking L.A. and Minneapolis. Besides, he's not that interested in me."

"Are you crazy?" Maggie yelped. "Your onetime intended who married on the rebound from you and just dumped his wife. Not interested? You've gotta be kidding."

"You can't jump to conclusions like that. I have no idea why he divorced Lucia. We haven't discussed it. We haven't really talked about anything personal."

"He's just scared," Maggie declared matter-of-factly.

"Kent Michaels has no reason, none at all, to be afraid of anybody," Christine objected. "He can have just about any woman he wants. He's good-looking, a successful surgeon, independently wealthy—"

"Ohhhh, how wealthy?"

"Very. Old oil money. His dad's family was hooked up with the Rockefellers for years. But listen, Maggie, there's just no way. I haven't even gotten over Blair yet. Maybe I never will."

Maggie suddenly found herself arguing against the very thing she had traveled halfway across the country to achieve. If this guy was worth sticking around the frozen North for, well—

"Sweet lips," she said, "now you listen to Aunt Maggie. If you're interested in this rich hunk, you go for it. Hear me? He's probably a

195

decent guy who could care deeply for you. That's more than you can say about any of the men you've met in Hollywood. Ninety percent of them are shits—just like Blair Montgomery."

Maggie saw the surprise on Christine's face, and when she continued, her tone softened. "Chris, face it. If it weren't for Blair, you'd be back in L.A. by now. You could have pulled through Jewel's report, even leaving the network. But that bastard let you down—and you crumbled. So if you've got a chance for a solid relationship with an honest guy who isn't dazzled just because you're in the spotlight—a guy you've known forever and can trust—do it, girl. Everything else will fall into place."

"But—"

"No buts. For once maybe your personal life should come first." She winked again. "At least for a little while. So I'm giving you a reprieve. An extra few days here in Minneapolis to hook this guy. We'll worry about moving him to the West Coast later."

"Maggie—" Christine began, then stopped abruptly. She saw no reason to argue.

— CHAPTER —

Nine

Sunday morning in Arlington, Virginia. Ominous black clouds gathered overhead, threatening to dump fresh snow on the expansive lawns and luxurious homes below, which were already covered in a thick blanket of white. A blizzard was forecast to begin by noon, and snow-removal crews had been called in from their warm beds at daybreak to stand by, waiting to do combat at the winter storm's opening salvo. An unnatural quiet had overtaken Arlington, a waiting quiet. Church services were sparsely attended, except for the stubborn faithful, and the streets were nearly deserted. Here and there, children staged snowball fights or built snowmen in front yards, but even their play was subdued, respectful, in hushed anticipation of the show mother nature was about to give them.

In one Arlington home, however, the perilous forecast had not been permitted to disrupt an important gathering. The driveway, shoveled clean and bordered by high ridges of snow, was crowded with expensive American automotive machinery, Cadillacs and Lincolns, a Chrysler New Yorker.

Inside, a man named George Steele glanced over the figures on the torn sheet of paper he'd just been handed. Almost instantly the crevices in his square, unyielding face deepened. His eyebrows furrowed over the bridge of his nose, creating one long, bushy white line above his deeply hooded eyes.

"Gentlemen, before we wrap this up, there is some disturbing news I've just received from San Francisco," Steele announced in a powerful, raspy voice.

The twelve men sitting around Steele's long mahogany dining-room table were somber in dark suits and ties. Most were in advanced middle age or better. They turned their heads to look at him. Clinking spoons in coffeecups were silenced. The Virginia ham and eggs on their plates, the country biscuits slathered with butter and grape jelly, were momentarily ignored.

If Steele was agitated about something, it was imperative that they listen. His closest friend was President of the United States.

Back in the seventies, Steele was practicing law in Arizona when his friend Raymond Sullivan asked him to head up his campaign to become governor of that state. A decade later he successfully orchestrated Sullivan's bid for the Presidency. When Sullivan moved into the White House, he brought Steele to Washington as Counsel to the President. Since then Steele had served in a variety of roles, among them the post of Acting Secretary of Defense and head of the Environmental Protection Agency. Sullivan sent him wherever he needed a hardheaded trouble-shooter he could trust.

Now Steele had left Government, for there was a more important task at hand—Raymond Sullivan's reelection. Steele was again running the campaign. The Sunday gathering in his three-story Colonial home was a weekly strategy meeting, a mandatory session for key members of the Committee to Reelect President Sullivan. Those who attended referred to it, half-jokingly, as the prayer breakfast.

This particular meeting had moved along more swiftly than most, in deference to the threatened snowfall. Steele had got things underway as soon as the freshly squeezed orange juice was poured.

In a freewheeling manner they'd covered several orders of business. The latest polls, handicappings of the President's Democratic opponents, declared and undeclared, were analyzed and discussed. There was the phone call which Steele had received a few days earlier from the Republican governor of Arkansas, warning of hazardous fallout if a local party rift was not quickly contained. A peacemaking mission, it was decided, would be on a Monday morning flight to Little Rock. Final approval was also given to the President's upcoming tour of key cities in early primary states.

When Steele's assistant handed him the hastily torn-off Telex, the prayer breakfast had almost concluded. Through the window behind Steele, at the head of the table, the men could see that it had finally started to snow. Large wet flakes were falling. Soon their automobiles would be smothered in individual icy-cold mounds of whiteness.

But Steele was no longer concerned with the impending inconvenience of a blizzard. The figures staring back at him from the Telex were cause for real concern.

Steele stood up, a commanding presence in the room. "It seems," he began gravely, handing the torn paper to Philip Albrisson, the committee's campaign finance chairman, on his right, "that Roland Williams was a sellout in San Francisco. Twenty-eight thousand tickets sold. He raised close to half a million . . . *in one night.*"

There were murmurs of surprise and disbelief. Steele paused dramatically.

"As I see it, gentlemen, the Democrats really have our cocks on the chopping block on this one," he said now. "As you know, under the revised federal campaign-spending law, moneys raised by entertainers for political candidates are matched, dollar for dollar, by federal funds. But this calculation is now based on the gross receipts of any performance. The gross—" he slapped a hand sharply on the table— "that's before the rent on the hall, or the cost of security, or any advertising, before *any* of that is deducted."

Steele swept the room with his eyes, letting the import of his words sink in. "That means that Roland Williams, just by standing up there and wiggling his ass for two hours, has added nearly a million bucks to the Democratic treasury. I don't have to tell you the potential of this thing. It's a monster."

The men looked at each other. One of them, a sixty-year-old mortgage banker named Matthew Rosenzwieg, an acknowledged genius at campaign fund-raising, said, "What's good for the goose—"

"Sure, Matt, sure," growled Steele. "But who've we got to trot out for us?"

A few names were tossed out. But the apparent quickly became the obvious. When it came to big-name, big-draw entertainers, the Democrats had a virtual monopoly. The hard reality was that Pat Boone or Wayne Newton couldn't begin to raise the kind of money a Roland Williams was capable of pulling in.

After about fifteen minutes of fruitless discussion, George Steele placed his hands on the table and leaned in toward the twelve faces before him.

"Listen up. I want every one of you to have this echoing in your skulls when you leave here today."

When he had won their complete attention, he said slowly and evenly, "Gentlemen, my information is that Williams will be doing several more of these concerts—just how many is not known at this point. There is, of course, only one Roland Williams. But between the thirteen of us, we should, and we will, come up with a combined celebrity drawing card to match the Democrats'. By Tuesday morning at eight o'clock I expect a list from each one of you of at least twenty performers you recommend contacting regarding fund-raisers for us. I cannot overstress this, gentlemen. This may be our Achilles heel. We must set in place our defenses before the opposition gets too much of a head start."

"Okay, DuRand," Kent commanded in mock military fashion from the kitchen. "I'll outflank the linguine if you'll attack the fire."

"Yes, sir!" Christine replied cheerily.

The living room of Kent's cottage was dominated by a huge fieldstone fireplace. The furniture was sturdy pine. And there were big bright-blue and green pillows everywhere. Christine liked the room's simplicity, its air of solitude.

Humming softly to herself, she went about her task. She felt light and uninhibited. It was as if a great weight had been lifted from her shoulders. And in a way it had.

The drive to Forest Lake had been almost a transcendent experience for Christine. The more miles they put between themselves and the city, the more serene the view. Huge pines lined the way. Farms peppered with grazing cows and horses glided by. Here and there a clear stream or small frozen lake appeared at roadside. The air was crisp and scented with the cleansing pungent aroma of evergreen trees. The pristine surroundings invigorated and energized her, renewed her, as though a part dormant since girlhood was just returning to life.

And when Kent caught her hand in his during a long walk late that afternoon, Christine found herself doing exactly what she'd vowed not to. Opening up to Kent. Sharing her innermost feelings.

It was remarkably easy talking to him. She was ready. She didn't think about how to say it. The words came in a steady, even stream, flowing from her: The Jewel Crosse report and how she had felt in Taubman's office; quitting the network, perhaps prematurely; Steven Jacobs's mysterious appearance.

"It seems odd telling you this now, after the way I broke our engagement," Christine confessed as they sat down on a huge, sun-dappled tree stump brushed clean of snow at the side of the road. He turned and fixed his pale-blue eyes on her, but made no reply. "Kent," she continued quietly, almost in a whisper, "I want you to know how impressionable and immature I was then. I didn't mean to hurt you. It was . . . I needed time . . . on my own"—she laughed lightly—"to make my own mistakes."

Kent took both her hands in his. "I know," he said. "It took me years to realize it. But probably neither of us was ready. What did we know about settling down to a permanent relationship? We were both still kids." He grinned at her and added, "And as you can see, once I took the plunge, it didn't work out anyway."

Christine smiled back, knowing this offhand reference to his failed marriage was a mask for his true feelings. From other comments he'd made, it was obvious to her that the divorce had affected him deeply. Just the fact that it had been the first marital breakup in his family's history was enough.

This seemed to be their time for honesty, for sharing in the painful disburdening of their souls. Yet she hesitated to approach the subject of Kent's marriage.

She didn't have to. As they headed back toward the cottage, Kent began. Soon he, too, was freely exposing the scars of destroyed hopes and lost love. In a tone of voice which could only be called sadly fatalistic, he talked of Lucia and the problems they'd failed to surmount during two years of wedlock.

"It was a mismatch from the beginning, I guess. About the only thing we really shared was a devotion to our separate careers. Lucia's an incredibly hard worker—assistant to the district attorney. But her hours were more regular than mine, and she wanted to see more of me. My schedule made that impossible." Kent picked up a stone exposed in a plowed snowdrift, examined it thoughtfully, and hurled it into the vast white distance. "She also wanted to have kids," he continued. "And I just didn't feel ready."

They said nothing for a few long moments. Kent watched the golden afternoon sunlight dance on Christine's thick black hair, streaking it with shafts of blue.

You want this woman, he decided then and there. You want her back for keeps. It was more than a stirring of the embers of an old love—he knew that. Over the past ten years they had both been through a lot in their own separate ways. The old love was gone, the ashes cold, the heat and light only a memory. And now they were different people, and this was a new warmth, a new kindling. They were learning to appreciate each other all over again . . . for new reasons.

Christine was more than he had expected. She was a television star without a star's ego. She was a woman now, a strong, determined woman who had proven herself and survived a devastating ordeal. He was sorry for what she'd gone through back in Los Angeles. But he was very glad it had brought her home to him.

"How's the blaze out there?" Kent called out, easing the fresh pasta into a pot of boiling water.

"Just about to happen," Christine yelled back, as the flame of the newspaper torch finally caught, with a stirring whoosh of fire, the twigs she had carefully arranged under the big pine logs. She moved back a little and watched in delight as the jagged, ever-changing peaks of orange and yellow shot upward.

Staring into the incandescent blaze, she remembered her father's words the first time he'd allowed her to help bring in the big dry logs from the garage. "C'mon, honey, your old dad is going to show you the only way to ever play with fire."

Playing with fire. She turned the words over in her mind. Is that what I'm doing now, here with Kent? A relationship with him would be such a long shot. And yet I feel it—something's there. Maybe it's been there for a very long time, smoldering . . . waiting? She picked up a long thin stick and prodded the logs. Oh, b.s., DuRand. You're such a dreamer. One afternoon in the woods and you're swept away. Just be glad you're here. And quit projecting into the future, for heaven's sake. Nothing ever turns out the way you want it to. Just cool it—play it by ear.

"Come and get it," Kent bellowed from the kitchen as he clanged a large ladle on a saucepan.

"Mmmm, smells divine," said Christine. She carried the steaming plates of linguine and white clam sauce, while he grabbed a large wooden bowl of green salad, two glasses and a bottle of red wine and transported them to the living room.

"How about over here?" Kent suggested, kneeling on the floor close to the fire.

"Great."

Kent poured the wine. "A toast," he announced, holding his glass up to meet hers. "To your good health and our good times."

Their eyes met as they drank in the earthy fullness of the Cabernet Sauvignon. Christine felt a warm glow. Watch it, she warned herself.

Not too fast. But she wasn't really listening to her own inner monitor.

They ate hungrily, appetites stimulated by their walk and the wine. After dinner Christine offered to wash the dishes, but Kent insisted they just put them in the sink. He led her back to the living room, where they finished off the wine and watched the fire in silence as it flickered, popped, and snapped, dying slowly down.

Kent placed his hand on the back of Christine's head and softly stroked her curls. She turned to him wistfully.

"What a wonderful idea this was, Kent."

"You could use about a month of it."

"That bad, huh?" She had hoped he'd noticed that her spirits had improved.

"Ummmmm. You're getting better," he said warmly, leaning in toward Christine and briefly brushing his lips across her cheek.

"And how do I gauge my progress?" she asked, reaching up to play with a tendril of his unruly blond hair.

"Oh, you can't. That's the doctor's department. You just have to follow his orders and continue to improve."

"I'm not sure I like that," she teased back, letting her hand drop down around his shoulder.

"I'm certain you don't, not right now. But in time you'll get used to it. You'll find you even enjoy it," he said, bringing his lips closer and placing them softly on hers.

Christine kissed him hesitantly at first, as though she were testing him, unwilling to accept the warmth of his gentle yet demanding lips. Then she tilted her head up ever so slightly to look again into his eyes. They were filled with tenderness and a certain magnetism. He looked at her with total acceptance. She knew with him there would be no games, no question of trust. Kent Michaels was saying he cared for her and that he wanted her. He was saying it with his eyes, and now she felt him saying it with his lips.

Christine wrapped her arms around Kent's shoulders, drawing him down on top of her, and returned his kisses, over and over, feeling each time that she hadn't gotten enough, hadn't savored all the richness and sweetness and pleasure that had been locked up in this man. And in her, as well—in them both. It was different now. The feeling wasn't the same as when they kissed years ago. Those kisses were each thrilling little explosions, but this . . . this was something she'd never felt before. Being held and being loved and knowing she needed this man as much as he needed her. It was like . . . finally coming home.

For the first time in years, perhaps in her entire life, Christine didn't want to let go. She was going to hold on to Kent for as long as this incomparably peaceful feeling lasted.

His hands moved to her waist and up underneath her sweater. The feeling of his flesh against hers gave Christine a quick little chill. His strong fingers gently massaged the nipples of her firm breasts until they stood hard and erect. She could feel the goose bumps rise on her body as Kent started to slip the sweater off. She felt woozy, wrapped in a soft cloud somewhere high and far from solid ground, where sound and light were dreamily muted, indistinct, unearthly. Like that odd beep, what the hell was that anyway? All but inaudible at first, yet nagging, insistent.

"Oh, fuck!" Kent said.

Exactly, thought Christine, leaning on one arm, sweater draped from her neck. Jumping up, Kent rushed to the windowsill over the kitchen sink and lunged for his beeper, cutting off the relentless noise.

"Sorry. I'll have to call the hospital," he apologized, grabbing his down parka and heading for the door.

"But there's no phone here," she protested.

"Yes, there is. In the car."

By the time Christine had straightened out her sweater and pulled on her coat, Kent was in his Porsche with the motor running. She heard the end of the conversation. "Right Charlie, but it'll take me at least forty-five minutes to drive in, and I'm sure we won't be able to operate until one or two in the morning. Alert the supervising surgical nurse, will you?"

That was that. Within five minutes they were driving away from the cottage, with Kent explaining that a donor had just been located for one of his patients. "She's only thirty-five, but her heart's a mess. She won't last much longer without a transplant. We've got to operate as soon as possible," he said as he sped down the narrow country highway.

Christine settled back in her seat and cinched her seat belt tighter. "I am really sorry about this," Kent said distractedly. "I'll have someone drive you to your parents' house once we're back in town."

She looked over at him, thinking of making a joke about bad timing. But when she saw his face, jaw set in rigid determination, forehead creased in concern, she realized Kent was already miles away. His thoughts had left the warmth of the fireplace and their recent moment of overwhelming desire for each other.

She thought about asking him if she could stay and watch the operation. She knew some hospitals allowed that and instinctually Christine now wanted to become further involved in Kent's work. But she didn't know if he'd like having her there. She decided not to bring it up.

And so, as they flew through the darkness, Christine sat in silence, trying her best to be sympathetic, understanding of the demands put on Kent as a doctor. But now those demands were affecting her, too, and resentment was building within her. Deep inside, she knew, she felt anger. Not with Kent, but with herself, for being so disappointed. Act like a grownup, she told herself. He's saving someone's life. What does it matter that you're left in the cold?

Yet all during the frantic drive back to Minneapolis, her wonderful getaway with Kent a memory before it really had a chance to happen, Christine could not escape facing how much she detested this feeling. The feeling of depending on someone for her happiness. Of being controlled, in a way. She hated the fact that Kent had to go back so abruptly. But more than that, she hated caring so much.

Kent still hadn't said another word. Pulling up at last in front of the hospital, stopping with a sudden lurch, he yanked on the hand brake and leaped from the car, expecting her to follow.

Like so much baggage, Christine fumed.

But as she trailed Kent through the glass doors and into the stark hospital corridor, one of her mother's favorite aphorisms came to mind: "Well, dear, maybe this is a blessing in disguise."

Maybe it was, she thought. Maybe this was a warning, a signal that she wasn't ready to throw herself into a relationship and risk abandoning her career.

Suddenly, she knew. Yes, Christine decided, watching Kent disappear through the double doors. It's time—time to go back to Los Angeles.

Blair Montgomery was on his stomach, stretched out on his redwood deck, enjoying the soothing cadence of waves pounding on the beach beneath him. The early-morning sun was already hot.

His eyes were closed and he felt tired. But it was a good kind of tired. The kind that comes with finally finishing a movie and knowing in your gut that you've got a winner.

Crackup had wrapped earlier that week. Principal photography had gone three million dollars over budget, but Blair was relieved. He'd expected Jason Kramer's coke-and-heroin dependency to cost the project a great deal more.

But at last Kramer had come around. They'd sequestered him at a private detoxification center for a week. Then Blair paid a local Dr. Feelgood to give Kramer B12 shots on the set throughout the rest of the shooting schedule. It was a stopgap solution. But it did get his star through the movie. When it was finally over, even Blair had to admit that Kramer was pretty damn good in *Crackup*. He almost wished he had the guts to sign him for a sequel.

But Blair was too smart a producer for that. *Crackup* could become a classic, but it would also be Jason Kramer's swan song. If he went back to the drugs, he didn't have another movie in him. What the hell. He'd done it to himself. And no matter what, Blair's cut of *Crackup* was 10 percent of the gross.

He smiled contentedly. Now all he had to do was oversee the editing and looping, plan the advertising and release campaign, keep an eye on the bookkeepers at the studio where he had his distribution deal, and count his money.

Last night he'd hosted the wrap party. It was the traditional way a producer thanked his cast and crew for their long hours and hard work. It had been a real blowout.

Poor Shanu had fled in a panic after a rowdy technician dumped a pitcher of margaritas over the houseboy's head. It was the first time Blair had ever seen the little guy get excited. After screaming Oriental expletives at the portly technician, he'd turned to Blair and announced that he was leaving and would not return until the cleaning service arrived the next afternoon.

Blair couldn't blame him. The place was a circus. Far more people had shown up than he'd anticipated, and apparently everyone had brought a date—and an extra friend. He'd found three women going at it in his shower.

Now his beach house was a shambles. Broken glass on the carpet. Ashtrays overflowing with stubbed-out cigarettes and marijuana roaches. Globs of guacamole on tables and chairs. Blair's silver ice bucket was hanging from the antlers of the moose head over the fireplace. Thank God he was leaving for the weekend. When he returned on Monday, everything would be squared away again. The house would be spotless enough for a crew from *Architectural Digest*.

He rolled over onto his side, squinted up at the sun and decided it was about nine-thirty. In half an hour he would shower and shave, then drive down to Newport Beach to meet his newest "lady."

Cara Collins was a stockbroker he'd met through his attorney shortly after breaking off with Christine DuRand. Cara had Bo Derek eyes and a Loni Anderson body. A pleasing combination, Blair told himself. He was due for a change of pace.

Women, he mused, closing his eyes once again. They're so accessible, so interchangeable. It's like getting new tires on your sports car, once the treads go . . .

Blair's daydream was interrupted by a sharp pealing of the doorbell. He groaned softly and turned over on his stomach, thinking it must be the boy with his delivery of firewood. He would go away.

But the second penetrating ring was longer, more insistent. And the third seemed as though it would continue indefinitely.

"Goddamn it!" Blair shouted, hoping the delivery boy would hear. He pushed himself up off the deck floor and wandered through the maze of party damage. When he reached the tall mahogany door, he yanked it open angrily.

But it was not his firewood delivery. Standing there before him were two stone-faced men in khaki uniforms.

The tall husky one with the wiry brown mustache spoke first. "Blair Montgomery?"

Blair nodded silently. He was aware that in these situations the less said, the better.

"Kevin Maloney and Mario DePanisis from the sheriff's department," the tall one continued. "We'd like to come in and take a look around."

Blair was stunned. The shorter one, DePanisis, started taking a step forward.

"Hold it," Blair said, blocking the doorway. He was thinking fast. He knew his rights. "You guys have a search warrant?"

Maloney pulled out a sheet of paper, unfolded it and thrust it at Blair. As he did so, his thin lips pulled back into a self-satisfied smile, revealing a mouthful of yellowed uneven teeth.

Blair scanned the warrant hastily. It appeared to be legitimate. Then he moved his eyes back up to the top of the page and pretended he was reading every sentence thoroughly. He was stalling for time.

None of this made sense. A search warrant? Why? Who had instigated that? The party had been pretty wild, sure, some grass and a little coke. But things hadn't gotten that out of hand. Two deputies waiting to search his house? It was like a scene from one of his movies. Then it dawned on him. Of course. These two poker-faced clowns weren't real cops. They had to be straight from Central Casting, acting out a scene. That fucking Bernie Zimmerman. His director on *Crackup* was a well-known prankster. He'd sent over these two bozos. What a relief.

"All right, boys," Blair said, beginning to chuckle. "I get it. Come on, you can cut the crap now. Tell Bernie I . . ."

But the two men before him just stood there impassively. "Listen, Montgomery," Maloney said firmly. "We're being extremely patient with you. But you're beginning to waste our time." He yanked back the warrant and waved it at Blair. "This warrant here says we can come in and search your house. You wanna know why? Well, I'll tell ya. Seems a couple of gentlemen, a Mr. Litvinov of Bel-Air and a Dr. Sauter from Beverly Hills, are kind of upset about the things that go on around here after dark. Now what these two gentlemen have in common is fourteen-year-old daughters, Maria and Nancy. According to the girls, they attended a party at your home last night. And both of them claim that they were raped during the course of the evening by a movie star in your employ."

"Who?" Blair blurted out.

"Jason Kramer."

"That's impossible!" Blair lied.

"Nothin's impossible," said Maloney, easing his way past Blair. "I think you better let us come in and look around, then answer a few questions."

"Omigod, what was that?" yelped Christine, feeling a cold, hard jab into her left hip.

"Hey, pipe down, will you?" shushed Maggie. "Somebody will hear us."

"Okay. Okay." Christine made her way unsteadily forward in the darkness. "But who's around at one-thirty in the morning anyway? I thought that's why we came so late."

"Never know. Night janitor maybe," Maggie whispered, groping her way, unwilling to risk turning on the overhead fluorescents. "Damn," she complained, stumbling on a swivel chair. "I think they rearrange this furniture every other day. Over here, girl, to the right . . . aah, voilà." Closing the door behind them, she switched on the supply-room light.

"All these?" asked Christine, surveying the rows of cardboard file boxes piled on the floor.

" 'Fraid so," said Maggie, kneeling down beside one labeled June 1979. "Here's where I left off. Why don't you take July?"

Christine stifled a yawn. She was still suffering jet lag from her flight back to L.A. And some sort of emotional lag, she thought—brought on by everything that had prompted her hasty decision to return. But Maggie needed her help, and she couldn't turn down her friend.

Still, she'd counted on getting a little sleep, at least, before pitching in to help at this ungodly hour. But Maggie had shown up early. So they'd sat in Christine's kitchen until almost one o'clock, sipping black coffee as Maggie outlined the plan she called Operation Billy Goat.

Christine extracted the first manila folder from the box marked July 1979.

"What we're looking for—" Maggie started to say.

"—is anything suspicious," Christine said in a mock mysterious voice. "Anything that will lead us to the villain . . . *dum de dum dum* . . ."

"Okay, wiseass. Cut the crap." Maggie chuckled. She was examining a tattered yellow invoice. "This may not be *Dragnet,* girl, but it is serious. Do you know what old Billy Goat would do if he caught me in here?"

"Hardly likely, my dear Watson," remarked Christine, flipping through a handful of restaurant receipts. "Your dear daddy is no doubt comfortably ensconced in his bedroom suite, fast asleep."

"You know what I mean," Maggie persisted. The thought of it brought an image of Billy's furious face glowering over her. Growing bigger and bigger, redder and redder. "He'd . . . well, first he'd have me arrested for burglary and then he'd disown me."

Christine wasn't listening. Her attention had been drawn to the canceled check she held in her hand. "Mag, who's Vic Paluski?" She waved the check at Maggie. It was made out to Paluski for sixty-five dollars on July 31, 1979.

"Sorry, Sherlock, that's nothing. Dad's barber. Gets paid in lump sums every so often. Comes to the office twice a week."

"Twice a week? I didn't realize Billy was so fastidious. What about Mabel Everett?" Christine asked, holding up another check.

"Manicurist. You must be in the personal care file. Better move on."

"You mean Billy has all these people come to him?" Christine asked in amazement, looking over an invoice for alterations from M. Joseph & Sons, Tailors.

"You betcha, kiddo. If nothing else, Dad is a world-class manager of potentially wasted time. Not a second slips by in an unproductive manner."

"Just like his darling daughter," Christine teased, with an affectionate smile. She was happy to be here helping Maggie. Even as tired as she was, it was kind of exciting, and it took her mind off her own overwhelming problems. She just wished her eyes would stop drooping shut.

"Eric Myers . . . invoice for five hundred dollars?"

"Sorry, girl. No sale. He's Dad's researcher. Been on the payroll forever."

Two hours passed quickly as Maggie and Christine rummaged through three of Billy Rafferty's dusty file boxes, unearthing nary a clue. Neither of them had said a word in half an hour, but they both knew it was about time to pack it in.

"Hey, Mag?" Christine, breaking the silence, startled herself with her own choice. "Is this anything? Keith Spechter. Electrical contractor. Two thousand dollars for rewiring the office."

"Uhhhh," Maggie grunted, straightening her back as she got up off her knees. She looked at the green slip of paper Christine handed her. "Oh, yeah, I remember this. Dad insisted on a completely new lighting system when he moved in here from down the hall. Studio wouldn't go for it. So he picked up the tab himself. Took this guy Spechter a helluva long time, too."

She continued to stare at the faded invoice. "Yeah, and I remember Dad bellyaching how he was losing so much valuable time 'cause he couldn't get in here to work." She thought for a moment. "Could be *Precipice* was lying around. Maybe, just maybe—"

"What—you think this guy Spechter picked it up? Stole it? Seems kind of far-fetched doesn't it, Mag?"

"Hon. I thought you'd lived in this crazy town long enough by now to realize that nothing—absolutely nothing—is unlikely." Maggie pocketed the invoice. "You can never be too sure."

"I know, I know, or too rich—or too thin," said Christine giddily, placing the lid on the file box with a thud of finality.

"Cruel, girl, very cruel," Maggie said, sucking in her tummy. She took Christine's hand and helped her to her feet. "Come on, Dick Tracy, let's get out of here."

CROSSE COVERS OSCAR/STAFF MEMO
Four runners on motorcycles
Hotel room Monday night at the Beverly Hilton for the Governors' Ball. Manned by researcher, runner, interns

Ring-down phone in Press Room for communication with office
Beepers and walkie-talkies for all
Two writers on duty Monday night—all night!
Crew #1 with Field Director Fred Hartley for Dorothy Chandler
Pavilion arrivals at 3 P.M.
Crew #2 with Field Director Sharon Sherman inside Press Room
at DC Pavilion by 5 P.M.
Crew #3 meets Hartley at Beverly Hilton Hotel by 7 P.M.
Crew #1 becomes party crew and travels to Ma Maison by
6 P.M.
Crew #2 travels to Spago for party after Awards ceremony is
over
Crew #4 arrives at Swifty Lazar's party by 9 P.M.
Note: Runners to pick up tapes from each location throughout
the evening. We must screen tapes immediately if we're to make
the 8 A.M. feed deadline.
Good luck! . . . Richard Lawson, Producer

For the third time that day Jewel reread the memo. It was her
battle plan, the carefully honed strategy by which her staff would
gather all necessary footage for *Crosse Covers Oscar,* her half-hour network special on Hollywood's annual celebration of itself. Jewel had
informed her producer, Richard Lawson, of her desire: nothing less
than the finest day-after Oscars show ever televised. They'd reviewed
the plan countless times. Making sure. Double-checking. Academy
Awards night was the Super Bowl, the World Series, and the Olympics,
all compressed into a few unbelievably pressured, incredibly insane
hours. The margin for error in putting together a show like Jewel's
was slight. The logistics were staggering. Even when the Awards ceremony dragged on, as it inevitably would, her coverage had to run as
smoothly, as efficiently as a German train.

And now everything was set, the moment was at hand.

It was five-forty on a sun-bright afternoon as Jewel's long white
stretch Cadillac snaked its way through the assembled throng to the
entrance of the Dorothy Chandler Pavilion. The show was to begin at
six on the dot. Time enough for a swift, dramatic entrance. A gracious
wave and wide smile to the television crews assembled from all over
the world. And then on to her seat near the stage, just as the orchestra
leader heard the order through his headset for the opening downbeat.

Inside the limo Jewel was flanked by her hairdresser and makeup
man. Before she stepped outside, the two men combed and puffed and

powdered in a simultaneous flurry. As she glided down the red-carpeted entranceway, nodding to fans and photographers, Jewel spotted a cluster of local TV cameras, broadcasting live. Deliberately slowing her pace, she wormed her way into each shot: on live TV, they can't cut you out.

Closer to the door she spotted her own crew. At a nod from her field director, Jewel swept by the International Network cameraman with a regal whoosh—an establishing shot for her own show. Jewel, looking divine, tall, dramatically curved and poured into her white-and-silver Halston gown, arrives at Oscars. Perfect.

Inside the massive auditorium, as Jewel settled into her seat, she noted with a tingle of pleasure that she was only touching distance from several of the nominees. Robert De Niro to her right. Jo Beth Williams and Julie Andrews to her left. Browsing through the program, she reminded herself to send a nice bottle of champagne to the publicist who had arranged for her credentials and tickets. The rest of the media, most of them, the hoi polloi, were jammed into the Press Room upstairs. There they would remain throughout the show, waiting for the parade of winners to file by and utter their few, not always well-chosen words for posterity.

Jewel had no need or desire to rub shoulders with the dreadfully disheveled techies or the cub scout *shleppers* who called themselves celebrity interviewers. No, her staff would handle that, thank God.

She had assembled an exceptional group of field directors, writers, editors, and cameramen. Several she'd stolen away from her old show. *Inside Hollywood* had devoted two columns to the way she'd raided that station. She was especially impressed with her new producer. Lawson was young, energetic, totally dedicated—a breath of fresh air after Howard Ruskin. So what if he was also a flaming faggot? Jewel loved surrounding herself with gay men. They were loyal, they appreciated her sense of style, tolerated her moods, her outrageousness. She didn't need more sexual tension at the office. Irving Taubman was quite enough, thank you.

Jewel sat back and savored her accomplishment. Here she was, seated with the stars—and as well known to millions of TV viewers around the world as any one of them. Those poor *shlemiels* in the Press Room. For too many years she had been part of those star gang bangs, shouting out questions at the top of her lungs.

No more.

Her work would come later, at all the best Oscar parties. First, the

Governors' Ball, the one must-show for the winners, always a lavish affair. No cameras were allowed inside, but since Jewel was an invited guest, she was free to roam the ballroom, cajoling stars to follow her outside, where her crew would be set up and ready to roll.

Afterward, on to celebrations at Ma Maison and then superagent Swifty Lazar's tony gathering. And, of course, she also couldn't miss Spago, where the trendiest roosters and hens would gather to cluck over who won, who didn't, and who should have.

The audience was applauding the best supporting actress nominees, but Jewel hardly noticed. She was oblivious to the mounting tension as the five actresses were announced and clips of their movies shown. Her mind had already jumped ahead to her own show, in which there would be one, and only one, real star.

Christine brought her Mercedes to a skidding halt for a red light at Century Boulevard. Damn, she thought, flipping down the vanity mirror and giving herself a scrutinizing smile. I'm going to be late. Satisfied that no lipstick marred her teeth, she reached for a brush in her leather bag and ran it quickly through her hair.

It was a cool evening, a Monday, in Los Angeles. A week had raced by since she'd returned. She'd spent every day making endless calls to friends and acquaintances, doggedly trying to track down leads on promising television jobs. So far, no real prospects. And she was growing increasingly restless. It was all Maggie could do to calm Christine down at the end of yet another dead-end, frustrating day.

"Jeezus God, you're unbelievable," her friend would complain over drinks at Joe Allen's, or dinner at the Hamburger Hamlet. "I thought we Irish were the ones in an all-fired hurry. You're more impatient than anybody I know. Give yourself a chance, willya, girl? You just got back to town, remember? Besides, you know you can go back to Channel 8."

That was true. She could have her old job again. But Don Winston wanted her to sign a two-year deal. That was the complication.

Christine leaned back, waiting for the interminable light, and thought again about that bitch Jewel Crosse. Pondering how to knock Jewel off her pedestal had become her singular recreational pastime. She was determined to find a way.

It was the radio that jolted her back to reality. An interview with Jane Fonda was blasting from the Dorothy Chandler Pavilion. The

Oscars, Christine remembered abruptly. I'd almost forgotten about them. A surge of adrenaline shot through her, triggered by memories of Oscar nights past. The crowds. The fabulous gowns. The heated competition to get the best interviews, the best camera positions.

She fought to put it all out of her mind, concentrating instead on the wonderful escape that lay ahead for her. Santa Barbara. And the Biltmore, no less. Everyone says it's absolutely, perfectly romantic.

But it was more than just where. It was also with whom.

Right now her mission was making it to the Los Angeles International Airport on time. She watched as the aggravating light changed at last, pressed her foot down hard on the accelerator and wheeled onto Century. Before leaving her apartment she'd called the airline. The flight was running on time. If it hadn't been for that damned overturned truck with its load of oranges cascaded across the 405 Freeway . . .

Christine glanced at her watch and saw she had five more minutes. Maybe I can still make it, she thought. And as she deftly snaked the champagne-beige auto in and out of the lines of buses, taxis, and airport vans, Christine said a silent prayer that he would not step out of the airplane before she arrived at the gate.

Kent Michaels. He'd called just two nights before, announcing his visit matter-of-factly, but not before chiding her about her hasty retreat from Minneapolis.

"I couldn't believe it," he carried on. "Sunday afternoon. A message on my service that you'd left. Just like that. The last time I saw you was at the hospital."

Exactly, she thought, saying nothing.

Christine couldn't tell whether Kent was actually angry or just surprised by her sudden departure. But she enjoyed the effect it had on him. Any reaction from cool Dr. Michaels is better than none at all.

Lightly, she laughed off his complaints, telling him she'd been anxious to get back and investigate a prospective television job.

"Did you get it?" he asked quickly.

"Well, I don't know yet," she fibbed. "I've only been back a few days."

"How about spending some time with me? I'm flying in Monday evening.

"Vacation?"

"Sort of. I'm due at a seminar in San Francisco on Thursday. Thought I'd give California another chance. I'd like to explore Santa Barbara. My friends tell me it's one of the few civilized places in the state. I'm flying Northwest. Gets in about six-thirty. Meet you at the gate?"

"Okay, sure," Christine replied, a little baffled. And unnerved.

How presumptuous, she thought after hanging up the phone. How does he know I have time for him? I could have work to do. I could already have made social plans.

She smiled to herself now. From the warmth she'd heard in his voice, Christine knew she would have made time for Kent, no matter what. It was clear he had decided to give their relationship a chance—on her turf this time. No emergency calls. No Dr. Michaels. Just Kent. And as she maneuvered the Mercedes into a snug spot on the roof of an airport parking garage, she could feel the butterflies fluttering madly in her stomach.

"Repeat that, you little fairy, and you better hope I heard you wrong the first time!"

"I said, the tapes are blank," repeated the anguished voice. "Empty. Nothing on 'em. Blank."

"How the hell could they be *blank?*" Jewel shouted into the telephone in the Beverly Hilton suite the network had reserved for Oscar night. Four floors below, the Governors' Ball was in full swing.

Jewel had been working the party nonstop for nearly two hours. Things had gone perfectly all night, and she had been on a high, managing to snare several of the winners and even some of the losers. Most of them had been cheerfully cooperative when she suggested they follow her outside the ballroom for a brief chat.

She knew these short yet exclusive interviews would add a special dimension to *Crosse Covers Oscar,* a personal touch, an intimacy to set her show apart from all the drearily similar follow-up reports using Press Room footage only. A few more one-liners from big-name stars was all Jewel needed to round out her special.

Then, suddenly, disaster struck.

It began with what seemed an unbelievable bit of good luck, a true Hollywood miracle. Just as Jewel finished interviewing Albert Finney, she spotted one of the most publicity-shy actors in town, a man who'd been known to run from TV cameras. Coming in her direction was Jack Nicholson.

Nicholson was walking quickly, eyes cast downward, obviously attempting to make himself invisible to Jewel and her crew. But with the agility of a tennis pro returning a hard, low crosscourt shot, Jewel lunged with her microphone, catching the actor off guard.

"Why was it important for you to show up at the Governors' Ball tonight?" she demanded.

Perfect ambush. Nicholson was trapped. The camera was rolling, and anything he said would be seen by millions of viewers the next day. Jewel was all smiles, enjoying his discomfort.

"Well, ah, actually—"

Deet-deet-deet-deet-deet! The videotape recorder whined its warning in a high-pitched staccato. As Jewel whirled around angrily, Nicholson hooted in triumph and hurried off.

"Battery problem, Jewel. Sorry," apologized the blurry-eyed videotape technician.

"Sorry? Sorry!" Jewel glowered at him. "I lose the coup of the night and you're sorry?"

She turned to her field director, Fred Hartley. "And what about you? You're supposed to be in charge of this Mickey Mouse operation! How could you let that happen?"

Before he could reply, there was another electronic interruption, this time a quick blast of static on Hartley's walkie-talkie. Then came the unsteady voice of the intern stationed upstairs in the network's suite.

"Fred Hartley, please call Richard Lawson at headquarters immediately. I repeat, immediately. Emergency situation."

The emergency had brought Jewel up to the hotel suite, where she was now screaming into the telephone at Lawson. The three tapes of Press Room coverage from the Dorothy Chandler Pavilion were completely blank. Lawson had informed Hartley, and now Jewel, that there wasn't a frame of action or sound on any of them. All the initial reactions of the winners, the quick quips, the spontaneous thankyous—every one of them was missing, vanished. She couldn't possibly track down every winner for an interview tonight. Without the Press Room footage to build her show around, she was in serious trouble.

"Richard, you idiot, are you certain you've got the right tapes?" She was incredulous. This could not be happening to her. She would not stand for it.

Lawson insisted he'd personally accepted the tapes from the runner. Each one had been properly marked DCP/PRESS ROOM.

"What about the cameraman? What's he got to say?"

Lawson sighed. This was the part that made absolutely no sense.

"Joe says," he answered wearily, "that he spot-checked each tape in the camera before messengering it back. And, Jewel, I know this sounds unbelievable, but he swears it was all there."

"But it *isn't* there now, is it, shmuck?" Jewel snarled back at him. "Well, I'll tell you what you'd better do, Mr. Hotshot Producer. You'd better get your index finger out of your ass and start phoning some local newsrooms to see what we can borrow. I'll be there in twenty minutes. And if you value your job, Lawson, you'll have some Press Room footage for me to screen by then!"

Jewel slammed down the phone. Down the elevator and out through the lobby she went, rushing so quickly that halfway through the sliding glass doors the heel of one of her three-hundred-dollar custom-made sequined shoes snapped off. Limping but undaunted, she shoved her way through the press of fans and photographers, searching for her limousine.

Dozens of luxurious stretch Cadillacs and Lincolns jammed the long driveway, but Jewel's white limo was nowhere in sight. Even if she asked the doorman for help, she knew it would be at least a forty-five-minute wait.

Furious, standing lopsided in her heelless shoe, Jewel was stymied, momentarily paralyzed by her predicament. Then, like an answer to a prayer, she heard the low rumble of a motorcycle off to the left. The driver's jacket was clearly marked "IN." It was one of the runners, on his way back to the network with tapes.

"Hey, you!" Jewel bellowed. "Over here!"

The startled runner looked, did a double-take, and immediately swung over to the curb directly in front of her.

Without a word, Jewel hiked up her long white-and-silver gown, gathering it in her lap, and hopped on the back of the cycle. Kicking off her shoes, she slid her long legs over the driver's and clasped her arms around his waist. Her breasts jutted into the small of his back.

The driver broke into a delighted smirk.

Several paparazzi recorded the historic scene with quick hits on their Nikons. Tomorrow they would sell the photographs to the *National Enquirer* or the *Star*.

Oblivious to the stir she was causing, Jewel shrieked into the driver's ear, "Listen, you, get me to the network in fifteen minutes, or you'll be heading right back to the unemployment line."

"Yes, ma'am, Miss Crosse," he said tamely, then lurched forward with such force that he almost threw his passenger to the ground.

But Jewel held on, all the way through Beverly Hills on Santa Monica Boulevard, up La Cienega and straight across Sunset. Her hair was flying, her gown was waving, her teeth were clenched so fiercely her jaw ached.

When she stamped into the office on bare, dirty feet, she was a sight. Her pantyhose were torn. Her dress was soiled and ripped. Her always-in-place hairdo stood straight up on either side, like two steel wings. But not one of the six staffers facing her had the courage to laugh. One look at Jewel's face told them that would be a mistake.

"Well, Richard!" she cried as she charged to her exhausted producer's side. "What have you got for me?"

Richard Lawson was in agony. He'd been up since four in the morning, fighting with his lover. Two hours later he'd arrived at the network. And it was now well past midnight. His throat hurt from chain-smoking. His tongue was sore from too much bad coffee. His eyes were bloodshot. His stomach was in knots. Richard Lawson was not ready to have a tirade unleashed upon him.

"Richard!" she repeated with vehemence.

Tell the truth. There was nothing he could do but tell the truth.

"Jewel," he began weakly, "I've tried. God knows." He draped a tired hand over his telephone. "I've called every local newsroom in town and all the networks. I even tried a station in San Francisco that has a crew down here covering the Awards. But the answer's always no. Nobody is willing to let us borrow the tapes."

It was the truth, but not the whole truth. He said "us"; he'd really meant "you." The more stations Lawson called, the more he realized what he was up against. Overnight editors had laughed out loud at Lawson's request. Jewel's fate to them was simple justice. Nobody was willing to help her out. Her ruthlessness had made her poison to her own colleagues. She had ignored one of the oldest adages in the business: Be nice to people on the way up, because you might meet them again on the way down.

Lawson did his best, but had exhausted all the possibilities. He had come to face the fact that Jewel was either going to have a very lame show, or no show at all.

"They said no?" Jewel exclaimed. "No? That is *unbelievable,* Richard, unacceptable. What about money? That usually makes a difference, you know."

"Of course I offered to pay . . . but . . ."

"But, but, but," Jewel mimicked him. "Richard, you are a pussy.

218

No wonder I have to do everything around here myself." She jumped off the desk top on which she had been perched. "Keep screening those party tapes!"

Retreating to her private office, she slammed the door. She collapsed into a pink satin-covered chair and stared blankly at a Manet painting, a sylvan landscape, across from her desk. Expensive artwork and imported antiques, ordered by Irving Taubman himself, filled her office, but tonight she barely knew where she was.

What she needed was a moment to think clearly.

A few seconds later, Jewel reached for the phone and with one long red nail punched out a familiar number. She had it now, the answer. There was always a way.

"Howie," she cooed coquetishly, "sorry if I woke you . . ."

"Uhhh?"

"It's me."

"Uh?"

"Me. Jewel. If Alice is there, why don't you take this in the bathroom. I have a crisis, Howie, and you're the only one who can help."

Howard Ruskin grumbled something inaudible and hung up the phone.

Jewel redialed immediately. "Howie, how can you be so cruel? Please, sweetie, I *have* to talk to you," she pleaded. "Just give me five minutes."

Howard was awake now, and, despite himself, he was curious. He'd never heard that note of desperation in Jewel's voice before. It pleased him. He gave his sleepy wife a garbled excuse and watched her hang up the phone as he picked up the extension in the bathroom.

"Yeah?"

"Sweetie, you have to help me out. I'm in a bind over here with my post-Oscar special. Can you believe it, all my Press Room tapes are blank! And I just know you have what I need in your news department." She waited for Howard to agree, but there was no response. "Howie? I mean it when I say I'm desperate. And you know if you do me this teensy favor I will repay you—you do know that, don't you?"

Howard Ruskin sat on the toilet cover scratching the stubble on his chin and thinking about the rare opportunity which had just presented itself. He knew he could get the footage—that was no problem. The news director at his station owed him. But why help the bitch? She'd not only dumped him, but stolen his key people away. Still, on the other hand . . .

Howard belched loudly into the phone. He did not bother to excuse himself. "Okay, Jewel," he said finally. "I'll get you the footage, but it's gonna cost you."

"Of course, sweetie pie," she sighed, vastly relieved. "Anywhere, anytime you like."

"That's not what I mean, Jewel," he replied gruffly. "I mean cash—dollars and cents, get it?"

"Of course I get it, Howard," she snapped. "How much?"

"Fifty thousand," he said, knowing she wouldn't go for it.

Jewel caught her breath. "Fifty is a little steep, Howie. Let's be sensible. How about ten thousand?"

"Forget it, honey lips. That's insufficient," he said with finality. "Twenty thousand dollars or nothing. A certified check made out to me personally. Take it or leave it."

Eight thirty-five. My God.

Christine had awakened with a start, not sure of where she was. Then in the next instant she knew very well where, and why it was so late.

Kent.

They'd made love until the early hours, collapsing into exhausted sleep well beyond three o'clock. Christine had counted on her inner alarm to wake her up, but this once it had failed her. And Kent had a noon flight out of Los Angeles International Airport.

If we leave in an hour we should be all right, she thought, walking to the bathroom and groping for her toothbrush.

Returning to the bedroom, she stopped for a moment to watch him as he slept. Kent was sprawled over three-quarters of the bed, lying on his stomach. His deeply tanned arms were dark against the crisp white sheets. His hair was tousled, more tendrils than usual grazing his forehead. On his lips rested a comfortable half smile, as if he were enjoying a pleasant dream.

She fought the urge to crawl back under the covers and cuddle up close. Their impromptu vacation had been wonderful and romantic and she didn't want to let it go. But she had known that all too soon Thursday would come. And there was a promise to herself to be kept. No disappointment would show, no matter how she felt inside. She would smile and say goodbye without hesitation. No long, sad looks. No regrets.

But she also knew that would not be so easy. Forget these marvelous two days in Santa Barbara? Swimming and playing volleyball on the beach. Wheeling along the magnificent bike path overlooking the Pacific. Holding hands on long romantic walks. Exploring the historic Old Mission together. Leisurely dinners at Penelope's and El Encanto, high in the hills.

Most of all, how could she forget the nights, here in this enchanting bungalow hideaway at the Biltmore?

Things had been a little awkward, a little tentative in the beginning. After the drive up from L.A. they were both famished, so they'd quickly shared a meal of veal and crusty bread at Rocky Gallante's on State Street. From there, driving the short distance to the hotel, she'd begun to feel uneasy, off balance, not at all sure her legs would work properly when she tried to get out of the car.

She knew why. Christine's self-confidence was at an all-time low. And here she was with a handsome, dynamic man who seemed to hold a certain mesmeric power over her. And it frightened her. She didn't want to relinquish herself to any man, not again. It had to be on her terms this time. But she wasn't sure she was up to the challenge. Christine felt more than a little vulnerable. She felt practically defenseless.

Hey, don't get so carried away, she warned herself as they pulled up in front of the red-tile-roofed Biltmore that first night. You're attracted to him, yes. But you know how to keep it light. This is no time for heavy romance. Just have a good time. You're not making any lifetime decisions here.

But as they checked in and were shown to their beautifully appointed bungalow on the manicured grounds, the memory of that night by the fire on faraway Forest Lake kept replaying through her mind. How she'd felt when he touched her. How much she'd wanted him.

This time the feeling—the burning anticipation—seemed even stronger. From the moment the door closed behind them and Kent reached for Christine, she was again pulled toward him by an irresistible magnetism of a strange and powerful sort. When he held her close, her head resting against his chest, his hands stroking her hair, her neck, and then, at last, when his lips sought out hers, the distant voice inside was so certain, so definite: Don't let this stop. Please don't ever let it stop. I want to hold on to this man forever.

Logically she knew that was impossible. He would go back to Minneapolis. She would stay. But by then Kent had begun unbuttoning her sheer blouse, and Christine was further away from ordinary logic than she had been in a long, long time.

Still, she struggled to hide the depth of her emotion. If he wanted her, he would have to win her.

"You, ah, don't have your beeper with you, do you?" she whispered as he nuzzled her neck.

"Threw the damned thing away."

"Yeah, I'll bet." She helped him remove his shirt.

"How 'bout if I promise never to have it around when you have your clothes off?"

They fell together onto the king-sized bed.

"Sounds fair to me."

"I want to devour you, Christine DuRand," he said, running his tongue down her cheek to her lips.

Do it, she thought. Devour me. Take me with you, wherever you go. Make me a part of you and make this feeling go on through eternity. But she said nothing. She couldn't.

Lying next to Kent, there were no words she could utter to let him know how she felt. She said it with her eyes and her touch and her lips, as he did. Their lovemaking went on and on, the minutes extended, their desire insatiable. Their naked bodies fit toegther so well that it seemed they'd made this tender, rapturous love before, many times. Synchronization in their movements was so graceful, their limbs entwined and stroked and touched with such fluidity, that it was as if a choreographer had directed them in their intimate love dance. Here at last they had perfected the scene, in this sumptuous retreat with the ineluctable sweetness of night-blooming jasmine wafting through the open windows.

The next two days passed like a romantic dream. Just the two of them, enjoying the city and each other. When they made love again and again, Christine felt herself lifted to a special place she had never known before. Sex with Kent was so exquisitely tender, yet intensely passionate. She could not have imagined it possible.

"Hey!" came Kent's sleep-deepened voice from the bed as Christine was toweling off from her shower. "Anybody home?"

"You betcha, sleepyhead." She flung open the bathroom door and emerged wrapped in the towel. "Your turn for the shower. And we're on a tight schedule. Better get a move on."

He bounded out of bed and faced her, naked, his hands grazing her breasts and finally settling on her waist. "I was hoping you'd join me."

"Uh-uh." She felt a thrilling quiver in her groin. "We have to leave in less than an hour if you want to get to San Francisco on time."

"In that case, I'll stay dry," he announced, yanking her towel away. And in one swift motion he swept Christine up in his arms.

"Kent!" she yelped in a voice full of surprise. "What are you doing? We've got—"

"At least twenty minutes to spare, that's what we've got," he said, carrying her toward the bed. "That foreign whirlybird you drive will get us to the airport in no time." Gently he put Christine down on the rumpled sheets and settled lightly next to her. "Before we have to say goodbye, let's at least take the time for a memorable morning."

Kent wrapped his arms around her and held her closely. And when they began to make love, Christine's resolve melted a little more with each kiss, every longing caress. She wanted to go on clinging to him, yet knew she'd have to let him go back to his world, as she carried on alone. Always alone.

She'd promised herself she wouldn't cry, but as their lovemaking ceased and Kent reached for the phone, she had to turn away to hide the tears. How could I do this to myself? she was thinking. How could I walk right into this knowing how empty I'd feel when he left?

She heard him arranging for a later flight and looked up in surprise.

"Hush," he said, leaning over to kiss her. "So I'll miss some boring speeches. I'd much rather relax and have something to eat with you. Besides we need time to talk—neutral turf where I'm not tempted to tear your clothes off."

Once they'd ordered breakfast in the nearly deserted formal dining room of the hotel's main wing, Kent took Christine's hands in his and looked at her determinedly.

"Christine," he began gently, "you might think this is a bit premature. But I think it's time for you to come back home where you belong."

Christine caught her breath. It was more of a choke than a protest.

"Now don't cut me off before you've heard what I have to say," he persisted. "I want you near me, Christine. And unless my powers of perception have failed completely, I think you want that, too. You're in a transitional stage right now. And you've been through a bad time. I know that fighting spirit of yours wants to forge ahead and show the world you can do it again. Be a big TV star. And maybe you can. But so what? What's that got to do with living life fully? What we have together and what we could have in the future is something very

223

special, Christine. We both know that. And there's no reason you can't continue working in Minneapolis. You know you could work for any station in town there—if you wanted to."

He paused as the waiter placed two heaping bowls of steaming whole-grain cereal before them.

Christine was stunned. She felt tongue-tied. Whatever her dreams of a relationship with Kent, moving back to Minneapolis had never once been part of them.

Kent watched the waiter depart and then continued. "I think we're good for each other, Christine. We've been apart for a long time, and now it's time to be together again. I want you in my life."

Christine's heart pounded wildly. Tiny beads of moisture lined her forehead and her upper lip. Her throat felt dry and clogged. Attempting to regain calm, she sipped at her ice water, then put the glass down carefully. Finally she looked up at Kent.

How she wanted to say yes. He loved her. That's what he was saying. And he didn't want to be without her. This strong, determined, great-looking, successful doctor wanted her, probably as his wife. Why couldn't she just make her life easy for a change and give in? Reach out for someone who could make her feel complete?

"Kent. I—I just can't move right now," she heard herself saying. "I really have to stay here in California. Rebuild my career. It's taken me so long . . ." Her eyes pleaded with him to understand. But she could see he wasn't going to.

"But you've got nothing in Los Angeles right now. And it's such a fucking competitive field you've chosen, Christine. You've *done* it once, sweetheart. You were a star, with your own show. An internationally recognized name. That's more than most people ever get a shot at. Why do you have to prove yourself all over again in Hollywood? What's the great satisfaction? I just don't understand."

She felt the dreamy mists of their days together vanish in the sudden glare of hot and unpleasant reality. She hated being put on the defensive like this. "What kind of satisfaction do you get when you perform a successful transplant?" she rejoined. "Don't you think I can reach those highs in my work, too?"

"Of course I do. But you really can't compare the two. I mean, medicine is—"

"Is what?" She cut him off. "Is legitimate and television inconsequential?"

"Well, no, it's just that . . ."

"What I do can't compare to what you do, so I should move, right?"

She tried to say it teasingly, in hopes of breaking the rising tension, but her words had an edge nonetheless. "Kent, I feel very strongly about you—about us. But I—well, maybe what we need is time."

"Sure." He lowered his glance and poked a spoon into the cooling cereal.

"Don't be hurt, please, Kent."

"Hurt? I'm not hurt." He pushed away the bowl in a gesture of frustration. "But you don't get it, do you? You say we need time. Time for you to find another job out here, or God knows where? And *then* where will we be? Don't you see, Christine? That's exactly why I brought this up now, before you sign your life away to some television station. Now at least you have a choice. All you have to do is make it."

— CHAPTER —

Ten

Tashi had made up her mind. One more day was too much, even if it meant giving back all the beautiful clothes and forfeiting the two thousand dollars a week she was being paid. She didn't care. She would confront Roland.

Turning a corner, she saw the entrance to the Regent Sydney Hotel and shivered, despite the typically mild early-winter temperature in the high sixties. The Regent was a magnificent high-rise located on St. George Street, overlooking the harbor. It seemed to climb straight out of the water, a proud and majestic monument to the modern-day Sydney that was young, brash, vigorous, with a population of more than three million—a thriving metropolis. And a far cry from its origins as a struggling convict settlement. The very spot on which the Regent now stood in splendor had been once occupied by an untidy huddle of tents and huts.

Tashi felt like one of the convicts who had first settled the site. Traveling with Roland Williams, as far as she was concerned, was comparable to being in prison, and this hotel was just another gilded cage.

At first she had tried to overlook Roland's coolness. He would surely come to accept her presence. She even deluded herself into believing they might grow to be friends. But by now she was thoroughly convinced Roland Williams was not going to bend. He disliked her and he was deliberately making her life miserable. When they were thrust together in public, he was barely civil. The rest of the time he shunned her, making it a point to exclude her altogether whenever possible. She was also off-limits to everyone else in the entourage; no one dared approach Roland's "fiancée." The only other member of the tour who knew the truth was the road manager, Dirk Andrews. And he hadn't said more than two words to Tashi since they left San Francisco.

For weeks now she had been alone. There was no one to talk to. No one to spend the afternoons with. No one to meet for lunch or dinner. She had plenty of money, an unlimited expense account and the allowance that Diedra had given her for more clothes. But she was tired of shopping. She was tired of doing anything alone. It was becoming a struggle to go out by herself every day, aimlessly walking unfamiliar streets. The museums, the standard tourist attractions interested her no longer.

Even at Sloane's Fish Market there had been a conviviality, a feeling of companionship. She wasn't lonely then; she'd had people to talk to. Now she had no one, nothing. She was spending more and more time in the hotel, wherever it happened to be, ordering from room service, watching television, reading. The isolation was driving her mad. It couldn't continue like this.

Now, after passing through the grand lobby and riding the elevator up to her suite, Tashi determinedly turned the key in the lock. A loud click, and the double doors swung open. She ignored the splendid furnishings, heading directly to her bedroom and changing swiftly into a smart emerald-green suit. Adding chunky silver earrings and a matching necklace, she gave herself an appraising glance in the mirror. Satisfied, she left.

She looked glamorous as she stepped into the waiting limousine. The outfit would photograph beautifully. Tomorrow her picture would appear in all the local newspapers. Tashi Qwan standing next to superstar Roland Williams, her fiancé. Holding his hand. Smiling devotedly at the man she loved.

She knew the scenario by heart. The media and Roland's fans couldn't get enough of Tashi. She was swiftly becoming one of the music world's most photographed trendsetters. *Rolling Stone* had already dubbed her "more exciting than Bianca Jagger or Alana

Stewart in their prime." *Womens Wear Daily* had assigned a special reporter to trace her every public footstep. By now Tashi was used to seeing herself alongside Roland in the newspapers and on the covers of the world's leading magazines.

Denny Bracken was overjoyed. "You're doin' great, kid," he'd congratulated her over the phone only yesterday. "They love ya. Just keep on foolin' 'em, sweetheart. You're one dynamite actress."

But Tashi was thoroughly disenchanted with her role. She wanted out. Making her way through Sydney's vast Entertainment Center, where she would co-star in yet another photo session, she told herself this performance would be her last.

"I need to talk to you," she whispered to Roland as the photographers clicked away. She knew she had to say it now, before the session ended. Immediately afterwards Roland was due at a sound check in the immense concert hall nearby.

"For crissakes," he snapped, struggling to maintain a tight-lipped smile for the cameras, "can't it wait?"

"No. It can't." She blinked back at the incessant barrage of flashbulbs, hoping she didn't look as strained as she felt.

"All right. My dressing room, after this. But only for five minutes."

Later, as the photographers were reluctantly led away, Roland said something in private to Dirk Andrews and stalked off. Tashi followed, a few steps behind. Her heart was pounding and her knees felt weak. The speech she had carefully rehearsed on her early morning walk had deserted her. Now, uncertain how she would find the words, she only knew she had to go through with it, that it was too late to change her mind.

Backstage, in the star's spacious quarters, Roland slammed shut the door after them. He poured himself a glass of mineral water, offering her nothing. When he turned toward her, Tashi saw the impatience of his expression and felt the rage boil up inside her.

"I know you don't want me here," she blurted out. "You've made that crystal clear. And I don't want to go through this any longer either. So I—I'm leaving tomorrow morning." She could feel the muscles in her throat constricting. "You'll probably want to tell Mr. Bracken."

She didn't expect him to argue, and she spun around to leave, eager to get away before she lost her grip on her emotions. But to her surprise, Roland moved with lightning speed. Before she could reach the door, he'd stepped in front of it and was blocking her exit.

228

He didn't know what this bitch was up to. He suspected it was a ploy for more money. No doubt she must realize the impact she was making. Burton and Bracken were pleased. Even Roland couldn't deny that a certain kind of electricity had been generated on this tour by his trumped-up relationship with Tashi Qwan. And the rumors about his sexual preferences had been buried, forgotten, stopped cold. Whatever she was doing, it was working, that was all Roland knew.

"Hold it," he commanded condescendingly. "What's your game, lady? I thought people in your business knew when they were well off."

It was the way he said "business"—she knew what he was implying. But she didn't fully realize what she was doing—didn't feel her hand drawing back. It was a spontaneous response. Not until she felt the sting of Roland's flesh against her fingers did she know she had slapped him hard on the face.

At first he stood there, unable to believe what had happened. No one had ever had the audacity to strike him—not since he'd left the unhappy foster home of Freddie and Mary Mae Williams had anyone dared to try. But here this vicious, for-rent female had just hauled off and slugged him.

He grabbed for her, taking hold of her slender shoulders and shaking her violently. "Listen, woman," he spat out, "I don't know who the fuck you think you are—"

There was a sharp knock at the door. "Roland? Everybody's ready to go. You set?"

"Not quite. Another five, man!" Roland yelled at the door, then immediately started in again on Tashi. "Where the hell do you come off insisting on talking to me and then—"

"Please," Tashi pleaded, trying to squirm away, "just let me go. You don't want me here. I know you don't like me. I just can't *take* it any longer." Her pent-up feelings demanded release, and she began sobbing miserably. "You can have your money and all the clothes. I'll even pay the airfare back to London. Just let me go!"

Roland released his grip on her shoulders and watched as she took a pathetic swipe at the tears in her eyes. Her mascara was smudged and her nose was red and shiny. The elegant exterior, the worldly facade, was ruined, and she suddenly looked young and utterly helpless. Roland was dumbfounded. Now he didn't know what to think.

"Just a second," he said, taking a step back. "Are you honestly telling me you want out?"

Tashi looked up at him with swollen but still lovely eyes and nodded. From a pocket in her skirt she pulled out a tissue and blew her nose.

"But I don't get it. You've got a great setup here. No one's making any demands on you. You're free to come and go. And all the money . . ."

Tashi shook her head in protest. "I don't want it anymore," she said in a voice still not under control. "I just want to go."

"What, you don't need the bread?" he asked, eying her skeptically. "Then why take this job? You knew what you were in for."

"No," she answered, staring at her feet. "I didn't. I—I did need the money, though, because my father—but you don't care, it doesn't matter."

"I asked, didn't I? Tell me."

"He died. Recently, I mean. My father died. And I had to drop out of veterinary school. This job would have paid for it all."

So it *was* true, Roland thought. He remembered Burton reeling off some background on Tashi, including this veterinarian business. At the time he'd figured it was just an obvious ploy, an attempt to make him more receptive to her.

"How long have you been interested in animals?" His curiosity was piqued. This undeniably beautiful young woman—so independent and detached at the parties and photo sessions, always cool, in control—now seemed a different person altogether.

"Since my father first took me to the London zoo." Tashi blew again into her tissue. "He always encouraged me to learn about everything. The animals I saw fascinated me. It just seemed natural that I would study veterinary medicine."

During the next few minutes Roland learned a great deal more about the woman the newspapers had been calling his fiancée. She told him about her mother's restaurant in Hong Kong and working at the fish market in London, about answering the classified ad and getting the cablegram that led to this assignment.

"I'm sorry I slapped you," Tashi apologized sheepishly.

"Forget it." The anger had drained from his face and he was smiling slightly. "I guess I was a bit of a jerk. I—"

It was Dirk Andrews's heavy-fisted pounding on the door.

"On my way!" Roland shouted, then turned back to her. "Listen," he began uncomfortably. "I . . . uh . . . understand now why you want to leave. But I just wanted to say one more thing."

She looked at him questioningly.

"That, well . . ." He appeared to be struggling to find the right words. "That, uh, I hope you'll reconsider . . . Tashi."

Before she could reply, he was gone.

Jewel slipped out of her limousine under the porte-cochere of the cheerfully pink-and-green Beverly Hills Hotel. She was dressed in a stunning translucent silk shirtwaist dress in a delicate shade of orchid. Bold slits ran up either side of the skirt.

"Pick me up at six o'clock sharp, Tom," she instructed her driver.

Strolling up the long canopied entranceway to the hotel's lobby, she was in no hurry, though already fifteen minutes late for her appointment. No need to rush things now. She had what she wanted.

With the Press Room footage, *Crosse Covers Oscar* had gone together beautifully. The show was a tremendous ratings success, Irving Taubman was happy, and there was talk of scheduling more special reports for her. All of this pleased Jewel immensely. Still, the memory of the absolute hell she had been forced to go through on Academy Awards night had not faded. It continued to rankle deeply. She would not be satisfied until she'd unmasked the culprit who'd stolen her tapes. And that was exactly what had happened. There was no doubt in her mind.

It could have been one of her staffers, but Jewel suspected this had not been an inside job. More likely the thief worked for another network. Whoever it was had to know television news. Stealing three tapes from the closely guarded Press Room inside the Dorothy Chandler Pavilion on Oscar night took considerable ingenuity.

Sweeping into the Polo Lounge, Jewel spotted the familiar figure in black ungracefully draped over booth number one. The very sight of him, waiting there patiently, disgusted her. I'm not sure I can go through with this. But she knew she would, and that it would be easy. She'd held him at bay for almost a week on the certified check. Howard Ruskin had no balls. He was a pushover.

Jewel smiled and nodded toward the afternoon maitre d'. Automatically her eyes gave the half-empty room a well-practiced scan. No important faces. Good.

"Howie, sweetheart!" She settled in beside him, simultaneously taking a quick nip at his thick lips. "How are you, dearest? You look wonderful."

"Fine, Jewy," he replied drily, using the nickname she despised. "I missed your Oscar show. How'd it turn out?"

"Ohhhh, Howie." She puckered up and planted a kiss this time on his left jowl. "You're such a sweetie. My show was wonderful, thank you, simply grand, with superduper ratings. Everyone at the network was so pleased and so complimentary." She nudged his black polyester jacket playfully with her elbow. "But *we* know the truth, don't we? Without you, Jewel couldn't have managed."

Howard grimaced. "Now," he said stiffly, not looking at her, "about that monetary matter."

The waiter appeared with a glass of white wine and placed it in front of Jewel. She picked it up immediately. "Thank you, Sal."

"Pleasure to see you again, Miss Crosse."

"I've got a joke for you, Sal." She winked at Howard, then turned back to the waiter. "It's as awful as the ones you tell."

"Yeah?" The waiter was wary. He shifted his weight uneasily from foot to foot.

"Ready?"

"I guess so, Miss Crosse."

"Okay. What's twelve inches and white?"

The waiter looked at Jewel, then helplessly over at Ruskin. "What?"

"Nothing, Sal. Absolutely nothing!" Jewel laughed wickedly while the waiter squirmed for a moment before excusing himself.

Howard let out a whoosh of air. "Jewel, are you finished with the Catskills *shtick?* Can we talk business, please?"

"Howie, darling," she said soothingly, "can't we just enjoy the moment? We have so many memories right here at this table . . . and upstairs." She winked at him again. "I'm in a horny mood. Want another tequila?"

"No. No, thanks." Howard took a long gulp of the golden liquid in his glass. "Jewel, I don't mean to sound doubtful or anything, but do you or do you not have the certified check?" As he asked the question, Howard felt the pressure of a small warm hand on his knee. Peering down, he saw Jewel's long red fingernails inching upward toward his thigh.

"Must we discuss money? Wouldn't you rather just talk about us and the things we used to do . . . to each other?" Her breasts were pressing up against his arm.

Howard cleared his throat and shifted in his seat, self-conscious about Jewel's roaming hand, yet unwilling to remove it. He still refused to look directly at her. He knew too well the powers of Jewel Crosse. She was unlike all the other women he had had during his fifteen years of marriage. Before Jewel, he had always initiated sex.

232

Always called the shots with women, always held the power. When Jewel abruptly ended their affair, she'd come as close as anyone to emasculating Howard Ruskin. He had come to hate her for it, but hatred alone did not provide immunity from her charms.

Her hand was now massaging his inner thigh. Soon, he knew, she would have his crotch firmly in hand. Oh, how he wanted that—wanted her. Just once more. He would screw her senseless, thrusting himself into her so savagely and for so long that she would scream, not in pleasure but in pain. Plead for him to stop, yet want him at the same time, need him, inside her, mauling her massive tits, pounding deeply into the soft dark-brown triangle between her legs.

No. Howard tossed down another gulp of tequila. No, he cautioned himself. Don't let her start. Don't fall into the old trap. Just get the goddamn check and sail out of here—fast.

"Howie, I was thinking," Jewel said sweetly as her hand continued its distracting massage. "Why don't we go upstairs and—"

"No!" He realized he sounded almost frightened. "No, Jewel," he repeated more evenly. "I want the money." He turned to look at her now. "The check we agreed upon, remember? Twenty thousand big ones—now."

"You can't be serious? I thought that—"

"You thought what?" he said gruffly. "That I would hop in the sack with you and cancel your debt? Is that what you thought, you calculating bitch?"

"Howard, please," Jewel implored, looking around nervously to make sure no one was listening.

"Please? Please? That's what you said in the middle of the night when you phoned and woke me up. 'Please get me the tapes, Howie. I can't do my show without your help, Howie.' I got you the fucking tapes. Now where's the twenty thousand?"

"Howie, really." Jewel feigned impatience. "I thought you'd come to your senses by now. What's a few videotapes between old friends—more than friends? Besides, that was such a hysterical night. I hardly knew what I was doing. It's not as if—"

"Oh, yes, you did, baby," he said harshly. "You knew *exactly* what you were doing, just like you know what you're doing right now." Then he raised his voice dramatically. "Take your goddamn hand off my leg!"

Half a dozen people looked up from their cocktails and private conversations to watch as Jewel Crosse's face turned a glowing shade of red that nearly matched the brilliance of her coiffure.

Howard rose brusquely, knocking against the table. A flustered waiter ran up to steady their drinks, but Howard was oblivious to the rescue attempt. His eyes blazed directly at the woman who had screwed him in private for the last time.

"Jewel baby," he said loudly for all to hear, "let me tell you something. No matter how many countries they beam that steel-plated puss of yours into, you'll always be small-time, a loser, a two-bit whore. I want that money, but I can see you have no intention of honoring your word. I should have known better, of course. But this much I do know. This time you're going to regret what you have done to me!"

Maggie was feeling a rush of triumph as she hurried down the long corridor toward Dan Campbell's office. It was the first time in years she'd been able to wear a size sixteen. Even though she'd had to hold her breath while zipping up the skirt of this newly purchased charcoal-gray gabardine suit—it fit, by God!

The pounds were rolling off. Maggie couldn't get over it. But the truth was, her appetite for food had all but abandoned her. She used to wake up dreaming of breakfast, but visions of consuming an entire coffeecake no longer tempted her. Since she'd begun falling asleep next to Nickels Yusorovic, her dreams had taken a more lascivious turn.

Maggie's life was full. Up at six-thirty each morning. The daily workout at Brad Larson's studio. Six or seven news stories to cover for the National TV News Syndicate. If she was lucky, a few stolen moments with Nickels before another long evening of poring over her father's files, still searching, still hoping for the vital clue that would ultimately clear Billy Rafferty's name.

Today she thought she had finally found it—another reason Maggie felt so elated as Campbell motioned for her to sit down across from his cluttered desk.

"Dan," she enthused, waving a slip of yellow paper in front of him, "this could be it."

The harried-looking attorney took the paper and held it close to the crookneck lamp on his desk. It was a copy of an invoice—four hundred dollars billed to Billy Rafferty by one Harriet Schmidt. The date was January 14, 1980.

"So?" he asked vaguely, looking up at Maggie.

"So!" she chirped back. "We've got our lead. I cross-checked this Schmidt person against Dad's Rolodex, and she's listed as a free-lance typist. A bill that big had to be a script, and the timing is right for *Precipice*. I asked Carol, and she doesn't remember for sure, but she thinks she was out with the flu about that time, which explains why she didn't do the typing herself. Don't you see? Someone outside Dad's office saw an early draft of the script years ago!"

Campbell shook his head. He was exhausted. It was eight o'clock at night, and he'd had a bear of a day. "Maggie," he began, leaning back in his big leather chair, "I really don't think it's worth the effort."

"But—"

He shook his head, holding her off. "Listen, there's probably nothing to this. And I just can't follow up every farfetched notion you get. Do you know how much you've cost your father already with your 'leads'? Fifteen thousand dollars, kiddo. My investigators get two hundred bucks a day, and you've had them going nonstop, sending them out on wild-goose chases as far away as Florida. When Billy finds out, he'll disown us both."

"No, he won't," Maggie protested. "He won't. He'll be overjoyed because we're going to win this lousy case for him!" She forged blithely on. "Now—I've tried contacting Harriet Schmidt at the number on the invoice, but she's no longer there. She isn't listed anywhere in the Los Angeles area anymore. So—"

"So." Dan Campbell was a patient man. He rarely raised his voice, and he almost never swore, but this was too much even for him. "You want me to track down a free-lance typist who's somewhere on this goddamn planet, hopefully still alive, on the slim chance that she might (a) have seen a copy of *Precipice;* (b) swiped same; and (c) have some connection with Leonard Rybar. What if she's in Alaska, for crissakes?"

"Dan, listen to me," Maggie pleaded. "More than likely this woman is nearby, and it will take less than a day to find her. We're only talking about a few hundred dollars more on Dad's bill."

The lawyer closed his eyes and massaged the lids with his fingers. "No, Maggie," he said finally. "I just can't follow another of your false leads. You know we're at a dead end on that aeronautics researcher—what's his name, Johnson?—the one your father first consulted regarding *Precipice*. He admits there was a disagreement with Billy over money, just as you said. But he also swears he never saw a script, and we know he has no connection with Rybar. Any other possible clues we could think of turned up nothing except a lot of time and expense. Johnson was our most promising lead."

"I know, but if we can only—"

Campbell waved her off. "Then you sent us to Seattle on that crazy hunch about the caterer," he reminded her. "And we're still checking on the electrical contractor who did that work on Billy's office. I think that's enough, Maggie. I really can't do any more without Billy's express go-ahead. Period."

"But, Dan," she continued to plead, waving the yellow invoice at him again, "look at this. The woman saw the script. She typed it and no doubt made copies of it. Now don't you tell me this isn't a solid lead."

Campbell merely turned up his palms in a gesture of helplessness. He had nothing more to say. He would go no further without Billy's consent, and, as Maggie knew, that was out of the question.

Maggie could feel her cheeks burning, her Irish temper rising within her. "Well," she announced, standing up, "I can see I'll have to take over from here. *I'll* find this Harriet Schmidt myself, Dan. And let me tell you something else. If she's the answer, you're getting only half your fee on this case!"

Campbell watched as Maggie thrust the yellow slip of paper in her handbag and stormed out of his office. He shook his head, slowly and sadly.

Christine reached for a piece of multiple-sheeted TelePrompTer paper and rolled it into the typewriter. She was back where she'd started in the business—in the Channel 8 newsroom.

Upon her return from Santa Barbara she'd found a message from Don Winston on her telephone-answering machine.

"Okay, crackerjack, you win," he'd grumbled good-naturedly when she returned the call. "No contract. Let's just say we have a gentleman's—er, gentle*person's*—agreement. A month's notice either way. Now get your ass over here."

The next morning Christine was covering an Ed Asner press conference and feeling like her old self. She knew she had missed being in the action, but hadn't realized how much. The lightning-fast pace of television reporting. The camaraderie of the camera crews, fellow journalists, even the public-relations flacks, the banter of conversation before a news conference, the competitive ordeal of firing questions faster and louder than anyone else. It was a small, cliquish group of highly skilled professionals that brought the world of show business to the world at large. And Christine was proud to be a part of it.

Her days went so quickly now that she barely had time to concentrate on anything but work. Even so, she also knew she was purposely avoiding thinking about Kent. It had been almost two weeks since their solemn goodbye at the airport. He'd kissed her, held her close, told her to consider seriously moving to Minneapolis, and then to call him.

"Give it a chance, Christine," he'd said before disappearing through the departure gate. "Give us a chance."

Kent had given her an ultimatum and he expected an answer.

But Christine had already made up her mind. In fact, there was never any serious doubt about how she really felt. Her career was too important to her, and she wanted it back too desperately. And if losing Kent Michaels was the price she had to pay, then so be it. Whenever she thought about their conversation in Santa Barbara, the way he'd trivialized her work, the hurt and anger welled up inside her all over again. In the throes of that anger she could easily imagine herself picking up the phone and blurting out, "No, absolutely not. There's no chance I'll ever move back to the Midwest."

But still she did not make the call.

Instead she also thought about making love with Kent. She thought about living with him and maybe having his children. These thoughts haunted her, too. Why must it always be so complicated? Why isn't real life ever simple and straightforward instead of an unending balancing act, a series of trade-offs and accommodations to conflicting desires, opposing interests? Does anybody ever have it *all*, she wondered.

She knew what Kent would say. "It *is* simple. What good is your old job going to do you? How long are you going to hang around there?"

Not for long, Christine hoped. Her plan was to take advantage of the on-air exposure, keep up her contacts, and find another, more challenging position by fall. While being back at the station was comfortable and the work stimulating, Christine could not dismiss the fact that by returning to Channel 8 she was taking several giant steps backward. For the moment, though, she was simply grateful to be working again, and trying to make the best of it.

The work had its rewards. Christine paused at her typewriter and sat back for a moment, smiling to herself. It was a dreary, rainy afternoon in L.A., the kind of day the tourist industry doesn't like to talk about, in which the best-laid plans are a washout. Yet a little more than four hours ago she had enjoyed a moment of supremely sunny irony.

Early that morning the assignment editor, Artie Turrell, had slipped Christine a City News Service wire report—a preliminary hearing on a drug bust case was scheduled in a few hours, at ten o'clock. Normally the story would be low priority, especially at this stage in the legal proceedings—just another movie producer caught with Lady Snow, Artie said. But he knew that Christine was preparing an update on Hollywood and drugs.

"We've got a crew available. Check it out if you like, Chris," he told her. "He probably won't talk, but maybe you'll get a bite from his attorney about how the cops are always trying to earn their stripes by picking on show-biz types."

Curiosity more than professionalism had convinced her to go. She didn't really need another lawyer spouting off for her series. But the chance to see the look on Blair Montgomery's face . . .

Christine had been astonished when she first heard about the drug bust at Blair's Malibu house. As far as she knew, he never used cocaine (the specific charge was possession of an ounce of coke, plus half a dozen Quaaludes). In its account of the arrest, the L.A. *Times* noted that there had been a raucous party at Blair's the night before. But, of course, the big story was Jason Kramer and the teenage rape allegations. All the newspapers, the trades, even *Time* magazine had carried that one; Blair's troubles had received scant notice toward the end of the Kramer articles. Yet Christine still couldn't help feeling a twinge of satisfaction. Justice had been served, in a way.

No other news crews waited outside the appointed courtroom. Kramer's hearing was next week, and every station in town would show up for that. By comparison Blair Montgomery was small potatoes.

But not to Christine. She stood quietly with her crew in a small alcove which had a clear view of the hallway outside the courtroom. When she first spotted the three men, she wasn't even sure Blair was one of them. The tweed jacket was unfamiliar, and his head was down, as if he were expecting a full-force assault from the Hollywood paparazzi.

Christine signaled her crew to roll. As he came closer, she saw those unmistakably handsome features and that curly black hair and—ah, yes—those adorable laugh lines around the eyes, just waiting to break into a smile. But not today.

With no warning, she was there. "What was your reaction to the sheriff's surprise raid at your home in Malibu, Mr. Montgomery?"

She had him. For those few seconds he was pinioned like a helpless animal in a large steel trap. A look of panic and horror clouded his face. Finally Blair blustered something about his attorneys and darted into the courtroom. The two lawyers tailed after him.

It was not the most admirable moment of her career—but it was one she would not forget. He had been at her mercy, if only for a moment, and she had loved the way it felt. From now on, whenever Christine flashed back to the degradation she'd suffered at the hands of Mr. Montgomery, she merely had to recall that stricken look on his face.

Better yet, she thought wryly, watch the tape. The cassette was neatly tucked away in her bag. She had already labeled it: BLAIR MONTGOMERY—BASTARD AT LARGE.

The ringing telephone startled Christine back to her current task. Every time the phone on her desk jangled, Christine jumped a little, thinking it might be Kent. Of course it couldn't be. He didn't even know she was working again.

"Right. I'll be ready to cut the piece by six," she told the tape editor at the other end of the line. She was in the midst of pulling together a story on Burt Reynolds, whom she'd interviewed the previous week. It would air on the ten o'clock news that night.

Christine put the receiver down but her hand lingered a second or two. All right, she promised herself, I'll call Kent tonight from home. But as she shuffled through the pages of her edit plan, Christine was already considering putting the call off until the next evening . . . or maybe the next.

The Japanese countryside passed swiftly by. Tashi felt calm, silly, and introspective, all at once. It had been a magical day.

Kyoto. What a fascinating, mystical city it had proved to be. A city with an aura, misted in ancient culture and religious tradition. Its magnificent shrines had made her lightheaded, giddy with their beauty. Kyoto had literally stolen her breath away. But the feelings that filled her heart now were due only in part to the wonders she had witnessed that afternoon.

For the first time, she and Roland had played tourist together. It had been a grand adventure. At Roland's insistence, they both took the precaution of donning a disguise. Tashi chose faded jeans, a long black shirt, and a wide-brimmed straw hat slanted down over her eyes. Drab, loose-fitting coveralls, silver mirrored glasses, and an unflattering stocking cap that completely covered the top half of his head gave Roland the look of a doughty merchant marine on shore leave. They made a strange pair indeed.

On the streets they were careful to walk single file. Not until they were inside the beautiful temples did they feel safe, as if granted a temporary respite by some higher power from an invasion of their privacy.

"Photographers rarely station themselves inside," Roland had explained. "Normally, they try to get you coming or going. If there's just one, we'll be able to get away fast." His face took on a pained expression. "But if a whole pack of 'em show up, they've got us for a while, until the guards move in."

All afternoon a cluster of Roland's burly bodyguards followed the couple at a discreet distance, tracing their path through the narrow and colorful streets. They sat at adjacent tables during lunch. Wherever Tashi and Roland went, the guards were never more than six feet away.

Tashi found the surreptitious sightseeing escapade dangerously exciting. At the same time, inside Kyoto's awesome sanctuaries, she felt somehow spiritually renewed. When Roland took her hand in his as they stood together in the Temple of One Thousand and One Buddhas, she was surprised, but took it as a sign that he, too, had been touched by the overwhelming wonder of the sight they were sharing.

They were on their way back to Tokyo now. As the countryside continued to rush past the windows of their small rented Mitsubishi—yet another aspect of their camouflage—Tashi glanced sideways to watch Roland at the wheel. She began to think about the touch of his hand and ponder its significance. He had never reached out for her voluntarily before. During photo sessions he'd held her hand, but that was a sham, as meaningless as a show-business kiss. But now—what did this simple human act mean to him? What was in his heart, and what was he trying to say? Roland's attitude toward her had certainly shifted dramatically, dizzyingly, since she had confronted him in Sydney. The radical change, in its own way, was as perplexing as his previous stoniness. His ability to make such a complete turnabout in so sudden a fashion left her more confused than ever.

At least this new Roland was much easier to be with. Tashi felt a little ashamed for even questioning the change. Her life was bearable now, more than bearable—it was actually quite exciting and wonderful. As much as she had hated Roland's iciness, she now felt gratitude for his warmth. As ready as she had been to leave him, she now felt fortunate to be his companion. Just let that be, she told herself. Don't question. Accept. A certain tranquility came with the silence. She turned to watch the sun start to dip below the Japanese landscape. The rigors of the tour seemed far way.

Since that morning in Roland's dressing room in Sydney, the two of them had spent more and more time together. He was allowing her inside his world. He was creating a space for her within his solitude.

Because of the security problem, rarely did Roland sample the usual tourist fare. His fear of crowds, of the crush of fans, kept him away. His need for escape, for moments of peace within the eye of his hurricane, took him on most free afternoons to remote and rural areas, where he could walk for miles. Tashi began to accompany him. The bodyguards were always nearby, of course, but she quickly became accustomed to their presence; soon they were almost invisible to her, as unobtrusive as shadows.

Most of the time on these hikes they walked without exchanging words. Roland seemed to need the silence. When he initiated conversation, they talked about music, sometimes books or the day's headlines. But their favorite topic was the animal world. Tashi would never forget the time Roland told her about his ranch in California.

It was only the day after they'd fought so bitterly in Sydney, and she was reluctant at first when he phoned her room to invite her on a "mystery trip." She didn't want to be tagging along just because he felt sorry for her. But Roland had persisted until she agreed to accompany him.

They began the journey in his limousine. The bodyguards followed in an Australian-built Ford. Roland spoke little, but he seemed relaxed and comfortable in her company. His attitude toward her had clearly undergone a transformation. A Sydney pop music station softly boomed from stereo speakers, and Tashi was content to view the sights from her luxurious vantage point.

At the outskirts of the city, the driver turned into a small private airport, where a twin-engine Cessna was waiting. Roland, Tashi, and the bodyguards boarded the plane, and within seconds they were airborne. Tashi still had no clue to their destination and dared not ask.

There was nothing to do but settle back and wait the ride out. Wherever they were going, she'd find out soon enough.

She watched as the coastal plain below gave way to the jagged, conifered peaks of the Blue Mountains, to woodlands with clearings tilled with vast rolling stands of winter wheat, and onward to sheep-grazed grasslands. At last, at the edge of the endless high desert known as the Outback, the Cessna dipped earthward, its wheels screeching as they settled hard onto a remote dirt landing strip.

Still too timid to question their mission, Tashi followed Roland into one of two Land Rovers parked nearby, and a driver in khakis and a battered cowboy hat led their small convoy along a rutted, dusty road. When, twenty minutes later, the Land Rovers finally came to a halt and Tashi climbed shakily out onto the parched soil, she at first stood stock-still in sheer amazement. They'd arrived at a government-run veterinary center. From what she could see it was immense, seemingly stretching on for limitless acres.

"How many animals do they have here?" she asked in wonderment.

"C'mon," said Roland, smiling. "We're expected."

Soon he was introducing her to the overseer, Sam Worth. A beneficent-looking man in his late fifties, Worth had a round face with rough, weathered skin that gave him the look of a wrinkled cherub. He had been with the center more than two decades, living alone in a modest prefab house on the premises. The animals were his life, and he took noticeable pride in giving—and remembering—a name to each and every creature he took in.

"All this was set aside by the government years ago expressly for the purpose of rehabilitatin' wounded and diseased animals found in the Outback," Worth explained as he began showing them around.

Tashi trailed behind the two men, astonished at the sights that surrounded her. It wasn't like a zoo. Since all the animals were native to the region, no special environments needed to be created for them. Fences and other barriers separated the predators from potential victims, but otherwise it was as if the entire panoply of the Outback's animal life had been called into assembly at this single spot. Looking over at Roland, she saw that his sense of excitement was equal to her own. His eyes were wide and bright, and there was a genuine rapture in his expression. And it was obvious he was also very fond of Worth.

"How many times have you been here?" she asked when the two men stopped talking for a moment.

"Oh, a lot, half a dozen times maybe. Right, Sam? I try to make a

trip out here every time I'm in Sydney. And usually I arrange to have
at least one animal sent back home. Last time it was Lolita."

"Lolita?"

"A wallaby. A small marsupial."

Tashi nodded. "Related to the kangaroo."

"You'd like Lolita," said Roland, grinning. "She's no bigger than a
rabbit, but is into more mischief than a barrelful of monkeys."

"Oh? And what makes you think I'd like that?" she teased back.

Roland was about to reply when the overseer shifted the conversation. "So, m'boy, what'll it be for you today?" asked Worth as they
passed by a grassy knoll pocked by the holes of a family of wombats,
small pointy-eared bears with fiercely sharp claws used for burrowing.

"I was thinking of an echidna, Sam."

"Is that the one with the quills?" Tashi asked, hoping she was right.

"Very good, m'dear," said Worth. He smiled at her benevolently.
"The echidna is an odd bloke. Small, egg-laying, yet a mammal. And,
yes, it is covered with sharp needles. I guess you could say it's the
Aussie version of the porcupine." He chuckled. "Be a bit o' a trek,
though. We've got the echidnas over in the far southwest corner.
Hope you're in the mood for a bit o' exercise."

They hiked on for another twenty minutes before Worth finally
led them to a pen housing what looked like a community of bristly
muskrats.

"Echidnas?" Roland asked.

" 'At's right, mate. Eight o' them, to be exact. And it'd be my
guess," he said, eying the group, "that you'd be most interested in
Edgar over there."

Tashi's eyes followed the direction of Worth's arm to a far corner
of the pen. Lying there, apparently asleep, was a tiny ball of dark
toothpicklike spikes. Little Edgar looked so weak and sickly compared
to the others that Tashi was certain Sam was mistaken. Why would
Roland choose the runt?

Roland walked over to Edgar's side of the pen and, wearing the
worn leather glove Worth had handed him, reached down and picked
up the little echidna. The wretched creature bristled slightly, but
otherwise made no effort to escape. Roland held it gently for a while,
talking softly as one would to a child. Tashi could not help but notice
the tenderness in his voice.

"Okay, Sam, where do I sign?" Roland said finally, returning the
baby echidna to his pen.

243

"Oh, I'll handle everything, per usual, Mr. Williams. Tell your vets to expect Edgar in about three weeks. We'll be buildin' 'im up with special vitamins and diet while all the ridiculous government paperwork goes through. Endless rigamarole, y'know, even way out 'ere in the middle o' nowhere."

Later, after saying goodbye to the kindly Worth, Tashi could contain her curiosity no longer. "I don't understand," she said as they walked back to the Land Rovers. "You have veterinarians who work for you?"

Roland nodded. "Uh-huh, on my ranch."

"Your ranch? Not in Bel-Air where you live?"

"Oh, no," he said laughing. "It's about an hour's drive from there, in a desert area called Soledad Canyon."

She could sense it was not going to be easy getting Roland to say more than he wanted to, but he didn't seem to resent her questions. His answers were short. He volunteered no information. But slowly Tashi was able to pry from Roland a glimpse into his other life, so apart from the one everyone expected of a music superstar.

"But why choose the sickliest echidna when there were healthier ones?"

It was then that Roland explained to her the true nature of his ranch. That he selected the weakest, not the fittest. Those poor, defenseless animals without much of a chance, the ones needing his help the most. "I guess you could say it's my way of giving something back," he concluded in a low voice. "My way of saying thank you."

Neither of them said much during the long trip back to Sydney. Roland stared out the window of the roaring Cessna. Every so often Tashi stole glances at him, wondering what he was thinking, reflecting on the events of this remarkable day. It was then that she realized how little most people knew of the complicated mind of this man. Today he had granted her a small peek, had allowed her to shine a thin shaft of light through the public facade of the flashy superstar. Maybe he wasn't as aloof and secure as he appeared to be. She remembered the tenderness with which he had talked to the little echidna, a helpless animal which could not respond, could not know the privilege it had been granted.

For the first time Tashi felt sorry for the man who appeared to have everything. How sad, she thought. How sad that he did not feel able to express as easily the same feelings toward his fellow human beings. How sad that he sang of love but lived closed off from normal human contact. How very sad. Roland Williams was the prisoner, not her.

"Are you tired?"

Tashi started, roused from her thoughts. Roland was glancing over at her from behind the wheel of the Mitsubishi, and the dense smog on the horizon signaled that Tokyo lay just ahead.

"No, just daydreaming," she said. "I hope you're not tired, either. I'm looking forward to a terrific concert tonight."

Roland laughed and shook his head. "I can't understand why you sit through every one. They're all the same."

"With some minor variations," she agreed.

"Yeah."

She noticed that he was frowning. "Is something wrong?"

"Sort of. What you said reminded me, that's all."

"Well?"

"It's my problem. You wouldn't be interested."

"Thank you very much for deciding for me." She said it lightly, but regretted it immediately when Roland shot her a wounded look.

"Hey, I was only kidding," she said.

"It's all right—I'll tell you. Did you notice anything unusual about last night's performance?"

She considered the question for a moment, mentally reviewing Roland's opening-night concert in Tokyo. It had all seemed to go smoothly. But, yes, there had been something.

"Do you mean when Pete missed his cue, early in the show? I think it was the 'Union Dues' number."

"You got it," he said, giving her a sidelong look of surprise, quickly replaced by approval. She was full of surprises, this one.

"What went wrong?"

"Pete's a great drummer, the best. But everything's been going wrong with him lately. He's been screwing up bad, though it's usually not as obvious as last night. In Melbourne he almost missed a sound check, and he's been skidding in at the last minute for performances. And he's always glazed."

"He's on something?"

"Yeah. I'm certain of it. 'Ludes or heroin, maybe, probably with booze," Roland said in disgust. Musicians who toured with Roland Williams knew the one inviolable rule. No hard drugs. No getting high before a performance. Alcohol or marijuana was all right, but only after the show.

"So what will you do?" Tashi asked.

245

"We've already warned him several times. Now we've got to boot him out. Dirk's arranging for a replacement."

"It won't be easy finding someone who measures up, will it?"

"I know," he said, surprised again by her perspicacity. "Especially in the middle of a tour."

They drove on for a while. Roland looked over at her again, as if he wanted to say more.

"What is it?" she laughed. "I don't play drums."

He began unsteadily. "I was, ah, wondering," he said.

"About what?"

"Tonight after the concert, would you like to meet me for dinner in my suite?"

Tashi tried to assimilate what she'd heard. Thus far they'd only spent afternoons together. The thought of being alone with Roland in his suite both thrilled and frightened her. First he holds my hand in the temple, she thought, now he wants to . . . well, what? We're becoming friends, that's all. Relax. You're making too much of this.

"Gee," she said finally, in a teasing voice, trying to hide her shame at jumping to an impossibly farfetched conclusion. "This is rather last minute, Roland. And, of course, I'll have to disappoint my steady date."

"Great."

For the rest of the ride he caught himself stealing glances at his newfound companion. Tashi had become a matter of intense curiosity to Roland. He marveled at her—at how she put others around her at ease, how she could accept new experiences without being threatened by them, how uncannily wise she often seemed, despite her age. To his amazement, Tashi could be both endearingly girlish and womanly at the same time.

Roland felt deep stirrings within him. He wasn't ready to call them sexual; the two of them had been no more intimate than a touch of hands, an accidental brush of warm body against warm body. But he found acceptance and comfort in that contact, and he realized he was no longer thinking of her as *not a man*. She was Tashi, his friend. Taking his courage from her, he vowed not to limit the possibilities of what they could share together.

Yet, try as he might, Roland could not escape emotional turmoil. He had begun the tour thinking he knew himself only too well. Now he was not so sure. And even as Roland recognized that he stood now at the brink, that the possibility existed that he might explore uncharted terrain in this rapidly blossoming friendship with Tashi, he was afraid. Afraid she might reject his advances. Afraid, most of all, that should she not, he would fail her as a man.

He smiled and reached out again to cover her hand with his.

Maggie could see it as she huffed and puffed up the steep hill to join her camera crew. The enormous blimp hovering maybe a half mile above. Moving so slightly it was almost lost in the dirty gray air. Maggie grimaced with displeasure at the sign on the blimp's bulging side.

WE DARE YOU, it spelled out in immense, brilliantly magenta letters.

Maggie was taking huge gulps of the hot smoggy air and imagining what it was doing to her lungs. The severe incline of this narrow, winding street in the Hollywood Hills was something she had never imagined when she parked and started walking.

Should have ridden with the damn crew. . . . Stopping briefly to catch her breath, she squinted up at the blimp once more, pulled the sunglasses down over her eyes and plodded upward. "Jesus God," she sighed in disgust. "What'll the loonies think of next?"

The "loonies" on this particularly bright, humid day were the producers of a new TV show celebrating would-be daredevils. The show was a get-rich-quick opportunity for bona fide risk takers and bombastic braggarts across the country. Thousands of them had written in, claiming they were capable of unbelievably perilous feats. The rewards were high—from a hundred thousand to half a million dollars for a successful stunt.

"More astonishing, electrifying, and exciting than *Real People* and *That's Incredible* combined," proclaimed the rumpled press release in Maggie's handbag. It went on to trumpet some of the show's first contestants:

A plumber from Davenport, Iowa, who claimed he could ingest sixty raw eggs in three minutes flat while hanging upside down in a pair of gravity boots.

A seventy-eight-year-old, self-proclaimed tri-athlete from Deerfield Beach, Florida, who would swim ten miles in the Atlantic, run the fifty miles to Miami and pedal a tricycle back.

And then there was Jamie Espin. He was the reason camera crews from every TV station, network, and cable bureau in town were now poised at the top of the hill, focusing their lenses on the famed HOLLYWOOD sign. Espin was a garage mechanic from Little Rock,

Arkansas, who—within the next five minutes, by Maggie's calculations—was supposed to leap from the blimp, parachute down and land smack on the letter H. It was a natural for TV news shows across the country, the perfect way to end the broadcast with an upbeat kicker that began, "Well, we saw again today why they sometimes call the place Holly*weird*. . . ." Which, of course, was exactly what *We Dare You*'s producers were counting on. Nationwide coverage. Guaranteed ratings boosters for their premiere show the following night.

"Gawd, it's hot," complained Maggie, shoving her way through the human chain of onlookers and finally sandwiching herself in beside her cameraman. "Y'know," she said too loudly, "I almost hope he misses."

"Why, Maggie, bite your tongue," the cameraman said.

"Rather it be yours, darlin'," she replied with a quick pinch on his well-worn jeans. "I'm serious, Clyde. If he misses, at least we'll have a story. I'm so sick of all this free publicity shit. Some days I feel like a walking PR firm. Why do they send us out on this stuff, anyway?"

"Because it moves, dummy," taunted a familiar voice from the right. "And because we're such terrific journalists. Experts at turning a sow's ear into a silk purse."

"Christine?" Maggie called out, looking for her.

"Down here, in the shade." Christine was crouched on the ground, wedged between several pairs of feet and holding a large sun reflector for her crew.

"How the hell did you draw this Z-off? I thought your assignment editor was a man of taste."

" 'Bout as much as there is represented here. I haven't seen so many hungry crews since we all witnessed the unveiling of the billboard for that horror film on Sunset."

"You mean 'the first Three-D billboard in the history of show business'?" Maggie intoned. "The one with the dragon that breathed fire and nearly burned everything down?"

There were groans and nods of pained remembrance from the other crews and reporters in the crowd.

"Oh, yeah . . ."

"You there that day . . . ?"

"What a pisser!"

"Hey, gang, we got company," shouted an alert soundman, hearing the faint rumble in his earphones. "Somebody called in an airstrike."

Soon the rumble became a roar, as three police helicopters moved in on the blimp and began circling it. Were they part of the act? Or trying to hold up the works? Ripples of conjecture circulated among the earthbound journalists as cameramen went to work recording the unexpected scene.

"Hot damn," Maggie hooted. "Looks like a bust."

And so it was. Within minutes the show's publicist, a chubby man wearing a tan suit and speaking through a bullhorn, announced that, much to his disappointment, Mr. Espin would not be skydiving down to the Hollywood sign that afternoon. Unfortunately, he said, the authorities had not informed the producers of *We Dare You* earlier that parachuting was illegal in the Hollywood Hills.

"What a blazing bunch of bumpkins," Maggie groused a few minutes later, walking back down the hill with Christine. "Blaming it on the cops. I loathe flacks. Especially incompetent ones. Hope that diphead Saunders loses his job over this one. Can't tell you the disasters I've been sent on, thanks to him."

"You mean the party for the John Wayne robot?" Christine asked. "And the unveiling of that specially equipped 'bullet car' for that TV series *Zoooooom?*"

"Yeah. Show committed suicide. Justifiably so."

"And let's see," Christine went on, warming to these journalistic war stories. "What about the opening of that new disco called Zipper? The one featuring all those punk stars nobody could recognize?"

"Oh, lord! Don't remind me. I was there till midnight because we had a new assignment editor. So nervous she wouldn't let me pull out until I *made* it a story."

"And you did, of course," said Christine, slipping into Maggie's dusty BMW.

"Sort of. A weird piece on kinky fashions." Maggie turned on the ignition. "Come to think of it, the crowd was rather, well, umm, interesting."

"Interesting?" Christine teased. "C'mon, you loved it."

"Well . . ."

"So you see, my dear, despite the hurdles, there are always rewards in our thankless business," Christine continued lightly. "I'm sure you had your fill of champagne that night, too."

Maggie laughed as she maneuvered wildly around a hairpin curve. "And that's not all, my little Midwestern innocent!"

"Oh?"

"Let's just say I've changed my tune since. Probably for the best."

"Probably?" Christine raised an eyebrow.

"Okay. Definitely," Maggie admitted. "It's just all so new to me. This thing with Nickels, I mean. Maybe it just feels better without the extra poundage. The fat cells have released my nerve endings or something. And I'm alive . . . I'm liberated . . . I'm *freeeeee*. . . ."

"You sound like Joanne Worley, for Godsakes. Careful, Maggie—that truck!"

Maggie swerved quickly to the right and hit the brakes, barely missing the garbage truck in front of them.

"Sorry. You all right?"

Christine nodded, catching her breath. "Close."

"And so it was," Maggie said, honking three times, then zooming past the truck and down Beachwood Drive. "And speaking of closeness and making love and men and all those top-priority things—what of Dr. Michaels?"

"What of him?"

"Must I spell it out, girl? Have you spoken to him? Have you seen him? Have you told him that you love him? In short, have you made any progress at all nailing the guy?" Maggie stole a sidelong glance at Christine.

"Nope."

"Nope? Why nope?"

"Because I'm a chicken. I swore I'd call him last night, but didn't. Maybe tonight."

"Why not now? Come, I'll take you home and you can—"

"No! Maggie! Just drop me off at the station. I have to make something of this parachute bust for tonight's show."

"All right," Maggie relented. "But when you're in the dark of the editing room, think about those wonderfully strong arms around you. Those surgeon's hands on your boobs. . . . Think of the way—"

"Maggie—lay off, will you?"

"On," Maggie persisted. "On is much better when it comes to laying . . . or getting laid—don't you think?"

Christine threw up her hands, laughing. "I give up," she said. "Unconditional surrender. Oh, maybe one condition—we change the subject. What's with Operation Billy Goat? Any news on the Schmidt woman?"

"Not yet. But I'm still hopeful. Planning on making a neighborly call to Harriet's old stomping grounds tomorrow. See if I can find a friend or two. Drop in on her landlady. Your basic Sam Spade stuff."

"Anything I can do?"

"Not yet, sweet lips," said Maggie, turning into the Channel 8 parking lot. "But I appreciate the offer. Maybe soon."

Christine gave her friend a goodbye peck on the cheek.

As Christine hurried into the station, Maggie shouted after her, "Volunteer your services to Dr. Michaels. I have a feeling he just needs a little intensive care!"

Industrious Tokyo was asleep, and the night sky was black and vast. At a low lacquered table the remnants of a feast: two *shokada* dinners in elaborately decorated, multicompartmented wooden boxes stuffed full of wondrous nibbles . . . fish cakes with cucumber slices, *tarado nomijiae,* cod roe on ringlets of squid, spiced chicken wings, a *yakatori* of plump skewered shrimp, eggplant, crisp scallions. . . . Nearby a glazed pottery container of sake, nearly empty.

The light in the hotel suite was low, diffuse, throwing hazy shadows against the bamboo wallpaper and the translucent screens that set off the interior spaces.

Through one screen two dark outlines appeared to be frozen in silhouette. The figures knelt opposite each other on a cushiony futon, at arm's length, not touching.

But they were not frozen, not inanimate.

Roland was trembling ever so slightly. And now Tashi gracefully opened her silken robe and let it glide slowly from her shoulders.

Her breasts were firm, perfectly contoured, with nipples erect and hard like two delicate pink Delft thimbles. Her stomach was flat, and her spine described a gentle arc to the fullness of her hips.

Tashi took Roland's hands in hers. She guided him in gentle exploration of her womanhood—perfumed hair, soft, smooth face, neck, shoulders . . . lingering at her chest, where Roland cupped the swelling of her flesh, transfixed by the contrast of hard and soft, nipple and breast . . . then down to her slim waist, her thighs, and, finally, to the dark, hot mystery of life itself.

She did this patiently, coaxingly, unhurriedly, pausing to show him where it felt good, offering tender words of encouragement.

His trembling had ceased, replaced by a pounding heart and breaths in short, rapid bursts. He broke free of her grasp and took her by the shoulders. He started pulling her toward him.

She stopped him. Roland opened his mouth to protest, but she touched a finger to his lips. Their eyes met and fused.

Tashi took his hands again and placed them firmly at his sides.

251

Nimbly undoing the knot on his robe tie, she slid open the garment. And gasped. A long throbbing shadow was cast upon the rice paper screen.

Oriental fashion, she bowed before this pulsating sign of Roland's desire for her, and taking him in both hands, let her lips lavishly give thanks—until he gave a low and raspy command for her to stop.

He was in charge now. Tashi smiled and submitted joyously. Lying back, she took him into her easily. He moved strongly inside her, without fear, without hesitation—as if he had been born with the certain knowledge of how to please this woman.

And please her he did, until the first slight slant of sun filled the hotel suite with its intimation of dawn. . . .

— CHAPTER —

Eleven

Inside the drafty, cavernous television studio the temperature registered at forty-nine degrees. Cameramen, electricians, and various technicians scurried about bundled up in heavy sweaters and coats. The floor manager wore woolen gloves.

"It's like the friggin' Klondike in here," complained a new soundman who hadn't been forewarned.

"More like Siberia," quipped a nearby electrician. "She likes it. The colder it is, the less heat she feels under the lights. Says her makeup will run if we warm it up any. We freeze our buns off, so what? Can't let the star look bad, now can we?"

Someone else muttered, "DuRand was an angel compared to this bitch."

The stage crew for *Crosse Covers Hollywood* was not a happy lot. Their taping sessions were endured with resigned indignation, in the hope of just getting through the show quickly. Rarely did that happen. For no matter how smoothly Barry Swanson, the new producer, had things running, there was always a snag, something Jewel objected to, which kept everyone shivering and stamping their feet in the frigid studio.

"Anytime, Miss Crosse." The announcement, in a singsong female voice, accompanied a short knock on the dressing-room door.

Inside, Jewel sat before her wall-sized makeup mirror. She was dressed in a sleek, peach-colored Ungaro suit and a soft pink camisole. To one side stood her makeup man, who was shading her nose. On the other, her hairdresser coaxed a sagging wave with the long tail of his comb.

Jewel's mood was uncommonly sunny. Today was the day. She had waited long enough, trying every way she could think of to flesh out what she knew, until finally she had simply decided, to hell with it. It was too good to waste. She'd run it blind. She just hoped that on Sunday, when the show aired, he'd be watching.

"Bruce, is my ice water on the set?"

"Yes, dear," replied her wafer-thin assistant. He was wearing baggy lavender pants and a light-green Lacoste sweater. Around his waist he'd tied a matching lavender down jacket for later use. Bruce was one of the few who enjoyed the arctic blast of the air-conditioned studio: so many fashion possibilities.

Five minutes later Jewel appeared in the studio and took her place on the set under the glaring white haze of light. She was seated, tall and serene like a reigning monarch, behind an elaborately scrolled antique French desk. Her chair, of the same style, was covered with crushed velvet of a dusky blue.

A bystander might have expected honeyed benedictions to flow from the moist lipsticked mouth of this regal vision.

"I'm hotter than a goddam hard-on up here, Barry! Tell them to crank it down about ten degrees," Jewel yelled into the inky blackness beyond the lighted set. From where she sat she could see only murky figures milling about in the middle distance.

Groans filled the air as the producer set about carrying out the orders. "All right, can the complaints," Swanson said. Jewel gave no sign of having noticed the exchange.

While the crew members buttoned and zipped jackets, she flipped through a sheaf of text that she would soon be reading from the Tele-PrompTer. These pages contained the short newsy items with which she always led the show. Studio shakeups, marital splits, actor's tantrums. Glitzy little stories to quickly catch the viewer's attention. Later she would move over to the satin-covered settee on her living-room set for a long interview with today's guest star.

As Jewel's eyes flicked speedily over the copy, she could feel her face growing increasingly hot. The lights were not to blame. By the time Swanson returned from his cool-down mission, she was livid.

"Barry, where the hell is that blind item, the one I personally handed you this morning?"

For a long moment no reply was forthcoming from the darkness. Finally a sheepish voice came from near the cameras. "Why, uh, Jewel, I think we'll have to pass on that one. Why don't we just forget it and go on with what's here?" A hush fell over the crew. This was trouble, and they knew it.

"Forget it? Forget it?" she repeated, standing and squinting into the black void, trying to locate him. "I can't see you, you imbecile. Get up here fast!"

Within seconds the nervous producer was at her side.

"Jewel," he whispered, so the crew would not overhear. "When the lawyers checked over your copy this morning, they really objected to that item. In fact, they strongly advised me to kill it. I was going to let you know, of course, but by then you were tied up with the manicurist and then in makeup, and I—"

"You chicken-shit horse's ass," she hissed at him. "Don't you know I'm boss around here? Who hired you, for crissakes? Listen, scout, get that item back into this show on the double."

"But, Jewel, I . . . the show is jammed as it is."

"So? Kill the Carol Burnett story. The blind item stays, got it?" She crossed her arms, as if the subject was closed, and glowered at him.

Swanson's face was crimson now, too—but with fear, not anger. "Please," he pleaded, "listen to reason, Jewel. We're already half an hour off schedule. Just dropping the Burnett visual and adding one for the blind item will take another twenty minutes, and with overtime costs we—"

"I don't care if it takes three hours, you pretentious asshole!" She was yelling again. "Just do it. And do it now!" With that, she turned quickly and marched back to her dressing room.

Forty-five minutes passed before Jewel returned to her throne-chair, fresh and unperturbed as ever, looking again like an elegant Royal at high tea. As she listened to her show's familiar theme music fade out and saw the floor director's hand come down, cueing her, Jewel's eyes gleamed.

"Good afternoon from Hollywood. I hope it's a lovely Sunday for you all. And here are some tidbits from Tinsel Town to get us started."

Smoothly she read from the TelePrompTer: A well-known actress had walked off the set of her recent movie; an extended holdup would cost the production company millions. An actor had fallen off a horse and broken his leg while doing his own stunt work; a lawsuit was expected. All the footage of an almost completed science-fiction movie being filmed in London had mysteriously disappeared.

Jewel sat up a little straighter. She looked directly into the camera lens. "And now I have a shocking bit of news," she said dramatically. "I can't tell you all of it—but I'm sure you'll be able to fill in the blanks." She paused a beat, took a breath, and then read the story she had been waiting to deliver.

"What former Big Ten athlete, who traded in his spikes for a run at television stardom, is now in danger of tripping himself up in the Hollywood fast lane? Yes, it seems this Midwestern beefcake is not only indulging in, but is also selling, drugs on the party circuit. If he keeps this up, his show-business career could take a very . . . speedy . . . nosedive."

She smiled like an avenging angel. "Stay with us. I'll be back in a moment to find out everything you've always wanted to know from talented actress Dyan Cannon. . . ."

As the lights slowly faded for a commercial break, Jewel Crosse stood and stalked imperiously over to her living-room set, confident that she had just squared her account with an impudent pup whose name was now mud.

Maggie woke up luxuriating in a warm glow. She felt like a contented caterpillar hidden safely away in its cocoon. In this case the cocoon was co-inhabited by Nickels. They'd fallen asleep locked together in a semifetal position, his legs tucked up tightly under hers. His chest pressed against her back, and she was keenly aware of the cushion of soft, furry hair that covered his muscular body. Slowly she slid her arm over and gently touched his hand. She wished for a moment that this was all there was to life, lying here listening to the steady, even breathing of the man who had transformed her.

Through Nickels, Maggie had gained a new sense of herself. It wasn't entirely the loss of weight. More had to do with the way they'd become friends, grown to trust and care for one another. No detail of her life was too small for him to notice, turn over in his mind, then make a pronouncement upon in his endearingly fractured English. She was equally enveloped in his world. They had become partners, sharing their days—and nights. As a result, Maggie felt more complete and whole than ever before in her life.

In bed he'd opened her up to a new world. Maggie had come to

256

realize that she'd never really felt anything before Nickels. She'd had sex, lots of it. But that was all, the brief physical elation that accompanied orgasm. It didn't matter to her then who her partner was. But with Nickels sex was an extended holiday at an uninhibited fantasyland. The joyful intimacy, the playful tenderness of his touch was something she'd never experienced before. He was so good in bed, she teased him about it.

"When did you have time to learn how to cook, Nickels, honey?" she'd say. "Was there a bed in your kitchen?"

"How did you know? We were very poor."

"I'll bet."

"Besides, is like cooking, making love. Exactly the right ingredients, perfect timing—and much fussing over." And he laughed uproariously.

Now, not wanting to wake him, she carefully inched over to her side of the bed and lowered her feet gingerly to the floor. But as she was about to stand up, he reached over and ran his fingers lightly down her back.

"Hey, little one," he whispered, knowing she loved this pet name for her. "You go to work so early?"

She turned to face him and smiled. "You were snoozing like a grizzly bear in hibernation."

"Me? I sleep like pussy cat. I can hear your dreams."

"Oh, yeah?"

"Is true."

"So? Tell me about them."

"No problem. But come closer."

She slid back under the covers and turned to face her handsome Slavic lover. Soon he began to stroke her gently, playing his fingers over her breasts, then slowly down.

When he knew she was ready, he moved up to mount her. Maggie's eyelids flickered shut and her breath came in short gasps as Nickels straddled her, his weight on his arms. As their bodies rose and fell as one, Nickels began kissing her mouth powerfully, demandingly, until Maggie again opened her eyes. He held them, lovingly, with his.

As the moments passed, however, he realized she would not reach the full height of ecstasy this time. She was his, yes, she would enjoy the strength of his body, but this morning she was not as much with him as he would have liked. She was clearly distracted, at a distance. Acceding to this fact, Nickels enjoyed to his own climax, crying out at its peak and falling upon her, satiated and spent.

"You, my tiny dumpling, are a driven woman. The more you do, the more you want to do," he said afterward.

Maggie noticed the hint of irritation in his voice. "Oh, Nickels, I only wish—"

"You wish you were not so filled with troubling thoughts? You wish you could truly enjoy making love?" he asked pointedly.

"I'm sorry." She traced his lips with her finger. "I want you, hon. You know how I feel. It's just this damn lawsuit. It's eating me up. I've just got to find this Harriet Schmidt woman soon."

"That I know—too well," he said, propping himself up on one arm. "Too bad her stupid landlady . . . Merble . . . Mervle . . . is that her name?"

"Merkle. Sonia Merkle, a case for the rubber room if I ever saw one."

"Yes, well, maybe if you tried talking to neighbors."

Maggie shook her head. "Did that. Knocked on doors all over the building. Those who answered never heard of Harriet Schmidt. The woman must have kept to herself."

"The landlady, is she worth another try? Maybe next time you catch her sober."

"Doubt it," Maggie said, remembering the glassy-eyed, washed-out soul who'd finally come to the door that hot afternoon in West Los Angeles. She was clutching a glass half filled with cheap Scotch. Sonia Merkle was fiftyish, with a flushed complexion, her teased brown hair unkempt. Once she had been pretty, probably the prettiest girl in her hometown, wherever that was, urged on to Hollywood by local acclaim only to find that it was literally overflowing with the prettiest girls from thousands of hometowns. Sonia hadn't become a movie star, but she played a convincing drunk.

"Harriet Schmidt? Schmidt? Nope," she said at first, until Maggie dug into her bag and produced a crisp fifty. "Oh, yes. Harriet. Sweet little thing. Always prim and proper. Neat, too. When she left, I hardly needed to clean up the apartment."

"Do you remember when she left? Did she retire or something?" Maggie asked.

"Retire? Hell, no. Not Harriet. She's young. Couldn't have been more than fifty-one. I 'member that she was a few years older than me." Self-consciously Sonia straightened the bodice of her flowered housedress.

"But do you remember when she left? How long ago?"

"Hmmm. Well. Lessee." She took a gulp from the glass. "Hey, wait

258

a minute here. What's it to you? Harriet ain't in any trouble'r anything, is she?"

"No, no, this is purely personal," Maggie fibbed. "I'm an old friend. She used to do some typing for my dad."

"Typin'? Oh, shit, yes. Harriet used to pound them keys all day long. Never rested till suppertime. Once in a while she'd come over 'round six—cocktail time, y'know. Come to think of it, I sorta miss Harriet."

"Please. This is very important to me. When did she leave, do you remember?"

"Oh, lord," she said, scratching her cheek, "'bout a year ago, I guess. No . . . no, make that a year and a half. I 'member, see, 'cause my grandson was visitin' at the time, and he helped Harriet with her stuff. She tipped him real good, too."

"Do you have any idea where she went?"

"Went?" Mrs. Merkle repeated, her eyes searching Maggie's face.

It was plain enough what the woman wanted. Maggie reached into her bag again and pulled out another fifty, holding it up in front of her like a carrot to a horse.

"Oh, Harriet? You mean where'd she go?" the woman said, not taking her eyes off the bill. "Yes. Ah, well, not exactly. I mean, she tol' me Arizona. Now I've got a sister in Flagstaff. And I think that's where Harriet went, too. But I get mixed up sometimes. Coulda been Phoenix. One or the other, I just ain't sure."

Maggie thanked the woman and walked sadly back toward her car. Dan Campbell was right, she told herself. Finding Harriet Schmidt was going to be much more than a one-day job. It might take weeks more work.

"So, you go back to phone books today?" asked Nickels, giving her thigh a quick squeeze.

"Guess so," she sighed. "Now that I know there aren't any Harriet Schmidts in either Flagstaff or Phoenix, I'm checking all the Schmidts in both cities. Maybe she's staying with a relative. I just hope it isn't an in-law."

"For both our sakes, I hope so, too." His expression grew pensive. "Maggie, I have idea for you. It might not work, but what you got to lose?"

"So, what is it? I've had enough mystery lately to last a lifetime."

"Listen. What do we in American restaurant business do to get customers?"

Maggie shrugged. "Don't know—serve good food, I guess."

"No, no, genius, I tell you what. We advertise! You do the same."

"Advertise for Harriet Schmidt?" she asked, puzzled.

"But of course. Take out ads in major newspapers of Flagstaff and Phoenix. You could say something like, umm, let me see . . . 'If you are typist named Harriet Schmidt who once lived in Los Angeles, call this number collect.' And you maybe offer money . . . say, five hundred dollars. Something like that, for the what-you-call-it—insensive?"

"Incentive?" She laughed. "You know, the bucks just *might* make old Harriet crawl out of the woodwork."

He leaned over to kiss her on the neck. "And for you," he said, "I treat. If this Harriet calls, I give her the five hundred . . . small payment to get my Maggie back to enjoying my bed."

Bbbrrriiiiiiing!

The noise startled Roland. His phone rarely rang. The front desk at the Plaza-Athénée had been issued the usual instructions: no calls were to be put directly through to his suite—they were to be rerouted to Dirk Andrews's room instead. Only in an emergency was Roland to be disturbed, and even then the concierge was to call first for permission.

"Damn," Roland muttered. He was just leaving and didn't want to be bothered answering it.

Outside in the hallway a pair of bodyguards flanked the suite's imposing double doors. At their stations through the night again, in shifts, these stony-faced fixtures no longer drew curious looks from the French chambermaids passing by in starched white uniforms.

Roland and his entourage had been in Paris for three days. Of all the visits he'd made over the years to this most romantic of cities, the city of lights, this had been the most enjoyable by far. In fact, he couldn't remember ever feeling so good on tour before. He could find only one explanation. Tashi.

The bond between them continued to strengthen. She was his companion, his friend, his confidante. Of that much Roland was certain. The two of them had not spent another night in lovemaking since Tokyo, glorious as it had been. Roland needed time, it was too sudden, too confusing. He had to sort things out.

What of Burton? More fundamentally, what of himself? Did this mean he was not really gay? Was he bisexual? No other woman had ever awakened in him the passion he had felt for Tashi—but had he simply been waiting for the right woman to come along? No. His feelings for Burton were real. His love for Victor was real. Why, then, did he want Tashi again—and more than he had ever wanted anyone before?

Roland did not know, and he felt the weight of his struggle for answers.

He had opened his heart to her. With astounding ease, and at length, he had revealed to her secret thoughts no one, not Victor, not even Burton, had heard before. About his early life. His struggle to cope with success. The faint but haunting memory of his mother. Did there need to be more between them than that?

He had to know. He had to be sure. He needed to take a step back, clear his head and see things as they really were. He and Tashi had talked all this over, too, and she understood immediately. Tashi wasn't the problem. She wasn't pressuring him. Roland was his own problem.

The amazing thing was, despite his mind being a jumble, he was still having the time of his life. He found himself feeling happier and more energetic than he had in months. Each new day had become an adventure. It had become a game to the two of them, slipping undetected out of their hotel through the servants' entrance, ducking into the waiting limousine. By now Tashi had become as adept as Roland at the art of masquerade, and even the bodyguards were astonished by their ever-changing disguises.

Paris. *Que será, será.*

Today they were going to Montmartre. Roland was eager to show Tashi its bustling cafés and talented street artists. A charcoal sketch of her would make a wonderful keepsake, if she'd agree to sit for it. He had been considering which room he might place it in back home in California when the phone began its irritating bleat.

"Monsieur Williams?" came the dignified voice of the hotel's concierge. "I have a Monsieur Ratchford from the States on the line. He sounds rather desperate to speak with you."

A few weeks ago Roland would have been pleased to hear from Burton. However, not now, especially not now. But what if it was important? "Okay, put him on."

"Ro?"

"Burton, how are you?"

"Great. Great. God, I'm glad I caught you in. Damn concierge gave me a hard time. I thought you always notified the desk to put me through."

"Andrews must have overlooked it, sorry."

"Ro? Jesus, this is a terrible connection. Listen, Ro, I've got tremendous news. I'm in Chicago, at the convention. And Senator Whittaker has just taken the nomination. Isn't that terrific?"

"Yeah, sure is," Roland replied with little enthusiasm.

"You know what that means, don't you? Whittaker really has the best shot at unseating Sullivan. We can do it, Ro! Now all we have to do is pull out all the stops on the fund-raisers. I've already arranged concerts in four cities for later this month. . . . Miami, Detroit, then Atlanta and Seattle. Jesus, think of it, Ro . . . all that money you'll raise. You'll be able to elect Whittaker almost singlehandedly!"

Roland cut him off. "I can't do it, Burton."

"God, this static is unbelievable. What did you say?"

"I can't!" Roland repeated, loudly. "I can't do the concerts. We're going into Germany three days earlier than we planned. I just won't have the time."

"You *gotta* be kidding!" Burton's distraught voice crackled through the phone. "Roland, you promised."

"I'm sorry," Roland mumbled. "It can't be helped." He wished he had never picked up the phone. This was the conversation he had dreaded. He felt guilty. There was a week to spare before Germany. But he wanted to spend it in France. It was all Burton's doing, these fund-raising concerts; Roland didn't care about politics. But it wasn't just that he didn't feel like trucking all the way back to the States. It was the thought of seeing Burton right now. He was already so confused. And he needed time to work out the ambivalence he was feeling—about himself, about Burton. He needed time to think.

"Ro!" Burton pleaded. "What's happening with you? You gave me your word. You signed the contracts."

"Talk to my attorney," Roland said coldly.

"But, Ro! What are you saying? It's me—Burton. I'm your friend— I love you! Listen, I know you're probably exhausted from the tour. But think of Whittaker winning and what that will mean. Ro, think of us."

"Burton," he answered wearily, "I said I was sorry. It just isn't possible."

"Hear me out. Please." Even through the static, Roland could hear panic in Burton's voice. He had never heard it before.

"I'm listening."

"I really need you now, man. Like you needed me so many times, remember? I've always been there for you, Ro. Every time. Is this too much to ask? Are you going to do a hundred-and-eighty-degree turn on me now—now, when I'm depending on you? I'm telling you again, Ro. I need you. If you love me . . ." His voice trailed off.

Roland listened to the far-away noises on the line and said nothing.

"What's wrong, Ro?" The desperate quality was gone; now there was suspicion.

"Nothing. I'm fine, really, other than the usual fatigue. It's just that I don't have the time, Burton. I can't."

"But you do have time. You know you do. I've set Miami and Detroit for the break before Germany. Two concerts in each city. Even with the shift in schedule you could squeeze them in. Roland, I know it'll be tiring, but I'm tired, too. What we do is not easy. But it'll be a lot easier if we help each other."

"Yeah, maybe."

"Roland?"

"Mmm?"

"I miss you. It's been hard for me, being apart from you for so long. But I haven't forgotten. You mean the world to me, Ro."

There was another pause, each expecting the other to speak. A lengthy, silent standoff.

But Burton was groping for a way to make sense of this sudden turnaround. They'd spoken before during the tour, everything was fine, the usual pledges and assurances to each other had been exchanged. Now this. This didn't sound like the same Roland. If someone's turning him against me, Burton thought angrily, I'll destroy the sonuvabitch. But who? Not that twerp Bracken. Not Andrews, he's just a road manager, a flunky. Who?

"How's it going with your, ahh—fiancée?" Burton asked finally.

"Okay."

"She still working out?"

"Yeah, sure. Nice lady."

"Oh, nice lady, is it? I thought you called her the Hong Kong hooker."

"Used to." Roland wanted to sound calm.

"So what's this change of heart, Ro? Is that slant-eyed tramp strumming your guitar at night, pulling all the right strings? Or is she doing your laundry?"

"Oh, shut the fuck up, Burton." He couldn't stop the words from rushing out. "I don't want to talk about her."

"All right, all right. I was just curious." Burton didn't need to hear any more. He made a mental note to check personally into the Tashi Qwan situation. No nineteen-year-old call girl was going to stand between him and Roland. Not with all that was at stake. No fucking way.

Roland was angry now, too, but he didn't know whether to hang up or apologize. Burton had done nothing to him, nothing but ask him to keep his word. It wasn't Burton's fault that his mind was crammed full of questions and doubts. In his entire career Roland had not backed out on a concert date unless he'd been ill. He had no respect for stars who refused to perform for insufficient reasons. They were selfish, childish—unprofessional.

"Burton? Okay, man," Roland said haltingly. "I'll do the concerts. But just Miami and Detroit—no more."

"God, Ro, that's great! That's wonderful. I'll arrange everything, make it the easiest I can on you. You'll see. I knew you'd come through for me. We're a team, Ro. And a damned good one. Never forget that."

"I won't."

"I'll call Andrews right now and work out the details. Let's talk again tomorrow. I love you, Ro."

"Yeah. Me, too." And Roland hung up the phone.

In his Chicago hotel room, Burton smiled and turned to the sandy-haired Georgetown University poly-sci major lying next to him.

"Sorry, Larry, just one more quick call."

He ran his hand down the young man's hairless chest. "Then we can forget for a while that either of us works for Mark Whittaker."

Neal Burgess kicked the wood paneling inside his elaborate motor home so hard that his toes stung through his heavy Adidas running shoes.

"She's not going to get away with it!" he sputtered once more, pacing the short, narrow distance of his on-location dressing room. His agent, Mort Lazaar, had been the first to phone last night with news of the Jewel Crosse blind item.

"Something about a Midwestern jock who's doing a series and getting himself screwed up with drugs . . . dealing the stuff," Lazaar had puffed over the phone. "Neal, you're the only Big Ten honcho with a series these days. What's Crosse got on you? More important, should I worry?"

Neal had gone a little crazy at that. Christ, if your own agent doesn't trust you . . . He'd chewed Lazaar out good, and even threatened to fire him.

Lazaar had reacted calmly, in full knowledge that Burgess's contract with the agency stipulated that the client is stuck paying his 10 percent even if he does "fire" his agent. "Listen, kid," he advised in a fatherly fashion, "forget about it. Everyone else will in a day or so."

But Neal didn't think so. And when he arrived that morning at the Long Beach location for his series, *Speed,* the item's impact became quickly apparent. No one actually said anything to him. It was those curious, scrutinizing looks which made him feel conspicuous. The hushed conversations that halted abruptly when he passed by. Even his co-star, Brian Wells, seemed uncomfortable and strained when they rehearsed. It also hadn't helped when Neal opened his copy of *Inside Hollywood* only to be greeted by Jacques Laffont's column: "Who could Jewel Crosse have meant with her blind item about the beefcake actor drug addict? There's only one Big Ten player on the tube—his initials are N.B."

That did it. Neal had run in a seething fury to the telephone in his trailer and summoned his three chief advisers to meet him during the lunch break. They had canceled appointments, rearranged schedules, and made the tedious forty-five minute trip to Long Beach with all due haste.

Brandishing the offending copy of *Inside Hollywood,* Neal faced Lazaar, his agent, Albert Shultz, his lawyer, and Mickey Klein, his publicist. They sat attentively in the air-conditioned trailer, shoulder to shoulder on a short couch. They looked like three somber, unhappy seals awaiting instructions from their infuriated master.

Neal couldn't stop pacing, and he was sweating heavily. Despite the chilled air, he could feel his pancake makeup streaming down his neck onto his T-shirt. It felt like hot lava.

"We've got to do something fast," he declared, firing the trade paper into the lap of Mickey Klein. "This could destroy me. I want to sue."

"Now, Neal," cautioned Klein, an old pro in the intricacies of good and bad publicity in Hollywood. "I've had these situations before, mainly with the *Enquirer.* You'll lose. You'll lose big even if you win the case. Just by acknowledging the item, your image goes down the toilet. Let it pass. Sooner or later things like this happen to everyone in the business. You've got to develop a thick hide."

"I'm just curious," interrupted attorney Shultz, a Beverly Hills entertainment specialist. "Why? Why would Jewel do this? We all know she's no cream puff, but I don't think she'd go with something this explosive, something this dangerous, if she didn't have some kind of reason—"

"Are you suggesting it's true?" shouted Neal, the veins on his neck bulging.

"No, no, of course not. Calm down. Of course it isn't true. Listen, everybody knows there's plenty of stuff around, at parties, on the set, but your reputation is clean. If you were a druggie, believe me, kid, the three of us would know by now."

Neal shot Lazaar a look of vindication and slumped into a chair facing the trio. "Okay, so she has a reason."

All three men perked up visibly at the prospect of hearing firsthand what everyone in Hollywood would have killed to know. Haltingly at first and then in animated detail, Neal recounted the entire story of the cocktail party at Jimmy's, Jewel's proposition, the suite at the Beverly Wilshire, and how he had failed to show.

"No kiddin'?" chuckled Mort Lazaar, running a hand over his shiny bald head. "You really stood Jewel Crosse up? Fellas, the guy's got balls."

"Yeah," agreed Shultz, laughing, "but only because the bitch didn't get ahold of them and add them to her collection."

"I hear she bronzes each set and hangs 'em in her trophy room," added Klein.

For a few moments laughter rocked the trailer. Even Neal finally gave in and joined the others.

"Well," said Shultz, red-faced and swiping at his watery eyes, "it looks to me like we've got a case here—taking Crosse's deposition on her lonely vigil at the Beverly Wilshire could be the most fun I've had in a long time. I'm in agreement with Neal. I say we sue."

Lazaar nodded. "Now that we know it was sour grapes . . . or sour balls." He laughed at his own wit. "God, that woman is something."

"It's agreed then," said Shultz, standing up. "I'll file by tomorrow in L.A. Superior Court. A nice round figure—fifty million in damages, how's that? Against Jewel and the International Network. Slander. Defamation of character."

"Great," enthused Neal, looking relieved. "When do you think we can—"

"—Hold it. Hold it." Mickey Klein, still seated on the couch, was waving his hands back and forth. He looked troubled. "Just hold up a minute here. I hate to break up the party, but I still think the whole thing could blow up in Neal's face. So you sue. So you've even got a solid case. So what? Let's not forget that Jewel Crosse is one tough case herself. She's gonna be looking for a way to turn this to her advantage publicitywise. And she's been in show business a lot longer than you have, Neal. She knows ways to hurt you that you never even heard of. You could be makin' a powerful enemy for life, remember that."

Neal stared hard at his publicist, then looked over at his lawyer and agent.

"Go for it," he said.

— CHAPTER —
Twelve

"Hi." He smiled down at her. "How about dinner?"

Christine could feel her heart miss a beat. "Well, actually I . . ."

"If you have plans, I think you should break them," he said firmly. "This is an emergency."

Now, a few minutes later, she still couldn't quite believe she was sitting across from him at Lucy's El Adobe. She'd planned to have a late dinner there with her cameraman friend who'd first encouraged her to go into television.

But suddenly there was Kent Michaels, towering over her in the newsroom. When she returned to her desk after doing an in-studio movie review for the ten o'clock news, he had simply shown up. Astonished, she'd phoned her friend to cancel, but kept the reservation at Lucy's, a popular Mexican restaurant across from Paramount Studios.

"Just as long as we aren't pummeled by paparazzi or smothered by starlets," Kent teased. "The quieter the place the better."

Christine assured him that although Lucy's could get loud, it was low-key. Without a doubt, famous faces had helped make the cozy hangout popular. Peter Falk. Linda Ronstadt—when she was dating former governor Jerry Brown. Assorted stars of the sitcoms and dramatic series produced on the Paramount lot. But it wasn't a place to be seen, like Spago or Morton's. Most stars who sampled the *enchiladas* or the *arroz con pollo* ("the Jerry Brown special") weren't looking to get noticed there.

Christine was totally unprepared to see Kent. They'd spoken only once since their trip to Santa Barbara, and that conversation had been chilling. After weeks of putting it off, Christine had finally called Kent, and he was obviously pleased to hear from her. But once she'd started explaining about her job, she could sense him backing off. His tone grew cool, and he brought the conversation to a swift close.

"What can I say, Christine? I'd hoped we could work things out," he'd announced stiffly.

"But there's no reason why we can't still see each other, Kent," she'd urged. "Airlines do exist, you know."

"Be honest," he'd snapped, making no effort to conceal his impatience. "You know it'd never work. You have a full schedule now, and I certainly can't go flying off whenever I damn well please. I'm a surgeon, for crissakes."

Their goodbye had had an empty note of finality. For days afterward Christine fought the temptation to pick up the phone again and try to reason with Kent. She did miss him. Even more than before she'd called—because now it seemed there was no hope.

She wasn't about to change her mind. Neither was he.

But that didn't stop her from thinking about him. Visions of Kent flashed to mind at the oddest times and in the strangest places. At her desk. In the car. In the editing room. Images lasting no more than a millisecond, but so real and vivid that they left her dazed, distracted from the task at hand: Kent handing her a pale-yellow flower he plucked at the edge of the pier in Santa Barbara . . . holding her hand as they bounded from rock to rock across a rushing stream in the verdant hills above the city . . . doing a silly impression of a waiter as he insisted upon serving her room-service breakfast in bed . . . the way his long silky eyelashes fluttered ever so slightly as he was about to kiss her. . . .

Sometimes she'd get so swept up in these shimmerings of memory that her eyes would moisten and she'd come close to breaking down. It was downright embarrassing. She felt like an emotional five-year-old. As much as she hated the feeling, she seemed powerless to control it.

If only he wasn't such a stubborn s.o.b., she'd say to herself. Can't have it his way, so that's it, we're finished. How could I live with a man like that anyway?

But could she settle for less? Hadn't the important men in her life always been strong and powerful? Steven. Then Blair. And now Kent.

But now she was determined to be just as strong. If only there wasn't such a heavy price to be paid.

"You know what, honey pie?" Maggie had advised. "Be just as stubborn, use that conniving femininity of yours and get him to move out here. It's time to reel the big guy in."

"You just don't understand, Mag. He has a very important position on staff at the hospital back there. He loves teaching at the university. And he's wild for Minneapolis. He'd never move. There's no way."

"Girl, there's always a way. How's the sex?"

Christine smiled at that question. "I told you," she confided to her friend, "it's the best. Supreme. Exquisite."

"Then not to worry," Maggie had proclaimed. "He'll be back. All you gotta do is tough it out. Get him to see the light about moving here. Besides, what's your alternative? You know the chances of meeting a decent guy in this ego-crazed city?"

Christine knew only too well. Finding a single, available, heterosexual man in Los Angeles was like looking for the proverbial needle in the haystack. Finding one she might be interested in was like having the haystack on the moon.

A successful career without a special man with whom to share it? It seemed a cruel joke. But Christine rarely allowed herself time to dwell on it. Instead she strived to keep busy, burying herself in her work, meeting close but "safe" friends for dinner afterward. She'd also struggled hard to regain control over herself and was making progress. The urge to phone Kent came less frequently. She hoped she was on her way to forgetting about him—and his ultimatum.

That's why his surprise visit was such an electric jolt to her system.

"Okay, so what's the emergency, Doctor?"

Christine was forcing herself to smile at Kent over a frothy margarita.

"The emergency?"

"That's right," she persisted. "You said it was an emergency."

"Ah, yes. So I did." He grinned at her. "Maybe I just needed to see you."

"Kent—"

"Hey, give me a chance, will you? I'm exhausted. I'm jetlagged. I'm—"

"For heaven's sake, Kent, you must have had something you wanted to say. Don't tell me you came all the way out here to buy me dinner."

"No," he said quietly. "The emergency," Kent answered her now, "concerns us. I'm not at my best on the telephone."

"And?"

He paused for a moment to trace the line of salt around the rim of his margarita glass with his index finger. "Quite honestly, Christine," he said, "I had to come to see you because I couldn't stop thinking about you."

Christine felt her cheeks flush. "I know," she said softly. "I think about you, too, a great deal. But I—"

"Christine," he interrupted, leaning into the table, "are you really all that happy working at that station?"

So that was it. Nothing had changed. They were headed for yet another standoff. She felt her heart sink.

"Yes," she answered firmly, "I like what I do very much."

"But is this what you want to do indefinitely? Up early, late news until ten-thirty? No life of your own?"

"Look who's talking. The surgeon who's at the mercy of his patients, on call twenty-four hours a day. And what makes you think it would be any different if I were working in Minneapolis?" she countered.

"I'm sure it would be," he said with an air of total confidence. "You *know* you could call your own shots there, they'd be so happy to have you."

"Kent, that's beside the point. I'm doing what I do best in the town I want to do it in. I don't think I have to apologize for that."

"I didn't say you should, sweetheart," he said, softening his tone, taking her hand in his. "Listen, I'm here because I'm in love with you. Isn't that obvious to you? And I don't want to lose you again."

Christine closed her eyes tightly, but she was hearing every word.

"I have to go back early tomorrow," Kent continued. "I have surgery late in the afternoon. Christine, are you listening?"

She nodded. His voice was searing her. She felt like crying out in joy. She felt like crying out in pain.

"I didn't come here to make love to you and say goodbye another time. I came here to plead with you. To tell you I need you in my life and I want you there. The longer you stay here, the more sidetracked you're going to get . . . and the less chance we'll have."

Christine opened her eyes and looked at their two hands clasped together. "I love you, too," she barely managed to whisper.

After a few moments Kent broke the silence. "What is it you want out of life anyway? Really, truly want?"

She looked up at his taut and handsome face. "Too much," she answered slowly. "I want my career . . . and I want you."

She hesitated briefly, then risked it all. "There is another way, Kent."

He seemed startled. "What's that?"

"What about the idea of you moving to Los Angeles?"

Kent's lips pulled back into a slow half smile as he stared at her, a look of complete amazement on his face.

"You must be joking."

She might as well have been.

Jewel was delighted. Awaiting her late arrival on this Tuesday morning was a message beckoning her to Irving Taubman's office. So it had worked—and very quickly, she thought, as she clicked briskly down the hallway in her high heels.

Apparently their little tryst in New York over the weekend was going to pay off sooner than she'd expected.

Taubman had flown there for a board meeting on Friday. Late that night they'd met in her suite at the Ritz-Carlton Hotel, a deliciously opulent setting with two marble baths and a huge Louis XIV bed.

Despite these sybaritic surroundings, more than anything else the weekend had been an ordeal for her. Keeping Irving Taubman happy was no picnic. He was like a bulldozer when it came to sex. She was still sore from the heavy plowing motion with which he had advanced himself inside her. The man had stamina, she had to admit that.

But she congratulated herself, walking toward his office, that in the end she'd won. That was the main thing. All weekend long Jewel had dropped little hints about increasing the frequency of her shows from two to three a week. At first Taubman had balked. But as the weekend and Louis XIV activity proceeded, she sensed a greater receptivity to the idea. By the time they left New York (clandestinely, on separate flights), Jewel was all but certain she'd get her extra show . . . and more money. It was only a matter of time.

Exhilarated by her success, she ignored the penetrating gaze of Taubman's secretary, Norma Scott, and flounced into his office.

"Irving, dearest." She closed the door behind her. "Ohhhh, how

272

smart we look this morning, so debonair. Is that a new suit? Let me guess—a Cerruti?" With a feline quickness she moved toward his desk.

Taubman didn't answer. Nor did he notice the black knit dress Jewel's long, tall voluptuousness was poured into. Preoccupied with the set of documents in front of him, he was scowling. He had the look of a man who had swallowed something sour. "Jewel," he said now, "come over here. I want to show you something."

"What is it, sweetie? My new contract?"

"No." He stood up and was holding out the papers. "This, my dear, is a complaint just filed in Los Angeles Superior Court, serving as notification that Neal Burgess is suing our collective asses off. By that I mean, the network's . . . and yours."

Oh, Christ, thought Jewel, her heart beginning to boom. Her face, however, betrayed none of her anxiety. "Suing us? Whatever for?"

"I assumed that you would know for what," he said. Then he reached for a sheet of TelePrompTer copy on his desk. "Tell me, does this look familiar? It should. I understand you fought Swanson tooth and nail to get it on your Sunday show."

"Did that little turd tell you that?" she demanded.

Never mind who tells me what," he replied quickly. "Don't be difficult. The point is, you used a blind item which Burgess finds damaging. So he's suing us for fifty million bucks."

"Fifty million? That's absurd. Totally ridiculous. It's a blind item, for crissakes. How can they sue us? I didn't even mention his name."

"Yes, I know, my dear. Come sit down," he said, guiding her to the leather couch and joining her on it. "Now, Jewel, we both know that this is nothing to become unduly alarmed over. You are a professional. No one is questioning that. And I'm certain—I am positive that when you ran that item you were very sure of your facts, confident in the credibility of your sources."

"Of course I was, Irving," she said adamantly.

"I'm certain you checked with not just one, but several informed persons on this matter of Neal Burgess dealing drugs," he continued in a soothing voice.

"I'd be an idiot not to, even for a blind item."

"Yes, you would. But you are not an idiot, Jewel. You are a very smart woman. That's why you have your own show. That's why you are a star. You do your homework, no one can deny that." He looked at her coaxingly. "By the way, my dear, just between us, who were your sources on this Burgess matter?"

"Irving!" she protested. "I'm surprised at you. You know very well that a good journalist does not reveal her sources. People in my profession have gone to jail rather than divulge their informants. I cannot cross over that line, dearest, even for you. It isn't done." She succeeded in striking just the right tone of righteous indignation.

"I know. I know," he responded calmly. "You have every right to protect yourself, Jewel. And you must, of course, remain loyal to your sources. I respect you for that. But please see it from my point of view. I am obliged to report this to Dollinger. He hates lawsuits, and fifty million dollars is nothing to sniff at, after all, nor is the publicity we will incur when this hits the papers. And when I call New York this afternoon, I must have something to tell Dollinger, something concrete to make him feel confident that we are in no danger. So, if you could provide me with at least one of your sources before that time, I—"

"No, Irving," she said firmly, standing and smoothing out her skin-tight dress. "It is out of the question. I can't possibly. Surely New York will see that this lawsuit is frivolous, a cheap publicity stunt. I said nothing about Neal Burgess. You have the copy."

She crossed her arms, sighed, and looking down at Taubman like a mother who was about to give an offensive child one more chance, she relented. "However, under the circumstances I will try for you, Irving. I will make some calls and inquiries. Perhaps my contacts will be cooperative. I cannot promise. But to tell you their names now and jeopardize them—that would be the kiss of death in my business."

Irving Taubman rose slowly to his feet until it was he who had the height advantage again. Towering over the shapely redhead whom he had ravished with such relish over the weekend, he said icily, "The kiss of death, eh? Let me remind you, Jewel, that the real kiss of death would be losing a lot of money for your network because of the noncooperation of sources, or a reporter's own negligence. Now, I strongly suggest you think about that and report back to me in a few hours. By then I expect you to enumerate your sources. And if they refuse to come forward, then you'd better make it your business to find some others, fast."

"Goodnight, see you in the morning."

Roland leaned over to give Tashi a kiss on the cheek. But as she turned toward him, their eyes met and slowly, as though being pulled by an invisible force, their lips came together and touched, however briefly. It was an uncertain kiss, a hesitant gesture.

"It's just that, ah . . ."

"I know," she said softly. "It's still difficult for you. But it's all right."

He took her long slim hand and kissed its palm, then each finger individually, until she touched his cheek tenderly and disappeared into her suite. When Roland joined his bodyguards at the end of the hallway, he could still feel the tingle of Tashi's lips on his.

He wanted to say goodnight again—he wanted to say at least that much and maybe more. Unlocking the door to his own suite, he entered and quickly dialed "O" on the phone.

"Hotel Pontchartrain, operator. May I help you?"

He stared blankly at the phone for a moment, trying to remember Tashi's room number. There had been so many hotels, so many room numbers. He was more tired than he had thought. Exhausted was more like it, from the Miami concerts and tonight's performance in Detroit. He desperately needed a good night's sleep.

"This is the operator. May I help you?"

"Ah, yeah, I—"

"Roland . . ." The voice came from behind the bar. He had been in such a rush and the room was so dimly lit that he hadn't noticed the tall, slender figure in the dark suit. But there was no mistaking that voice.

He put down the phone and focused now on this intruder, who was pouring himself a tumbler of vodka. He made no attempt to conceal his surprise. "What are you doing here?"

"Ro," said Burton cheerfully, ignoring the question. "Great job tonight. You had them camped out on the sidewalks begging for tickets. And Miami, my God, do you realize what you brought in? More than six hundred thousand. That's a record, and Uncle Sam is gonna match it. I think we should celebrate. Want some champagne?" He walked toward Roland, a broad smile on his lips.

"No. No, thanks. When did you get in?"

"Just a couple of hours ago. I guess you were detained at the party. I didn't want to get tied up in that, so I came here and waited for you. I really thought you'd be back earlier."

"Yeah, well, I had dinner."

"With the charming fake fiancée?" Burton asked, still smiling. "Sorry. I know you don't want to talk about her. And that's not why I'm here."

"And why are you here?" Roland asked again, settling onto a long rust-colored couch.

Burton reached into his shirt pocket and pulled out a thin hand-rolled cigarette. "Want a joint?" he asked.

"No," Roland said quickly, looking suspiciously at the marijuana. Burton loathed the stuff. Why would he bring it here?

"Oh, come on, Ro," Burton urged. "Take it. You look very tense. And we both know grass is the only thing that mellows you out."

"File the joint, man, I'm not interested. Now are you going to answer my question? Why are you here all of a sudden?"

"Okay," Burton relented, tucking the joint back into his pocket. "Just trying to help." He sat down next to Roland. Close, his long leg almost touching Roland's.

"Why am I here? You might ask why I didn't show up in Miami. I wanted to, Ro, but there were a few fires to put out back in L.A. Minor stuff, but they had to be taken care of." He leaned closer and placed his hand on Roland's thigh. "The reason I'm here," he said with sudden emotion, "is because I miss you, and I want to be with you. It's been a long time, Ro . . . almost three months. And I've found it very difficult without you."

Burton began massaging Roland's leg, working toward the inner thigh. "Don't," Roland said, getting up abruptly. "Not now."

"All right," Burton sighed, depositing his glass on the coffee table. "Okay. I get the message. Loud and clear."

He placed his elbows on his knees and his head in his hands. "I'm afraid I've failed you, Ro. I haven't been able to get away and spend time with you. And now our relationship is suffering. I know it. I can feel it, the way you sound on the phone, the way you're treating me right now." He looked at Roland imploringly. "Don't you know how I still feel about you? What do you think I've been doing these past three months? Working, yes, but also hurting, Ro, missing you and knowing things weren't the same. It'll take some doing, bringing us back to where we were, I mean, but—"

"Maybe I don't want to go back," said Roland defensively.

"I've considered that," Burton said, getting to his feet. "And the thought sickens me. Look, strange things happen on tour. They go with the strange cities, the strange hotels, the strange beds. But that isn't reality, you know that. Reality is when you come home, after it's all over. Reality is when you face the old familiar surroundings again, the old familiar you. You know the kind of man you are, Ro. You know what brought us together in the first place, what kept us together." His voice cracked. "Is it another man, Ro?"

Roland started at the question. When he didn't immediately respond, Burton rushed on, the words tumbling out hot. " 'Cause if it's another man, Ro, I could almost understand. I understand loneliness. I understand need. But if that's not it, if I have to suffer the double humiliation of being dumped for no one else in particular, or if—if—"

"Burton," Roland said, almost inaudibly, "I don't know what to say."

They were standing side by side now, in front of an immense window with a nighttime panorama spread beneath them. They both stared out in silence at the bright lights of the nearby Renaissance Center and the shimmering Detroit River beyond.

Burton reached over and placed his hand on Roland's shoulder. "You could say that you still care for me, that in time you might love me again."

Roland continued to stare at the cityscape below.

"Ro, look, you're tired. You've been flying all over the world performing, and now you're spending your brief hiatus working to help me. Don't think I'm not appreciative, Ro. I know what it took for you to drag yourself back here. I know what kind of loyalty and endurance that demands. But maybe now you're just a little too worn out and, well . . . a little confused because you're feeling resentful. I don't blame you for resenting me. I put a lot of pressure on you to do the fund-raisers. I just want you to know that I understand, in part, what you're going through. But I don't think it means we're at a dead end, Roland. We're too good a team."

"Burton, you're not—"

"No. Don't say anything more now. I've caught you at a bad time, that's all. You need rest and some solitude. I'll leave you alone for tonight. Maybe tomorrow we'll have lunch and talk some more." He began walking toward the door.

"I have plans tomorrow."

"Fine. I'll see you after the concert then."

"Burton . . ."

"And we'll discuss the other fund-raisers, all right?"

"I don't know," Roland said as Burton Ratchford left the suite.

"Jacques Laffont returning your call, Miss Crosse."

Jewel breathed a sigh of relief. Although she didn't believe in God, she said a silent prayer of thanks to whatever power was responsible for finally forcing the hand of Jacques Laffont to the telephone.

More than twenty-four hours had elapsed since Jewel had placed the first call to Laffont's office. She'd left several other messages and spoken to his answering machine at home as well. It was obvious that he was stalling, deliberately trying to irritate her. But at this moment she could not allow herself to react to that. Jacques Laffont was her only hope. If he wouldn't cooperate, she'd be at a dead end. So far she'd managed to keep Taubman at bay, but she knew that could not continue indefinitely.

"Jacques, darling!" she said in a saccharine voice. "How are you?"

"As well as can be expected at eleven in the morning." He yawned loudly into the phone. "Not my favorite time of day. What's with you, *chérie?*"

"Oh, couldn't be better. I just wanted to tell you how much I loved your column yesterday. The description of the Van Richies' party for Marvin and Barbara Davis was marvelous. Pure genius, Jacques."

"Yes. The action did sort of jump off the page, didn't it?" He waited for her to continue.

"Uh, Jacques," she obliged, "as long as we're chatting, I was just curious. You know that brief conversation we had over lunch at the Bistro Garden? When we spoke of Neal Burgess and that drug business?"

"Neal? Oh, yes. I read about your lawsuit this morning. My God, it even made the *Times*. Fifty million. Jewel dear, you must really have laid it on thick," he said.

"I did no such thing!"

She cleared her throat self-consciously and softened her tone. "Jacques, as you know perfectly well, my story was a blind item. I did not name names. I accused no one. But Neal is a young man on his way up, a very talented young man, and he's trying to protect himself. I understand that. But, you see, I'm sort of unfairly caught here between pressure from the network and my loyalty to you, Jacques."

"To me?" Laffont replied ingenuously. "What in the world do I have to do with it?"

"Well, during lunch you did tell me that Neal was dealing drugs."

Laffont took a sip of the steaming *café au lait* his assistant had placed before him, a dramatic pause before launching into the speech he had been waiting to deliver.

"Why, Jewel," he began, his voice full of reproach. "I said nothing of the kind."

"Wha—?"

"Now, now. If you'll take a moment, I'm sure you'll recall that it was you who introduced the subject of Neal Burgess and drugs. It was you who asked if I knew that he'd been dealing. One's brain cells do decrease with age, my dear, but I would strongly suggest that you try very hard to joggle your memory bank. You might try taking some choline tablets. They're in all the health-food stores, and my nutritionist raves about how they help you remember things . . . correctly."

"Are you telling me," Jewel asked slowly, struggling for calm, "that you are denying what you said about Burgess? Are you actually going to lie about this, Jacques? Are you saying you didn't tell me that Burgess's drug problem was a known fact?"

"Fact? Why, Jewel, you've added a new word to your vocabulary. I had no idea you knew the meaning of 'fact.' Congratulations." He took a large bite of the chocolate croissant accompanying his beverage.

"Jacques, please," she implored. "I really need your help on this. I'll even—"

"But, Jewel dearest," he said. She could hear him chewing. "I *am* trying to help you. This is a good lesson in journalism. Never break your story if you aren't sure of your sources. In this case, you were apparently so eager to nail young Mr. Burgess that you didn't have any. You've hung yourself, my dear, singlehandedly." Laffont chortled loudly.

"You rotten s.o.b.!" she screamed into the phone. "You'll be sorry. I still have power in this town, you shriveled old fag!"

"Easy, my dear. One slander suit at a time is quite sufficient, don't you think? And as for your power, it's fading quickly. Going fast. Better hang on tight, especially to our boy Irving. The man is notorious for his roving dick. He might find someone younger. And smarter."

Jewel was too angry to speak. "I—I—I swear I'll—" she sputtered.

"Goodbye, Jewel. And good luck with the lawsuit. Of course, I'll be following it closely in my column. The whole town is talking about it."

By the time Laffont finished, Jewel had already hung up.

It was nearly midnight in New Orleans, and still oppressively hot. Sweet strains of Dixieland jazz drifted through the French doors off the bedroom balcony of George Steele's suite at the Royal Orleans in the French Quarter. Shouts of gaiety rang out from crowds strolling below. In Steele's sitting room the heavy, humid air was stale with the smell of cigarettes and alcohol.

The four men gathered there might as well have been sitting around a cinder-block motel room in the middle of Indiana for all they noticed their surroundings. They were in New Orleans on business—the President's business. Raymond Sullivan was here to deliver a speech to the Crescent City's business leaders. It was expected he would be challenged about huge federal deficits run up by his administration. As Sullivan's key campaign strategists, it was important that these men be at the President's side.

Despite the unbearable heat, each man was dressed in a business suit and tie. Only Frank Lombardi, chief of security for the reelection committee, showed signs of discomfort. His face was bathed in sweat, and his oxford-cloth shirt, strained at the belly by his imposing girth, was dark with dampness. As Steele got the impromptu meeting underway, Lombardi held a paper napkin to his glistening brow.

"Gentlemen," Steele said, "I had no intention of calling this meeting tonight. You'd much rather be enjoying dinner at Antoine's or the Commander's Palace, I'm sure. But I've just met with the President, and our conversation necessitated this session. He is very upset."

The others exchanged glances, wondering what this was all about. Sullivan's public image was that of a kindly grandfather who loved to spin amusing yarns about his years as a rancher and politician back in Arizona. But these men knew that in private he could be tough, demanding, and impatient for results. He was a chief executive whose personal popularity far exceeded the public's fondness for his programs. And although it was still early in the race, his Democratic challenger, Whittaker, was showing surprising strength. The nation's best political pundits were predicting a closely fought campaign, with the incumbent Sullivan having a narrow edge.

The men searched their minds for the probable cause of the President's ire—and Steele's obvious agitation. Was it some foreign-policy development? Another gaffe by his unpredictable Secretary of Human Resources? A damaging news leak?

"It's the Roland Williams business again," grumbled Steele. "We've all heard the rumors—that he might cancel his European tour to devote his full energies to raising money for Whittaker. Well, the President has become obsessed with that possibility." Steele looked at each of the men in turn. "He has instructed me to have a full report on Williams's Detroit and Miami concerts by tomorrow morning. You know as well as I do that the President is not going to like what he hears. I want some good news to help take the bite out of the bad."

The three men stared back at Steele, speechless.

"Norm?" Steele persisted, turning to the President's private pollster on his left. Norman Sklar was a tall, wiry man whose face was set in a permanent grimace. There was no way to read his expression, for it was always the same. But tonight Steele was hoping for at least a flicker of optimism.

Sklar rubbed his hands together nervously and shook his head. "Sorry, George, nothing positive. Maybe after Tuesday."

"What about the results of the special mailing?" Steele asked, switching his attention to the fastidiously dressed jowly man on his right. Philip Albrisson was a fabulously wealthy Texas businessman and the campaign's finance chairman.

Albrisson ran a hand through his thinning sandy hair and looked at Steele apologetically. "So far only marginal response, George. Something less than one percent."

Steele scowled back at him. "Apparently the Barbarian didn't hit people where they live," he said sourly.

A few weeks earlier the committee had sent out a nationwide appeal for campaign contributions under the signature of actor and body-builder Arnold Schwarzenegger. He was a conservative Republican and active in party causes.

"I thought you said it was a sure hit, Phil," remarked Sklar, who had been skeptical of the scheme. "I expected a couple of million in return at least."

"What's the dollar total to date?" demanded Steele.

Albrisson avoided Steele's penetrating gaze. "It's in the half million range."

"Christ, that barely covers our mailing costs. All right, let's move to the very bad news. Phil, what do you estimate the Democrats can potentially raise if Williams does go balls-out for the rest of the campaign?"

Albrisson brightened slightly. "First off," he replied, "our information is that the European tour—to Germany and Italy—is still on. I checked through sources in Rome and West Berlin as recently as last night."

"That's a relief," said Steele with a tight smile. "Maybe he'll choke on a bratwurst." Mild chuckles filled the damp air. "But all bullshit aside, what's your best projection, Phil, assuming that he won't be available until the home stretch of the campaign, September, say?"

Albrisson took a deep breath. "Maybe you shouldn't tell the President this, George. . . ."

"I'll decide that," Steele snapped. "Let's have it."

"Okay. I calculate that Williams could singlehandedly raise as much as twenty million. Much more, of course, if he shitcans the trip to Europe."

Steele let out a low whistle. The overwhelming figure hung over them like a specter. They didn't need anyone to tell them what a number like that could mean. In a tight contest, it could mean the ballgame. After several moments of silence, Steele got up and poured himself a Scotch.

"We'll have to do better than this, gentlemen," he said finally. "But it's a little late to work any miracles tonight. I'll see you all tomorrow at ten for the prespeech rundown. Oh, and Frank—uh, stick around for a drink, will you?"

As the others left, Frank Lombardi pushed himself up off the couch and walked over to the bar, where Steele was already pouring him a Budweiser. The two were old friends. They'd met years ago, when both attended Duke University. In all the time Lombardi had known Steele, including the twenty-five years Lombardi worked for the CIA, he'd observed his tough-minded friend in action countless times. There weren't many men who could ramrod their way through like George Steele. Not much got to him. When Frank was an undersecretary of Defense, he'd seen Steele take on the flintiest generals in the Pentagon and walk away victorious, not even breathing hard. But he'd never seen him quite like this.

"Hey, George," Lombardi began, "you been workin' too hard, ol' buddy. C'mon, let's go out and see the town, grab something to eat, chase some pussy."

"Nah, too tired," Steele said, collapsing into a chair and kicking off his loafers. He eyed his friend as if he had something important left to say. "Frank, remember how we used to joke back at Duke about the way things would be different when we ran the world?"

Lombardi laughed and sat down across from Steele. "Yeah, sure I remember. When was that, a hundred years ago?"

"Feels like it. But now, Frank, we do run the world, don't we?" He emptied his Scotch.

Lombardi's eyebrows arched. He knew more was coming. All he had to do was wait.

"You know," Steele continued in a low voice, "this Williams thing has got the President and me spooked. It's a real threat now, Frank. We've got to make certain that Raymond Sullivan gets another four years to complete all he's begun, to set in concrete the kinds of changes that won't be undone for the rest of this century, at the least. And I'll be damned if—"

"Hey, George, whoa there, buddy," Lombardi interjected. "Listen to yourself. Old friends can say anything they want to each other, but even friends have to remember that there could come a day when a conversation like this might be misconstrued by some reporter or a congressional committee."

"Aw, shit, Frank, nobody's listening in."

"I used to work for the CIA, remember? The whole world could be listening in, for all we know."

The intensity on Steele's face vanished for a moment as he began to chuckle softly. "Yeah, right. If Watergate taught us anything, it was to keep our mouths shut. But I have to be able to tell the President that we're leaving no stone unturned on this."

"I know," said Lombardi, nodding somberly.

"Just let me be able to say that we're carefully considering all of our options. Understood?"

"Options, huh?" said Lombardi with a half smile. "That sounds like something you learn about at the Harvard Business School."

Thirteen

011 49 30 88 1091.

Burton punched the numbers on his office phone in rapid-fire fashion. He'd already dialed the Bristol Hotel Kempinski in West Berlin so many times that all the digits were etched in memory.

Christ, it's two in the morning there now, he thought, anxiously checking his watch and adding nine hours. *He's got to be in.*

Burton's previous messages to Roland had gone unreturned. On the last attempt, an hour ago, it was obvious that even the hotel concierge was becoming impatient with him.

As he waited for the connection to go through, Burton tapped on his desk with a pencil, reviewing once again what he would say.

"Concierge, please. This is Burton Ratchford calling from—"

"*Ja,* Mr. Ratchford." There was resignation in the voice, and the German accent was thick. "This is the concierge speaking. *Eine Minute, bitte.*"

Burton's pencil taps increased to a quick staccato.

A click on the line. "Yeah?"

"Ro!" Burton exclaimed, standing up as though Roland had just walked into the room. "God, it's good to hear your voice. Sorry if I woke you."

"Just got in," said Roland. "What's wrong?"

"Wrong? Oh, yeah. Nothing really. I mean, us. We've gone wrong, Ro."

Roland was incredulous. "You left a zillion messages and called at this hour to tell me that?"

"I miss you, isn't that enough? And I was hoping that by now you'd had some time to think things through."

"Don't start, Burton," Roland warned.

"But, Ro, we agreed back in Detroit that we'd talk again. It's been more than a week. And, well, I just couldn't go another day without—"

"—Without asking me to do more fund-raisers?" Roland's voice had an edge to it. "I already told you, Detroit was it. The end. I'm wiped out, man. This tour is taking its toll."

Burton sat down again, closed his eyes, and spoke quietly, tenderly. "Ro, I'm talking about us. I know you needed time . . . to think about things. That's why I deliberately kept my distance in Detroit, even though I wanted to be near you."

"Burton, things have changed," Roland said hesitantly. "And I . . ."

"How? How have they changed, Ro? I don't know what's going on with you. I feel so cut off. I just wish I could fly over there and convince you how much you mean to me."

"No!" The word had a surprising, nearly an electric, force. "That would only make things worse. Leave it, Burton. This was inevitable."

Roland tried to soften his tone, wanting to spare any hard feelings while at the same time making his point. "I'm just not as—well—not a political animal like you. I tried to help you while I could. But I've got my own work, my own career . . . my own life. We were good for each other for a time. Very good. But people grow . . . move on, you know?"

"And just who decides that?" Burton demanded, allowing his anger to surface now. "Who decides when we move on, huh, Ro? You didn't discuss it with me. Didn't give me a chance. Who was there to give you advice after Victor died? Who did you depend on to steer you in the right direction when you were down? Who is it that really cares about you? It's me, Roland." Burton was nearly shouting into the phone. "Me, not her!"

"Hey, hold it, man—"

"No, you hold it! Don't you think I know all about that Oriental whore, fawning all over you? Don't you think I know how she's messing up your head?" The words boiled over in a mad rush. "You think maybe you're turning straight, don't you? Well, forget it, Ro! It just doesn't work that way. She's bad for you. Look how cleverly she's managed to separate us. Imagine what she'll have up her dainty sleeve once she's in full control of your life."

Now Roland was screaming into the phone. "You shut your dirty mouth, Burton! Just shut up! You don't know anything about me—about how I feel. All you care about are your fucking fund-raisers, and what you can get out of me! Well, I'll tell you what you can do—"

"Yeah? What can I do, you slimy faggot cocksucker?"

"What did you call me, man?"

"You heard me. Don't you go playing superstar with me, pal. You just remember that I orchestrated this goddamn tour for you when you were too insecure to get off your ass. If it hadn't been for me, you'd still be stoned back there in your Jacuzzi, feeling sorry for yourself. So don't tell me shit!"

Roland had heard enough. "I'll tell you whatever I goddamn please. And right now I'm telling you to fuck off, Burton. Find yourself another sucker to work for the Democrats. And get this straight, asshole—don't you ever call or come near me again—or I swear you'll be sorry you did!"

Roland slammed down the phone, then picked it up immediately again to alert the concierge. There would be no more "emergency" calls from Burton Ratchford.

Back in Los Angeles, Burton paced his office, outraged, his mind churning with expletives. Soon, however, his fury turned cold, and the white heat was replaced by a surgically precise determination. Whatever their personal relationship, Roland *must* do the concerts. He had to. Burton's reputation, his future, were at stake. This was too big to blow.

He hadn't expected Roland to change his mind immediately, but he had hoped at least to state his case and perhaps convince Roland to see him in person. But that damn bitch—she was a fucking sorceress or something. . . .

Burton grunted. Goddamn fucking broads, he thought. He'd been down that road. Roland would do his own U-turn soon, but it might not be soon enough. He had to get Roland away from her, out from under her spell. Then he could handle him. But Burton had to do it now. Whatever it took. While there was still time.

Returning to his desk, he picked up the press release that had been prepared for distribution to the media the next morning. Once again, his eyes traveled to the key paragraphs.

> Music superstar Roland Williams, who has already raised nearly $1.6 million for Democratic Presidential candidate Mark Whittaker, has agreed to perform in an unlimited number of additional fund-raising concerts starting later this month, it was announced today by Burton Ratchford, chairman of the Democratic Party Finance Committee.
>
> Williams, now on tour in Europe, will begin the fund-raising tour immediately upon his return to the United States, Ratchford said.
>
> It is estimated that by playing some twenty cities, Williams could raise in excess of $11 million for Senator Whittaker by mid-October. Matched by federal campaign funds, that could mean an infusion of as much as $25 million for the Whittaker campaign.
>
> Williams has expressed his willingness to add still more concert dates to his schedule.
>
> "He has pledged to work for Mark Whittaker's victory up to election eve, if necessary," Ratchford said.

Burton picked up the phone and dialed press aide Todd Armstrong. "Todd . . . Burton. About the Williams fund-raiser release. It's a go. That's right, he's agreed to do them all. Great, huh? Listen, handle the press on this, will you? I'll be out of town for a few days. Flying to Rome tomorrow. I want to go over the itinerary with Roland personally."

Impatiently Christine riffled through the pile of phone messages stacked on her desk. There were message slips from PR people, story sources, her manicurist, even a bona fide star or two. But nothing from the one man she wanted most to hear from.

Give it up, DuRand. He's not going to be the one to back down. She yanked her handbag off the chair and headed out the newsroom door. Just get on with your life.

It was an impossible situation. She knew that. Two adults, grown-ups who really cared for each other, loved each other—and neither one would pick up the telephone to try and work things out. At times Christine almost had to laugh, it seemed so ludicrous.

She turned the ignition key of the Mercedes.

I should have been born in the 1920s. There'd have been no contest then. At thirty-one I'd have been the dutiful doctor's wife with a houseful of kids, two cats, and a collie dog named Shep. I'd be baking Toll House cookies, not struggling to maintain my independence and at the same time hold on to my man.

She let out a short, sardonic laugh. *Much simpler. Less traumatic . . . and dull.* She turned off Sunset Boulevard and headed down Doheny. *I'd probably have gone bonkers.*

On this particular brisk, sunny day she wasn't feeling bonkers at all. In fact, she radiated energy. Christine was on her way to the Beverly Wilshire Hotel, where the monthly Hollywood Radio and Television Society luncheon was just about to get underway. Usually she avoided these dreary talkathons. Listening to network executives drone on about programming or standards and practices was not her idea of a stimulating afternoon.

Today, though, was different. Christine had a mission.

With a sharp right she guided the car onto the Beverly Wilshire's bricked driveway and thought again about her plan. *What impeccable timing it had been bumping into Albert Shultz at that premiere earlier this week. Uncanny luck.*

Swiftly she moved through the hotel's heavy glass doors. She was wearing her new carmine raw-silk suit. With a hasty glance she caught her reflection in the glass and smiled approvingly. *The drop pleats gave her a refined, classic look.* Christine felt confident, optimistic.

Oh, good. Still cocktails, she observed, scanning the smoke-hazy room of blazers, open shirts, gray suits, and striped rep ties. As was the case at most official Hollywood gatherings, men outnumbered the women. Christine nodded in the direction of several sets of cold eyes and tight-lipped smiles. Then, in the midst of a clammy handshake and the beginning of a boring conversation, she spotted him—the middle-aged man dressed in black.

He was across the room, at the cash bar, ordering a drink. Probably at least his third, Christine figured, as she deftly made her excuses and began wending her way toward the throng of bodies between her and the bar. As she drew closer, she could see that the shoulders and neck of his black velvet jacket were heavily flecked with dandruff.

God, what a seedy loser he is.

Nonetheless, Christine tugged on her permanent television smile and thrust her hand forward in greeting. "Howard! Christine Du-Rand. How are you?"

Howard Ruskin squinted up from his double tequila and smiled. It was always nice to see a pretty girl, but even better to be recognized by one.

"Hassler Villa Medici, *per piacere*," Diedra Davis instructed the driver as the tiny Fiat taxicab sped like an angry gnat away from Leonardo da Vinci Airport. As she braced herself for what was sure to be a harrowing half-hour drive, she thought again about what Denny Bracken had told her.

She'd been groggy and half asleep when they spoke. The early-morning phone call had woken her up, but she couldn't mistake the urgency in Bracken's voice.

"Rex there, honey?" he'd asked as soon as she yawned her way through "hello."

"He's in Acapulco."

"Shit. Have you gotta number for him?"

" 'Fraid not, Denny," Diedra replied sleepily. "He just left a few hours ago, and I won't hear from him till tomorrow around noon."

"Oh, Christ . . ."

"What is it?"

"I really need Rex to shoot over to Rome as soon as possible. We got a big problem over there, and your little girl Tashi is smack in the center of it."

"Really? Then I'll go."

"I dunno, Diedra," Denny said uncertainly. "I think that Rex should—"

"Denny," she interrupted. "Rex won't be back for a week. Whatever's going on over there I can handle. Now what is it?"

"Okay, then, sweetheart, you're on. Now, listen, Diedra. Ratchford just called me, the man is absolutely frantic. He claims Roland is goin' nuts, won't do any more fund-raisers, and is threatenin' to cancel out of Rome. He swears it's all Tashi's fault—that she's got some power over Roland and is turnin' him into a monster."

"That's nonsense."

"I know, I know. But now Ratchford's about to take off for Rome himself, and I want you to get over there first to check out the situation. Make sure Roland's all right. I'd go myself, but I can't get away."

"Have you spoken with Roland?" she asked, rubbing her eyes.

"No, can't get him on the phone. That's why I'm so damned nervous. He's usually a pretty levelheaded guy. Listen, Diedra, honestly, I don't know what's goin' on. But when you've got two fags fightin', and there's a woman involved, it's gotta be major trouble."

She was fully awake now. "Just how involved are Roland and Tashi?" she asked. "Did Ratchford say?"

"He implied that Roland's gone straight on 'im. But I find that hard to believe, if you get my meanin'. When they met, Roland hated Tashi on sight. And I can't imagine him crossin' over the line at this point in his life. Anyway, it won't pay us to sit around gabbin' about it. Sorry I woke you up, but get yourself on the first flight, willya? They're at the Hassler. My secretary already booked your room. And Diedra . . ."

"Yes?"

"Call me soon as you get there. And watch your step, okay? Ratchford's actin' like a ravin' lunatic. Says he's going to get rid of your little girl."

A chill worked its way up Diedra's spine as she reflected on Denny Bracken's last words. Get rid of her? What could that mean?

If necessary, of course, she would send Tashi home. But she prayed it wouldn't come to that. Please.

Diedra sighed heavily and closed her eyes, oblivious to the taxi's near miss with a dusty truck impossibly overloaded with household furniture.

The sun shone hot on the Via Veneto. The fashionable boutiques were abustle with activity. On either side of the famous street, shoppers and tourists crowded the sidewalks. Burton watched the flow of humanity, a continuous stream, from the backseat of the rented Mercedes, irritated by their smiles and affectionate glances at one another. They all looked too happy to suit him.

The crawl through Rome traffic continued until Burton's driver made an unintelligible sound, motioning toward the imposing stone building ahead. *"La,"* he said then, "Hassler Villa Medici." Rome's most distinguished hotel perched majestically atop the Spanish Steps like an immense castle resting on two endless winding staircases.

Burton stared hostilely at the sumptuous structure. "You're going to love the Hassler, Burton," Roland had said one night months ago, after they'd made love and were dreamily planning a romantic rendezvous during the tour. "It suits you."

And now he's up there with that slut, Burton silently fumed. Okay, time to get hold of yourself. Be in control.

He approached the front desk. "Burton Ratchford," he announced, scrutinizing the clerk, a slender, sallow young man with beady eyes behind yellow-rimmed glasses.

"Ah, *si*. Ratchford. Here we are. Room 516. And you have a message, *signore*."

Burton's eyebrows shot up. Who knew he was here other than Bracken and the press aide, Armstrong?

The clerk handed him a white slip of paper. "The bellman, he will—"

"That isn't necessary," Burton interrupted, scanning the note.

> Please call me in room 423 upon your arrival. Denny Bracken
> suggested we speak.
>
> DIEDRA DAVIS

Bracken? Diedra Davis? He pocketed the message. What the hell is going on here?

"No bellman, *signore?*" asked the clerk.

"No, there's just one bag. And I've got business to attend to first." He smiled at the clerk. "I wonder if you would be so kind as to tell me which room my client, Mr. Roland Williams, is staying in? I'm his attorney, and I must speak with him immediately."

Returning the smile, the clerk shrugged. "Terribly sorry, *signore*. We cannot give out our guests' room numbers. Hotel policy."

"This is urgent, an emergency. I've just flown all the way from Los Angeles. Unfortunately, I left in such a hurry that I couldn't phone Mr. Williams to alert him to my arrival. I'm certain that under the circumstances . . ."

"I am very sorry, *signore*." The clerk shrugged again, raising his palms in a gesture of helplessness. "The rules are very strict. I could lose my job."

"All right, who else can I speak with?" Burton's patience was wearing thin. "My client will be very angry if I don't see him immediately. The concierge—or the general manager, perhaps?"

"Unavailable at the moment, I'm afraid," the sallow man answered with an unctuous finality. "I suggest you try again in about two hours. Now please excuse me, *signore*." The clerk turned away and busied himself with a stack of mail.

Two hours—shit! Resisting an urge to lean over and grab the clerk by his lapels, Burton managed a curt "Thank you," then spun around furiously and collided head on with a bellboy.

"Sorry, *signore*," apologized the short, plump young man who was clearly not at fault.

"S'okay," murmured Burton. "Ahhh . . ." he began as the boy started walking away, "Could you show me to my room?" He held out the key.

The boy nodded, reached for Burton's bag and led him to the elevator. Once upstairs Burton gave him ten thousand lira and waved another sixty thousand under his nose. "It's yours if you can find for me the number of *Signore* Roland Williams's room."

Ten minutes later Burton took the elevator to the twelfth floor and marched determinedly toward room 1260. He knocked softly on the door, then waited. He knocked again, then put his ear to the door. No sound from within. Probably still sleeping, it's only ten-thirty here, he thought. He rapped harder. But still there was no response.

"Roland!" He was pounding on the door now. "Are you there? It's me, Ro. Burton. Come on, open up!"

A maid and a room-service boy passed by, and they stared at Burton suspiciously. He waited until the hall was clear again. "Goddamn it, Roland, this is childish. I can't believe you're acting this way!"

By this time it had occurred to Burton that no one was in the suite. Either the bellboy had intentionally given him the wrong number or Roland was out.

Enraged, Burton kicked the door with a thud that resounded up and down the long corridor and stomped off.

Roland reached for Tashi's hand before she could pick up the phone. "Don't answer it," he said.

"Why not?" she asked, playfully biting his fingertips.

"It's nobody you want to speak to. Who would call you at this time in the morning?"

"Only Roland," she giggled.

Last night, when they'd made love for the second time, Roland was afraid. The first time, in Tokyo, it had just happened. Last night he wanted it to happen. He had no doubts about that anymore. His feelings toward Tashi, he'd finally come to realize, did not negate his past, did not betray Victor, did not mean his love for Burton wasn't once strong and genuine. The past didn't matter. Whatever he was as a man, he was irresistibly drawn to Tashi as a human being. He wanted her, and, yes, loved her. But could he be a man to her again, this time deliberately, consciously, without reservations? Failing her physically would mean an end to their relationship, he'd decided. He couldn't stand the thought of not being able to love her totally.

But as he nestled nervously into Tashi's arms last night, slowly giving in to the feelings trapped within him, responding to her patient touch, to her long, graceful hands moving across his body, Roland experienced a palpable sensation of release. Suddenly he was floating somewhere above the bed. It seemed as though he were in a trance, wrapped in the most ecstatic caress of his life. His fear left him.

In its place there was a primitive force. It overtook him. He moved effortlessly then, this magical power guiding him, spurring him on. He no longer worried about who he was, what he was doing, what their bodies were doing together. All doubts vanished. He tasted Tashi's kisses hungrily and returned them, on her mouth, her neck, the deep crevice between her breasts . . . everywhere his lips touched seemed sweet beyond all knowing.

Running his hand over her taut stomach, he inched lightly downward. With a renewed sense of wonder, he explored again her most private contours, remembering what she had taught him, coaxing paroxysms of pleasure from her silken depths. She was honeyed with wetness, ready for him. When he moved over and into her, they came together within moments. But it was a magnificent, extended rush, filling them both with the warmth and well-being they'd wanted so badly to feel . . . and had been so afraid to reach out for.

Afterward they'd held each other tightly for a long time, unwilling then to let go, for fear the marvel of what they'd just shared would disappear.

"Tashi?" Roland said after the phone finally stopped ringing.

"Umm-hmm."

"I was thinking . . . after the tour . . . if you really want to study veterinary medicine . . . is there any reason why you couldn't do it in Los Angeles?"

Tashi leaned over and pressed her nose against Roland's, then kissed him softly on the lips. She smiled. "No reason at all," she said.

• • •

Diedra led Burton to a pair of armchairs near the balcony of her small suite. "Nice view," he commented drily, looking out briefly over the city.

"Yes, isn't it?" she replied, relieved to see Ratchford's apparent calm. If anything, the tall, slender blond man sitting opposite her seemed unnaturally cool. Diedra lit a Players cigarette and offered one to him.

"Thank you, no," he said, watching her exhale a billow of blue smoke. "So you work with Denny?"

"In Europe, mainly. In fact, it was me he turned to when it was decided Roland—Mr. Williams—needed a woman on his arm. I hired Tashi."

What passed as a half smile darted quickly over Burton's face. "I see . . . that explains why you're here."

"Yes," she said, placing the cigarette in a small ceramic ashtray. "Tell me, Mr. Ratchford, what exactly is the problem?"

"The problem, Miss Davis," he began evenly, "is the woman you selected for Roland. I'm not criticizing you. Please don't interpret it that way. But I think you underestimated the manipulative instincts of Ms. Qwan. There must be a Machiavellian quality to her character. Roland Williams is a musical genius, but like many highly creative people, he is also naive, insecure, and easily led. She has managed to gain control of him. And she's apparently convinced him that a lot of things being done in his best interest are not really so."

Burton leaned back in the chair and stared out at the rooftops of Rome. "He won't listen to reason anymore," he said, the words oddly cold and flat.

Diedra noticed that Burton's knuckles were white on the armrests. "Could you be more specific? Exactly what is it you think that Tashi is doing?"

"Think?" he said, acting startled, returning his gaze to her. "I'm not just imagining this. When Roland began this tour, his head was in the right place. He wasn't looking forward to the rigors of performing all over the world. But he was behaving like a professional. Now he's totally out of control, breaking engagements he's already agreed to do. Did Bracken tell you Roland is threatening to cancel out here in Rome? He's booked for the whole week, for crissakes. I don't know what to make of it except that she's pulling his strings."

"I find that hard to believe, Mr. Ratchford. It seems to—"

"And what do you know about Roland, Miss Davis?" he demanded. "I'm telling you he's behaving like a two-year-old. It's totally unlike him. I can't remember Roland ever canceling a concert date before. And it's her—that woman—she's dangerous. You've got to dump her, right now."

Without warning, his face had taken on a terrible intensity, and Diedra was beginning to feel as though what she was really facing was a volcano threatening to erupt. "Mr. Ratchford," she said reassuringly, "I know you're concerned for your friend Roland. And it may be true that he's refusing to follow through with some of his performances. But I am quite confident that Tashi is not responsible for his actions. She's an unaffected young woman, a child herself, in whom I have total trust."

"Oh, sure, total trust!" Burton nearly shouted the words. He got up and was moving away from the balcony. "Like the way you trust all the whores you deal with!"

"Mr. Ratchford—"

"She is wrong for Roland. How else do you explain his crazy attitude? The man is in outer space somewhere!"

"Why don't you let me look into the situation? I'm sure everything will work out."

"Damned right it will!"

He turned toward her now and pointed a threatening finger at Diedra. "What a jerk I was for hiring you and that bitch in the first place!"

Diedra looked up at the man who had seemed so controlled only moments ago. He was perspiring now, his cheeks scarlet. It occurred to her that he might be manic-depressive. Or maybe he was on drugs. Whatever the cause of Burton's intemperate outburst, it was *he* who seemed dangerous. Would he try to do something to Tashi? Was the girl in real danger?

His rage kept on building. He seemed unable, or unwilling, to stop it. Burton was pacing now, gesticulating wildly, the words spewing out, uncensored, uncontrolled, as if Diedra were no longer there. "Roland's crazy to think she can give him what he needs," he ranted. "I *know*. I know what he needs. He's just confused right now, that's all. He'll come around. He can't deny who he is . . . what we are. Goddamn it, it's her, it's that sneaky, back-biting, gold-digging cunt, she's taking advantage of him! He's mine, and I won't stand for it! I won't, I won't, *I won't!* . . ."

His frenzied glance alighted upon a wooden pedestal near the entrance to the hotel suite. In a single, swooping motion, he seized an exquisite porcelain figurine of a ballerina in *jeté* that rested atop the pedestal and hurled it to the pink marble floor of the foyer, where it smashed into shards.

He wheeled to glare again at Diedra. "If you won't stop her, lady," he hissed, "then *I* will!"

Diedra was stunned. But in as soothing a voice as possible, she managed to reply, "Mr. Ratchford, please. Take it easy. There's no need for threats." He continued to glare at her, frozen in his rage, saying nothing. She got up and gently guided him to the door, ignoring the broken bits of porcelain that lay strewn all over the floor.

"You obviously feel strongly about this. As soon as I can locate her, I will send Tashi home."

"The faster, the better," Burton said, refusing to be assuaged. He slammed the door as he left.

— CHAPTER —

Fourteen

"You okay?" came the drowsy, feminine purr from the other side of the bed.

"Yeah, sure. Just a little restless. Go back to sleep, hon."

"Mmmmm." The woman turned over, tossing her long silky hair across the pillow, and drifted back into a deep slumber.

In the chilly darkness he continued to wrestle into his jeans. By the time he reached the front door of the cottage, Kent Michaels had slipped on a heavy sweater and zipped up his dark-green parka. With his first deep gulps of biting, cold air, his immediate impulse was to leap into his Porsche and drive hundreds of miles—at hundreds of miles per hour.

But that wouldn't be fair to Mary Ellen.

Mary Ellen Riley was the very prototype of Kent's ideal woman. Pretty and bright, a physician herself, and thus understanding of Kent's unforgiving schedule. Raised in northern Minnesota, with not the least inclination toward relocating out of state. Mary Ellen was not only fond of, but also quite skillful at, skiing and tennis, Kent's two favorite sports. And she had a graceful, easygoing manner that made people gravitate to her as naturally as water flows downhill.

Everyone agreed they were perfect for one another, she and Kent. Everyone, even Kent's mother.

More importantly, Kent very badly wanted this relationship to work. He'd taken time with it, orchestrating their friendship slowly, building to a gradual crescendo of shared experience, making sure to find each common note of interest, every point and counterpoint of harmony. For two months he'd been seeing Mary Ellen regularly, the last few weeks almost exclusively. Tonight they'd slept together for the first time.

Even that he had planned masterfully. Kent decided they should make love in his rustic, peaceful cottage on Forest Lake. It was there, he told himself, that he felt the most free, untethered by the pressures of his profession and the plasticity of condominium life. But of course there was another more important reason why Kent had chosen the cottage.

Now, gazing up at the awe-inspiring maze of stars that swept across the limitless black Minnesota sky, he was truly honest with himself for the first time in months. What he'd been doing was senseless. It was useless suppressing his real feelings. It didn't do a bit of good refusing to deal with the emptiness and frustration gnawing at his insides.

Yes, he had brought Mary Ellen here to the cottage for one reason and one reason only. Once and for all, he wanted to erase a memory. He thought he could do that by making love to another woman under the same roof where he'd first started falling in love with Christine.

But what he'd just had with Mary Ellen Riley was sex. Despite all his hopes to the contrary, it had been the same kind of detached, uncaring act he'd shared with numerous women since his divorce.

And now, in the wake of that disappointment, sleep would not come. Kent had lost a great deal of sleep lately. When all else failed, the tiny white pills he kept next to his bed helped. But he hated resorting to them. In an emergency, a surgeon who was drugged might not be able to perform at his best. Christine haunted his dreams anyway. And during the day she dropped unsummoned into his thoughts.

Nothing seemed to work. Not the ski trips to Sun Valley and Aspen or the medical convention he'd combined with a European vacation or the growing list of women he'd attempted to begin relationships with.

For the first time in his life Kent Michaels was faced with a problem he could not solve. He couldn't wish her away. He couldn't think her away. He couldn't even screw her away.

Not even the perfectly lovely, perfectly suitable Mary Ellen Riley could free him of Christine DuRand.

Aimlessly he wandered down the dirt road in the starry darkness. Sometime around three in the morning he turned and headed back toward the cottage. Slipping quietly into the kitchen, he went directly to the freezer, withdrew an iced bottle of hundred proof Absolut vodka and poured himself a tumblerful.

Quickly he knocked it back. And then he poured another.

The white-jacketed room-service boy stood stiffly, awaiting instructions. Balanced above one shoulder was a silver tray on which rested a pot of espresso, two small cups, a plate of *amaretti,* crunchy Italian macaroons. In the golden-red light—for through the open balcony doors the sun was just beginning to set—the boy's face looked fiery.

"Sulla tavola, per piacere," said Tashi, indicating a shiny teak coffee table with an ivory inlay pattern.

"Grazie," the boy said. He beamed as Tashi handed him a twenty-thousand-lira tip and made a swift and silent exit.

"You're sure?" Diedra's voice was troubled, insistent. She was pacing a shadowy corner of the elegantly furnished suite, an overflowing ashtray nearby bearing evidence of her chain-smoking. "You're sure he hasn't said anything about canceling out here in Rome?"

"No," insisted Tashi, sitting cross-legged on the bed. "Just the fund-raisers in the States. The only thing that upsets Roland these days is Burton Ratchford. He refuses to have anything to do with him."

Diedra stubbed out her cigarette, poured the steaming espresso, and handed Tashi a cup. She sat down beside her. "And what about you and Roland, Tashi?" she asked. "How are you two getting along?"

Tashi took a tiny sip of the rich, dark coffee and then looked up, blushing slightly. "We're ah . . . extremely close, Miss Davis . . . I mean Diedra. I care about him very much."

Diedra said nothing for a moment, but smiled warmly and then took the girl in her arms. "Tashi," she said finally in a low, almost trembling voice, "I'm happy for you—for you both." Regaining her composure, she placed her hands on Tashi's shoulders. "We must work fast. Ratchford is threatening to do something drastic. I'm afraid you may be in danger."

"What can we do? Roland says he's uncontrollable sometimes."

"Yes. I'm sure of it. Tashi, I've already told him that I'm sending you home."

"Home? But Diedra—"

"Of course I won't, honey. Don't you worry. I've been in the business of handling men for a long, long time. But we can't take any foolish chances. To be safe, I've arranged for you to move to another room, under an assumed name, and you must stay there, out of sight. The front desk will tell anyone inquiring that you've checked out. It's already taken care of."

"I won't be able to go to the concert?" asked Tashi, disappointed.

"Not tonight, honey, I'm sorry. But if my plan works, the coast will be clear by tomorrow or the next day. I'm going to try to convince Roland to meet with Burton and swear that you're gone—and even pretend to agree to those fund-raising concerts. Anything to get him out of Rome. Once we're back in the States, we'll let Bracken take over. He'll put the muscle on Burton to keep him away from Roland for good."

She winked at Tashi, forcing a smile out of the crestfallen girl. "Now, when do you think I might be able to speak with your new squeeze?"

Tashi looked at her watch and shook her head. "Not until after the concert. He's at a sound check now, and he isn't coming back to change. And once the performance is over, he's usually pretty difficult to get to. Oh, Diedra, I hope this works!"

"Honey, we'll have to find a way."

"Ro–land! Ro–land! Ro–land!"

Rome's Sportivo Palace was a madhouse of shouting, clapping, adoring fans. It was more than pandemonium; it was mass hysteria. A phalanx of anxious-eyed security guards in bulging black blazers lined the edge of the stage, keeping a wary eye out for those who might decide to rush the proscenium, knowing all too well that a riot would be totally beyond their power to contain.

The houselights had dimmed, and the crowd was working itself up to a new height of frenzy in anticipation of the moment they had come for—Roland Williams's arrival onstage. Here and there, fans held aloft ignited Bic lighters, pinpoints of light in the darkness, individual welcoming beacons scattered in this sea of rapturous faces.

It was just past eight-thirty.

Suddenly there was shadowy movement onstage, a flicker of light as curtains parted to allow the small troupe of musicians to grope for their places in the darkness, guided by memory and the glowing red lights of their amplifiers.

A reverberating, thrilling beat began to thunder offstage, washed now in a hazy red-and-blue light, and the Sportivo Palace rocked with a deafening shriek of adulation. A single white spotlight locked onto a staircase which divided the stage and disappeared somewhere high above it, its uppermost reaches lost in the night.

A cloud of red smoke scintillated and billowed at the bottom of the staircase. Then another. Another. Red. Blue. Red. Up the edges of the stairs, another and another, past the vacant circle of white light, up higher, explosion after explosion of colored smoke.

And then the voice—high, sweet, loving, not male, not female, not of this earth—an angel's voice, come down from the heavens. The crowd heard and went wilder, but as yet the possessor of the voice was nowhere to be seen.

At the base of the stairs, another explosion. A brilliant flash of light and sparks and white smoke, blindingly bright. And in the next instant he was there. In the center of the white spotlight. The unmistakable profile. Gleaming white teeth against golden skin, green eyes flashing fire, chin tilted back, hands firmly on hips, guitar slung across his chest.

His song—the new song he had written especially for this world tour, the song that already had eclipsed his previous platinums—a song of soaring hope and unshakable faith, of love and life and the dream of a global community united by its differences, its people joined by music—this song he sang, joyfully, inimitably, but his words were all but drowned out by the incessant screaming of the fans.

> *All together! All! All! All!*
> *One forever! One! One! One!*
> *That is what—what—what we can be! . . .*

Diedra sat in the front row, captivated. She had never witnessed anything like it. She had never seen such an outpouring from the stage—and back onto the stage. Even though her mind was troubled, she found herself mesmerized. Roland Williams was everything she'd heard, and more.

As he spun and whirled on stage, singing, pounding out the pile-driving rhythms of his anthem on his guitar, she wondered how he would react later on when they met. The plan was deceptively simple: After the concert, Diedra, not Tashi, would be waiting in Roland's limousine. She had, in fact, switched roles with Tashi for the night.

So far it was working. Diedra was dressed in one of Tashi's outfits— a long mauve jersey gown with a large cowl collar that doubled as a hood. She'd draped the hood fashionably over her head. Since she was approximately Tashi's size, it was even possible that no one would spot the ruse. Certainly the two silent rent-a-guards now sitting on either side of her hadn't.

Roland didn't allow the intensity in the Sportivo Palace to dim even slightly for more than two hours. He seemed inexhaustible. Immediately after his second encore number, as the shouting and screaming continued, Diedra was guided backstage by one of the guards, a short, stocky Italian who appeared not to speak much English.

She was shepherded out through the Sportivo Palace's artists' entrance, where a noisy crowd was already gathered behind police barricades. *"Ro–land! Ro–land!"* they chanted incessantly as a small army of Roman police in riot gear manned the perimeters. The guard, his eyes wide, brusquely shoved Diedra into the waiting limousine.

The door slammed shut with a heavy thud and the electric locks clanked into operation. The motor was softly idling. Even inside the limo, shouts from the crowd seeped through, muffled and distorted like noises heard underwater. Slightly disoriented and a bit riled by her rough treatment, Diedra was about to complain to the driver, a huge beast with no neck and a tiny chauffeur's cap. She thought better of it. Her voice—it might unmask her.

Even if they were heavy-handed, she wondered at the efficiency of Roland's protectors. Peering out through the tinted-glass windows, she watched the screaming mob strain against the barricades and noted that two other heavyset men, apparently also Italians, were leaning up against the limousine's front bumper. They seemed to be continually checking their watches. She assumed Roland kept a tight schedule and hoped that he would be joining her soon. It was unsettling, sitting there in the back of the locked limousine all alone.

But another fifteen minutes passed. Then, suddenly, a newly frenzied chorus of shouts rose from the crowd, which began to surge forward into the riot shields of the police. The outnumbered officers struggled mightily to hold them back. *"Ro–land! Ro–land! Ro–land!"* Before she could turn to see if he had come through the artists' entry, the limo doors flew open. Diedra jerked her head back, facing straight ahead, trying to make certain the hood hid her profile.

The noise and bedlam were unbelievable. Diedra dared not look anywhere but directly in front of her, where she saw one of the Italians who had been leaning against the car slide into the front passenger's seat and slam the door shut.

Someone plopped heavily onto the soft leather seat beside Diedra. She heard labored breathing, as if the person had had to run a gauntlet to reach the sanctuary of the limousine.

An instant later, all hell seemingly broke loose.

The police barricade couldn't hold the crowd. The limo was converged upon from several directions and instantly surrounded by scores of crazed fans.

Roland! Chè bellezza! Un angelo! Roland! Eeiiii!!

Fans began pounding loudly on the hood and sides of the limousine, and suddenly Diedra heard what sounded like a scuffle just outside the still-open door to her left.

"Hey, please . . . don't!" It was unmistakably Roland's voice.

"Ayyy, Roland! Roland!"

The beast in the chauffeur's cap, twisting his body around to see what was happening, let out a bellow. *"Cacchio! Cogliona!"* With surprising quickness, he pushed his door open and jumped from the car.

Diedra could resist no longer. She had to see what was going on. What she witnessed in the next few moments was nothing short of horrifying.

A fat-cheeked young Italian, a girl no older than fifteen with stringy black hair and a totally wild look in her eyes, had managed to climb far enough into the limo to grab Roland by a sleeve. Her other hand was locked in a vise grip around the armrest of the car door. The burly chauffeur was pulling at her violently, but she stubbornly refused to give up her prize catch.

"Don't . . . don't . . . don't," Roland kept pleading. He had changed into street clothes, jeans and a black leather jacket, and a white towel was draped around his neck to soak up the perspiration that still streamed from his temples.

The chauffeur pulled a small black pistol from his trouser waistband and raised it high above his head. Diedra screamed. The thud the weapon made against the girl's skull was sickening.

Her body went limp—but still she hung on.

Cursing furiously, the chauffeur wrapped both arms around the unconscious body and heaved it into the back of the limo, where it landed in a heap, head first, on the thick carpeting, blood trickling from the girl's scalp. The limo door closed with a crash, and the chauffeur leaped back behind the wheel and tromped down on the accelerator. The limousine shot forward, fishtailing wildly.

The screams outside turned to cries of outrage and terror as the driver plowed through the throng of fans, oblivious to all in his path. Several were struck and thrown to the side; one young man was catapulted over the windshield and bounced off the trunk lid before crashing to the pavement.

"Hey, for crissake! Stop! What the fuck are you doing?"

The glass partition was already up, and if the driver heard Roland's impassioned command, he didn't respond. Roland sprang forward and glared angrily through the glass.

"What the hell is going on here?" he said, punching the button at his side to lower the partition. "Who are you, and what are you doing in my car? Where's my driver? Where's Vinnie?"

Again there was no response from the no-neck man at the wheel. Instead he pressed his foot down even harder on the accelerator, and his companion produced a compact Uzi submachine gun and leveled it menacingly at Roland's chest.

"Silenzio!"

The driver made a sharp, screeching right into an alley, and then they were racing down darkened, unfamiliar streets. He was definitely not going in the direction of the hotel.

"Holy Jesus," said Roland. He looked down at the girl on the floor, who had not stirred.

Leaning close to her, struggling against the lurching turns of the limo, he put a hand to her neck, searching for her pulse. "Thank God, she's alive," he said. "Tashi, help me get her up on the seat."

Diedra froze.

"Tashi?" Roland got no further. He stopped talking as soon as Diedra turned to him.

"Who the hell are you? What have you done with Tashi?"

"Don't worry, she's fine. I'm Diedra Davis," she said in a frightened voice. So this is what Burton meant, she thought, trying desperately to make sense out of what was happening. He had planned all along to kidnap Roland and Tashi, scare them into doing what he wanted. God, this is the work of a psycho.

Roland was nearly blind now with rage. "You damn well better hope she's fine! If your animals have touched a single hair on her head . . ." He spit the words at her. "You'll never get away with this, you know. My security squad is on our tail right now. And, lady, when they get hold of you and your goons here, they're going to squish you all like bugs—like filthy cockroaches!"

"But I'm not . . . you don't think I did this?" she said as the car careened down a dark and bumpy street. "Denny Bracken sent me. I thought—didn't he get in touch with you?"

"Why don't you just cut the crap? I don't—"

Before Roland could finish his sentence, the limousine stopped short, sending them both hurtling forward. The chauffeur and the man holding the Uzi pulled open the passenger doors. They dragged the unconscious girl out in the darkness, then Roland and Diedra were yanked from the limousine, blindfolded, gagged, and handcuffed.

They herded the two of them into another vehicle, a van or panel truck; whatever it was, it had a loud muffler. One of the men drove while the other rode in the back with their prisoners. Both Roland and Diedra were in a disbelieving daze, and time seemed to be suspended; the ride, while seeming to take forever, in fact lasted no more than half an hour.

Finally the driver braked hard, bringing them all to a punishing stop. Led by the Italians, Roland and Diedra were forced out and made to walk several yards up a steep incline. They were shoved roughly when they faltered. Diedra stumbled and moaned loudly as the hard steel of the handcuffs dug into her wrists. The no-neck man with the pistol struck her across the temples with his weapon, felling her to her knees.

"Tu parli quando pisciano le galline!"

Behind them, they heard the roar of the faulty muffler receding into the night. Diedra was pulled to her feet again. They kept on walking, and Roland tried to clear his head and concentrate on any clues he could glean concerning their whereabouts. By the sharp, cool, clean air in his nostrils and the sounds of night insects he figured they were in the countryside. He knew by the crunch under his shoes that they were on a dirt road, apparently at some distance from the nearest busy highway or residential neighborhood. The uphill march suggested a mountainous area.

"Fermi!"

At that, they were pushed into the back of a small four-wheel-drive pickup. Then their captors apparently walked off some distance, almost out of earshot.

Diedra and Roland lay there silently in the dark and dewy air, shaken and thoroughly frightened. Off to one side they heard the men grumbling lowly in Italian. There seemed to be more of them now, and soon they were arguing. A briefcase or a suitcase snapped open. The talking stopped. They heard heavy footsteps move toward them.

Diedra's heart was pounding. She couldn't catch her breath. She felt as if she were suffocating. What were they going to do to her and Roland? What had become of that poor girl? And was Burton really that insane that he would kill for revenge? She felt a hand grab her arm and roll up the loose sleeve of her jersey dress. Then the sharp prick of a needle. She heard Roland groan, and as she tried in vain to call out to him, everything went black.

Jewel sat bolt upright in bed.

A moment earlier she was about to doze off, but when his face flickered onto the television screen, she was awake instantly.

Uh? My God, it's Williams!

She clicked up the volume on her remote control to hear an announcer's somber voice:

"We interrupt this broadcast to bring you a special Eyewitness News bulletin. . . . An Italian news agency in Rome reports that it has received a letter from a leftist terrorist organization known as the Nucleii Armati Proletari, which claims responsibility for the kidnapping of music superstar Roland Williams. According to the news agency, the group has demanded release of its fifty-seven members currently being held by Italian authorities, and safe conduct out of the country. . . . Repeating, an Italian terrorist organization says it is holding superstar Roland Williams captive and has demanded release of its members now in Italian prisons. Reaction from Hollywood, which views the Williams kidnapping as a warning to all celebrities who tour or work on films abroad, tonight at eleven . . ."

Jewel pressed the "off" button on her remote control and picked up the telephone. Hurriedly flipping through her small bedside phone book, she dialed Denny Bracken at home.

"Denny dear—Jewel. I'm so glad you're in. Any more developments? Why would a terrorist group pick on Roland Williams? Denny, what else can you tell me for tomorrow's show? I could really use an exclusive."

"No can do, sweetie," replied Bracken, curtly. "I got nothin' more than the latest wire-service reports. Like to help you, doll. Sorry. Gotta go now." He started to hang up.

"Wait! Denny! How about a quote from you?" she pressed. "Something different from what you've been feeding the media all day. Something personal about Roland."

"Jewel baby, I just can't right now. I'm too strung out. Been yackin' into a microphone all day long. I've really gotta hang up now, sweetheart. You caught me at a bad time."

"Look, Denny . . ." Jewel was pleading now. "I'll level with you. This Neal Burgess suit has truly become a pain in the ass. A bummer, you might say . . . ha, ha! Seriously, darling—any little tidbit about Roland would be a real boost right now. How about it, for old time's sake?"

"Tell you what, Jewel. Gimme a call at the office early tomorrow. First thing in the morning I should have something, and it'll be just what you need, exclusive—very big. Talk to you then, kiddo. Bye."

Jewel hung up the phone, satisfied. On his end, Bracken picked up his suitcase and raced out of the house, into a waiting limousine. "LAX, and make it fast," he ordered. "I only got an hour to catch a plane to Rome."

Tashi was distraught. All night long she'd tried calling Roland and Diedra, using her code name (Diedra had told her to identify herself as "Nancy Johnson"). Then, around six in the morning, she'd picked up the *International Herald Tribune* outside her door and nearly collapsed with shock. There, spread across page one, was the story of Roland's kidnapping. Since then she'd been frantically ringing Roland's road manager's room. It was 10 A.M. before she finally reached him, and by that time she was sobbing uncontrollably and quaking with fear.

"Dirk! Wh–where have you been? It's Tashi. What's happened to Roland?"

Dirk Andrews gripped the phone as if he'd gotten a call from the grave. "Tashi?" he gasped. Even in his excitement, his voice sounded flat and exhausted. "Where are you? Are you all right? Is Roland with you?"

"No," she cried. "I didn't go to the concert last night. I had to stay here because—"

"Tashi, listen to me," he interrupted. "Now just tell me where you are and stay put. Don't move. I'll be right there."

Five minutes later Andrews was comforting Tashi in his arms, and at the same time trying to fit the pieces of this increasingly bizarre puzzle together.

"So this woman, Diedra . . . she was with Roland last night?" he asked, trying to follow Tashi's emotional retelling of the arrival of Burton and Diedra, of Diedra's fears and plan to talk with Roland. He was astounded and more than a little confused, to put it mildly.

"Yes, yes, yes . . . that's what I've been trying to tell you!" Tashi blurted. "She works for Denny Bracken, and she had to talk with Roland."

"Hmm," Andrews pondered, handing her a wad of tissue from a box on the bed table. "Here. Blow." He shook his head. "Sounds fishy to me. Maybe she was in on it."

The same thought had already crossed Tashi's mind, but she wouldn't let herself admit it. "I don't think so," she said, slowly, sitting down on the edge of the bed. "No. I'm sure Diedra wasn't involved."

"But, Tashi, if—"

Just then there was a pounding at the door. Andrews rushed across the room to open it.

"Burton?" he said in amazement. "How did you find—"

"Out of my way." He pushed past Andrews, his eyes fixed on Tashi. He looked haggard, drawn, like he'd had no rest. His eyes were bloodshot. He was unshaven. And when he came close, Tashi could smell the sourness of liquor on his breath.

Before she knew what was happening, he drew back his hand and slapped her hard across the face.

Blood, a thin drizzle, began to streak down her chin, and her eyes went wide with terror.

"Where's Roland?" he demanded as she cowered, trying to move across the bed away from him. "I know you're behind this charade, you conniving bitch. You'd do anything to keep him from me!" Burton leaped to the other side of the bed, grabbed Tashi by the shoulders and brought her roughly to her feet. "Goddamn you!"

"Hey!" Andrews broke in, trying to separate them. "Lay off, man!

What the hell are you doing? She's been here alone all night."

"Yeah, hiding out," Burton said snidely. He still refused to loosen his grip on Tashi's shoulders.

"You—you're hurting me," she protested weakly.

"Why didn't you leave?" he ranted on. "Go, like you were supposed to? Back to whoring in Hong Kong, where you belong."

Tashi was gaining strength from the anger rising inside her. "You shut up!" she lashed back now, twisting and squirming with all her might until finally freed from his grasp. She retreated a few steps. "You're the one who's causing all the trouble! Everything was fine before you showed up. You're just jealous because Roland cares for me."

"Cares for you?" taunted Burton. "He doesn't know what he cares about anymore, you've messed him up so."

"That's a lie!" she screamed. "You're the one who's always meddling, trying to win him over so he'll do more of your lousy fundraisers and make you a big hero. You don't care one bit about his feelings!" Her body was tensed, fists clenched, her eyes on fire.

"Hey . . . hey," Andrews tried again to intervene. "Can't we just sit down quietly and try to figure things out? Calm down, both of you. Tashi?" he admonished. Then he turned to Burton. "When did you last see Roland?"

"I didn't see him at all," Burton said bitterly, still glaring at Tashi. "She monopolizes all his time."

"And that's why you had him kidnapped, isn't it?" Tashi rejoined angrily. "Think about it, Dirk. Who else had a better motive? And he knew Roland would be alone after the concert last night. Where is he, you bastard? What have you done with him?"

A penetrating ring interrupted, and they all turned anxiously toward the telephone. "I left word that I'd be here," Andrews said, lunging to pick it up.

"Hello? Yes, this is Andrews . . . Oh, no—all night? Jesus, are they all right? Okay, ah, listen—Tashi Qwan, Roland's fiancée—she's here. No, she wasn't with him. . . . Sure, sure. She's a bit rattled, but she's okay. . . . What? Yeah, I'll be at the hotel all day. Thanks."

"That was the detective who's in charge of the investigation," Andrews said somberly as he hung up the phone. "They've just located Vinnie, Roland's driver, and the four bodyguards. They were drugged and tied up all night in a makeup room downstairs at the Sportivo."

. . .

Blurry. Everything was blurry at first.

As edges became sharp and furry outlines came into focus, Diedra realized her head was aching terribly. She was dizzy, nauseous, and totally disoriented. It was as if she'd just emerged from a deep, dark well filled with icy-cold water. She'd been spinning down farther and farther, helpless, gasping for breath. Then all of a sudden, by some miracle, she was propelled upward, back to the top, where, finally, there was light again.

It was a narrow stream of brightness, slanting through a window high on her right. Iron bars, four of them, stood sentry in the small opening. She saw that they looked new compared to the blackened stone walls, as if they'd been added only recently. The room—not large, about the size of an average bedroom—was chilly and damp. It smelled of mildew and long-undisturbed mustiness. She guessed it was a very old structure.

Diedra was lying on a lumpy straw-filled mattress atop a rusty iron cot. There was one door, directly across from her, made of rough-hewn wood. It was closed. The room had no sink, no sanitary facilities. She noticed two wooden buckets near the door. At the moment she felt too weak and too frightened to investigate.

Diedra shifted to examine the rest of her new and unwelcome surroundings. There, on another small cot, was Roland. She was trying to recall just what had happened to them when he turned to her and their eyes met.

"Where are we?" he whispered.

"I don't know," she said with difficulty. Her mouth was parched and her tongue felt like sandpaper. She longed for a glass of cool water. "How long have you been awake?"

"Not long," Roland said, examining the reddish abrasions on his wrists. "Must have been sodium pentathol. I feel like I've been under for days."

She caught him searching her face suspiciously. He was wondering how she could be an accomplice in this, since here she was—locked up with him. Nothing made any sense.

"What's your name?" he asked groggily, unsure of what she'd told him last night.

"Diedra Davis," she replied, almost inaudibly. "Denny Bracken sent me to check up on Burton Ratchford, make sure there wasn't any trouble."

"Burton's in Rome?" Roland abruptly sat upright on his cot, only to fall back again when a wave of dizziness swept over him.

"Uh-huh." Diedra had shifted her eyes toward the doorway. "Did you hear something?" she asked nervously.

Roland listened for a few seconds, then shook his head. "If you work for Denny, why haven't I ever met you?" he persisted, watching her closely.

"Because I don't work in the States for him," she said, glad she had rehearsed this speech for their aborted meeting in the limo. "Only in Europe when he can't get over here. I guess you'd call me a public-relations troubleshooter." Diedra sighed and looked around their dismal quarters. "Do you think Ratchford did this? Is he that weird?"

Roland stared at her blankly. He had no idea who would kidnap him, or why. He still wasn't sure she hadn't been in on it, but he certainly hadn't suspected Burton. "Why would he want to hold me captive? What good would it do him?" he asked, testing her.

Diedra shrugged. "Who can say? But you know how erratically he's been acting lately. That's why Bracken sent me to Rome. Burton was threatening to get rid of Tashi. When I talked to him yesterday, he was behaving like a lunatic. I thought Tashi was in danger, so I convinced him she was on her way home. That's why—"

"She's all right, isn't she?" he asked sharply.

"Yes, as far as I know. She stayed in the hotel last night. And I was—" Diedra stopped abruptly and held her breath. She knew she'd heard something this time.

Then they both heard it—the sound of heavy footsteps coming closer and closer. Diedra swung around and put her feet on the floor. Her hands squeezed the iron frame of the cot. Her headache pounded relentlessly, keeping time with her heart. Were those Italian thugs coming to get them? Would they be carrying the submachine gun? Was this an execution?

Roland froze and clenched his teeth. Why was this happening? What did they want? Money? His life?

There was the snapping sound of a key freeing a padlock. The door flew open with a rusty screech, and a hulking man dressed in black filled the doorway, facing them stonily. It was no one they recognized from their abduction. He had short curly dark hair, a bristly mustache, and massive arms and shoulders. But his most prominent feature was a black eye patch over his right eye. He was cradling an Uzi in one arm.

The man took in the dim cell with his one eye. Then he turned his head and gave an order in Italian.

There was a scraping sound, as if something heavy was being

dragged across the hard dirt floor outside the cell. The man in the eye patch backed away, and another man, short and unshaven, could be seen straining with a badly soiled burlap sack, the bottom of which was indeed cutting small furrows through the dirt. At the cell's entrance, the man summoned all his energy and lifted the burlap bag, heaving it several feet inside. It landed with an ominous splat.

Roland and Diedra watched with mounting terror. The bulky, oddly shaped bag lay no more than a dozen feet from where they sat on their cots, rigid with fear.

The man in the eye patch was back in the cell now, standing astride the burlap sack. He grinned broadly at the two frightened prisoners, exposing yellowed uneven teeth.

Leaning over, he slit the sack open neatly with a stiletto, then stepped back.

Diedra recoiled, putting her hands to her mouth to hold back a wave of nausea. Roland's facial muscles began to twitch involuntarily and his face was drained of color as he, too, fought to control himself.

The sack's contents were a mystery no longer. It was the girl—the young fan who'd had the misfortune of getting caught up in the kidnapping. She was clearly, inescapably dead.

"No—no—no," Diedra heard herself saying.

The girl's lifeless eyes stared obscenely, there was a gruesome expression on her face, and huge bluish bruises on her neck. Her hair was matted and crusted with dried blood. But that wasn't the worst she had endured. She was stripped naked. Her stomach and thighs were pocked by cigarette burns, and across her adolescent chest a stiletto had carved out the letters "R–W."

Roland struggled to speak, sickened beyond words that the sad young thing had paid for her overzealousness as a fan by becoming the macabre plaything for these sadists.

"Y–y–you . . . y–you . . ."

The man in the eye patch cut him off. *"Silenzio, culo!"* He squared off against the two of them, glowering stormily and brandishing the Uzi in the direction of the dead and mutilated girl.

"Non rompermi il cazzo. . . . No . . . fuck . . . with . . . me!"

Irving Taubman yawned. It was only eleven o'clock in the morning, but paperwork made his eyelids feel like lead weights, and today he had mounds of it—policy memos from New York, the latest Nielsen reports, budget reviews—to sift through. He glanced at his watch, anxious to keep his one o'clock lunch date at Trump's.

As he was returning to his reading, he noticed a three-quarter shot of Jewel on one of the half-dozen television monitors across from his desk. She was beginning to tape her show for transmission later that day via satellite.

He noticed that she was wearing something frilly in pink with a white taffeta sash. Irving frowned. He wasn't fond of the look, no matter who the designer. Tell her to stop dressing like a prom queen, he made a mental note to himself.

He continued working, but then something she said—the audio was turned down so low that he couldn't quite make it out—caught his ear. He pushed a button on a small console built into his desk.

"—Two weeks since music superstar Roland Williams was mysteriously kidnapped in Italy," he heard her saying now. "And few clues have surfaced, apart from the initial communiqué from the terrorist group which claimed responsibility for the act. Italian authorities have so far balked at negotiating with the group, and if authorities are any closer to discovering Williams's whereabouts, they are keeping it to themselves. . . ."

The screen flashed with scenes of Roland Williams's fans, as Jewel continued reading: "All over the world, vigils like these have been staged, some urging the Italian government to meet the terrorists' demands for release of their captive members, others simply praying for Williams's safe return. This adoration of the elusive and enigmatic singer, who always seemed safely flanked by bodyguards and was obviously uncomfortable in public places, is not surprising. Even before the kidnapping, Williams generated a mystical aura, a mysterious quality. Seldom posing for photos. Almost never doing interviews."

Taubman was ignoring the papers on his desk now and was watching intently as the camera returned to Jewel: "But I have this evening a very exclusive interview with this same Roland Williams, as he appeared last winter, discussing his difficulties in adjusting to stardom . . . and his tremendous fear of the crowds which inevitably surrounded him. I think you'll find it touching, and in light of what has happened, terribly, terribly sad."

A closeup of Roland appeared onscreen. He was sitting on a royal-blue velvet couch, wearing a shirt trimmed with silver.

"I was always afraid of the fans coming at me," Roland was saying

313

slowly and uneasily. "Reaching for me. Like hundreds of spiders trying to get me. And all I wanted to do was run . . . escape."

"Jesus Christ!" Taubman reached for the telephone so fast his
coffeecup was upended, sending a flash flood of cold Sanka over the
memoranda, budgets, and Nielsen numbers. "Get me Swanson in
Studio Two!" Silently he began counting to one hundred. He got as
far as forty-eight when Jewel's producer came on the line. "Swanson,
you stupid son of a bitch! What the fuck are you doing down there?
Where'd you get that tape? Stop it . . . stop that tape immediately!
I'm coming down!"

Fewer than two minutes later Taubman marched into the frigid
studio looking angrier than anyone working on the show had ever
seen him, including Jewel.

"Irving," she greeted him innocently. "What's wrong? Why did you
make us stop?"

"That Williams tape, you can't use it," he blustered. "Where is it?
Will somebody give me that fucking tape? Right now!"

Barry Swanson came rushing out of the control room waving a
cassette box. "Here you are, sir. I have it right here. Ah, sorry."
Swanson looked totally confused.

Jewel, equally at a loss to explain Taubman's unexpected outburst,
was nonetheless not about to give up so easily. "But Irving," she
purred, "I went to a great deal of trouble to get that tape from Denny.
I know you never aired it because Christine was fired. But Denny
told me I could use a soundbite as long as it was less than a minute,
and as long as I didn't use the part where Williams jumps up and
leaves."

"And why wasn't I told?" he scowled at her.

"I wanted to surprise you. This is exclusive footage, Irving. Nobody has anything like this. I thought you'd be thrilled." Besides, she
told herself, Bracken is in Rome so there's no way you can check up,
you old toad.

"Well, I'm not. I am most definitely *not* thrilled." Impossible, he
thought. She could never have gotten it from Bracken.

"Oh, please, Irving—this would be a major scoop. Think of the
reaction, the print it'll get us. You're always telling me we have to
stand out . . . have fresh material. This is as fresh as it gets, unless
you want me to find Williams myself."

"No!" His voice reverberated through the studio. "No, Jewel. You
may not run the Williams interview, even the teensiest soundbite,

until I speak with Denny Bracken personally. I know he's in Italy, but I'm going to track him down."

He clutched the tape cassette box to his chest and started to leave. "And, Jewel," he said suddenly, stopping to face back in her direction, "for your sake, I do hope that you are not lying to me."

Fifteen

Each day without rescue made the likelihood of their salvation seem more remote—even impossible. An aura of unabating horror hovered over Roland and Diedra, circling them constantly like a ghostly vulture, silently, patiently awaiting its prey. Roland couldn't shake the feeling that they were going to die.

The days had passed with agonizing slowness, the hours marked by the angle of sunlight through the small window of their gloomy cell. The two of them had been stripped of their valuables, including watches, so they had no means of measuring time exactly. Yet a routine had emerged.

The only welcomed interruption of their anxious monotony came from the appearances of the short, unshaven Italian they had nicknamed Bozo. He was clearly the gofer in the operation, not very bright, and clownishly clumsy. Twice a day he shoved a tray of food at them, and he exchanged the wooden buckets for fresh ones each morning, usually muttering to himself incoherently in Italian.

It was their other daily visitor they had grown to despise and live in constant fear of—the huge Italian with the eye patch. His arrivals were on no set schedule, and often they came in the middle of the night, as if he was deliberately heightening the terror.

To Roland, his manner clearly suggested that it was only a matter of time. That it wouldn't be clean and quick. That it would be slow and brutal, like the way this same monster had finished off the young girl.

Any lingering hope Roland harbored that they would not be harmed evaporated after one visit in the first week of their captivity. For no apparent reason, the man with the eye patch had blindfolded and handcuffed them both, and Roland could smell the stale odor of garlic on the man's breath as he felt the cold hard steel of the Uzi pressing against his temple.

So this was it. He tensed for the fatal impact. Then he felt his head exploding. He slumped down onto his cot.

Is this how it feels? Am I dead?

He was not dead. When his ears stopped ringing, the first thing he heard was the man's coarse laughter mixed with Diedra's anguished sobs. The blindfold was torn from his head, which throbbed painfully from the noise and power of the gunburst. He looked up into the yellowed teeth of his tormenter, which were bared in a smile of the purest malevolence. It was then he noticed the splintered trail the Uzi slugs had left in the heavy wooden door of the cell. An instant before firing, the stubby barrel of the submachine gun had been lifted an inch or two, splattering the door instead of human bone and flesh—this time.

Their captor clearly enjoyed this deadly play. His English was limited to a few rough curses, but there seemed no mistaking his intentions. The very breath in their bodies was offensive to him. He cared nothing for their lives. He was amusing himself with this war of nerves, evidently awaiting only an excuse, the right moment, an order from someone higher up.

If these men didn't get whatever they were after, Roland decided, their own deaths were inevitable. Maybe they were dead either way.

Such a dire conclusion had led Roland to withdraw for hours on end into his own private shell. He blamed himself for everything that had happened, especially the young girl's death—with a sharp pang of regret he realized he would never even know her name. If he hadn't come to Rome, she would still be alive, her friends and family would have been spared the terrible pain . . . and the woman beside him also would not be in mortal danger.

Roland had long since discarded the notion that Diedra was somehow involved in the kidnapping. A bond born of their shared adversity had formed between them. When Roland could muster the spirit to talk, he was surprised, in fact, at how well they communicated. He found himself opening up to Diedra almost as easily as he had to Tashi. She was a willing listener, patient and sympathetic.

Their most common subject of conversation, of course, was the reason behind their abduction. Roland was convinced they were being held for a huge ransom, and that the sum was certainly being raised and arrangements made. "The record business is heartless, but not so heartless that Lightning wouldn't try to buy me back," as he put it. "Besides, I'm still worth more alive than dead."

Diedra continued to believe Burton was to blame. She couldn't forget the insane look in his eyes when they'd met in Rome. He had wanted to punish Tashi, and maybe Roland, too. And if he was so hungry to make a name for himself in the Democratic hierarchy, it made a crazy sort of sense that he'd also want Roland out of the way rather than have to admit he couldn't deliver his big ticket draw for the additional fund-raisers.

They'd both theorized for hours about the possibility of escape. But it seemed useless. The door was always locked, constantly guarded, and the barred window was the only other exit.

Soon after waking from a short nap on this particular late afternoon, Roland sat up on the uncomfortable cot and stretched. Then he brought his hands down to grab his ankles and began bouncing his head toward his knees.

"At it again, huh?" Diedra said, watching him spread his blanket on the cold stone floor. Several times a day Roland would use the thin wool covering as an exercise mat to do a series of stretches and calisthenics.

"Keeps me sane," he replied glumly.

Diedra turned to gaze out through the iron bars of their prison. From the vantage point of her cot, she could see two gnarled olive trees. They stood close together, their twisted branches entwined. To her, they looked like two old friends, contorted by age, taking a walk up a desolate hillside.

She had spent many hours staring at the knotted olive trees. They had become so familiar that by now she almost didn't see them. Instead she often wondered about Rex, and what he must be going through trying to locate her. And her mind, too, was clouded by constant fear. *Why* was it taking so long for the authorities to find them?

Surely someone must have seen something. How could one of the most famous faces in the world be locked away without a trace? The thought haunted her—also because she sensed that their captors could ill afford to keep someone like Roland Williams alive indefinitely. Every day increased the risk. Besides, what was their alternative? To turn him loose in the countryside, where he would be recognized in five minutes?

She tried not to dwell on the awful possibilities, especially as Roland became more withdrawn and depressed. She fought to remind herself that things could be worse. They were fed regularly: If not delectable, their usual fare of bread, cheese, coffee, sometimes salami or fruit was at least filling. They had been given two changes of clean clothing. They were both in good health—for the moment.

Her job, as she saw it, was to cheer Roland up as best she could.

"What, no deep knee bends today?" she teased him as he refolded the blanket.

"Later," he puffed. "Got to change the routine, or I just might get bored."

Diedra shook her head in frank admiration. The thought of working up a heavy sweat without being able to wash properly held no appeal for her. Diedra longed for her pink marble tub back on Fifth Avenue and the luxurious bubble baths in which she liked to soak for hours.

There was no tub here, no shower, no washbasin, no toilet. The wooden buckets were all they had. One was for washing. The other had a metal lid, and they used it as a chamber pot. They both had been terribly embarrassed to perform these routine but necessary tasks within their cramped quarters. Diedra had refused to use the toilet bucket for the first two days, until finally forced by absolute necessity to do so.

Soon, however, the worst period of humiliation was over, as they both adjusted to the inevitable and discovered that privacy can be a state of mind. Within their newly forged society, they respected each other's dignity, and that was all that mattered. Against the specter of imminent torture or even death, a sacrifice of modesty seemed a small thing.

"Exercise time officially up now?" she asked, as Roland flopped down on the cot.

He didn't answer. Instead he stared up at the high ceiling, focusing on nothing.

"Do you want to talk about it?"

"You've heard it all," he said finally. "What the hell. It's just that I can't get her off my mind. Before she came along, I thought my music was everything. But look where it's got me. . . ." He gestured to indicate the cold stone walls that encircled and trapped them. "Now I know she's the thing in my life that's real—that means something beyond everything I've accumulated—and I don't know if I'll ever see her again."

The sunlight was slipping from their cell.

"Funny, isn't it, Diedra? That old cliché, it's true. You really don't know what you have until it's gone."

Diedra nodded silently. They'd talked many hours about Tashi. It was clear to Diedra that he wanted to share his life with the girl. Something about his determination gave her hope.

"Hey," she coaxed, leaning over to touch his arm. "Think positively, remember? If you love her so much, you'll be with her. I believe that. There'll be a way."

"Right." He said it without enthusiasm.

The light was fading quickly now. Neither of them knew what to say next, so they sat in silence for a long time, until Diedra could stand the inactivity no longer.

"Time to turn your back, honey," she said, rising up off the cot. "Before it gets any colder and darker, I'm going to take my fabulous minibath."

Diedra started unbuttoning her blouse, and she reached for the coarse sea sponge next to the washbucket, then stopped to examine the water. "Hey, Bozo never brought the fresh stuff today," she complained, picking up the bucket and marching over to the door.

"*Aqua!*" she shouted. "Hey, you out there. *Aqua. Aqua dolce, capisci?*" She pounded on the door. "*Apri la porta!*"

Several minutes passed as Diedra continued her pounding and loud pleas for fresh water. Then, finally, they heard the heavy lock click open, and the short, stocky guard stood in the doorway, gripping a new bucket. He was scowling like a beast rudely awakened from a long sleep. Motioning for Diedra to back up a few steps, he set it down between them, all the while glaring at her, red-eyed.

Diedra returned the glare. She had by now worked herself up into a fit of anger, her fears, her frustrations all having been distilled and concentrated into the dregs of yesterday's water, in the bucket she still held in her hand.

"About time, you ignorant wop," she cried. Harshly she threw the nearly empty bucket at him with such speed that it hit him with a resounding thwack squarely in the groin. Murky water slopped over his chest and protruding belly.

"*Cazzo!*" he groaned in pain, doubling over briefly, then raising his face in an ugly mask of rage. Immediately Diedra regretted her imprudent action. But before she could try to mouth an apology, the jailer was on her. With an angry swipe, he knocked her to the floor, then raised the bucket of fresh water up in the air and dumped it over her head.

"*Scopona!*" he roared.

Instantly Roland was on his feet. He shoved the beefy guard back. "Lay off!" he ordered, stepping between them, trying to protect Diedra. "Leave her alone!"

Stumbling backward, his eyes wild, the guard muttered an oath in Italian. Then, with one swift motion, he threw down the bucket and yanked his small pistol from the waistband of his trousers. Raising the weapon, he pointed it toward Roland and squeezed off a shot.

The impact of the bullet sent Roland reeling back, and he crumpled to the floor. "Diedra, stay away from him!" he shouted. "He'll kill us both!"

A bright-red stream of blood was running down Roland's right side.

"Oh, my God!" exclaimed Diedra, as the guard hastily retreated through the doorway, slamming it and fumbling furiously with the lock until it snapped shut again. Dripping wet, her long hair swept back over her shoulders, Diedra rushed to where Roland lay sprawled and knelt to examine the wound.

Working quickly, she helped Roland off with his blood-soaked shirt. A small round hole gaped in his chest in a fleshy area near his right armpit. The small-caliber bullet had gone completely through, exiting through a jagged gash just below the shoulder blade. She grabbed the sponge, sopped up a small puddle of the spilled water, and hurriedly washed the two wounds. Tearing a strip of cloth from the long jersey gown she had worn the night of their abduction, she tied the soft stretchy material around his chest and back to stop the bleeding.

"Don't worry, baby, it's gonna be okay. Just a scratch," she lied, kneeling over him, cradling his head in her arms. "As long as it doesn't get infected, you'll hardly notice it."

"Thanks," Roland managed weakly, looking up at her. He was still dazed by what had happened. At first he had felt nothing, but now his whole right side was beginning to hurt. It was a throbbing, caustic pain. But at this moment Roland also felt an overwhelming surge of relief—and gratitude to this kind and tender woman who had become his friend.

"You know," he said with effort, "I don't think I would have been able to—"

"*Shhhhhhh.* Don't waste your energy." Tears were welling up in her eyes as she held him.

"B–but I—"

"Hush now." She began to stroke his brow with smooth, gentle fingers. Suddenly, without thinking, a melody sprang to her lips. She started to hum it softly.

Roland closed his eyes. His breathing was slowing.

Still stroking his forehead, Diedra now found herself adding words to the tune, words from her distant past. She sang in a soothing, almost hypnotic contralto.

> *Todo mi afecto puse en una ingrata:*
> *y ella inconstante me llegó a olvidar.*
> *Si así, si así se trata*
> *un afecto sincero,*
> *amor, amor no quiero,*
> *no quiero mas amar. . . .*

Before she was finished, Roland's eyes fluttered open. A single tear tracked down his cheek.

"What is it, hon? The pain?"

"That song," he said hesitantly. "What is it?"

"Oh, I don't know. Just some poem, it used to be a favorite of mine, by a South American named Melgar, and a long time ago I put it to music and sang it to—"

Diedra's body stiffened. In her confusion, she had been completely unconscious of what she was doing. She began to stand up.

Roland's hand stopped her. "Don't."

She felt his eyes burning holes into hers.

"*Amor, amor no quiero, no quiero mas amar* . . . Love I do not want, I do not want love anymore," he said now. Memories flooded over him, momentarily extinguishing the pain, carrying him away to a time and place that had dimmed but had never died. "My first hit came from those two lines. I'd forgotten the rest of it. Where—where did you learn it, Diedra?"

"Oh, y–years and years ago," she stammered, looking away. "From my mother."

"Funny," he said softly, reaching up to touch her chin and turn her gaze back toward his. "I remember learning those words from my mother, too. I'll bet you haven't sung them in a long time."

Diedra's eyes were glistening with tears and she trembled as she nodded in agreement. "No, my darling," she whispered to her son. "Not in a long, long time."

Not wanting to risk being late, Howard Ruskin had allowed himself extra time for the drive from Hollywood to Beverly Hills. He arrived at the large mahogany doors fifteen minutes early. A brass plate read Shultz, Korman and Rieger: Attorneys at Law. Howard smiled. He had been looking forward to this appointment for weeks.

After speaking briefly with the pert dark-haired receptionist, he took a seat at the end of a long bleached-oak bench, giving a nervous glance of approval to the classy Tudor decor. He picked up an out-dated copy of *Time* magazine and began leafing through it distractedly, his thoughts turning again to a review of the dirt he'd be dishing up in a very few minutes.

There had been so many outrageous accounts to choose from, all true, and each more appalling than the last. Howard had finally settled on three doozies. Now he went over their order in his head. . . .

Start with the time she had that fairy assistant of hers, Bruce Whatshisname, slip a miniature tape recorder into soap star Harry Walder's dressing room. The poor bastard Walder was about to meet with his manager during a break, and they'd discussed the terms of his new contract. The next morning she not only reported Walder's million-dollar deal but his hidden perks, as well. Little things, like a new Audi for his mistress and the monthly mortgage payment on her penthouse condominium on Wilshire Boulevard.

Yeah, Howard thought with a wry smile—that one was a perfect opener.

Next, the time she went down on . . . nah . . . too juicy, save it for last. Go with the "drug bust" now. When was it, two years ago? She had developed this extreme dislike for that Australian actress, Lileth Finley—probably because Lileth was no dummy and had refused to answer her embarrassingly personal questions during a live interview. Lileth had made her look like an ogre. But that's off the track a little. Stick with how she sweet-talked that actor into offering Lileth coke at a party in Pacific Palisades.

As soon as the actress lifted the tiny spoon—Christ, it was only a powdery baby laxative!—to her magnificently restructured nostrils, the others in cahoots on this, two extras posing as undercover narcs, nailed her! Gave the broad the shock of her life—especially when she heard the whole hilarious episode repeated on the air the next day.

Yeah. That should raise a lawyer's eyebrows. Talk about unscrupulous.

And finally! Case History Number Three: "The Limo Driver Gets Road Head." In glorious detail, just like I heard her brag about it to Brucie baby that night in the office. She must've been drunk or stoned, but who gives a shit? The bitch is capable of anything.

The faggot was giggling, I remember that. "So how'd you talk the driver into stowing you away next to him on the floor?" he asked her.

And she boasted, "I unzipped his fly and went to work, of course. You would've loved it, Bruce. The guy had a prick like a flagpole, and he went off like a cannon. When we drove away with Cash Crawford and his new honey in the back, I found out that Crawford's wife had a private detective on their trail. Naturally I shared this with my viewers the very next morning. My contract was up for renewal then. Better believe I wrote my own ticket on that one, sweetie pie!"

Howard could still hear her laughter. Guess who's got the last laugh now, Jewel baby? If this guy is in the mood for a little character assasination, he had the right boy. . . . Who'd have thought that cute DuRand cookie would have come up with such a hot idea?

"Mr. Ruskin? Mr. Shultz will see you now." A tall woman with frosted hair had appeared at his side.

Howard stood up, absentmindedly adjusting his red silk pocket scarf and running a hand over his black linen jacket. It was a brand-new Giorgio Armani. Normally he didn't feel comfortable in designer clothes, but this was a special occasion.

"Believe it or not, this is the first deposition I've ever been asked to give," he told the woman as she led him down a long corridor toward the office of Neal Burgess's lawyer.

It was minutes away from eight o'clock on a smoggy Thursday night in August. Christine was on deadline. Typing away furiously in the Channel 8 newsroom, she was behind schedule on a piece about a meeting of Hollywood stuntwomen that she'd attended earlier that evening. Viewing the videotape footage had taken twice as long as usual when the machine jammed, almost chewing her story into shreds in the process.

Now her mind was a jumble with the technical process of preparing a news story for air—sorting out the soundbites she would use, the bridges she would write to string the visuals together. Only minutes remained to prepare an outline. If she didn't start working with the tape editor by eight-fifteen, there'd be no chance to get the piece on tonight's ten o'clock broadcast.

Fortunately, Christine had already written her Entertainment News Updates, a smattering of show-business briefs with which she always closed her on-air segment. She'd taken particular care with tonight's final item.

The item began by stating that Jason Kramer's lawyers had failed to win further postponement of the film star's rape trial—and that jury selection would finally begin in early September. But then it segued to news of none other than Blair Montgomery. His trial was also scheduled to begin in a few weeks. A guilty verdict on the drug charges could bring him up to three years in jail and a ten-thousand-dollar fine.

There was more. The item concluded with official confirmation from the Los Angeles County D.A.'s Entertainment Industry Task Force that it was looking into allegations that Hurricane Films, Blair's production company, had resorted to the use of forgery, embezzlement, and kickbacks in dealings with at least three motion-picture studios.

Neatly packaged in bold TelePrompTer type, the account of Blair's mounting legal problems now lay on Christine's desk, ignored for the moment. She was checking her notes for the final outcue time on her stuntwomen piece. Glancing up, she happened to notice a flurry of activity near the wire-service-machine room on her left. Such sudden commotion was not unusual, so she glanced only briefly before returning to her work. Probably an update on baseball scores or a late-breaking but minor story, she thought as she resumed her typing.

But she knew something much bigger was afoot when News Director Don Winston came charging out of the wire room, clutching a fistful of yellow paper and shouting orders in stentorian tones.

"Cut out of the movie! Get Allison on camera! We've got a news-breaker!"

Quickly the station's longtime news anchor, a white-haired man with apple cheeks, took his place on the edge of a desk reserved for just these live "cut-ins"; the controlled chaos of the newsroom played effectively as his backdrop. When the camera's red light flashed, Allison, tie loosened and in shirtsleeves, paraphrased the wire copy that Winston had thrust at him.

"This is Curt Allison in the KQV Newsroom," he said with the aplomb of an old pro, looking squarely into the eye of the camera. "The Associated Press in Rome reports tonight that music superstar Roland Williams has been rescued after three weeks of captivity in Italy. Italian authorities reportedly carried out a successful predawn raid on a seventeenth-century citadel in a remote mountainous section of Caserta, thirty miles outside Naples, in which Williams and an unidentified woman were rescued and two of their captors arrested. The captors were tentatively identified as Angelo Raffini and Carmine DiApolo, presumed members of the Nucleii Armati Proletari, the terrorist group which earlier claimed responsibility for Williams's abduction. A body, believed to be that of the teenaged girl last seen being forced into Williams's limousine in Rome on the night of the kidnapping, was discovered in a shallow grave near the citadel. Italian police would not reveal how they learned of Williams's whereabouts. But Williams was said to have been rushed to a hospital in Naples, where he is listed in stable condition following treatment for a gunshot wound to the chest. It is not known at this time how the recording artist was injured. Repeating . . ."

As Allison recapped the news bulletin, the newsroom was erupting. Editors issued orders, reporters ran to find their tape crews, and phones began ringing everywhere.

Christine had stopped typing to speak briefly with Winston. He told her to dump the stuntwomen story and start preparing a lead-in to the background report on the Williams kidnapping, which she'd had on standby for exactly this moment. Her other standby report—a Williams obituary—could remain in the tape library unless the star's condition took a turn for the worse.

It was twenty-five to nine when she returned to her desk after consulting with the news producer to make certain her story did not overlap the others being hastily stitched into tonight's script. She found that her own phone was now among those still filling the air with their maddening rings. Her hand shot out to silence it.

"Christine?" The strong, resonant voice was immediately familiar to her.

"Steven!" she gasped. "Where are you?"

"In town, princess. At Matteo's right now—you know, in Westwood."

"I'm sorry, but you couldn't have picked a worse moment to call. I—"

"Christine, wait. I want to speak with you privately, as soon as possible."

"God, there's no way right now. It's a funny farm here. Have you heard the news about Roland Williams? He's been rescued, we're all going crazy, and I have to—"

"Princess! Listen to me." He said his next words slowly, carefully. "Never mind what you have to do. You know the Tail o' the Pup hot-dog stand on La Cienega at Beverly? Be waiting there in your car in twenty minutes. You'll be back in plenty of time . . . and you'll have the lead story, I guarantee it."

"Steven," she sighed in aggravation. "I told you—it's impossible."

"Chrissie, baby," he insisted, "this is more important. I've got something that'll catapult you back to the top, sweetheart—where you belong. Trust me. Tail o' the Pup. Twenty minutes. Be there."

And he hung up.

Traffic on Sunset Boulevard was crawling at a snail's pace as usual. Christine took a shortcut down Fairfax Avenue, then shot across Fountain to La Cienega. The whole way she was thinking she should have her head examined. Sneaking out of the newsroom in the middle of one of the biggest stories of the year? Meeting the man who cost her her last job—at a place fashioned out of chicken wire and stucco to resemble a gigantic frankfurter in a bun slathered with mustard?

She reassured herself that Steven was right about one thing. She'd still have time to do the lead-in when she got back. And with all the commotion, Winston might not even miss her.

There he was, the silver limousine idling on an adjacent corner.

"Hello, Miss DuRand, nice to see you again." The short, balding chauffeur held open the door for her.

"Shaeffer!" she greeted him. "Nice to see you, too." She slid onto the white leather seat.

Steven looked the same as always. Beautifully tailored suit. Impeccable grooming. The Great Gatsby, not the Godfather. He was smiling. "Princess," he said approvingly, "the pearls are terrific. You look sensational."

"Thank you," she replied, as he lightly bussed her on the cheek. Could this be happening, really? After all these years, sitting in the back of a limo with him again as if nothing had ever changed between them?

"Steven," she said pointedly, "what's this all about?"

"Wait a bit," he said softly. The car was gliding up the steep incline of La Cienega Boulevard, heading north.

"Steven—"

"Shhhh . . . please. A few minutes more."

Christine noticed for the first time that he seemed uncharacteristically nervous. As they moved across Sunset, over to Doheny and into the elegant residential area of Trousdale, he kept turning around to steal furtive looks out the back window.

Finally she could stand the wait no longer. "Steven, will you *tell* me just what the hell is going on?"

He took one last look through the rear window before turning to her somberly. "Okay, princess," he said. "I know you're going to think what I'm about to say qualifies me for the loony bin. But listen closely, because if you don't report this tonight, you can rest assured that somebody else will break it by tomorrow morning. The leak is out, Chrissie. I just happened to be there when the first drip came through. So just hear me out—deal?"

She nodded silently.

"Uh . . . maybe you should take notes."

Christine pulled a reporter's notebook and a pen out of her bag.

"It's about the Williams kidnapping."

"Well, what about it?" She still felt uncomfortable being here, and it showed as impatience.

"The two guys. The captors. They aren't members of any terrorist group."

"They aren't? Well, just who are they, then?"

"Italian Mafia."

The two words stunned her. Her first thought was that this must be some kind of perverse joke, a Byzantine form of revenge—but for what? Having had faith in him once?

Then he offered further explanation. When he had nearly finished, she could restrain herself no longer. "Jesus Christ, what is it with you?" she demanded. "Steven, it's not enough that you get me fired from one job? Now you want to make sure I never work again?"

Anger—a sense of betrayal—these quickly displaced the numbing incredulity. It was a preposterous tale. She told herself she should never have come, should never have listened to him.

"Do you realize what would happen if I went on the air with something like that? Do you? Assuming, of course, I even got on the air! My butt would be on the sidewalk as soon as I mentioned it to my boss!"

He put up his hands as if to fend off her verbal assault. "Hey, hey— princess!" he said. "Calm down. Our deal, remember? I'm not finished yet."

Bending to grab a briefcase, he snapped it open. He winked at her and handed her a large flat manila envelope, sealed shut. "Here's your 'visual.' Do I know TV?"

"What's this?" she asked edgily.

"An eight-by-ten glossy taken at the Leonardo da Vinci Airport in Rome the day before Williams was kidnapped. Raffini, DiApolo— and him."

"Really, the three of them? Together? Are you positive?"

"It's your proof, princess. You pop this on the screen, and there's nobody can say you haven't got a story. You've got the story of the year!"

Now she was dumbstruck. The enormity of this revelation suddenly hit her like a thunderbolt. All she could think to do was to lean over and kiss him loudly on the cheek.

He looked at her and smiled again, his eyes betraying a sadness. Touching her cheek with his smooth palm, he said, "This makes up for the way I mucked up the London deal, right, princess?"

As the limousine turned down La Cienega again, she sat back and took a deep breath. "Now I just have to convince my news director to go with it."

"That shouldn't be hard," Steven reassured her. "Not for you. Remember, baby—shoot for a star!"

"Where's Winston?" Christine had just raced into the newsroom.

One of the news writers looked up from his phone call. "In his office, watching the feed on Williams from New York," he called over to her. "Not in the greatest mood, Chris. Interrupt at your own risk."

"Thanks, Benny," she said, moving quickly toward Don Winston's closed door. She stared at the door handle for a moment before reaching for it. Then, knocking once, she pushed the door open. "Don," she said breathlessly, "sorry to break in like this. . . ."

Winston scowled up at her and motioned to a chair. "Sit down, Chris. Where the hell you been? Be with you in a—"

"No. No, Don. This can't wait." She stepped between him and the

TV monitor. "Don, Roland Williams was not being held by terrorists. It was the Italian Mafia, in conjunction with—"

"Stop! Cut! Hold it!"

Winston shot her such an outrageous look of disbelief that for a brief moment Christine thought she'd imagined it all. "Chris, what the hell has gotten into you? Where's your lead-in? We've got a show to do in twenty-five minutes."

She knew Winston wouldn't sit through a long explanation. But the photo might work—shock him into hearing her out.

"Please," she pleaded, "I know what you're thinking, Don. But look at this." She leaned over his desk and pointed out the three subjects locked in conversation in the black-and-white photograph. "These two are Williams's captors, Raffini and DiApolo. My source swears they're members of the Italian Mafia, Don. And this guy—do you recognize him?" In a few terse sentences, she summarized what Steven Jacobs had revealed to her.

Winston looked at her skeptically. He'd been in the news business for eighteen years, long enough to know there are times when you just have to go with your instincts. What he saw in front of him seemed impossible. But as much as he wanted to dismiss Christine's story, he knew he couldn't. He believed in the old journalism adage: You're only as good as your best reporter. This one was onto something so hot it scared him.

"Miller!" he called out. "Get me that wirephoto of the two terrorists who kidnapped Williams—fast."

As they waited, Christine filled in the gaps of the story, just as Steven had told it to her. "Trust me on this one, Don," she was saying as David Miller, the newsroom intern, walked in and handed Winston the wirephoto. "My source is infallible."

Winston was busy comparing the two pictures. One of the men, a behemoth with a mustache, had a patch over one eye.

"Miller!" Winston bellowed again. He wrote down a name and job title on a memo pad and handed it to the young man. "Try to locate a picture of this guy right away. Get me any research we've got on him, too. Oh—and if anybody asks, tell 'em it's routine. Hurry!" He turned back to Christine. "So your source is infallible, huh? Chris, this is just too big. Who's your source?"

Christine felt her mouth go dry. It was a huge risk. But she knew he'd ask, and she'd already decided what to say. "I have your word this stays between us, and us only?" she asked.

"You got it."

"All right," she began shakily, going on to tell Winston quickly the entire story about Steven and his connections, including the details behind the Princess Diana mess.

"So Jewel Crosse was right after all?" Winston said after she'd finished.

Her back muscles clenched into knots, and her head felt hot and woozy. She'd lost.

Winston shook his head. "I'm sorry, Chris. I know you think this guy is shooting straight with you. But I can't put dynamite like this on the air if—"

"Here's the photo you wanted, sir," interjected the nervous young intern. "It was taken last month at a political fund-raiser here in town. And here's the research file on him."

"Thanks, Miller . . . good job," Winston said gruffly as the boy left. Then he scrutinized the material for what seemed like an eternity, saying nothing.

"Well, is it—?"

"I dunno. Give me another minute."

When he'd finished, Winston looked up at her intently, as if peering into her soul. Christine shivered slightly.

"We'll both be up shit creek if this photo turns out to be dummied, you know that, don't you? Now tell me again what you intend to say on the air," he said.

"Don, my God . . . does that mean—?"

Winston raised a hand. "Christine," he said, "you know I've always admired your work. But tonight, more than anything, I admire your guts. You put a lot on the line, telling me what you did. I don't approve of your friend, but a source is a source, and now I believe he's telling you the truth. We're going with it."

Tears of relief and gratitude welled up in Christine's eyes, and she rushed over to Winston and hugged him with all her might.

After dashing off her copy, she'd run a brush through her hair and freshened her makeup as best her trembling hands would allow. She knew she looked drained and exhausted. And although she felt confident in her material, there was always that chance . . .

At two minutes to ten, Christine took her place beside Curt Allison on the news set. She looked into her camera for a lighting check, feeling weak-kneed. There were sharp pangs in her stomach—dinner had been forgotten tonight, but that wasn't it.

Under the glare of the hot lights, Christine knew that stomach-churning fear all reporters know. It strikes as they stand at the parapet, about to shout their revelations to an unsuspecting world. Maybe Steven had been misinformed after all. Maybe she was going with a story that would demolish her credibility. Maybe tomorrow she'd be out of a job.

"Five . . . four . . . three . . . two . . . one!" The floor director pointed to the set, and Allison looked up from the sheaf of papers he clutched in his hands and dispensed a toothy smile to the camera.

Christine sat dazed. Nothing seemed real. There was a roaring sound in her ears.

"—And Christine DuRand has that startling report." It was Allison's voice, introducing her. Camera Two flashed its red light. In that instant, her face appeared on the screen of thousands of homes, neighborhood bars, TV store-window displays.

Christine stared into the camera but said nothing.

Up in the control booth, Don Winston pleaded with her lambent image arrayed before him on a bank of monitors. "Come on, Chris! Just read the TelePrompTer!"

She took a breath, and suddenly some inner resource brought the world back into focus for her. As the camera zoomed in closer, she began in a strong, clear voice:

"Curt, we have learned exclusively tonight that Roland Williams may have been kidnapped not by the Nucleii Armati Proletari terrorist group, as has been widely reported, but by the Italian Mafia . . . working in conjunction with the Committee to Reelect President Raymond Sullivan.

"According to a highly informed source, a top-level Republican working for the Sullivan reelection committee arranged to have Williams abducted, apparently to prevent him from undertaking further fund-raising efforts on behalf of the Democratic challenger, Senator Mark Whittaker. . . ."

All activity back in the newsroom had ceased as every eye was transfixed by the nearest screen. The control room was filling up fast with station personnel until the technicians at the boards of buttons, switches, dials, and levers were in danger of being too crowded to perform their tasks.

"Hey, everybody out who doesn't belong!" shouted Winston. He turned back to the monitors. "Doin' fine, Chrissie," he urged. "Come on. Doin' fine!"

"I know this shocking news seems almost incomprehensible," she was saying now. But this . . ." The photographic evidence popped up, full screen. ". . . This is a photo of Frank Lombardi, chief of security for the Committee to Reelect Sullivan, with Williams's captors, Angelo Raffini and Carmine DiApolo. The photo is believed to have been taken in Rome three weeks ago, one day before Williams was abducted following a concert. . . .

"Anna Maria Leone, the young Williams fan whose body was found near the site of the rock star's captivity, was apparently accidentally swept up into the real-life melodrama, only to be brutally murdered in an attempt by the kidnappers to add further authenticity to the terrorist cover story. . . ."

As she concluded her report, Christine turned to the white-maned Allison. "What we seem to have here, Curt," she said, "is a situation which is a step beyond Watergate. Kidnapping and murder—make that several steps beyond."

Sixteen

Over the next several hours Christine found herself swept up in the maelstrom she had created. Almost from the moment she walked off the news set, she was besieged with requests for interviews. The calls began coming in from all over the world. The BBC offered transportation to London on a private jet. She spoke with newspapers and radio reporters from as far away as Taiwan.

Around midnight Don Winston set up an impromptu press conference at the station for the Los Angeles media. At three in the morning he finally insisted that Christine go home. She arrived at her apartment with barely enough time to bathe and change for early morning appearances on the *Today Show* and *Good Morning America*.

Somewhere in the midst of all this frenetic activity, Maggie had caught up with her. And it was five-fifteen in the morning when the two of them slipped into the back of the limousine provided by KABC-TV, where Christine had just spoken to David Hartman via satellite.

"God, you were good! Fantastic! Dynamite! Terrific!" Maggie was carrying on proudly as she settled into her seat.

"Mag." Christine squeezed her friend's arm affectionately. "I'm just so glad you were there with me."

"Wouldn't have missed it for a leap in the hay with Warren Beatty, sweet lips." Maggie beamed back at Christine. "My, my, how celebrity becomes you. You're aglow, girl. Overnight sensation. Won't the networks be clamoring now!"

"We'll see," Christine said softly, leaning her head back on the pillowy black leather. She'd had no sleep. But rest was out of the question—she was still too wired.

"Got the papers up here, ladies, 'case you want 'em."

"You have?" Maggie said excitedly, leaning forward toward the chauffeur. "Well, pass 'em back here, sugar. We've got a current-events quiz to study for."

She eagerly accepted the heavy stack of morning newspapers. And by the time they pulled away from KABC, Christine and Maggie were avidly studying the front pages of the *Los Angeles Times* and *The New York Times*.

Christine's eyes were immediately drawn to the prominent photograph of Frank Lombardi with Raffini and DiApolo in Rome. It was the same picture she'd used on her newscast the night before. Seeing it in newsprint struck her as affirmation that her story was solid.

"Great," she sighed with increasing satisfaction while scanning the accompanying *L.A. Times* article: ". . . Lombardi, who was recruited personally by George Steele, chief of the Committee to Reelect . . . The pair were classmates at Duke University some three decades ago. . . ."

"Hey, listen to this from *The New York Times*," Maggie said enthusiastically. " 'Ties between the Central Intelligence Agency, where Lombardi worked for twenty-five years, and the Italian underworld can be traced back to the era immediately following World War Two, after Mafia 'soldiers' had sided with the wartime resistance movement in its efforts to sabotage Axis rule.' Girl, are you ever going to shake up the stuffed shirt brigade in Washington! I can see it now. 'Christine DuRand, *Time* magazine's Woman of the Year.' "

"Right . . . right," Christine agreed distractedly. She was already reading the accompanying story over Maggie's shoulder. It quoted a press spokesman for President Sullivan, who was stumping in the Texas panhandle, as saying the White House disavowed all knowledge of Lombardi's "alleged adventurism," while Mark Whittaker, in St. Louis, issued a statement that called for American voters to "repudiate the old politics, including corrupt echoes of the Watergate era, in favor of fresh voices of change." Political pundits whose opinions were solicited were unanimous in believing the Williams kidnapping could weigh heavily on voters' minds, especially among the young and undecided, and could possibly propel Whittaker ahead in the race for the first time.

"God, if he wins, Whittaker ought to appoint you to an ambassadorship or something," Maggie continued to gush. "Paris would be nice, don't you think? Switzerland, maybe . . . I mean, you're dumping millions of votes in his lap."

Christine chuckled and scanned more of the news reports. Obviously there was no stopping her dear, giddy friend, and besides, who wanted to?

"Well, they *did* spell your name right in America's 'newspaper of record,'" Maggie chattered on. "Five mentions in *The New York Times* so far . . . and still counting."

"Maggie, look," gasped Christine, holding up page three of the *L.A. Times.*

"Hmm, not a bad shot, either," Maggie said, scrutinizing the picture of Christine in the far right corner. "Harry Langdon could have made you a bit more 'glam' . . . better yet, Helmut Newton, don't you think? . . . Christine, are you there?"

"What? Oh, yes, Helmut Newton . . . but only if I posed with you," she answered without looking up.

"And in the buff."

Christine shot her a look.

"Just checking to see if you're still on the planet," Maggie teased.

"I am, I am. Here's a sidebar about Roland Williams."

They'd already heard snippets of the latest development in his kidnapping. *Today*'s Bryant Gumble and *GMA*'s Joan Lunden had each referred on the air to the newest unexpected turn of events, but there'd been few details.

Quickly, Christine's eyes sought the paragraphs she was looking for. "'In perhaps the oddest twist in the Williams kidnapping,'" she read aloud, "'the unidentified woman freed with the superstar recording artist has turned out to be Williams's mother, Diedra Davis.'"

"His mother! Sweet Jesus," Maggie yelped.

"Yes," Christine went on. "And look at this . . . ' "She often shows up unexpectedly at his concerts as a surprise for Roland," stated Williams's publicist, Denny Bracken, who also explained that Williams changed his surname early in his career for "artistic purposes." ' "

"Artistic! What a bunch of bull," Maggie interrupted. "I can't believe that Ro—"

"Mag, will you hold on? There's more. 'Williams just had a better ring,' said Bracken. Mrs. Davis, who is divorced, lives in New York and visits her son in Los Angeles frequently. . . .' "

"I'll bet," said Maggie. "Something very fishy there, honeybunch. You know anything Bracken says is straight from fantasy land. I'd sure like to know what the real scoop is on that mommy-sonny relationship."

"Mmmm, me, too," agreed Christine. "Now look at this." Near the end of the article was a reference to the reunion of Roland and Tashi: "Miss Qwan, following her visit to Williams's bedside, said through publicist Bracken that she and her fiancé will return to California immediately upon Williams's release from the hospital, which is expected in a few days. Miss Qwan said she will live at Williams's Bel-Air home while studying veterinary medicine in Los Angeles."

"Now that's *got* to be a piece of Bracken's work," said Maggie. "I mean, how in hell else do you explain it? One night he's humpin' Big Burt Ratchford and the next he's blissed out over this Oriental chick? I don't buy it. The guy's gay."

"Maybe," Christine offered with a wry smile, "but other people have been known to alter sexual allegiances—almost overnight. And he could be bi, you know."

"Wonder whatever happened to old Burt anyway?" Maggie asked. "You see anything about him?"

Christine shook her head, turning a page. "Oh, yes. Here we are. Down at the bottom."

Maggie leaned over to read the short mention:

"Burton Ratchford, Democratic finance chairman and former prominent entertainment lawyer, held a hurriedly organized news conference on his return from Rome at John F. Kennedy International Airport in New York last night. Ratchford noted that, although singing star Williams remains one of Senator Whittaker's staunchest supporters, he will make no more campaign appearances on behalf of the Democratic presidential candidate.

" 'Roland Williams literally put his life on the line for the Democratic ticket,' he said. 'And we will be eternally grateful for his terrible sacrifice. Ironically, it may have done more for the Whittaker campaign than any of his prior fund-raising efforts. This shocking revelation of Republican complicity in Mr. Williams's kidnapping should sweep aside any lingering doubt voters may have had as to which party best represents the traditions and values of the American people.'

"Before boarding a flight to Washington, D.C., Ratchford said he was in the process of shifting his base from Los Angeles to the nation's capital for the home stretch of the campaign 'and hopefully beyond.' "

Maggie shook her head in wonderment. "Whew, what a turn of events," she said. "You know, girl, all of this has the ring of one terrific TV movie. If I were you, I'd get on the horn later today and call Aaron Spelling. He—"

"Maggie, please," Christine pleaded, holding up a hand. "My brain is already on overload."

"Okay, okay. But now's the time. Tell you what, I'll call. 'Course, I'll want my fifteen percent—"

"Fifteen?" Christine protested. "I thought the going rate was ten."

"It is. Extra five is for my gut instinct. And I'm worth it. Trust me. Only have your best interest at heart."

Christine laughed and reached over to give Maggie a big hug. "You always do," she said. "You always do."

As the limousine sped through the early-morning mist toward Christine's apartment, she dropped the papers to the floor and allowed her eyes to close. But sleep would still not come. Before long, though, a series of tangled yet vivid images began intruding upon her thoughts. She flashed briefly on that hot afternoon at Lightning Records when she'd interviewed Roland Williams. Was it only six months ago? she reflected drowsily. My God, it seems like a lifetime.

"Time for your medication, Mr. Williams."

Roland stirred from a light sleep. He was groggy, and his bandaged side ached. The hospital room was flooded with the light of mid-afternoon. A cool breeze rustled the venetian blinds at the open window.

He was on the third floor, and he could hear the knot of fans still gathered in a small grassy park across the street below as they continued their celebration of his safe return, serenading him with his music on their tape players and shouting up well-wishes. The Naples police, who ringed the hospital with a security net befitting the Pope or a head of state, had offered to clear the area. Roland said no. The noise of their happy partying didn't really bother him. In fact, he was buoyed by it. It was like a welcome back, a joyous refrain from the realm of the living.

338

He had survived, and life never looked sweeter.

"Mr. Williams, be a good boy and take these or I'll tell your mother."

He looked up at the nurse.

"Tashi."

"Pretty nifty disguise, huh?" She was smiling broadly. "The hospital lent it to me. You should try getting past all those fans—and the paparazzi! It's unbelievable. The police found a twelve-year-old boy crawling through a ventilating duct this morning. And last night they pulled some guy with a telephoto lens off the roof of the building in back of the park. You'd think you were famous or something."

"Like I said in that hellhole," he replied with a grin, "I'm still worth more alive than dead. Thank God I'm here to prove it." He reached out for her hand, drew it to his mouth, and kissed it tenderly. "How are you, baby?"

She bent over to return the kiss, lightly, sweetly. "Couldn't be better—now. How's the patient today?"

He found her tone amusing. "Save the bedside manner for your four-legged customers, will you? Is this what I have to look forward to, being treated like another one of Dr. Qwan's sick puppy dogs? How 'bout a simple, 'I love you'?"

"You're acting more like a horse's backside than a pup. I love you."

"Don't ever talk to the star that way. I love you, too."

They kissed again, this time long and lingeringly.

"Did you do like I said," he asked then, "and stuff my mother with spaghetti and meatballs last night?"

"Not only that, but she finished off with a luscious *zabaglione*." Tashi leaned close again and whispered, "Is there anything I can get for you, Mr. Star?"

He pulled her even closer. "You could shed that nurse's getup and hop in here beside me. I'm in desperate need of comfort and affection." Roland reached up and started to unbutton the starched white uniform.

"Roland!" Tashi stole an anxious glance at the door. "Not here. Somebody's bound to come in, and besides, what about your wound? You were shot, remember?"

As if he didn't hear, he continued to undress her.

"Roland!" she repeated.

"Hey, if somebody walks in, they'll just do a one-eighty and march on out of here again. And as for the hole in my side, if you nurses can change the bedsheets with me still in the bed, then I guess you can work around that problem."

"Wellllll," she murmured, stepping out of her low-heeled white pumps, "I guess we could say it's part of your therapy."

"Yeah. And, baby, I'm gonna need plenty of that."

Sea gulls swooped and dipped overhead, shrieking greedily at the man who was tossing bits of bread, dried fruit, and other remnants of a now-empty pantry onto the small sandy patch that served as a front yard for the beachfront apartment building. A small U-Haul truck was parked nearby.

Despite a light ocean breeze, the heat of the afternoon sun was withering, and from where Nickels stood feeding the gulls he could look longingly at the sunbathers, windsurfers, and volleyball players, all of whom were actually enjoying this blast-furnace heat. Definitely this was not the day he would have chosen for the task at hand—moving Maggie out of Hermosa Beach and into his hilltop aerie, one of those modern split-levels overhanging a cliff in Laurel Canyon.

Returning to her nearly barren living room, he sneaked up behind her, wrapped his large hands around her waist, and planted a kiss on the back of Maggie's neck.

"Sweet Jesus!" She wheeled around and reached for him, but he was already kneeling near a high-tech bookshelf, hurriedly jamming paperbacks into a box.

"You get more skinny, you're going to ruin my business," he complained good-naturedly. "People think you hate my cooking."

Maggie beamed. "God, what a sweet-talker."

"So this Harriet Schmidt," he said after a few more moments, swiping at his brow with the back of his hand, "she was what, Rybar's girlfriend?"

"Not exactly," said Maggie, gently wrapping a delicate blown-glass vase in newspaper. "She and the charming Lenny Rybar only went out three times."

"Why then did she give to him the copy of your father's screenplay?"

"She says she didn't. He apparently lifted it from her garbage can."

"Garbage! Is your father's hard work only fit for garbage, like carrot peelings?"

Maggie sailed a flat metal ashtray at him but missed. "She'd run off several copies of the draft for Dad, but spilled something on one. So she tossed it in the kitchen trash, dummy. Harriet thinks Rybar was over at her apartment for dinner that same night."

Nickels glanced up from his book packing. "Now it makes perfect sense. He went to kitchen looking for script to—what you say?—rip up?"

"Rip off." She laughed. "She asked Rybar to fix her a drink or something. He had to go into the kitchen to do that. So he copped the script, changed a few lines, put a new title page on it, and started planning how to take my dad to the cleaners." Maggie removed a framed *Star Wars* poster from the wall.

"To cleaners? This means what?" he asked.

She laughed again. "Means—take his money. What's the matter? Can't get the hang of those good old-fashioned American idioms?"

He smiled sheepishly. "This Harriet, she has good memory, yes?"

"No. I mean, not at first." Maggie stopped what she was doing, turning toward him in a boxer's crouch, her fists raised. "I had to work her over pretty good," she snarled.

It was his turn to laugh. "American women," he said, shaking his head. "They like to act like peasants! So what happens now, my little gangster?"

"Private eye, not gangster—you've got your Late Late Show movies mixed up," she retorted. "Campbell took her deposition this morning. If she told him what she told me, I think this is one plagiarism case out the—"

"Maggie," Nickels broke in. "Excuse me. But what about these?" He was still emptying the bookshelf, but the three book-sized items in his hand were not reading material.

She looked to see what he was talking about. "Holy shit, I'd forgotten all about those!"

Rushing over to him, she stared down at the trio of video-cassette boxes. "I'll take care of these babies," she said, chuckling. "They have sort of a sentimental value, I guess you might say."

Retrieving the cassettes, Maggie moved quickly to the small stone fireplace on the other side of the living room, where she tossed them onto the charred remains of a redwood log. She turned the gas jets underneath on full, lit a match and flicked it at the tapes. The fireplace erupted with a loud roar, and soon the yellow-red flames had engulfed the cassettes.

"Maggie!" Nickels protested. "It is oven in here!"

"Burn, baby, burn!" she cried, ignoring the heat, fascinated by the spectacle. "My dear Nickels, do you know what these are? They belong to Jewel Crosse. I stole them on Oscar night. You should have seen Christine when I told her. I thought she'd hyperventilate, she laughed so hard!"

He looked perplexed. "But how did you do that—steal them?"

"Ah, a simple bit of Rafferty trickery, angel face. See, I was in the ladies room, and there was Jewel's field director, Sharon something, I forget her last name. Anyway, she made the big mistake of going into one of the stalls and leaving her huge bag of tapes outside. Faster than a speeding bullet, I grabbed the buggers and tucked fresh blanks into the boxes! I hear Jewel went bananas when she found out."

She smiled gleefully and poked at the fire with a curtain rod. "The deep satisfaction in my decadent soul is enough to allow me eternal serenity."

It was a race. Christine and Kent were both trailing puddles of water as they bounded pell-mell up the steep stairway to their room at the Sonoma Mission Inn and Spa. Squealing and taunting each other, ignoring the stares of other guests, they were carrying on like two wonderfully spoiled children. They'd just taken an invigorating twilight plunge into the Olympic-sized pool, and then it was off to the Spa's magnificently frothing Jacuzzi, where they'd lingered until they felt their bodies begin to melt.

Christine had never been happier. All of a sudden she had it all. And this time she was determined to hang on to it. Especially to this thoroughly beguiling gentleman at her side.

Their romantic reunion had come as another total surprise to Christine. Early Friday morning, shortly after she'd returned from doing *Good Morning America,* Christine had received an unusual delivery. Standing there on her doorstep was a tuxedoed young man holding a magnum of Piper Sonoma champagne in one hand and a miniature wooden dollhouse in another.

Christine stopped laughing long enough to open the envelope attached to the champagne and then she collapsed on the couch. She'd expected to see Steven's name, Maggie's, or maybe even her parents'. But the note read:

> Okay, so you're a star. If I can't hold you down, I might as well live with you. Arrive LAX at 6:30 P.M., Northwestern. How about the wine country this weekend?
>
> I love you,
> KENT

"The truth is," he'd teased her at the airport, "I don't want all this celebrity going to your head. Figure you need a leveler . . . nice folksy guy like me to set you straight."

"And to help me get level, too, I'll bet!" Christine had laughed delightedly.

Within three hours they were in northern California's scenic wine country, where they felt drunk simply from the earthy aroma and deeply rich colors of the harvest season and the rejuvenating fresh country air.

"Now this is a whole other California," Kent marveled as they drove through the mountains that separated the Sonoma from the Napa Valley. It was a stunningly clear day, and the rolling view of green touched with gold seemed to go on forever.

"Not half as nice as Minneapolis, of course," Christine said with a mischievous glance.

"Oh, I'm not so sure." He was squeezing her hand.

They'd spent Saturday visiting wineries, sampling their sights, smells, and wares. Christine had happily related to Kent the news of the TV offers she'd received. ABC, NBC, and CBS had all contacted her regarding a position as Hollywood correspondent. Four independent producers were hot to discuss reviving *The DuRand Report*.

Returning to the stately California Mission-style hotel, an elegantly restored beauty blushed in the palest peach, they eagerly took their swim and then a look at the modern spa, where they'd discovered the Jacuzzi.

Now Christine was drying her hair, having celebrated her victory in the 100-yard dash by showering first.

"You know," Kent bellowed over the whirring noise of the hair-dryer as he stepped into the bathroom, "about those offers—there's one you haven't considered."

"What, darling?" she asked, clicking off the dryer.

"I said, there's one package deal you haven't mentioned yet."

"Whose?"

"Mine." He let his towel drop to the floor and stood grinning at her, stark naked.

"Hmm, looks pretty interesting," she admitted, looking him up and down. "Exactly what might it include?"

Giving her a sly wink, he moved close and began to untie her terry wrapper. "What would you like it to include, you luscious temptress?"

"Oh," she said, returning the wink, "a move halfway across the country on your part, for starters."

"To California?"

"To Los Angeles," she corrected, slipping out of the wrapper.

"Mm-hmm. Can you be more specific?" Kent placed his hands around her trim waist and drew her toward him.

"Well, let's say to a home in . . . why not Beverly Hills?"

"Why not?"

Christine nibbled on his lower lip.

"Mmmmmmm . . . will you share it with me?"

Now she kissed him gently. "Can you be more specific?"

They looked into each other's eyes, as if searching for an answer. "I love you, damn it," he said finally. "I want to be with you. Is that specific enough?"

A prickly sensation rushed through Christine's body. Hearing those words made her feel lightheaded and buoyant. "This, ah, package deal," she managed to say, "does it come with a ring and a ceremony?"

"If you want it to . . . yes."

"Oh, Kent." She held him close, hugging as hard as she could. "You know I do. I want us to—" She stopped abruptly. The damn phone was ringing again.

Kent frowned and looked down at her helplessly. "Aw, hell, let it ring," he said. "Nobody knows I'm here."

"But it might be important."

Moving across the room, he yanked up the receiver. "Yeah, who is it?" he asked angrily. "Oh, Maggie! Sorry—sure, sure she's right here. . . ."

As he handed her the phone, he whispered, "Your personal beeper service."

Christine sighed. "Maggie? What's wrong? How on earth did you find me?"

"I have ways—and nothing's wrong," chirped her friend excitedly. "Sorry to disturb, girl. Lover boy sounded upset. But what I have to tell you could not wait another millisecond."

"What, for heaven's sake?"

"Two glorious developments! First, Jewel Crosse is *finis!*"

"No!"

"Oh, yes. Cross my heart—pun intended. She's been canned and so has Taubman."

"It's about time. When did you find out?"

"Seconds ago, sweetie, and I wanted you to hear it from me first! It was the Neal Burgess lawsuit. You know damned well she had no source for that blind item, and the network knew it too. Guess who swung the ax that chopped off the witch's head?"

"Couldn't have been Howard Ruskin, could it?"

"Wha—" For once Maggie was almost speechless. "How the hell did you know?" she finally sputtered.

"Oh, I have my ways, too. Actually, my dear," she confessed, "I put him up to it."

"You? You did that? Well, hot damn, honey pie. Guess old Mag can still take some lessons from the teacher. So you know everything?"

"Not exactly. Just the part about the deposition."

"Well," Maggie bubbled on enthusiastically, "once the network's attorneys got a whiff of what Ruskin was telling Burgess's side, they advised the board to settle fast. Still cost 'em plenty, but as a bonus to us, ol' Jewel got sacked this afternoon! Taubman got it in New York this morning. There's one hell of a celebration going on right now at El Coyote. That's where I'm calling from—can you hear it, girl? The place is crawling with deliriously happy IN staffers! It's a real blowout!"

"Maggie, I've got a feeling I'm going to remember this day a long time," Christine enthused. "What's the other good news?"

"Jeezus, almost forgot! Remember that Kahala Hilton trip you owe me?"

"Well, yeah, sure. I've been so—"

"Skip the excuses, honeybunch. I have the plane ticket right here in my bag. And the hotel's all booked—for a month!"

"A month! Wha—"

"What's going on? Hold onto your hat, girl. It's a present to Nickels and me. From Big Daddy! That's the other news, hon. I helped him expose that phony plagiarism suit, and he's finally decided he loves his little girl after all!"

Christine smiled and said softly, "He's always loved you, Mag. And so have I. I'll call you when I get back, okay?"

Christine hung up the phone. "What was that all about?" Kent asked.

"Oh, nothing," she said, wrapping her arms around his waist again. "Just a little shop talk."

He kissed her long and lingeringly.

"Thought I should know," he whispered in her ear, "just in case someone should ask at one of those fancy Hollywood cocktail parties you're bound to drag me to."

"Mmmm, that's a laugh. First I'll have to drag you out of surgery."

"I'd rather drag you off to bed."

In a single motion, he picked her up and swung her up over his shoulder. "Now are you going to tell me or—"

"Okay, okay!" she relented, arms flailing. "If you must know, a woman who worked for the International Network—replaced me, in fact—she just lost her job. Her name is Jewel Crosse. Ever hear of her?"

"Nope."

"Then will you unhand me, for Godsakes?"

Kent carried her over to the bed and placed her on it, carefully. "Thank you," he said, snuggling his blond head against her shoulder. "I just wanted you to know I'm interested in your work."

"Great."

She pulled his body down on top of hers.

"But right now," she said, "I'd rather hear more about that package deal you were telling me about."